Dedication

This book is dedicated to the men and women in the Armed Forces who unselfishly serve our nation and protect us every day, particularly, *the forgotten,* those who fought in the Vietnam War. Your sacrifice and bravery will live forever.

Prologue

On a moonless summer night, a Greyhound bus rushes along a lonely stretch of road, its headlights penetrating the blackness. In the thoughts of Men, a bus is an innocuous conveyance, transporting all sorts of strangers. But, in that single moment, all are joined in an unspoken united purpose: to reach their destination. The simple act of moving from point to point is taken for granted. It is on these rare, unintended occasions when paths cross, lives intersect, and the Fates intervene. Directions, once solidly set, change. Destiny is fickle, humbling human arrogance. It spins, It weaves, and It cuts lives on a whim.

PART ONE

Chapter One

June 1st, 1967 – Houston – Greyhound Bus Station

The image of Papá waving good-bye still scorched Raquelita Muro's mind. She tried to swallow, but it was impossible. After last night's tears, her mouth was dry and raw. Desperate to erase the painful memory, she stared around the unkempt waiting hall, her gaze hopscotching from person to person, reading the emotions of her fellow travelers: excitement, fear, exhaustion. Marité, her younger sister, was lost in her comic book. But Mamá's irritation, intensified with every grating heel tap on the tiled floor. The wooden benches, the incessant crisscrossing of travelers, and the jarring noise of the loudspeakers did nothing to ease Mamá's tense disposition.

The two-hour connection seemed endless, and all destinations had been announced except theirs. Not that she was eager for her bus to arrive; given the chance, she would turn back to her father in San Antonio immediately. Their farewell had been rushed and ultimately ruined by another volcanic quarrel between her parents. Papá had wanted to take them to the station, but Mamá refused, arguing it was best to say good-bye at the horse farm. They'd still be arguing if the ranch workers hadn't stopped to listen in.

"Raquelita, I'm so sick of the pathetic face. Take this," Mamá said, waving a tissue.

Raquelita took it in silence. As she dabbed her eyes, her attention returned to the activity in the room. The traveling frenzy had slowed, and the evening light filtered through the windows, splashing a curious tint on the distressed walls. Outside, tired golden rays had dimmed into hues of rose and light fuchsia, foreshadowing what waited ahead: a dark, lonely road. As if on cue, a green light above Gate 5 blinked. Bus 5570 was docking. Her fate had arrived.

***

Thirty yards from Raquelita, the transport opened its door, and a crowd of people dashed out in all directions like crazed ants. A lone soldier considered disembarking, but at the last minute opted to stay, enjoying the silence before the next array of whimpering children, admonishing parents, and grumpy passengers boarded. He needed peace from his memories and the mocking caption under his yearbook photo: *Matthew J. Buchanan, Honor Society, Football Star, Most Likely to Succeed.*

He should have enrolled in college to earn a student deferment. Instead, he'd allowed his youthful passions to overwhelm his judgment and delay his decision while he mooned after Kathy like a lovesick puppy. Now he was paying the price.

Any other man his age would've been terrified by such a cavalier throw of the dice, as thousands scrambled to dodge military service any way possible. But Matthew suffered no such fear. He was raised to believe serving his country was an honorable duty and a source of pride. When the Selective Service called, he enlisted.

And Kathy dumped him.

She'd expected a stellar life with a successful career man, a power broker, a shaker and a mover, not a rancher or a military man. In her opinion, hesitation equaled worthlessness. Matthew Buchanan was found lacking. His last recollection of Kathy Miles had been a lengthy tirade: *"How'd you let the scholarship offer run out, Matthew? Well, don't think I'm gonna sit at home waitin' for ya..."*

Thumps and shuffling of feet ended his brooding, and he was back in the present, staring at a man built like a linebacker, blocking the aisle. Luckily, the man spotted an empty seat away from the one beside Matthew, and with the incongruous lightness of a ballet dancer, twirled and sat down. His immensity now gone, the passage was cleared to reveal three beautiful females, a mother with her two daughters, waiting patiently.

The youngest almost made him laugh. In her short-sleeved blouse, plaid Bermuda shorts, and summer sandals, she shuffled along in happy, preadolescent innocence. A pace behind, the other young woman followed with hunched shoulders and a hesitant step. He couldn't discern her features, but her pale yellow dress highlighted the golden color of her skin and her mahogany ponytail. The mother was a handsome woman, yet her features were distorted by a deep scowl as she scanned the length of the aisle in search of seats. Other than the empty spot next to him and one vacant row at the back, the bus was full.

When the women reached his row, the mother murmured in the oldest daughter's ear. The young woman nodded, and for the next second or two, she barely moved. But then she took a decisive step forward, stood under the cone of his reading light, and her face emerged out of the shadows. Through a veil of dark lashes, a wondrous pair of caramel irises gleamed at him. It was a three-way punch: belly, solar plexus, and lungs. Matthew was suddenly mute.

"Is the seat taken?"

Her melodious words jolted him out of his stupor, and he jumped to his feet. "No, ma'am. The seat *is* available." In seconds, Matthew had removed his hat and duffle bag to the overhead rack.

***

Raquelita couldn't help but smile at the soldier's diligence. Apparently he wasn't fast enough for Mamá, who grumbled with impatience.

"Ah, Mamá," Raquelita huffed, jerked her shoulder and cringed, expecting Mamá's barrage of invectives to follow. To her surprise, none came. Her mother must have been distracted, because she mumbled something and prodded Marité onward to the back of the bus.

All her life Raquelita had feared provoking Mamá's anger. Somehow, with the exciting prospect of sitting next to this attractive stranger, she'd forgotten caution. Perhaps when she'd crossed the boundaries of the ranch, a benevolent magic had loosened some of her instilled reserve. *It is possible.* The real world was about adventure and discovery. She was ready to leave shyness, hesitation, and doubt behind.

The young man gestured to the seat. But she didn't move, her attention focused on his hands. They seemed strong and capable, and she knew hands never lied. Her thoughts traveled to long-ago days when Papá's hands guided hers during her first riding lessons. She remembered their warmth, and shape, their sense of care and affection, their quiet command and easy authority when he showed her how to hold the reins and guide the noble beast.

"Take your seats!"

The announcement boomed, Raquelita blinked, and the vision vanished. Feeling a little foolish, she gathered her traveling paraphernalia to her chest and settled down.

"Hi there," the soldier said.

"Hello," she whispered, caught by his resplendent smile.

God, he's beautiful. The thought rose unbidden. *Are men supposed to be beautiful?* What did she know about such things? As she had been raised and educated strictly within the limits of the horse farm, never allowed into town or public school, her frame of reference was limited to that tiny universe. Well, Mamá had opened the door to this journey of discovery, and discover she would. Behold, here was her first subject.

Her soldier had gone silent, ostensibly involved in a thorough examination of the front seat-back pocket. It was a perfect opportunity to study the charming man surreptitiously, and yet, with his attention elsewhere, an odd emptiness descended upon her. *Quick! Say anything.* Her mind churned. *Make him look at you.*

Instead he spoke first. "Is that your momma sitting behind us?"

She nodded, once. First she wanted his attention; now she didn't know what to do with it. She could blame his dazzling smile with the small dimple, the deep emerald eyes, and the straight nose with its quirky tiny bump at the bridge for taking her speech away, but it was something else, an insubstantial feeling. His gaze was warm and reassuring, almost intimate.

"Darn, I've no manners tonight. I'm Matthew Buchanan."

"I'm Raquel…Raquel Muro. My family calls me Raquelita, or Lita." The stammered response was rather weak, but he didn't notice. He seemed intent on saying her name.

He tested, struggled, and finally rolled it. "R-Raquelita?"

She rewarded his effort with a good smile. It was an awkward sound for many, but in this young man's light Texan accent, it was extremely pleasing to hear.

"I like it. It suits you. Did I say it right…Raquelita?" he asked with a hopeful look.

"It's perfect. I like how you say my name. "

"Doesn't it mean petite Rachael in Spanish?"

"Why, yes." Her fingertips flew to her lips as they rounded in wonderment. "You must be good with languages."

"A little." He shrugged. "I tried my luck with Spanish but gave it up for French. I found the guttural R easier. Okay…how did I do?"

"Great." The enthusiastic answer sounded strange to her. Even stranger were the bubbles bursting inside her chest. "You did great."

***

At the back of the bus, Isabel Muro fumed. This wasn't in the plans. How could she keep control of Lita sitting so far apart? She almost slapped the armrest in frustration. The only available seat was next to a young soldier, who, for the moment, appeared serious. Surely he would see Raquelita for the wet-behind-the-ears girl she was and disregard her entirely. However, soldier or not, his kind rarely restrained their sexual urges or salacious ideas. Men were such animals.

Her thoughts flew to her so-called ex-husband. Emilio the fool. This sham American divorce he'd forced upon her was a travesty, and illegal in their homeland. He could never return to Jerez if he remarried. He'd be declared a bigamist and shame the illustrious Muros. They were irrevocably tied. Spain and the church did not grant divorces. *Until death do us part...*

In retaliation, she'd absconded with their two beauties. From now on, Lita and Marité would remain under her strict supervision. She'd do everything to keep them pristine, unsullied by men's desires, and far, far away from their father's influence and reach. Revenge was a dish best served ice-cold.

* * *

Matthew glanced out the window and smiled. Night had fallen upon them. He'd lost track of time and forgotten his troubled thoughts thanks to the young woman sitting next to him. Her mirth and exuberance were infectious. She used her hands to speak, creating curious shapes in the air, which he visualized with total enchantment. While the minutes and hours passed imperceptibly, they had covered all sorts of topics, from the weather on the road to his assignment at Fort Benning's Airborne School. Even the odd color of the lady's wig two rows ahead didn't escape their happy commentary. Raquelita was a delicious combination of naïveté and awareness and was delightfully engaged in every word he said. This genuine attention was much needed sustenance for his soul.

"Let's forget about everyone on the bus," he said. "Tell me more about you. Where were you born?"

"San Antonio. My parents are from Spain, born on the outskirts of Jerez de la Frontera."

"The land of Don Quixote and Sancho Panza," he said. "A legendary country full of history and romance. I've seen pictures and read a ton of books. I hope to visit one day."

"Gracious, you've heard of *El Ingenioso*?"

"You bet. *Don Quixote* was a reading elective in school. Darned difficult, but I managed." Matthew paused for a moment. "Jerez isn't close to La Mancha, is it?"

"Not at all. Jerez is near the coast in the province of Andalucía, south and west of La Mancha," she explained, adopting a cute tutorial attitude. "The region is known for its music, historical monuments, its prized sherry wine, and majestic horses."

"Mysterious Andalucía. The Moors fought so hard to hold it." His eyebrows gathered as he spoke. "Lorca was from Granada. His poetry was musical and raw in one breath, like *The Sleepwalking Ballad*, or *La Guitarra*. It's a pity he died so young."

"Yes, a tragic casualty of the Spanish Civil War." Speaking to Matthew was like sifting through a treasure chest full of surprises, one more enticing than the last. She had the oddest desire to touch him, ensure he was real. "So you know *La Guitarra?*"

"Oh no. I'm not going to embarrass myself by reciting Spanish." A faint flush rose on his face. "It's bad enough I mix up my locations."

"My father and I used to recite it together." In her softest voice, she spoke:

Empieza el llanto de la guitarra.
Se rompen las copas de la madrugada.
Empieza el llanto de la guitarra.
Es inútil callarla.
Es imposible callarla.

Words flowed out of her lips, her fingertips flitted like butterflies, and notes filled Matthew's ears, full, vibrant, and warm. "You have it, *el duende* comes to you," he said.

"Me? No."

"Yes. You. I know Lorca's poems, but I've never heard them in Spanish. The genie glimmers on your face and moves through your hands. The music comes to you. *He* comes to you."

"How do you know so much? Very few people outside Spain know about the genie, much less feel or hear it."

"The teacher who helped me survive *Don Quixote* knew my admiration for Lorca's works and lent me several books. One had a lecture Lorca gave in Buenos Aires. It was outstanding. The images Lorca presented inspired the reader's imagination. He spoke of dark sounds. According to him, *el duende* is the hidden spirit of a doleful Spain. Please, please say more."

Raquelita smiled and continued:

Useless to silence it
Impossible to silence it.

"That was lovely," he whispered. "You *are* enchanting."

"Oh." She blushed.

"Lita." The stern sound sliced the air. Isabel and her deep scowl stood next to their seats. Her gaze shifted suspiciously from her daughter to Matthew. "Is *everything* all right, Lita?"

"Y-yes, everything's fine. Mamá…this is Matthew. We've been talking for a while. I've told him a little about us and our family."

"Lita. Do *not* pester people with your little stories and inane fancies. Travelers like privacy. Uh…nice to meet you…Matthew, is it? I hope Lita doesn't annoy you *too* much." Isabel arched an eyebrow at Raquelita, and before Matthew could speak, she pivoted and headed to her seat.

Matthew watched the angry woman go. Why would a mother humiliate her daughter in public? If her purpose was to smother her daughter's spirit, she'd managed to do so. He'd spent the past few hundred miles relishing Lita's joie de vivre; he didn't wish to sit through the next hundred without it. He blurted the first thing that came to his mind. "Lita, you can say anything you want. I love your voice."

"You do?"

"Yes, and I love our conversations. Heck, I can't remember the last time I discussed music, geography, and poetry in a single exchange."

"If I bore you, will you tell me?" Her expression was serene, but her earlier mirth had disappeared.

"Impossible. You could never bore me," he murmured, hoping *his* sweet girl would return. "How far are you traveling? Where's your last stop?" Matthew continued, but seconds after he asked, he knew the subject was trouble.

"We…we are going to Ocala."

"Ocala?"

"Yes."

"Are you meeting your father there?" Her grimace deepened, and he wanted to kick himself. "Raquelita, if you don't wish to talk…"

"Please, don't think… I really like talking to you… He's not coming. My parents are divorced. We're moving to another state." She choked out the three statements, and turned to the aisle.

He murmured reassurances to no avail. She still looked away. He placed two fingers under her trembling chin, and she did not resist when he turned her face toward his. Her cheeks were damp, her irises sparkled like gems, and her lashes were heavy with moisture. She looked at him with undiluted trust and an emotion he couldn't identify.

This guileless young woman with her soulful eyes, shimmering brown locks, and golden skin had captured him. The pull was inescapable. Matthew slipped his hand under hers. "I would give half my soul to take your pain away." He lifted the delicate fingertips for a feathery kiss.

Raquelita stared in fascination. The strong hands she'd admired earlier had grasped her hand as if she were a fragile porcelain doll. She felt safe. She felt protected. She felt secure. Other than for rare moments with her father, Lita lived in a cold, affectionless wasteland, under the strict rule and discipline of a rigid mother. With a simple brush of his lips, Matthew had infused her soul with life-giving warmth. She knew then, to the marrow in her bones, she was bound to him. She would never feel this close to anyone in life again.

"Talk to me, Lita. I'm on your side."

Their gazes locked.

"I believe you, Matthew."

Hovering above, the ancient women watched.

Chapter Two

San Antonio – June 1st, 1967

At this late hour, the tack room was deserted. No ranch hands lingered with last-minute chores. Not even Xavi—always the last to leave—was around. Emilio scoffed. Xavi had likely fled to one of his mysterious hangouts to avoid Emilio's wrath. Yes, Emilio was ticked off at his friend, but he was furious with himself. Xavi's sin was to drive Isabel and the girls to the bus station. Emilio's sin was far greater: he'd permitted Isabel to take his precious girls away without a single remonstration. He looked at his numb hands. In his fury, he'd gripped the bridles so tightly his fingers were almost white.

Taking heavy steps, he approached the dark paneled wall where multiple rows of riding accessories were arranged in orderly fashion. Thomas Ferguson, the owner of the ranch, was fastidious with his equipment. Emilio forced his stiff fingers open and hung the two bridles on their hooks. With the same restrained pace, he turned to the center of the room. Side by side on their respective stands were two saddles—Xavi's and his—a study in contrasts.

His was hand-tooled Peruvian leather, exquisitely embossed. He touched the intricate work, appreciating the artistry of the maker. Indeed, it was a showpiece, but for all its beauty, the saddle was stiff and uncomfortable. Emilio rarely used it. In juxtaposition, Xavi's saddle was highly functional, with its low profile and elegant, simple lines. It was the perfect trainer's instrument. The smooth leather, supple from constant use, had molded to Xavi's form in some areas. His friend conditioned and buffed it with loving care, and would likely maim anyone who touched it. Had Emilio missed the symbolism?

Actually, he'd missed all of it. His hand tightened on the cantle as his forehead fell upon his knuckles. What a terrible mess they had made…

In January 1928, Emilio Muro arrived in the world "feet first," a sure sign of good fortune. Indeed, he *was* fortunate. The Muros were famous throughout the region of Jerez de la Frontera for horse training and breeding excellence, and young Emilio inherited every last gene. No colt or filly could resist him. Without resorting to harsh roping or standard breaking methods, he turned the young horses to butter in his kind hands. The venerable, and highly spirited Pure Spanish Horse was his specialty. To his family's consternation, job offers from competing breeding farms arrived daily, which Emilio good-naturedly refused. The blessings didn't stop there. Emilio inherited the Muro charm and bearing: Vandal, Visigoth, and Moor ancestry endowed him with splendid looks. The townsfolk—most especially the ladies—flocked to him.

In contrast, Emilio's childhood friend and training partner, Xavier Manel Repulles, had been accosted by innuendo and suspicion from boyhood. Not even his fair, angelic features could endear him to the town's biddies. Xavi's northern origins, his taciturn and irreverent personality, deemed him the neighborhood's *niño terrible.*

Xavi's fortunes growing up should have been similar to Emilio's. Repulles was a respected name within the legal profession in Barcelona. But the political climate had grown unstable. Cataláns were demanding independence from Spain. From the hallowed halls of the *Generalitat* to the average citizens, dissatisfaction and dissension raged like a wildfire.

Xavi's father, the brilliant young attorney Jordi Repulles, subscribed to such ideals. Despite his family's reputation, his career was abruptly truncated when authorities learned of his separatist efforts. Threats to desist ensued. Already, the more outspoken partisans had been detained, and some vanished without a trace. At the behest of close friends and the pleas of his elderly parents, Jordi and his wife packed their belongings and their young son and left their lives and beloved Catalunya behind.

They moved to Jerez, a distance of five hundred miles. The couple's savings were enough to purchase a modest wine-and-tapas bar in the new neighborhood. The business thrived, but it didn't satisfy Jordi's soul, which pined and languished in silence for his now forbidden profession, his old lifestyle, and his ancestral home. A dark shadow fell upon the Repulles's home.

This shadow accompanied Xavi daily to school. It would disappear in the company of his buddy Emilio, yet resurface with the end of school. It trailed him all the way home. It gave Emilio the willies to watch the hovering black cloud over his friend, knowing something ugly was going on at home.

One auspicious afternoon, whether it was from a desire to lighten Xavi's mood or simply extend their playtime, Emilio dragged his friend to the family stables. In the midst of their games, shrewd trainers observed that the boys shared more than a close friendship: they could both speak to the horses. On the spot, Xavi was offered an apprenticeship, and from then on, the boys were inseparable.

Until Isabel Llorenz appeared, and Emilio fell in love with her.

Isabel was the most breathtaking creature Emilio had ever seen. From a distance, she was beautiful. When she came close, he was lost. A mysterious light danced in her almond-shaped eyes, a shade of caramelized sugar promising a delicious dessert. She was lovely, with lustrous dark brown curls and a tempting figure. Despite Emilio's charming advances, however, she remained distant and aloof.

"You are wasting your time," Xavi said. "Isabel is not for you. She's cold and remote. Isabel needs two things: either the touch of the switch, or to be left alone entirely. I'd say the latter. I wouldn't tolerate such behavior. You'd do better looking elsewhere."

Pretending shocked amusement, Emilio rebuffed Xavi's suggestion. "That isn't my style. I prefer a gentler approach. Besides, I have the talent. Isabel will eventually respond. You'll see. ¡Dios! Look at her. I'm bewitched."

Xavi would shrug in response. He obviously had different ideas. When it came to the ladies, Xavi was an enigma. Whatever his tastes, he was not one to tell. Whatever his preferences, not even Emilio knew.

Weeks later, Xavi arrived at Emilio's doorstep, surprising him with the offer of a new venture. A large horse farm in Texas was seeking experts to train and breed Spanish and other purebred horses. The opportunity was better than anything they would have in Spain, and it paid in dollars, not *pesetas*. After involved negotiations, both men accepted job offers. Emilio stipulated one condition: he would stay behind in a last attempt to gain Isabel's hand in marriage. With the urgency of the impending move, he pressed his pursuit of Isabel by recruiting the assistance of her mother.

Doña Alicia Llorenz, *La Viuda*, was no fool. She had a good eye for economic position and wealth. When Emilio presented the full monetary scope of his venture, her sharp mind evaluated her daughter's future and, by default, her own. She knew an advantageous match when she saw it. In a flurry of activity, unceremoniously and completely unprepared for the intimacies of marriage, Isabel was wedded, packaged, and shipped onward by her shrewd mother.

Meanwhile, Isabel was fearful, which made their wedding, and especially the wedding night, a disaster. Inexperience, enthusiasm, and a measure of masculine impatience conspired against the couple. In Emilio's loving hands, Isabel reacted to his initial caresses with pleasure. She struggled, had almost vanquished her conflicting shame, when he whispered a passionate request. "Touch me, Isabel. Touch me now, woman." And disaster struck.

He reached for her hand and pressed it against him. It should have felt right. It did not. Isabel tumbled down the dark alley of hidden memories. Shocked by the distastefully familiar gesture, she heard another horrid voice and felt that other cruel hold. Her fragile arousal dissipated instantly.

Emilio missed the sudden change and the signs of her distress. Instead of guiding his wife sensuously through the light pain experienced at first possession, his passion urged him onward, and he rushed her. Hours later, a brew of ugly emotions boiled within Isabel. Shame mingled with self-disgust in a strangling poisonous knot around her soul.

Unaware of his wife's tribulations, Emilio was delighted. The elusive Isabel Llorenz was finally his. Their wedding night belonged in fairy tales. Their joining was blissful, man and woman united as one soul, one heart. It was days later before he noticed Isabel was quiet and reserved. With his usual lighthearted attitude, he blamed it on the initial jitters of married life.

By the time the couple arrived in Texas, Emilio felt the emotional distance. He might have been able to reverse the disunion, but Isabel was pregnant, and her symptoms were so onerous they widened the chasm between them. On the happy day when Emilio received his daughter into the world, he saw no love for him in his wife's eyes.

The years passed, the family stumbled along, and the horse farm prospered. On the evening of a big sale, the men decided to go into town to celebrate. Emilio begged Isabel to join them, but she turned down the invitation. Her refusal was their undoing.

Rejection is lousy company, and Emilio's mood was as dark as the bar. At the Black Brew, he tried to vent to Xavi the sorry state of his marriage, but his friend's focus was on distant thoughts. Left alone to wallow, Emilio caught the admiring glances of the bar owner, Julianna, and on this disappointing night, his bruised ego lapped it up.

Roused by the lady's interest and uninhibited by the booze, Emilio determined he wouldn't be denied by his wife. Not on this night. He missed Isabel. He loved and desired her, and his alcohol-addled mind was confident he could seduce her. She was his wife and the mother of his child. When he returned home, he would have her.

The following morning, Emilio was appalled. He'd forced himself on Isabel. Her glaring resentment shamed him without mercy. Defeated and weary, Emilio accepted the disaster they'd become. He left the marriage bed, never to return.

Nine months later, the arrival of María Teresa caused the estranged couple to strike an unspoken truce as they navigated through diaper changes and feedings. But their animosity couldn't be repressed, and soon disagreements spread to all topics. The fights raged on. In their self-absorption, the combative parties failed to notice the effect on the silent witness. Five-year-old Raquelita watched and kept it all in.

Experience is an excellent instructor. If years ago Emilio had missed the signs of change in Isabel, this time he recognized his child's distress. He embarked on a campaign to deflect the damage, lavishing his daughter with love and affection. Except Isabel's tenacity to oppose him was stronger. Her intimidating scowl and her tireless censuring of Raquelita neutralized and defeated his efforts. Emilio watched impotently as his vivacious girl turned silent and docile. She brought less attention to herself and no longer sought his affection. She became the lost child, and her journals were her sole refuge. She retreated into a tiny private world, hiding all emotions and curiosities, and constantly criticized notions.

To his relief, as Marité grew up, the sisters became each other's companions. He knew they understood and shared each other's needs and heartaches. What he could no longer give them, they supplied to each other: nurturing, sympathy, and friendship. Through the ensuing years, life at the Muro household continued on its established unhappy pattern, until Sunday, February 9th, 1964. On that night, the world's popular music and Emilio's life changed forever.

"Everyone's at home watching The Beatles on TV," Emilio said after a quick scan of the unusually empty bar. He tried to sound casual, but Xavi must have perceived his anger. The question in his stare couldn't be ignored for long.

"The way Isabel treats the girls it's infuriating," he explained, shuttling his beer from hand to hand. "She won't even let them watch the boys on TV. She called them 'long-haired degenerates.' Can you believe that?" Emilio wiped the sweating bottle. A few drops fell on the countertop, making a wet spot. He spread it around absently with his forefinger.

"Isabel's a difficult woman to manage. You know this, Emilio."

"I never thought it would come to this. She once responded to gentleness, I think. Damn, I can't remember anymore. I've tried and failed repeatedly."

"You didn't fail, Emilio. You never spoke a language she understood. I told you what to do once. Did you listen?"

"What could I do? I can't kill her."

"Certainly not. But she needs a handler. One who can heal the hidden pain and tame that nasty biting habit."

"Tame her? She's not a mare. *Dios santo*, I hate what she's doing to Raquelita."

"*I* see the pain. She behaves like an abused mare. *I* can control her. And *I* don't like the way she treats my goddaughter either."

"What is that supposed to mean? *You* can control her?"

"Okay, guys. These are on me." Armed with two frosted mugs and a wide smile, Julianna Black halted the discussion with her version of peace negotiations. "Let's cool the spirits a bit."

"I'm sorry, Julie. Were we getting loud?"

"Nah, I could use the company. It's a ghost town in here tonight. Not a big disagreement, I hope?"

"I just...needed to vent." Emilio offered an apologetic smile.

"Oh, what about? In addition to libations, I offer mediation services. It's well known bartenders have the most sympathetic and impartial ears in the world. It's a requirement."

Emilio stared at the warm bottle in his hand. Noiselessly, he propped it against the counter. Xavi shifted and rolled his shoulders in obvious discomfort. Suddenly, he blurted, "It's his wife, she..."

"Stop. I don't want to talk about her anymore."

Julianna nodded. "I may not be the most experienced person to offer advice, but I can sympathize with the difficulties of relationships. Robert and I weren't married long, but we had our share of arguments." As she spoke, she replaced the bottle Emilio held with the icy glass.

Torn between his innate sense of privacy and a burgeoning desire to talk, Emilio stammered, "We...we aren't important. I'm worried about the girls and our continuous disagreements. I can handle anything, but they're young and full of life. They need...they need..." He paused. "I don't wish to burden you or anyone else with my problems, Julie. Somehow, we'll work this out."

Xavi snickered. "Oh yes. He's been saying this for years now. But it's an impossible task, as Isabel is difficult. Emilio has an easy, persuasive hand. It's not what Isabel needs."

"Xavi, please, don't start again."

"I don't have children," Julianna intervened. "It doesn't mean I can't offer a woman's perspective. It's scary out there. Our country is in a state of flux. We've been shocked by Kennedy's assassination, the war in Vietnam is escalating, and the hippie movement is on the rise. The easygoing fifties are over. In defense of Isabel, I'd say she's worried about the future and uncertain how best to raise the girls."

Emilio stared at Julianna. Her tone was gentle, yet she spoke assuredly. She was aware and informed about the political and societal changes in the country. The knowledge freed her to be compassionate and nonjudgmental, offering another woman, perhaps a worried and frightened mother, a generous lifeline of empathy and understanding.

To Emilio—a man exhausted with the constant struggle at home, drained by the fighting, starved for affection, desperate for even the smallest of intimacies between a man and a woman—Julianna's easy assessment was a revelation. Her words and perspective fell around him gently, a soothing salve he wanted to spread over every aching inch of him.

To his amazement, she wasn't trying to change his mind about Isabel's obstinacy. Instead, she argued in her defense, presenting facts, prompting understanding, and offering compassion. This was exactly what he'd always wanted and needed from Isabel, an exchange of ideas and thoughts, a dialogue without a battle. Physical intimacy was the ultimate gift, yet what he needed to survive was a simple conversation. This easy communion of minds was an epiphany.

In Spain, he'd flirted, danced, and played around with the ladies, in happy ignorance of the fundamental needs of his soul. When he first saw Isabel, he gave physical beauty precedence and failed to observe the spirit. In penance, Emilio had lived a lonely life.

And now, wise Julianna Black beckoned him out of the emotional desert. Isabel no longer filled his mind and heart. Lord, he did not love her anymore, and the knowledge ripped painfully at his heart. But was he grieving the broken marriage or the lost prize? *Maldición*, he'd doggedly pursued a woman who never wanted him. Emilio stared at Xavi, realizing his friend had known all along. Earlier tonight, he'd stumbled along a dark road, but a distant beacon flashed ahead, guided by Julianna's unexpected kind hand.

***

A wave of fresh anger filled Emilio's belly. The past disappeared, and he was back in 1967, staring at the paneled walls of the tack room. Isabel's coup had been brilliant; by the time he learned she was taking his daughters, he was unprepared to stop her legally. The element of surprise had been on her side. Not anymore. If she thought he wouldn't fight for his girls, she was wrong.

Isabel misjudged his passivity in court for weakness. It was guilt. Insidious and implacable guilt for loving another crushed the fight out of him. He knew the courts favored the mother in custody matters, especially when the man was living in dubious circumstances, as her rapacious attorney threatened to use against him. Fury surfaced hot and steamy again, and he slapped the saddle hard. What did anyone know about his life with the kindest and most loving woman he'd ever known? Nothing.

His ex-wife was in for a huge surprise. Tonight he'd propose to Julie once more. As soon as they were married, he was going to appeal and modify the custody decree, one way or another.

***

The unexpected lights in the room crushed Xavi's reverie. He squinted, pissed off with the interruption, and stared at the almost forgotten beer bottle in his hand. It was a miracle it hadn't slid out and made a mess on the table, or worse, on his pants, adding embarrassment to an already outlandish day. The illumination came from a small stage on the far wall where a couple had started a scene. Xavi shook his head. Exhibitionism was not his bag.

Now that the club's darkness had disappeared, so had his privacy. And sure enough, a cute blond dressed in skimpy clothing swished before him, offering submissiveness with properly lowered lids. Impatiently, he waved her away. No substitutions tonight, thank you; he was sick of them. Tonight, *she* was strong on his mind, and he would dwell in the fantasy of her.

This was a part of him not even his best friend knew about. He could never explain the forces driving his needs. He liked his intimacy hard and rough; the urge to control another's responses always surfaced. It frightened some women, while others enjoyed it. With time, he learned to select his partners carefully. To Xavi, sex was not about fear. He was a dominant, not a sadist. Training horses offered an outlet of sorts. The powerful beasts sated the unspent desire to control and dominate. But he was always left with a hollow space in his chest. Training horses could never replace a relationship with a woman.

Moving to the States saved him from prison. Spain had been under the rule of ultraconservative, über-religious Franco for long years, and folks landed in jail for any behavior deemed immoral. People like himself, who indulged in this kind of sexual activities, were considered deviants and menaces to decent society. America embraced all kinds, more or less. As long as everything remained between consensual adults, the authorities did not intervene. To his great fortune, a few years ago he was invited to a private club catering to his tastes. It was a relief to meet others like him.

Frequenting regular bars was pointless. In such places he would rarely find a lady who would enjoy the pleasures he offered. He was grateful for these clubs and the folks who created them, offering him somewhere to go when the need arose.

And the need assailed him every time he saw Isabel. From the first day, he'd looked into those whisky eyes and had fallen. *Fate. Nasty little word, that.* No wonder the Greeks feared the Fates. Love had struck Emilio as well, and he could never interfere in his best friend's happiness. And so, through almost twenty years, Xavi burned for Isabel in silence, knowing her marriage to his friend was destined for ruin.

From the sidelines, Xavi watched Isabel's beautiful sexuality wasted. She had the same dark passions that ruled him, the savage animal need, the raw sexuality. She was his perfect match. What a ride he could show her. He would make her tremble in delight and scream in satisfaction.

Now she was free, and he was moving in to claim her. And when he did, he could only hope Emilio would remember he'd always kept his distance and respected his marriage. No one, except his other close friend, Jonas, knew about the love that crazed and blinded him. However, explaining his part in Isabel's move to Florida, his motive, and most of all his silence, would be tricky. *¡Hostia!* Xavi was tired of sacrifices. The speech to Emilio had to be good. He was determined to keep both his friend and his woman.

The scene on the little stage finished, and the principals emptied it. The lights dimmed, indicating the end of the evening's entertainments. Like his spirits, the club darkened. Xavi took another sip of his beer and, finding it tepid, put it back down with a grimace.

Chapter Three

Along Interstate 10 – June 1st 1967

"Are you warm? Would you like some air?" Matthew reached for the air vent and pointed the stream toward her. "Do you mind if I open my jacket? This tropical uniform is supposed to be cooler, but it's getting stuffy in here with all these people. I have a perfectly respectable T-shirt underneath, promise."

"Oh, so formal," she teased, noticing the faint trace of perspiration on his forehead. "Go ahead, please."

"Regulations call for the jacket to stay on. I only need to open a few buttons to cool off." Matthew's fingers were already busy with the buttons.

"Silly. Look around, none of these people know or care about the rules. It's going to be ruined by the time you arrive."

"Agreed. Come morning, it'll be one wrinkled mess."

"I won't tell any of your superior officers, cross my heart." She laughed, signing a cross over her chest.

"Why, thank you, ma'am. Mighty kind of ya." Matthew tugged, and the garment slid right off. In seconds, the jacket was folded and placed in the overhead rack. "Oh man, that feels better. It's hot in here, A/C and all. You must be exhausted, Lita. This has been a long, trying day for you."

"Yes, I'm a little tired."

It took her a moment to answer. All his shifting around had released his personal scent in a delicious sensory invasion. She didn't want to ogle but could barely conceal her fascination with the proud lines of his jaw and neck, how the regulation T-shirt delineated his chest and the flat line of abdominal muscles. Her gaze swept from the expanse of wide, rounded shoulders, past the curve of sinewy biceps, on to tightly corded forearms dusted with glimmering gold hairs. The glint of his dog tags finished the hypnotic effect.

Welcome to the world of discovery.

Matthew had awakened every feminine nerve in her system. He spoke to her in a language she supposed was the most basic communication between man and woman. Her reaction had been swift and thorough. Her mouth became dry as an exhilarating heat wave rushed through her body and took residence in her belly and regions below. She'd once envisioned her first experience with a man to be fraught with shyness, discomfort, and a host of other issues. With Matthew, not a shadow of discomfort bothered her. Everything was easy, perfect, and natural.

Careful as you tread, remember where you are...

Yes, discretion and subtlety. She paused in admiring her subject, and slowly turned toward the back of the bus.

There was no movement from *that* direction, which was a good sign. The rest of the night and the following day would require finesse and tons of praying, anything to keep her mother unaware of this precious friendship. Until she waved Matthew farewell, she would protect it any way she could, even if it meant sending her mother misleading clues. It would be dishonest and contrary to her character. But had honesty ever helped with Mamá? Shaking her head, Raquelita turned back around and was met by Matthew's careful regard.

"I think she's asleep," she offered as explanation.

"You seem relieved. Is she always like this? Is it travel anxiety?"

"Mamá is always anxious. She rarely smiles, and she trusts people even less often, including me."

"You? Honestly?"

"Yes...me," she murmured, turning away.

"No, please. Stay with me." He lifted her chin. "I understand if you're not comfortable talking. It's just... I want to know all about you and help you anyway I can."

"I can't explain how good it feels to talk to you, how comforting. Other than my sister, I didn't have any friends growing up. Mamá restricted our activities. She believes too much freedom leads to depravity."

"Depravity? She's raising two ladies, not delinquents."

"Yes, well, she does have her reasons for everything. Like, this move. There's something odd about it. She told us two nights ago, with barely enough time to call Papá and pack. Why Florida? She could've held the same position in Texas."

"Maybe." Matthew hesitated. The question seemed to burn his lips. "Do you think it's because of your dad? Was he bad to you?"

Raquelita's response was fierce. "My father is the best man in the world. He loves us. There's nothing he wouldn't do for us both. It's her, Mamá. She hates him. She wants to keep us apart. I didn't want to leave him, Matthew. I didn't want to leave him." A sob exploded, and she slumped toward him.

He propped her up, but another deep sob rattled her body, and without thinking, he sought her mouth in a full, silencing kiss…and the world tilted. Her shy, tentative lips molded to his. Her delightful breath filled him with a joy he'd never known. He now understood why poets wrote about heaven in a kiss. He'd discovered his. He deposited tiny kisses along the edge of her mouth, savoring the salty tears, learning the silky skin of her cheeks. In response, her body yielded to his, and the dizzying sensation returned. When Matthew pulled away, she uttered a little protest.

What is happening here? Matthew didn't see himself as the world's most profound thinker or a romantic. He was a jock; his friends would laugh if they saw him. But he was reevaluating and relearning. Once he believed Kathy was the pinnacle of beauty. No sir. The simplest things are the most beautiful: the less artifice, the brighter the beauty. Here it was, displayed in the most limpid gold eyes he'd ever seen. Eternity and the mysteries of life were revealed through them.

Beauty is eternity gazing at itself in a mirror.

Lost in her eyes, he ran his knuckles gently along her cheek. In response, she leaned her face trustingly upon them. The gesture was so pure and disarming, he felt weak.

"Did I offend or scare you? I can't ask you to forgive me for kissing you, because I desire it too much. But I'll beg you to forgive me if I overstepped my bounds."

"You didn't offend me. I want your kiss too."

He cupped her face, relishing her adorable, sudden flush. His thumb caressed the edge of her lips. "I'm so relieved. I fear I might have pushed you beyond your limits, angel. Do you feel better?"

"Yes… I guess leaving my dad affected me more than I thought. Mamá managed to push my father beyond endurance. They had a lifetime of nonstop strife. He asked for a divorce a year ago."

"And your momma? How did she take it?"

"Badly."

"Can you tell me?"

"Okay, I'll be brief. It's not a happy memory. It was last year, days after my birthday. Papá arrived from the farm, but instead of greeting us first, he went directly to Mamá's room, which was already unusual. They no longer slept together." She took a deep breath and forged on. "I thought another fight would explode, so I ran to Marité's room. As time passed without a sound, I ventured out. I found her sitting in the family room, staring out, silent and remote. She told me then, Papá was leaving, abandoning us, and moving out forever.

"I didn't believe her. Papá would never abandon us. But she ranted anyway about the devious nature of men and how it applied to me. When she lost steam, I was ordered to my room. I went to Marité's instead. I knew she would be worried.

"As soon as Marité calmed down, I scrambled out the window in search of Papá. When I found him, he did his best to convince me nothing would change except the living arrangements. We'd see each other every day. But the fear squeezing my stomach spoke the truth. Our protector was gone. There'd be no buffer between her and us.

"Hours later, he walked me home. He kissed me good-night and promised he'd see us the following day, while Mamá watched in silence. I swear, as soon as Papá left, the house turned cold, like a blast of winter had swept through. Her expression had changed, it was frightening."

"Your momma's not very forgiving, is she?"

"Nope, and now she's getting even. Mamá's pride could never forgive his two sins: leaving her for another woman, and finding happiness while she had none."

***

At the back of the bus, Isabel had fallen asleep. Through the indistinct shadows of a dream, a man's horrid voice threatened. Fingers, cruel and hard, pulled and tore her clothing away. She wanted to scream for help, but the cold, bony hand pressed her lips shut. She was accosted with painful stabs everywhere—her chest, her arms, her back. Her mind screamed, *run, run, run...*

Isabel awoke with a gasp. Disoriented, she looked to her lap. Marité was still sleeping, thank goodness. With a trembling hand, she wiped the dampness from her own forehead. More rivulets of perspiration ran between her breasts, but she could do nothing about those. She lowered her lids, allowing her heartbeat and breathing to calm down. Weakened by the punishing dreams, she thought of the man who could fill a room with his presence, and the name she'd refused to say slipped past her lips: *Xavi*.

Emilio's best friend never hid his antipathy. For years he'd been critical of her every word, step, and gesture. That same Xavi had made a bewildering turnabout. Days after Emilio moved out, he stopped by every day, as if his animosity had been her delusion. These unexpected visits were unsettling, and definitely puzzling. Initially, she'd feared Lita was his quarry. In the end, the truth astonished her. Xavi didn't want Raquelita at all. He wanted Isabel.

She remembered how Emilio's move with Julianna was *el tema del día*. The ranch was a roiling cauldron of gossip. The humiliation felt like a tsunami wave. Each time Isabel reached the surface for a breath, she was pulled under anew.

In a daring move she questioned months after, Isabel waited for one of Xavi's daily visits and seized the opportunity. The gamble backfired in ways she never anticipated.

"You seem preoccupied, Isabel. What is it?"

She explained how their life was unbearably public, and she couldn't take the side-glances and whispers anymore. She even complained it could make a person drink.

Xavi growled under his breath, "What do you want, Isabel?"

And so she told him. She wanted to move away. Start fresh, in a new town, in a new life. Xavi's eyes flashed. In a single motion, he reached for her neck. Threading his fingers possessively through her hair, he twisted her face under his.

"Isabel, if you need to move, I'll make it happen for you." His breath was hot on her face. She gasped, and his lips crushed hers. His voracious tongue possessed her mouth. His kiss was fierce, thorough, and disconcerting, and Isabel Muro—cold, stoic, and detached—trembled. Before he pulled away, he bit her bottom lip as a parting caress. Without another word, Xavi left the house.

In the following weeks, their conversations were limited to the move. He did not try to kiss or touch her again, nor did he offer an apology. Isabel was obsessed; she couldn't stop thinking about the kiss. Like an addict seeking the next fix, she would amble about the house recreating the moment, pressing her fingers to her lips, to the tip of her tongue, reliving the heat, the febrile sensation of his mouth on hers.

Her sexual life with Emilio had been a duty. This hardly felt like a duty. When Xavi's lips captured hers, fresh desires roared to life, in turn creating a new conflict. He was the sort of man who would make her look in forbidden areas and watch right along with her, learning her secret yearnings. Worse, he would demand she embrace them. And she simply couldn't allow it; her sexuality and the horrible past were entangled. What was so carefully concealed would be revealed, and she could never survive it.

She'd attempted a game of manipulation with Xavi. Was she crazy? No one manipulated the man. How would Xavi react when he realized she had no intention of taking him to her bed?

Pushing aside her prickly thoughts, she examined her surroundings. In the gloom, the headrests lined up like crowded monoliths; the stygian aisle yawned. Isabel amused herself with the odd patterns of strewn feet, heads, and elbows in midair, or out in the aisle, victims of the cramped space. The scattered beams of reading lights added a ghostly illumination. The occasional rumble of a snorer or the low mewl of a dreamer interrupted the silence.

She looked farther ahead. Raquelita's light was off, but her traveling companion's light was still on. She frowned. He better not keep her awake. Their journey was long, and she would need Lita's help on arrival. Maybe she would pay them another impromptu visit. Just then, his light flicked off, and she settled back in her seat, relieved that both daughters were sleeping as they sped farther and farther away from her troubles.

***

"When they send me overseas, will you write to me?" Matthew asked in a whisper.

Raquelita vowed firmly, "Yes. Of course I'll be there. I'll be everything you need."

Matthew leaned his forehead against hers. "I don't know what has brought us together. Whatever the forces—fate or destiny—I can only be grateful. Less than twenty-four hours ago, I was sure I had taken several wrong turns. Now, I know I was meant to be here, on this bus, next to you. Just before you arrived, I was looking at my life through very dark lenses. Not anymore. Am I scaring you?"

"Why, because you're articulating my emotions, is that supposed to frighten me? I only know this feels right and perfect, and that's enough for me. Same as you, twenty hours ago, I hated this move, but now…"

In a bold move, Raquelita held Matthew's face between her hands and brushed his lips with hers. Surprised by the unexpected act, he gasped but recovered, returning the caress.

Matthew reached up and turned off the reading light. Darkness descended, enfolding them in its protective embrace. They knew each other's thoughts. *Release the love; the night won't last forever.* With an unfamiliar hunger, they crashed into each other's arms, kissing deeply and thoroughly in a desperate bid to imprint themselves on each other. With every passing mile, Raquelita left behind the remaining traces of the girl she had once been.

Chapter Four

Louisiana – June 2nd 1967

"Wake up, angel."

Raquelita's lids stirred open. She lifted her head from Matthew's chest and looked out the window. The sky had paled; dawn was stretching her greedy fingers over the land, and morning was not far behind. Neither was reality. Time was passing much too quickly.

"Where are we? Are we near New Orleans?"

"We've crossed the state line, and we're coming up on Baton Rouge. We should be in New Orleans in an hour or so." He brushed a thumb over her lips. "Look at the sunrise. Like you, it's breathtaking."

"Matthew…"

"No, angel, don't think about it. It's only dawn. We still have hours together."

"You're right, I'm cutting our time short by thinking ahead."

Raquelita inhaled and closed her eyes. Last night had been a wondrous fairy tale. They had pushed all worry and doubt aside until the morning. And now here it was, and although it was rife with anxiety and uncertainty—Matthew's destination and their impending separation—it also offered possibilities. They would talk and make plans as a couple, together, no longer single and alone.

"Sweetheart, you might wish to use the facilities before the rush begins." He gestured at the surrounding sleeping heads.

"You're right." She reached for her carry bag underneath the seat. Seconds later, she held up her toiletries case with a triumphant smile. "Who needs people knocking at the door and interrupting your personal business? What about you, Matthew? Do you wish to join me?" She almost slapped a hand over her mouth. She didn't recognize this brazen Raquelita.

"Hmmm...what if Momma is awake? We don't wanna tip our hand yet. Go ahead, darling. I'll wait for you right here."

Raquelita headed to the lavatory, taking slow, cautious steps. In spite of the faint aisle lights, the back of the bus was ominously dark. Soon she would come upon her mother's row. She picked up her pace, hoping to pass unnoticed. No such luck. Her mother grabbed her wrist, quick as a striking cobra, giving her a start.

"Mamá...what?"

"It's too early, Raquelita. Why are you up?" Isabel shot her daughter a piercing look. "Is that young man keeping you awake?"

"Who? No, I just woke up. I need to use the facilities." She squirmed in indignation. "I'm in a hurry."

"If you must, but be careful back there."

Oh, it was going to be a trying day. The need for caution was imperative. And yet, the notion of hiding her budding romance was distasteful and irritating.

Play the game, Raquelita.

She reached the haven of the small lavatory, secured the door, and stood before the mirror examining her reflection. She felt different, and now she knew why. Her smile was brighter, and her cheeks were flushed. If *she* noticed, would Mamá notice as well?

"Finesse is the name of the game," she spoke to her image. "Smoke and mirrors, learn to use them." She would do anything to protect her love. Anything.

His scent lingered on her skin, making her feel giddy and silly. Happiness was an amazing emotion, unique to each human, and brand-new to her. It was an intangible treasure. It couldn't be held, weighed, or measured, and yet, like all treasures, it was highly coveted and envied, especially by those who never had it.

In her situation, one wrong word or negligent gesture would wipe happiness away. Her time to enjoy it openly was not yet upon her. Her day would come, and until then, she and Matthew would be the sole keepers of this treasure. Discretion and vigilance would be their biggest weapons.

With a sudden hurry, she finished her ministrations and quickly left the lavatory. She stepped lightly up the aisle, returning to her lover's side. As she passed her mother's seat without a glance, she tucked a small smile to herself. Matthew was waiting.

***

Matthew was in trouble. Happy trouble, but trouble none-the-less. The night had been a test of control and restraint. Raquelita regarded him with so much trust and undisguised desire, it almost drove him mad. He had stood at the edge all night. Were it not for the bus and the public location, he would have showed her his love, and marked her deeply, body and soul, indelibly and forever. From that moment forward, no matter what happened, she would always know she belonged to him, as he belonged to her.

Watching her efforts to stay awake with him had incited a new round of protective feelings. The urge to hold her in his arms and never let go was problematic. He did not want to leave her. Months ago, he'd accepted his future. As far back as he could remember, the men in his family had served honorably. One day it would be his turn, and he'd be bound to carry on the Buchanan tradition. And now a fundamental transformation had occurred. Matthew wanted to serve his country, but his duty rested with the young woman who had slept in his arms.

He'd sworn to serve, and he kept his word. Between now and Tallahassee, he would have to think of something. Evading his duties was not an option. He would never lay that shame upon himself, his family, or, worse, on Raquelita. If he soiled his name, their future was gone. If they were to have a life, his conduct had to be irreproachable.

A beautiful, smiling face yanked him out of his reverie. "I'm all done." She scurried in and placed her bag under the seat. "It's your turn now. The coast is clear."

"Yes, angel. Now tell me, are you gonna let me out, or should I climb over you?" With a wink and a quick kiss to her lips, he unfolded his long legs and stepped right over her.

***

Inside the busy New Orleans station, the three females stood before the women's lavatory. Isabel pressed a hand on the door, staring at her daughters. "Are you two sure you don't need to use the facilities?" Marité and Lita shook their heads silently. "All right, stay together and don't move from here. I'll be right out." Isabel hissed the threat and, with unnecessary force, pushed the door and disappeared inside.

"Marité, please. I need your help."

"What is it, Lita? You look scared."

"It's Mamá. Let me explain. See that young man standing by the boarding door? The one I've been sitting next to since yesterday?"

Marité nodded. "Yes, he's cute."

"Yes, sweetie, and he's really nice. I want to stay next to him until we reach Florida. I need your help. I'm afraid Mamá is going to change my seat. She probably guesses I like him."

"She will? But, Lita, the bus is full. How could she change anything?"

"You know Mamá. I don't know if there will be any empty seats. There may be some, but it wouldn't change anything. I would still have to sit with another stranger."

The ladies' room door swung open, and Isabel stepped out, signaling to her daughters imperiously. "Come along, girls. Follow me." She pivoted and, with a brisk step, headed in the direction of the ticket counter. She looked every few steps to check on her daughters as she dodged the scampering throngs. "Come on, hurry," she yelled through the pandemonium.

Marité whispered, "I don't know what she's up to..."

Raquelita's answer was a sharp nod. As worry began to chill her, she searched for Matthew. He leaned on the bus next to the boarding door. His bland smile and expression were unreadable. She turned forward again, chasing after her mother.

They got their answer the moment Isabel reached a ticket window. She presented their itinerary to a pleasant-looking clerk. "I'm traveling to Ocala. These are our tickets. I want both my daughters seated next to me. The bus from Houston was full. Can you help me?"

Raquelita stopped breathing, waiting for the answer from the nice man behind the window. A loud roar filled her ears, like carts on a roller-coaster ride plunging down the first steep drop. Did she hear loud screeching, or was it her mind?

"I'm sorry, ma'am. The bus is still full," the clerk explained with an apologetic look. "It's June, and lots of folks are on vacation. Perhaps if you wait for the next bus, I could find y'all closer seats. You wouldn't be seated together anyhow. There're only four seats per row, ma'am."

"I see," said Isabel. "When does the next bus arrive?"

"In two hours, ma'am. It takes a different route and arrives much later. I can switch your tickets, if you prefer." The man's expression never wavered in its pleasantness.

Cold sweat ran down Raquelita's back.

"Thank you. I appreciate the help. People are meeting us, and we must arrive on schedule." Isabel snatched up the tickets from the counter and walked away from the window. Abruptly, she turned to Marité. "How would you like to swap seats with your sister?"

Raquelita thought she would faint.

But the bond forged through years of strife came through. "What? No." Marité bristled in character.

"Come on, Mari, you've been with me for hours. Give Lita a break."

"No, Mamá. I don't wanna sit next to a stranger." She stomped the floor in a perfect whine-plea combination. "I really don't wanna. Lita's older. It doesn't bother her. Pleeease, say yes, Lita?"

People around started to look. Raquelita could barely breathe for fear of giving anything away. She'd never loved her sister more than she did now. She wanted to hug and kiss her but settled for squeezing her hand tightly, hoping she understood.

"All right, Marité. I thought you might give Lita a chance to switch, but if you hate it so much…"

Isabel didn't finish her statement. Shaking her head, she marched out of the station's main room with her daughters in tow. She spoke over her shoulder, "Raquelita, you'll go back to your original seat. The young man may be a stranger, but at least you're a little more comfortable with him."

Mamá had no idea. Blood began to rush back to Raquelita's limbs as she breathed in relief. She waited for Mamá and Marité to climb ahead and followed close behind.

***

The bus driver gave several reminders to stay seated, and with large circular motions, he turned the wheel, driving the bus smoothly away from the station onto old cobblestone streets. Soon New Orleans would be a memory, happy to some, frightful to others.

"She wanted to change the tickets, didn't she?" Matthew stared ahead as the question escaped past his lips. He pressed her hand against his hip in reassurance.

"Ye…yes. She inquired about another bus. I was so scared. If she'd changed the tickets, I wouldn't have seen you again."

He turned to her at last, his expression fierce. "Do. Not. Say. That." Matthew punctuated each word, tightening his hold of her hand.

"When she asked Marité to change seats with me..."

"I would've found a way to speak to you and tell you how to find me. Before we reach Tallahassee, you'll have all my addresses. My family will always help. I'll tell them all about you in my next phone call. Angel, I promise"—he released a low chuckle—"unless I lose my mind, you'll always have a way to find me. Come on, sweetheart. The day is still young. Let's enjoy it." He kissed her knuckles, transferring his warmth into her, replenishing what she'd lost in New Orleans.

Matthew leaned back in the seat. Unconcerned with who might watch, he reached for her shoulders and brought her head to rest on his chest, threading his fingers through her silky hair. Lita might need his warmth, but he was desperate for hers. He'd followed Isabel Muro's resolute maneuvers in icy panic, making one contingency plan after another, anticipating her moves and planning his countermoves. He smiled when Lita's body relaxed. The world was sane again.

"Tell me more about you, Matthew."

"Anything you want, angel. Anything at all," he said. "My folks were high school sweethearts who got married as soon as my dad returned from the war in the Pacific. They wanted a ton of kids, but Mom got sick during the next pregnancy and lost the baby. Doctors said no more children. It was sad for them, but good for me, because they gave me all the love in the world and spoiled me rotten. In school, my grades were good—you know I like to read—apparently I have a talent for languages and football." A light flush colored his cheeks. "Kathy—my ex-girlfriend—sent me packing when she learned I lost the scholarship and had to enlist. And here we are."

"Seriously, she broke up with you because you have to serve? I don't understand. Didn't she love you?"

He shrugged. It was ancient history to him. "She had high aspirations, and the army was not included."

"I'm so sorry, Matthew." She pecked him lightly on the lips.

"What are you sorry about?"

"Well, about your breakup."

"Angel, I would've been miserable studying some absurd degree only to make her happy. I'm a farmer at heart. I wanted to attend Texas A&M, become an Aggie, help out my dad, improve and upgrade the farm. It wasn't glamorous enough for Kathy. We would never've worked."

"Her rejection must've hurt. And now with the service in the way..."

"Knowing you and being here is everything. I wouldn't change a thing. Nah, the service is only a temporary impediment, a slight bump on the road. I'll take advantage of what the army has to offer. When my tour is over, I'll pick up where I left off, with a significant improvement—you'll be at my side."

"Yes, I will... Wait, I have something." She reached inside the neckline of her dress and pulled out a gold chain with a small gold charm. Unclasping it, she presented it to him. "I want you to have this, please. Keep it with you at all times. It'll make me feel better."

The pretty medallion was just shy of an inch. One side displayed a crowned Madonna and child set within a ring of starbursts. The back had two inscriptions, *Raquelita* and *3 de Mayo 1950*.

"What's this?"

"*La Virgen del Pilar*, the patron Virgin of Spain. My paternal grandmother had it made after I was born."

"I can't take this from you, angel." He protested, though he was deeply touched. "This is too valuable. You shouldn't part with it."

"All the more reason. From now on, she'll watch over you. Will you make me happy and wear it? This way you'll be taking a little of me with you. Hopefully it'll make you smile."

He nodded, captivated by the significance of her gesture. "I'll keep it close to me always. Please, put it on me."

Holding both ends of the chain, she reached around his neck, clasping it in place as she murmured, "I commend him to your care, *Virgencita*. Keep my Matthew safe." Setting his dog tags aside, she pulled the neck of his T-shirt and released the medal inside.

"There. Now I feel better."

***

Five hundred miles away, Emilio Muro woke full of purpose and vigor. He jumped out of bed and marched into the shower, ready to seize the day and outline a plan for his daughters' recovery. During his conversation with Julie last night, they agreed to retain an attorney and move swiftly. And after she accepted his heartfelt apologies for not calling throughout the day, Julianna agreed to marry him. He owed her flowers and some serious loving.

As the energizing rush of water pelted his skin, the anguish of the past forty-eight hours tried to resurface. He pushed it away. He wouldn't look to the past anymore, only to the future with Julie. The dull roll of the shower door alerted him to Julianna's presence.

"Coffee, anyone?" She waved a mug of steaming coffee.

"Coffee, yes. And more." Emilio grabbed the mug; with the other hand, he pulled wrist, arm, and owner inside the stall.

"Emilio, no, you're getting me all wet."

"Emilio, yes," he answered, setting the mug on the side shelf. He enfolded her into his arms and brought Julianna right under the spray.

"Don't you want coffee?" she spluttered, half-drowned.

"I do, but I want you more." One hand held her lower back; the other cradled the base of her head, tilting it gently back. He kissed her, hungry and intent, silencing any possible objections. The moment her tongue joined his, Emilio chuckled in delight and plundered deeper still.

He slipped the hand from her lower back to her abdomen, trailing under the hem of her sodden blouse. He began a slow caressing journey up, toward her silky bra and the treasures underneath. Emilio grasped the edge of a cup and, uttering an impatient groan, yanked it down, releasing her breast. Her arms tangled around his neck, pressing her body tightly against his. The first round of serious loving would begin now.

***

Emilio loved Julie's kitchen. Like her, it was small and sunny. The corner apartment allowed for windows on two walls, and light streamed in all day. The first time he visited her, he was astounded by her choice of décor—the straw-colored walls, spotless white countertops, and azulejos backsplash made him feel he was back in one of his relatives' kitchens. To cap the overall Mediterranean feel, a sidewall displayed a collection of authentic Talavera plates.

Emilio stood at the entrance as he finished buttoning his shirt and breathed in a lungful of air, amazed at how much brighter the world looked this morning. He smiled at his soon-to-be bride shifting to and fro in the small space with breakfast preparations. He decided then, as soon as they got married, they were moving into a house with a huge kitchen.

He approached her silently, set aside her long, still-damp tresses, and kissed the juncture of her neck and shoulder.

"Scoundrel," Julianna accused without turning around.

"Scoundrel? Me?"

"Yes, you. You made me change clothes twice."

"Darling, if it were up to me, you'd be wearing no clothes at all."

"You're impossible." She whirled around, and Emilio took advantage. He pecked her on the lips and reached around her back, aiming for the coffee mug on the countertop.

"What? I'm a guy, and you're beautiful. Can you blame me if I want to see you naked?" He shrugged, unaffected by her jesting scowl, and took a seat at the tiny kitchen table.

Julianna snickered as she followed behind him, holding a large platter of scrambled eggs, crispy bacon, and toast. "If you don't behave, I won't feed you," she said airily, setting the platter on the table.

"Aww, baby. Don't be sore. I can't help it if I can't get enough of you."

"If you continue down this path, lover, you'll be really late for work."

"At this moment, it may be a moot point," he said with a distant look.

"Would you care to explain?"

"A curious notion popped into my head the moment you left me so ignominiously alone in the shower. It's really all your fault."

Julianna couldn't tell anymore if he was serious or joking. The lopsided smile and tight expression were reminders of the early days, when Isabel used to hound Emilio constantly. She waited while he chewed on a rasher of bacon. Eventually, he would tell her.

"Isabel's sudden move... When did she get the job? How did she contact the Reynoldses?"

"She didn't know the Reynoldses personally?" Julianna's eyebrows shot up.

"Isabel met Coralina in Spain, before our marriage, but they've not spoken since. This move was well put together, efficiently organized and prepared. By the time Isabel was ready to leave, everything was in place to ease her transition."

"You think someone helped her?"

Emilio shook his head, his lips a solid line. "There's only one man who knows all the parties and could make this move easy for Isabel. But I refuse to accept it."

"Who?"

"Xavi."

Julianna gasped. "Why wouldn't he tell you?"

"I don't know. But today, before I do anything, I'm going to find out."

***

While he drove to the ranch, Emilio's mind was in turmoil. He anticipated Xavi's arguments and pondered his possible motivations. He was really worried. Xavi was his brother, the right hand he was unwilling to lose. Enough had been taken away, and a Judas kiss would be the coup de grâce. Damn, it would hurt.

The farm was the right location if the confrontation turned ugly. The grounds offered privacy and distance. Even if Xavi tried to avoid him today, he couldn't do so forever. This face-to-face would happen. Emilio had barely descended from his truck when the rumble of a familiar engine approached. Minutes later Xavi walked toward him at a fast clip.

"Emilio, I'm glad you're here. We need to talk."

"Is that a fact?" Xavi's direct approach threw him. Why had he envisioned Xavi evading him?

"This is important and private. Where should we go?" His tension was palpable.

"Let's take that bench," Emilio said with more calm than he felt. "If it starts to get busy, we'll go somewhere else."

There was an edge to Xavi's stride. His gestures were sharp, his usual coolness and detachment absent. He sat down with a jerk.

"There's much you don't know. Things I've never told you, from the old days, in Jerez. With Isabel."

"Isabel? What the hell…"

"Please, sit down. You're too restless. This isn't easy to talk about."

"Restless. I'm not restless. I'm outraged."

"All right," Xavi raised both palms up. "Allow me a minute, please." He slid to the end of the bench and patted the area next to him. Emilio hesitated, a sudden dread rising. They were about to discuss a lot more than his daughters. Exhaling a large breath, he sat and braced for the worst.

"I've been in love with Isabel since the night at the plaza. Remember that night?" Xavi clasped his hands together and leaned his elbows against his knees.

"Yes," Emilio whispered, blindsided by the revelation. Slowly, feeling much older, Emilio reached for the edge of the bench and sat, assuming his friend's pose. They stared at the floor, both minds traveling to the same place, the same fateful evening.

Isabel, lovely and playful among her friends. The late-evening breeze carried her joyful laughter to their ears. A perfect rose, a Spanish rose.

"But—"

"Let me finish," Xavi interrupted. "Let me pull out this twenty-year-old thorn."

"You didn't like her."

Xavi ignored his comment. "The night we met Isabel, she stole my heart. But in typical Emilio haste, you staked a claim immediately. From then on, I had to keep silent. How could I interfere in your happiness? You are my best friend, the brother I never had. Your happiness would always come first."

"You said Isabel was difficult and she needed a strong hand. You argued we shouldn't have married. You didn't like her at all."

"I hid it well, didn't I?" He scoffed. "It's all true. Isabel is everything I said and more. She was never right for you. Think of it. You needed someone like Julie. She's your ideal partner. Isabel needs a determined son of a bitch like me. When others give up, I persist. No matter how wild the stallion or mare, I always bring it around."

Emilio nodded. Since the first day of apprenticeship, everyone had observed Xavi's unusual talent. Indeed, he managed the worst, most skittish mounts without breaking their spirit. In turn, they accepted his dominance at once. None of the master trainers understood how it happened.

"Now you are divorced, and I'm free to speak about my love and explain why I helped Isabel move. I pray our friendship will survive."

In slow cadence, Xavi revealed why he'd acted with such antipathy toward Isabel. He told of his unilateral decision to help her move, his suspicions about her past, and the firm conviction he was the one man to heal Isabel Llorenz and make her happy.

Emilio listened with apparent interest. Encouraged by his behavior, Xavi explained with ease. He hadn't expected it and was relieved by his friend's understanding. It was the most liberating experience in Xavi's solitary emotional life.

"Emilio, I always respected your marriage. If you hadn't divorced, I would've taken my secret to the grave."

"Does Isabel know how you feel?"

"Not openly. My control failed once. Knowing Isabel, it sent up all sorts of red flags. Right now, she's plotting ways to avoid me."

"I'm sure she is. Look, I understand you respected our marriage, but your silence is inexcusable. You're supposed to be my friend. Why didn't you warn me? I should kill you for that."

"Kill me if it makes you feel better. Heaven knows I deserve it. I didn't tell you because you would've stopped me. I've watched Isabel for years. Something haunts her. It sits heavy on her shoulders, making her irascible and abusive. Since you left, your daughters have taken the brunt of her pain. It has to end. Isabel must be healed, and I couldn't do it while she remained here, where there is too much past history and resentment.

"One afternoon, she mentioned she longed to get away. She thought she was so clever, trying to use me. I hated keeping you in the dark, but there was no other way. The girls are safe. Jonas is on top of the situation, and I've made arrangements with Ferguson for a leave. I promise, all custody issues with your daughters will soon cease. You'll have free access to them. It's my vow to you."

Emilio didn't respond. Minutes passed without a word between them. They sat, two men side by side, a lifetime of friendship hanging in the balance. An occasional spark of tension crackled. Finally, Emilio straightened and turned to Xavi.

"I've suffered this shadow. Isabel needs help. You raised an argument which saves you from a black eye—my daughters' welfare. I'll try to understand why you kept silent, but knowing you didn't trust me makes me question our friendship. For the moment, I'll play this your way. If it gets complicated or Isabel remains obstinate, I will act and you *will* help me. I want my daughters. You owe me, Xavier Manel. Do we have an understanding?"

"We do."

"God, Xavi. All these years, and you never said a word. I'm still angry, but you deserve to be happy, and I hope you win. But be warned, Isabel can be treacherous. I speak from personal experience."

"I've always loved her, and now she's mine. Isabel knows it and wants it, much as she tries to hide or pretend otherwise. I know what I'm up against." He straightened and clasped a hand on Emilio's shoulder. "Knowing our friendship stands gives me strength. I would've been lost without you, my brother," Xavi said, sincerity and truth beaming on his face.

Chapter Five

Alabama – June 2nd 1967

Matthew had to find a way through Isabel Muro's impenetrable reticence. Soften her, somehow, before the end of the trip. *Talk about strategic military operations and dealing with hostiles.*

Mobile, Alabama, was the next and longest stop, with enough time for a sit-down meal at a proper coffee shop instead of a snack at a convenience stop. Perhaps if he extended an invitation to the Ice Lady and she accepted, he might endear himself to her. Maybe.

"Matthew? Are you all right?"

The prolonged silence hadn't escaped Raquelita. She stared at him.

"Everything's fine, sweetheart. I was plotting how to soothe your momma. I'm thinking of inviting y'all for breakfast when we reach Mobile. How does that sound?"

Raquelita smiled despite her doubts. "Mamá accept a breakfast invitation? Well, she might," she said, lowering her lids pensively. "With her, one never knows."

"Sweetheart, this is an investment in us." He tucked an errant lock of hair behind her ear. "If she agrees, we'll spend time together in a friendly environment, not rows away with all kinds of suspicions running through her mind. It makes me real, instead of the stranger next to her daughter. It gives me a face and a name. We'll be at the station in about forty minutes. Tell you what. I'm heading down the aisle on recon. I'll evaluate your momma's attitude. If it's safe, I'll spring an attack invitation. The surprise just might stun her to accept." He grinned, and the dimple flashed, eliciting her smile in response. "Ah…better. I love your smile."

Raquelita stared at Matthew, and a wave of elation swept through her. He really wanted a permanent place in her life and was taking the first steps to engineer it, neither afraid of nor deterred by her mother. His optimism was infectious, and she could do nothing other than hold his hand and let him lead her on this brand-new road. He was her miracle.

"Don't worry, angel. It's gonna be just fine," he said, his Texan accent reappearing. "You'll see. I've a mighty good feeling about this." He hunched under the light panel, leaned on the seat rests for leverage and, with his long legs, stepped over her and into the aisle.

Here we go, Operation Charm Mrs. Muro underway.

As they said, *extremis malis extrema remedia*. Matthew Buchanan deserved a pat on the back for bringing his dress uniform. His intention had been to change before arrival at Fort Benning. Now he prayed he could impress Mrs. Muro with a polished image. He straightened to his full six foot two height, reached inside his duffle, and removed the garment bag his mother had so carefully packed for him. Armed with all the necessary items, he marched to the lavatory.

The scene he encountered bewildered him. Marité slept soundly on her mother's lap as an enrapt Isabel caressed her face and hair with surprising gentleness. Isabel appeared vulnerable and lost, and Matthew felt a strange pang of sadness. Her forlorn expression cemented his decision to extend the invitation.

"Good morning, Mrs. Muro. I hope you rested during the night? It's difficult while sitting in a crowded bus, is it not?"

She smiled at him pleasantly. "Good morning to you, Matthew. Yes, to both questions. Traveling can be challenging, but I was able to get some sleep. Marité, as you will observe, had no difficulty."

"I'm glad to hear it, ma'am. If you'll excuse me." He tipped his head in a light salute.

Once inside the lavatory, Matthew leaned on the washbasin. He could use a moment to gather his thoughts and fortify his resolve. He turned on the faucet, threaded his wet fingers through his hair, ran a comb through the spiky tips, and dried his face. With great care, he unfolded the uniform, shirt, and tie. He shed the tropical-issue uniform, folded it into the bag, and changed garments. Satisfied with his final appearance, he stepped out.

"Excuse me, Mrs. Muro," Matthew said when he reached her seat. "Please allow me to start over from the beginning. I'm Matthew Buchanan from Round Rock, Texas, on my way to Fort Benning. I know you're on a long trip, unescorted and with two young daughters."

Isabel's lips opened slightly, but the frown stayed in place. Undeterred, he pressed on.

"I started thinking about my momma. If she were traveling in similar conditions, I would hope one of my military brethren would offer assistance. We'll soon be arriving at Mobile, and the stop is long enough for a decent meal. It would be my pleasure to invite you and your lovely girls for breakfast."

The invitation was clearly so unexpected, Isabel did not answer, and Matthew continued. "Your daughter Lita is most charming. I'm certain she learned from her momma. As for myself, I'm heading to a new base, and her enchanting company has distracted my thoughts from what lies ahead. It's my way of thanking you. I sincerely hope you'll accept."

It was quite the speech, and Matthew knew he had her. He wasn't Ernestine Buchanan's son for nothing. He crossed his fingers, waiting for her response.

"Why, I'm flattered, but it is totally unnecessary."

"It would be my pleasure if you accepted."

Isabel regarded him with a sharp eye. "I don't wish to impose on you." She paused as her brain did a one-hundred-meter sprint. She could use the distraction, and it was a perfect opportunity to observe Raquelita's companion and their chemistry together. She'd scented an air of interest between them last night. "If you are so certain, we accept."

"Thank you, ma'am." He pivoted and headed to his seat with a light step.

***

Forty minutes later, the bus pulled into the Mobile bus station. With a loud whoosh, the boarding door opened, allowing the stampeding passengers to scatter out in desperate search for food and other necessities.

Raquelita's nerves were on edge, yet she took one look at Matthew's serene face, and her jitters stopped. He appeared calm, as if nothing out of the ordinary was happening. If he could be at ease, so could she. It was time she gathered some courage and demolished her timid shell.

Seconds later, she was Dorothy in Oz, the peaceful ranch long gone. She tried to inhale a deep breath but couldn't. The air was warm and so thick it stuck to her lungs. The cacophony of street sounds and the hustle from the station attacked her ears. The city was awake, and its sounds reverberated in a dissonant symphony of horns, beeps, and human shouts. Was this the harbinger of her new life?

"I asked the driver where to eat." Matthew paused, looking at Marité. "Is this little flower your sister?" He smiled, bending to the girl's height.

"Say hello to Matthew, Marité. He's invited us for breakfast." Isabel pushed her forward. The girl extended her hand to Matthew with a giggle.

"Nice to meet you, Marité." He grasped the small fingers and shook them gently. "Okay, the driver recommended a diner around the corner. The food is good and the service is fast. Shall we?"

They passed through an alley and exited onto a busy street, skirting busy pedestrians and trying to stay together. Raquelita had no difficulty following Matthew. Taller than most, he stood out. Handsome in his dress uniform, he was a composed sentinel, his alert gaze searching his surroundings for the diner. Observing Matthew filled her with amazing pride. Out here in the world, he was stately, confident, and all hers.

The diner was busy, but they were seated quickly. At Matthew's urging, they ordered omelets, meats, pancakes, and grits. An odd aura of anticipation clung to the air as they sipped their drinks. Fingers tapped on the table and hands played with utensils and glasses as the opponents measured each other.

A mother can't be fooled for long, and Isabel was no different. Raquelita was doing her best to hide her attraction to Matthew but failed. If he moved or spoke, her expression changed, and her body turned to him ever so slightly. Isabel wondered if her daughter was aware of her behavior. Despite these signs of infatuation, Isabel was confident their arrival in Ocala would erase Matthew from Lita's mind. The young man, however, was a different matter.

"Matthew, how long have you been in the military? You seem young to be enlisted."

"Yes, ma'am. In these days, it's either enlistment or the draft. I chose the first."

Isabel nodded and pressed on, "Right, nineteen, then... Where's your next assignment?"

Lita wanted to yell at her mother to stop the Torquemada act. Why must she bring up the service or ask about future assignments? Why ask about his age? She searched for a sign of discomfort in Matthew, but other than a light sparkle in his eyes, he betrayed none. He answered with ease. He leaned against his chair, tipping it slightly back with his long legs.

Matthew had opened the door with the invitation, and a persistent Isabel took advantage. He seemed unaffected when he told her about high school, his family's ranch, and upcoming training at Fort Benning. He explained his choice of Special Forces and the inevitable Vietnam. He finished and waited for her next question.

"I see." Isabel's brain dashed into a mad sprint. Matthew was going to be busy. The likelihood of a leave before he shipped out was nil. There was the age gap as well. Almost-twenty-year-old men lost interest with inexperienced seventeen-year-old girls. Everything translated to Matthew fading from Raquelita's life forever. Whatever bloomed in Raquelita's heart, the flow of life would end it, and Isabel wouldn't have to dirty her hands terminating an inappropriate affair. "I wish you good fortune in your assignments and hope everything works out well for you," she said sincerely.

"Thank you, ma'am. You are very kind."

Matthew flashed a sample of his devastating smile, and Isabel almost choked on her coffee. Raquelita's enchantment had a sound basis. Matthew had an understated, masculine charm, an air of assuredness, and a peaceful steadiness, rare in a man his age, and much too dangerous in her opinion.

Their meals arrived, and they plunged in ravenously. As soon as their empty plates were removed, Matthew checked his watch. "Sorry, ladies, we need to return before the hour is up. I'm afraid our fun is over." He paid the tab, and once again they were thrust into the busy foot traffic. They returned to the station's loading bay without another word.

Matthew stopped at the door. "If you'll excuse me, ladies, I need to check on something inside the station." He tapped his forehead with his fingers. "It was a pleasure having breakfast with y'all. I'll see you back on the bus." He turned on his heel and disappeared inside the station.

"Hmmm," Isabel murmured.

***

Matthew returned to find Raquelita in his seat by the window, staring out and ignoring his arrival. He pressed a hand for leverage against the seat back and leaned close to her face. His lips brushed her earlobe.

"Nope. This ain't gonna work. You're going back to the aisle seat. That's where I want you, with your full attention on me, not out the window."

Something about the terse order gave her a vision of Matthew in command, and her stomach quivered with a strange excitement. Lita turned away from the window to find his intent regard.

"Please, get rid of that look. I want my smile back, the smile I love so much. We have about five hours before we part in Tallahassee, and I want you seated as close to me as possible. I want to drown in your scent, your beauty, and warmth. I'm gonna kiss and caress you at every opportunity. You and I are going to live days in these five hours. Don't you know I love you?"

She jerked at his comment. Matthew leaned in closer. The warmth of his breath bathed her face, and she lowered her eyelids. Nothing on this earth could've stopped his next move. He slanted his mouth and took hers in a deep, long, savoring kiss.

"Now. You need to return to your seat so I can get to mine." He winked, and Raquelita laughed.

"Care to tell me what happened?" he asked, once settled. "I could see it growing at the diner. Please, tell me."

"It's me and Mamá. She presses, I jump. She pulls, I hide. It's the only dance I've ever known. She suspects something between us but isn't certain. So she threw the verbal digs and jabs, and I fell for each of them— your age, the service, the distance."

"What about my age?"

"There is a huge age difference between us. I'm seventeen years old."

"It's less than three years. I'll be twenty in three months, angel. It may seem a lot right now, but when you turn twenty, I'll only be twenty-two. I realize it's too soon, and you've been mistreated for a long time. The only way we'll survive is to believe in each other. What I feel for you is alive in here." Reinforcing his words, he pressed her open palm above his heartbeat. "You are the keeper, no one else. Do you understand?"

His regard was serene, and she nodded. Age, distance, war—even interfering mothers—were excuses for hearts not truly engaged, when commitment, intention, and love were just words. He took an envelope out of his jacket and presented it to her. There was a card inside. The title read *Mobile, Alabama*, just above a gorgeous photograph of an ornate fountain surrounded by colorful trees in full bloom. And his dedication:

A little memento of Mobile.

Don't forget I love you,
Matthew

P.S. I do.

P.P.S. The photo is of Bienville Park in Mobile. It's a beautiful place, not nearly as beautiful as you, Raquelita. Let's return when we're older.

She held the card against her chest, and smiled. "Matthew, I could never forget. You are my heart."

Chapter Six

Florida – June 2nd 1967

The afternoon skies darkened without warning. Wave upon wave of blinding water blanketed the windshield of the bus. Despite their steady metronome-like effort, the wipers couldn't keep up; the hazard lights clicked in incessant counterpoint. Silence thickened inside the bus as the vehicle's progress became slow and laborious. Lightning flashed ahead, jagged threads connecting earth and sky. Thunderclaps rumbled and rolled in quick succession like angry, growling beasts.

Raquelita and Matthew sat huddled in the tight knot of each other's arms, her cheek pressed tightly against his chest as he nuzzled her crown of silky hair. The unexpected darkness was a willing accomplice to their intimacy. Tallahassee lay ahead. The final countdown had begun.

Lita's throat ached. Tears clamored to be released. Matthew remained silent. His breathing kept a slow tempo. They were past worry of discovery. This was stronger than either had imagined, and their separation was imminent. They couldn't stay apart, not now. He needed her as much she needed him.

She looked up at him. "I'm not ready to say good-bye. Not ready at all. I've not yet learned enough about you. I need to know more. There hasn't been time for…" Her voice cracked, and tears began to roll. It made speaking so much harder. "I haven't told you about me either. There's so much I want you to know."

He brushed her cheek as he returned her head to the cradle of his chest. "Tell me, angel. Tell me everything."

"I like to write poems. I didn't have time to show you, but I have this notebook. And…I didn't tell you…I love kids. I want to work with children who n-need help." The knot in her throat tightened, allowing no further words. She pressed her face against his chest.

"That's wonderful, sweetheart. You're so kind. I know they'll adore you. I'll be looking forward to your beautiful letters. You'll write to me every day, won't you?"

He knew her desperation. Time was running out. Every minute without a word was wasted. Could they each compress enough of themselves into the other before they said good-bye? Was this the send-off the Fates had planned for him before he shipped out? Was this his brief taste of happiness before the ruin of war, like a modern-day Moses granted a fleeting glimpse of the Promised Land, though never allowed to enter?

He had to believe Destiny brought them together for a firm purpose, not idle entertainment. Rocky or not, this was their beginning. This would be his focus. One day followed by another, and before long, she would be in his arms again. The vision came to him in a quick flash— in four weeks, between Fort Benning and Fort Bragg. Yes, they would see each other again.

"Angel, listen to me carefully. You now have my APO address. Write to me as soon as you arrive, okay? I'm counting on you."

He reached into his pocket and pulled out his wallet, extracting a fifty-dollar bill. "Take this. It's important."

Shaking her head, she fisted her hand, refusing the bill. "No. I can't accept this money. You need it."

"No, I don't. This is more important. I've been figuring things out, and this is our contingency plan." His fingers touched hers. Raquelita opened her hand, and he pressed the bill on her palm. Slowly, he folded her fingers back over it. He smiled at the still-stubborn frown on her face.

"You're going to ask your relatives if we can use their address for our correspondence. If they deny our request, or if you have any other difficulties, use this money to rent a box at the post office. Are you following me?"

Yes, she was. Clearly.

"This is our last resort, okay? When you write, send me the address and phone number in Ocala." He pulled out a sheet of paper, folded it, and tore it in two. "This half has my parents' address and phone number. By tomorrow, they'll know about you. Use it if you need to. They're loving people and will always help. When you meet them you'll understand. Use the other to write down your father's address and phone number in San Antonio. I must have more than one way to find you."

He deposited a light kiss on her lips. "It's not going to be easy, but we'll do everything to make it work in our favor. Let's keep the possibilities in mind, rather than the impossibilities. Are you with me?"

Her smile was steady, her expression serene, and with every breath she seemed to relax.

The storm abated while they spoke. The late-afternoon sun caught suspended drops of water at a perfect angle. A full rainbow arced ahead, the ancient symbol of the Creator's covenant with mankind, and the omen he needed—a sign of hope and second chances. "Time will pass faster than you think. Please, wait for me. I am coming back for you."

Just below the rainbow, the city's skyline was growing larger. He pulled her hands to his lips and kissed them tightly. Her face was composed. At least he'd managed to erase her trepidation.

A slight peripheral movement caught his eye, and he turned to the aisle to see Isabel approach. "Your momma's here, my love." In silent accord, they released each other's hands, reluctantly returning to their separate seating positions.

"Hello, Matthew. Wasn't that a wild storm?" Isabel addressed him with a light smile. "Raquelita, we're almost at Tallahassee. Get your things together. We don't stay in the same bus. This one continues east."

"Yes, ma'am, this bus goes to Jacksonville. I have to transfer as well."

Isabel ignored him. "Make sure you have everything ready. I want to get off as soon as possible. I need to stretch my legs before we transfer. Are you listening, Raquelita?"

"Yes, Mamá. I'll be ready. I need to go to the ladies' room now, before we pull in." She swiped at her carry bag, stood with a jerk, and without a word passed her mother on her way toward the lavatory. Isabel looked at Matthew questioningly, and he answered with a shrug.

"Matthew, it was a pleasure meeting you. Thanks again for your generous invitation, and I do wish you the best of luck with your new assignment. I'll be praying for you." With a skewed smile, Isabel slowly turned for her seat, but not before her gaze sent him a silent message: *Be gone forever.*

"Thank you, ma'am. I appreciate the sentiment. The pleasure was all mine, I assure you." He tilted his head and flashed his own riposte back: *Don't count on it.*

Raquelita returned silent and stiff, same as when she left. "Are you all right, angel?"

She nodded, staring toward the large windscreen. They were almost at the station. In seconds, the bus came to a full stop. Instinctively, they turned to each other, their hands joined one last time.

Everything around them went into slow motion. Lita searched inside her carry bag, pulled out a folded sheet of paper, and presented it to Matthew. His eyes flicked from her to the paper and back. She mouthed *I love you,* and tapped his chest, right above the medal.

Travelers around them milled about, gathering their belongings. One by one, they marched up the aisle toward the exit. Matthew looked to his right as Isabel and Marité approached. The moment had come.

"Please, let me help you with your bags." Without waiting for Isabel's response, he reached out and grabbed their bags. He allowed the three women to pass, pulled his duffel and hat, and stepped into the aisle. Once outside, their little group moved away from the door, letting stragglers exit the bus.

"Mrs. Muro, do you know which bus you're taking to Ocala?"

Isabel looked perplexed. Tallahassee was a large station, busier than Mobile and almost as insane as New Orleans. Peering around, she moved onto the main platform. "Matthew, would you be a dear and stay with the girls for a few minutes? I need to locate our bus."

"It'll be my pleasure." Matthew watched her disappear within the crowd and turned to Raquelita. They stood in silence, immersed in each other, inhaling every last bit.

Good-bye.

Isabel returned as quickly as she'd left, breaking the spell. "I found it. Let's go, girls. We need to make sure everything's ready."

Matthew picked up their bags and trailed after Isabel's quick steps. The bus awaited, the engine primed, the huge transport ready to gobble up its passengers and head onward to the next destination.

"Well, this is where I take my leave," Matthew said, placing their bags on the floor. "It has been a pleasure. I hope y'all have a safe journey." He reached down to Isabel's hand and brought it up to his lips for a courteous brush.

He turned to Marité, and she surprised him with a tight hug around the waist. Isabel shrugged in a silent apology. Raquelita was still, ghostly pale. Her lips were a thin line. Her eyes glittered. She fooled no one.

In a bewildering move, Isabel pushed Marité ahead of her. "Come on, Mari. Let's go. Say good-bye, Raquelita. Quickly." They clambered up the steps.

Matthew grasped her hand and pressed it against his lips. Unlike Isabel's, this kiss was hot and fierce. "I love you. You know it. Keep it in your heart, Raquelita. Don't let go. Don't forget. We'll see each other soon, I promise."

"Yes, I won't forget. Don't *you* let go."

"Never. Raquelita, never! Farewell, my angel, till we meet again." Matthew released her hand, touched his forehead in salute, and pivoted around.

***

Raquelita took a tentative step into the bus, but her leaden legs refused to obey. She tried again and barely managed one step. How could she do this without him? She turned to the left just as Matthew walked away. He was so beautiful. So elegant in his stride, so august. She was filled with pride, longing…and pain. Acute pain dug a hole in her chest. Raw, stinging pain. It burned, singed, and scorched. The need to stop him was so powerful she almost turned on her heels and ran outside to the shelter of his arms.

How she reached the back of the bus, she would never remember. Here she was, face-to-face with her new reality—the road without Matthew. On one side of the aisle sat Isabel, the embodiment of determination and sternness. Across the way, her sister offered comfort and solace. Raquelita settled in her seat and reached for Marité's hand, squeezing it in silent gratitude. She looked out the window, and was granted one last glimpse. Matthew had reached the loading area for his bus. In two more steps, he disappeared behind it.

Good-bye. I love you.

***

Time was a blur of highway lines and speeding vehicles. When Matthew finally focused, hours had passed. The empty seat next to him was the stark reminder. He thought about placing his duffle bag and hat on it, same as he had when he left home. No, the seat would remain symbolically empty. He remembered the folded piece of paper and pulled it out of his front pocket. *For Columbus,* it read in her beautiful script. He had no clue where he was. He leaned toward the man sitting in front.

"Excuse me, where exactly are we?"

"We're close to Blakely, mister."

"Thanks." Blakely. He was halfway there and couldn't wait another minute. With extreme care, he unfolded the neat white sheet of stationery.

Remember

I'll beseech a gentle wind
Entrust it to do my bidding
Through the miles to offer
Precious thoughts of love
Whispers of longing and need
The night's spirits will witness
The perfect union of our hearts
In the realm of our dreams
The dominion of our love
Remember, we are one.

My Matthew.
My heart.
My love.

Raquelita.
June 2, 1967

Matthew folded the paper and slowly returned it to his front pocket. He patted the medal hanging above his heart. As he succumbed to sleep, her beautiful face filled all the spaces of his mind.

***

"Lita, wake up. We're here."

Raquelita bolted upright and stared at her sister. Moved by deep affection, Raquelita held Marité's face and placed two loud kisses, one on each rosy cheek.

"Thank you, Marité. Without you, I wouldn't have made it this far."

"Lita, it's not going to be easy." She nodded in the direction of Isabel. "I promised I'd help you, and I will." She affirmed with a thoughtful look, much older than her years. "I get a nice feeling from Matthew."

"Thank you, sweetie. I needed to hear it." Raquel leaned forward, massaging her temples. "I was beginning to fear it had been a dream."

"Oh no, Matthew's real and very cute." The little girl giggled. "Really cute."

"Girls." Isabel interrupted.

Raquelita glared back, brazenly tangling with her mother's harsh stare. Isabel's head tilted in careful regard. "Raquelita, what sort of look is that?"

Lita sneered. "I'm sure I don't know, Mom."

"Did you just say 'Mom'?"

Raquelita nodded, slowly and deliberately. She'd changed.

***

The welcoming committee in Ocala was effervescent and boisterous. Inside the receiving hall, Aunt Coralina, Uncle Jonas, and Cousin Lorrie waved, while Cousin Michael stood at the entrance of the station holding the leash of an eager, smiling Lab.

The sisters stepped down as Isabel gave orders to stay put. They complied, glancing through the glass doors at the exuberance of the welcoming group. If this was the other side of their family, they couldn't be any more different. Raquelita looked to her mother. There she stood, as usual, scowling, arguing, and gesticulating at the man unloading the bus, while she pointed from item to item.

Isabel returned holding two huge suitcases and frowned at her two spellbound daughters. "Well, if you're not going to help. Go. Say hello to your relatives." The words had barely left her lips before the sisters picked up their carry bags and rushed out.

Uncle Jonas dominated the group with his tremendous height. He wore jeans, boots, and a white button-down shirt folded mid-sleeve, reminding her of ranch owners back home. *Home.* The word made her tremble. Where was home now?

"Welcome to Ocala, ladies. Welcome." Uncle Jonas's powerful baritone rumbled through the room. He reached for Isabel's hand and, with a dazzling smile, shook it effusively.

"My word, you've grown into a beautiful young lady." Coralina spoke from behind Raquelita.

Aunt Coralina's resemblance to Raquelita's father, Emilio, was so surprising that Lita threw her arms around her aunt's waist, holding on for dear life. Her embrace was warm, comforting, and steady. A scent of orange and jasmine—the sweet fragrance of tropical summer mornings—enveloped her senses.

Overwhelmed by the unexpected connection to her father and moved by pure instinct, Raquelita buried her face into her aunt's chest and wept, releasing it all—separation from her father, loss of her home, sundering from Matthew.

"Shhh, child. It's okay, I know. It's going to be okay," she murmured, rocking Lita in place.

Isabel seethed, uncomfortable with the forgotten similarity between brother and sister and stunned by her oldest child's embarrassing display. She would address this outburst and her insolent behavior on the bus later.

"Raquelita, stop blubbering at once." Isabel had to suppress the impulse to physically intervene and separate the two women. "I'm sorry, Coralina. I don't know what's come over her."

"There is no need to apologize. Raquelita is my niece, and it's wonderful to finally hold her," Coralina countered, halting the rain of kisses on Lita's hair. "Don't fuss over the behavior of children. She seems exhausted." The words were uttered lightly, but the veiled challenge in her glance was impossible to mistake. "Lita simply needs a moment. Take all the time you need, child, all the time you need."

Her aunt's expressed tenderness was so alluring, that Raquelita couldn't help envisioning how wonderful it would be to grow up under her care. Her aunt was one of those people who commanded with gentility and elicited devotion with love. With a last sniffle, she pulled away. "I'm sorry, Aunt Coralina. I got your blouse all wet." She touched the dampened spot.

Coralina's laughter took flight, filling Raquelita's ears with musical enchantment. "Oh, it's nothing. In Florida, we're used to a lot more. Feel better?"

Lita nodded vigorously. Coralina couldn't fill the emptiness nor close the distance to home or Matthew, yet she offered a connection to her father through the mystery of blood ties. More importantly, she offered a promise—Lita wouldn't face her ordeal alone.

"Lorrie has been waiting anxiously for your arrival." Her aunt steered her gently by the shoulders to her cousin.

Lorrie took after her father, tall and pretty, with lustrous dark brown hair cascading past her shoulders. Her bright blue eyes—a testimony to paternal genes—sparkled in the light, and a cute smattering of freckles adorned the bridge of her nose. Raquelita admired the fashionable bell-bottom, hip-hugging jeans she would never be allowed to wear, and a multicolored tie-dyed T-shirt. Lorrie opened her arms wide, and in the welcoming embrace, fashion was forgotten.

Isabel watched the scene, questioning if Ocala had been a wise choice. At first glance, the contrast was significant between the Reynoldses' philosophy and the neatly ordered system she'd established for her daughters. Perhaps she'd swapped her troubles in Texas with a new set in Florida, the uncontrollable real world.

"All right, let's get on the move," Jonas interjected. "I'm sure you want to go home and get some rest. Besides, Michael and Sam are waiting their turn to meet y'all."

"Michael? Sam?" Marité asked.

"Why, yes." Jonas smiled, bending down to address his niece, the disparity in height almost comical. "Michael's your cousin, and Sam's the impatient Lab drooling outside." Changing his direction and purpose, Jonas reached down and swept Marité in his arms, cradling her against his side.

"Let's go meet them. You'll love Sam." He explained as he strutted outside with Marité. Coralina, unfazed by her husband's zest, watched the scene while stroking Lita's shoulders.

The interaction between dog and little girl was adorable to watch. Michael greeted her first, with Sam the Lab following close behind. Marité bent to pat the handsome head, and her cheek was thoroughly licked for her efforts. She giggled, which got Sam going, nudging her hand with his head for more. Marité relented, and Sam leaned against her, enjoying the little girl's gentle strokes.

Raquelita realized she was smiling. Life was full of twists and unexpected surprises. The painful separation from her father had brought her the love of her life. She'd dreaded and feared Ocala, but after meeting her family, it wasn't as intimidating anymore. There was shelter and solace in the home of her aunt and uncle. She might even receive precious help in corresponding with Matthew. Perhaps this town would be good.

***

And so, directions once solidly set changed.
What was not intended, happened:
the young lives were now irretrievably entwined.
The Ancients were pleased.

Chapter Seven

Ocala – June 2nd 1967

With much merrymaking, the van was loaded with luggage and family. Once everyone was settled and strapped in, Jonas pulled away and drove off in the direction of IH75. Everyone spoke at the same time, and Marité, overexcited by it all, chattered incessantly.

"Michael, how long have you had Sam? You are so lucky to have him. I wish I had dogs. They're so much fun. I love them even more than I like horses. My Papá trains horses in Texas. Did you know—"

"Marité, stop your babbling this instant," Isabel snapped, and the conversation froze.

Michael remained impervious. "I don't mind at all, Aunt Isabel. Mari, you can ask me all the questions you want. We've had Sam about five years. There's also Nina, a border collie, and she's very sweet." He laughed, mussing Marité's hair affectionately. "Just like you."

"We train horses as well," Jonas chimed in, his tone kind and patient. "Tomorrow, I'll show you around. I'm sure you'll find it similar to the ranch in Texas. We hope you'll like it."

At the next exit, Jonas took the off-ramp onto a country road. He continued a few miles, made a right turn, and drove through a stately gate guarding the entrance of a long winding road. Minutes later, he stopped before a single-story house. With a set of jangling keys in hand, Coralina descended quickly and rushed to open the door. Jonas followed on the other side, instructing the kids to collect the bags and belongings.

"Welcome to your new home, Isabel." Coralina breezed around, flicking lights on to illuminate a pleasant living room. In the center, a set of plush sofas arranged in an L shape faced a wood-burning fireplace.

Isabel walked over to the mantel. "A real fireplace?"

"Sure. They're great for Central Florida winters. Follow me, and I'll show you the kitchen." Coralina ushered her through a connecting hallway to a well-appointed kitchen. A paneled door accessed the backyard, while a large pane window took up half the sidewall. Under the window, a table and two small chairs were neatly arranged.

"The pantry is this way." She pointed to a closed door. "I'll take you food shopping tomorrow. You should have enough essentials to get you through the morning."

"I really appreciate what you're doing to help us. But I can't put you out like this."

"Put us out, how?"

"The house is charming, but a little small to accommodate everyone."

Coralina's laughter filled the air. "Dear, this is the guest house. There's plenty of room. I've not shown you the rest yet. There are three bedrooms through that hallway."

"I don't know what to say. You're being so generous."

"There's nothing to say." Coralina touched her forearm gently. "We want you and the girls to be comfortable. You'll find several phones around the house, so the girls can call their father. Goodness. Before I forget, Xavi called. He wanted to know if y'all had arrived. He'll call you tomorrow."

Isabel paled. Her purse and bag fell on the floor.

***

Isabel paced in little circles, unsure of what to do first, unpack or collapse on the bed. Her new bedroom wasn't a bad setup. It was clean and neat, but with zero personality, much like a blank canvas, a good analogy for her new life. Here she could draw her own picture. She didn't have to share her space or justify where her clothing fell, and had no man to answer to. It was only herself, her responsibilities, and her capricious dreams.

After long hours and miles, the trek finally weighed her down. Ditching her shoes carelessly, she slumped at the edge of the bed. *Time for some much needed privacy.* Privacy: an overrated word. Solitude would only bring her rash decisions and disconcerting thoughts into sharp relief. She began to unbutton her blouse, but her shaking fingers made it difficult. Abandoning the garment, she bent her head, taking an honest personal inventory.

What had possessed her to leave Texas without studying the consequences? In a remarkable display of immaturity, she'd thrown a tantrum, and here she was—a divorced woman with little money, no steady job, and two needy daughters to support. Pressured by gossip, pride, and shame, she'd moved without a single cautionary thought. Shame, in all its noxious permutations, had forever been a ruthless companion, the dictator of her decisions, and she'd submitted again, accepting Xavi's option.

Xavier Manel Repulles. The slightest thought of the man stirred flustering thoughts and feelings. Despite all efforts to ignore him, he pulled at her, dazzled her with his inner fire. Her fingertips tingled with the desire to touch him. *¡Cielo santo!* Now she really owed him. Thanks to Xavi, they were settled in a safe place, assisted by kind, helpful people. What would he require in return?

Enough. She needed rest. Her brain was turning to mush. In the morning, she might devise a strategy with room for gratitude, but excluding her as payment. Relieved by this decision, she quickly undressed and donned a sleep shirt. Her last thought was her nightly prayer: *Please, keep the nightmares away tonight.*

***

Raquelita raised the window and tilted her temple against the frame. *No star wishes tonight.* Their twinkle dimmed by a dense layer of clouds. A breeze wafted through the metal screen, sultry and thick, redolent with an unfamiliar floral and piquant scent. It elicited languorous desires, sensuous memories of strong arms, warm hands, long, full kisses, and the man who, in the course of a night, had awakened her womanhood.

Tomorrow, she'd begin all the necessary steps to communicate with Matthew. She'd received from her aunt an encouraging message of empathy. Still, the endeavor required extreme caution. It would be disastrous to confide in her aunt only to have her plans betrayed to her mother. At the first hint of vacillation, she would squash the request and use her ace card—the money Matthew had given her to open the post office box.

To endure their separation, constancy, creativity, and faith were required. The journey couldn't be hurried, for the military controlled it. She could bear it, as long as she held a connection with Matthew.

***

Isabel awoke with a gasp. She pulled stiffly at the twisted sheets around her body. Her mouth was dry, her body a furnace, and her drenched nightgown was stuck to her limbs. It was the same terror each night, but when she awoke, details eluded her, and only frightful shadows remained. One day—she promised herself—one day she would challenge the demon and win, or lose her sanity trying.

The clock on the nightstand read 5:05. Too early to rise, yet impossible to fall asleep again. Thoughts of her new life were slowly overtaking the remnants of her nightmare. Maybe a long, hot shower would help.

Twenty minutes later, feeling restored, she dressed and began her explorations. She peeked quietly in her daughters' rooms. Everything looked normal. Satisfied, she proceeded to the kitchen and ambled about. The décor was simple: white countertops and cabinets with pale yellow appliances. She found a full complement of pots and pans, dishes, flatware, glasses, and coffee mugs stored in cabinets and drawers. Coffee and a percolator were in a cupboard, which she quickly set up on a burner.

She turned toward the fridge and forgot everything. In the rising dawn, the huge side window displayed the full panorama of the Reynolds Ranch. The fields extended to infinity. Interspersed in the distance, hulking silhouettes of laurel oaks broke the lines of the terrain. Wispy blankets of mist floated above the emerald lawns. Tiny drops of dew hung precariously on pointy blades of grass, waiting for their moment to sparkle like early morning diamonds under the sun. Out on the horizon, barely distinguishable, a white fence demarcated the property line of the immense ranch.

Isabel longed to inhale a lungful of air and plunge into this new environment. The scent of coffee brewing tantalized her more. After pouring herself some of the aromatic beverage, she sat down and prepared to enjoy the show the sun was about to perform on the earth. The phone's insistent rings interrupted her reverie, and she rushed to the living room before its inopportune sound awoke the girls.

"Hello," she answered breathlessly.

"Isabel?"

Her legs buckled, and she dropped her full weight on the sofa. Xavi's resonant baritone spread like wildfire through every cell in her body. She quivered, self-conscious and delighted at once.

"Yes," Isabel whispered.

"Good morning, Isabel. It's good to hear you. I trust you're rested."

Isabel had the oddest need to check her robe and ensure she was presentable. "Good morning. I d-did rest, though not as much as I would have liked." She gave a nervous titter. "And I'm so grateful for all your help. Everything is perfect. Jonas and Coralina have arranged a very comfortable guesthouse for us. They're wonderful, and your touch is everywhere." There, she'd been suitably grateful.

Dead silence at the other end. Should she speak?

"Isabel, I promised, anything you needed, I would make happen. I keep my promises," he said with a slight edge. "I'm not pleased you've not rested. Is your bedroom adequate?"

"Oh yes, it is. I was overly tired last night." She paused again. "Xavi, it's all so different here. In Ocala, I mean."

"Of course, Florida is different," he murmured. "It's lush and humid like a woman at her peak, ready for her lover's presence. Nothing on earth is more beautiful, sensuous, or mysterious."

Isabel's brain came undone. His softly spoken suggestion aroused her on the spot. She could feel the humidity he spoke of. He was slowly unveiling his charms, spoon-feeding her the real Xavi while demolishing her barriers. She had the odd vision of a rustling snare coiling about her ankles.

"Err..." was the extent of her articulation.

"Listen, Isabel," he interjected. "I have to cut this short. There's business I must attend to. Before I go, how are the girls?"

"Tired, of course. They're still sleeping."

"Good. Kiss them for me, especially Raquelita. I'm sure Emilio will call later." Suddenly, his tone turned hard, the admonishment clear. "Isabel, Emilio wants to speak with his daughters. Don't interfere."

"Sure, Xavi. Whenever he wants," she agreed without a protest.

"Good girl. I'll call later. Try to get some rest. Whatever you must do, it can wait until tomorrow. Isabel, I miss you."

The line went dead on the earpiece, and she was left alone to relive his words and examine her unprecedented reactions. She'd joined a tiger inside his cage, had she not? And she was in over her head.

***

It was a fine Central Florida morning. Puffy white clouds, like huge cotton balls, dotted the bright blue sky. Coralina arrived, chatting incessantly. The morning and afternoon were all planned. She drove them around the center of town, from Silver Springs Boulevard to Pine Avenue and Ocala Square. From there, she proceeded to the nearest supermarket for supplies. When Isabel offered money to the cashier, Coralina stopped her.

"I'll explain later, Isabel." She paid the bill without further explanation.

Back at the ranch, they ate on the shady side of the wraparound porch under huge ceiling fans, enjoying a selection of exotic salad greens and roast chicken, along with sweet iced tea and a fresh fruit salad. While the kids cleaned up, the adults moved inside to the large family room to while away the hottest hours of the day in easy conversation.

In the late afternoon, the ranch tour began, and Jonas, always a gracious host, was full of information. He didn't balk at the myriad questions thrown at him, explaining in detail the workings of the ranch and how the business was run, making comparisons and pointing out the differences between his ranch and the one in Texas.

By the time they visited the last paddock, Raquelita was past anxious. The afternoon was growing late, and her plans remained idle. She leaned against the tall fence, her mind consumed by her dilemma. How and when to address the Matthew issue?

"Penny for your thoughts?" Her aunt imitated her stance. Their elbows touched lightly. "Who's troubling you? Is it the young man or your father? Perhaps both?"

Raquelita's head snapped around. "How did you know?" Holding on to the fence, she pushed up and stiffened, preparing for battle or escape.

"It's not difficult to figure out. Earlier, Isabel mentioned a young man, and then I remembered last night's tears, which I blamed on the trip and the separation from your dad. Today, however, your face tells a different story. Your heart is far away, and it's not Texas."

Gently, Coralina placed a hand on Lita's arm. "It may surprise you, but I remember how it felt when I met your Uncle Jonas. You have the same wistful look."

"Aunt Coralina, I know you're going to say it's impossible. How can I explain? I know we just met, but we love each other. We do."

"I know you're in love, *querida*. Maybe it's our gypsy blood. Muro women recognize their men on sight. I suppose he's nice and cute?"

"Oh, he is. He's wonderful. I hope one day you'll meet him." Releasing a new rush of words, she elucidated about her Matthew, how they met and fell for each other, what transpired during the trip, and at long last, she articulated her request. "He's the world to me, and he's waiting for my letters. Can you help us?"

"I gather you don't want Isabel to know."

"No, she can't." She gripped her aunt's arm, squeezing it harder than she intended. "You don't know my mother. If she learns we're writing to each other, she'll destroy it all. He's too important. He needs me. He *will* need me, when he's shipped overseas. Please, will you help us? Will you help me?"

"I'll accept your judgment of Matthew, for now. I agree he's going to need support from home and loved ones. All the men in the military will. He's asking for yours in particular." She paused. "I have to discuss this with your father. Emilio is a fair, levelheaded man, and I'll follow his rule. Until then, you have my permission to write to Matthew. You may use the business address. It's more private. However, if I sense any mischief, or if your father decrees otherwise, the privileges stop. Agreed?"

The wave of relief was so huge she threw her arms around Coralina. "Thank you. Thank you so much. Matthew asked for everyone's addresses and phone numbers, in case of emergency. Is that all right? He really dislikes all this subterfuge but knows it's necessary. He met Mom."

"Matthew's request shows character. I like that. I'll also talk to Jonas. Don't worry, he's a true romantic." She winked. "Why do you think I fell for him?"

Raquelita almost started a happy dance, uttering words of gratitude. She'd received permission and was anxious to begin her letter, to be close to him again and hold him within the imaginary circle of her arms. Already her mind composed her opening words:

Sweetheart, here I am, as promised. Aunt Coralina and Uncle Jonas have agreed to help us. We may use the ranch address for our communications. My relatives are loving and wonderful, just as you predicted. But you know this, my love. I feel you with me.

She almost blushed, thinking of her next words:

I miss you so much, every minute without you is intolerable. I long for your touch, the feel of your hands caressing me. Are you as needful as I am?

"What's going on?"

Like the grating sound of a needle scratching a record, Isabel's question jarred Raquelita out of her daydream. She stepped away from her aunt and stared at the ground.

Arms tight across her chest, Isabel stared at her daughter. "Raquelita?" Her heel tapped the ground impatiently.

"Nothing, we're just talking."

"Hey, Isabel," Coralina intervened. "I was suggesting we should call Emilio. The girls would love to speak to their dad. What do you say?"

"Do you miss him that much, Raquelita?"

"Of course, Mom. I love Papá. I miss him."

Isabel froze. The "Mom" word remained. Lita had been distant and petulant since Tallahassee. She dedicated a fleeting thought to Matthew, but rejected it. The time they'd spent together had been too brief. It had to be Emilio. "I suppose you do," she stated carefully.

"Great. Let's return to the ranch. We'll have something to drink, cool off, and call Emilio. How does that sound?" With perfect timing, Coralina's chatter ended the awkward exchange.

***

Isabel followed the conversation between Emilio and Raquelita from a distance, seemingly offering privacy while hearing every word. Several times she had to squash the desire to yank the phone away and tell her ex to shove the handset in his nether regions. But she controlled herself, observing instead this stranger, this almost mutinous and insolent young woman who claimed to be her daughter.

Why was she so suddenly consumed with her daughter's behavior? She'd never cared before. It bothered her; in the span of twenty-four hours, Lita had sought emotional relief with an aunt she'd just met, and now with her father. Ludicrous or not, Isabel felt like an outsider. The corresponding stab of jealousy made a rare mark on her soul.

They might be mother and daughter, but they were utter strangers. In all her seventeen years, Raquelita had never reached out to her for comfort. For that matter, had Isabel ever started a conversation, offered a gesture of affection to her oldest child? It had taken a move across several states and a phone conversation for Isabel to grasp the truth: an abyss yawned between herself and her firstborn.

***

"Mamá. Please, wake up."

Isabel bolted upright. Marité's fearful, teary eyes stared right up into hers.

"Mamá?" Her daughter's small hands held her forearms tightly. "You were having a bad dream. It scared me."

"Did I wake you?" Isabel could barely speak. Her mouth was a desert. "I'm thirsty. Please, Mari, get me some water?" Her nightly flailing was a constant worry and one day would betray her. These dreams had to end. Next time, it could be Raquelita awakening her with pointed questions, and this was not an option.

Marité left and then returned, holding a glass of sloshing water in her trembling hands. "Are you feeling better, Mamá?"

Isabel took it and gulped greedily. "Yes, thank you. Mari, you can go back to bed now. I'm fine."

Her daughter's gaze, with irises as dark as those of her father, remained fixed on Isabel. "Mamá, why don't you let me sleep with you?"

"Mari, you know my rules. You sleep in your own bed," Isabel replied, returning her daughter's stare with a level look.

"But tonight you need my company," she pleaded. It was obvious the child needed reassurance more than she did.

"All right, Marité, but just this once." She relented, sliding to the center and lifting the coverlet.

The girl crawled in. Isabel reached over and turned off the light as Marité burrowed close to her. Soon she was emitting tiny, raspy breaths. Slowly, Isabel stroked her youngest daughter's hair. Affection always flowed easier with Marité. She remembered her earlier thoughts of Lita, and a tinge of regret began to surface. Isabel pushed it aside. She was not about to change her philosophy. The oldest received the sternest discipline. It worked best this way.

***

Isabel had been dozing in and out of sleep when the phone rang. She knew who was calling. She stared at it, tempted to pick it up but unwilling to submit to Xavi's mesmerizing influence, or the irritating ease with which he diminished her control. It rang and rang, and still she didn't move. She winced, remembering who slept with her. The little bundle stirred, nestling deeper. It would wake her up.

She glared at the contraption. He was so self-possessed, so secure. What would rattle him? Crack his shell? While she continued to ponder all the ways to bring the confident man down a peg, the ringing stopped. Feeling confusingly bereft in the ensuing silence, she remembered her vision: Xavi's alluring snare.

"You're going back to your bed," Isabel whispered, and with a light grunt, she lifted Marité. Soon she wouldn't be able to carry her daughter, she was heavier and growing fast. She entered the girl's room, pulled the covers, and rolled her upon the bed. Once she was tucked in, Isabel left quickly.

On her way out, she noticed the light under Raquelita's door. She lifted her hand to knock, but let it fall. Matters pending between them could wait. Rather than engage her daughter in an early battle of wits, she directed her thoughts to the week ahead. So many details to work out—the teaching job, transportation, budgeting. The phone went off again, and her traitorous body thrilled in expectation. Her heart bolted as she rushed to answer.

"Hello," she answered, breathless with anticipation.

"Good morning, Isabel."

She almost screamed in frustration. "Hey, Coralina," she said modulating her response. "What can I do for you this morning?"

"How about coming over for lunch? We'd love to see y'all. I'm sure you're anxious to discuss the teaching job."

"Yes. Lunch would be great."

"Come over around noon?"

"Sure. Thanks." Glaring at the handset, she slammed it on the cradle. She wanted it to ring; she didn't want it to ring. Jerky shadows brought her attention to the dining room mirror and the reflection of a wild-eyed, anxious woman. Her. Why had she allowed him to get so close? She needed to stop him or, more effectively, stop herself.

When the phone rang again, she steeled her heart. It rang and rang.

***

"Lita, come, come." Lorrie greeted her arrival with an excited squeal. She rushed to Raquelita, kissed her on the cheek, all the while dragging her to the bedroom. "I want to show you the tops I bought. Mom, do we have a few minutes before lunch?"

"Sure, don't linger. Lunch is almost ready."

Lorrie released another excited little squeal, and in seconds, the cousins disappeared down the hallway.

"Lorrie, I love your room. Gosh, I wish my mother allowed posters. She's just too rigid and old-fashioned. Anything related to hippies and modern music, it's forbidden. With her, there's never a balance. It's always one extreme or the other." Raquelita sighed, ambling from one wall to the next. Her fingers brushed the wildly colored paper, and her hungry regard devoured the imaginative, psychedelic graphics. Lorrie had them all, The Beatles and Rolling Stones, in addition to groups she'd never heard of, such as The Who and The Animals. On a small shelf, she saw a stack of LPs. First on the pile was *Pet Sounds*. She'd entered rock-and-roll heaven.

"Mom thinks it's messy. I try to please her cleaning up once in a while. Take a look. What do you think?" Lorrie upended a shopping bag, and a variety of items spilled out: multicolored T-shirts, some tie-dyed, others in flowery patterns, a miniskirt, and an oversize pair of bright pink sunglasses.

"I love these," Raquelita chirped in delight. She donned the sunglasses and held up the miniskirt in front of her. "So cute. I love the front pleats, and it's not as short as I thought it would be."

"Mom will let me go only so far. One has to know when to concede. I'm taller than most girls. It'll be *just* perfect."

"All these albums. I'm not familiar with some of the groups." Raquelita dropped the skirt and sunglasses on the bed, and knelt before the stack of LP jackets. She flipped through the covers, naming each one. "I could never own any. I love music."

"You're always welcome to hang out in my room. Wait till I show you my brother's collection. His stuff is as eclectic as his temperament." Lorrie sat facing Raquelita. Pressing her hands together, she leaned forward. "Mom told me about Matthew."

Lightning quick, Lita dropped the album and placed two fingers over Lorrie's lips. "Shhhh, please, Lorrie. If my mother finds out, it's over."

"She won't. I'm going to help you."

"Girls," Coralina called out. "Lunch is ready."

"Be right there."

Lita crawled to the bed, reaching for her small bag. "I have two letters." She pulled out the envelopes. "I don't want to rush anyone, but I would love to mail them by tomorrow, if possible."

"They will, the postman comes around three." Lorrie smiled, extending her hand. Lita grasped it and stood. Lorrie pivoted to her dresser and opened the first drawer. "Drop 'em in here. We'll mail them after lunch."

***

In keeping with their personality, Sunday lunch at the Reynoldses was boisterous and full of laughter. Today, in honor of the Muro ladies, Coralina had gone all out preparing her delicious seafood paella. The oversize pan was brought steaming to the table and was received by admiring whoops and Jonas's piercing whistle.

"*Muñeca*, you've outdone yourself," Jonas exclaimed with a beaming smile. Blushing with the compliment, Coralina tilted her head shyly.

Not everyone celebrated. Ignoring the raucous feast, Isabel mulled Coralina's earlier bomb: *"Isabel, don't look so worried. Soon the girls will go to school, and you'll have a job... Oh, I almost forgot. Xavi sent money to help out. I used some to pay for your groceries."* Isabel had almost choked on the spot. Emilio provided alimony and child support, but until she got a job, expenses would mount steadily, and her girls could use the money. *It's not for me*, her mind protested. The rustling sound of Xavi's snare grew louder.

By the time her thoughts stopped churning, lunch was over and the kids had cleared the table for dessert. Jonas walked over to a small cabinet and returned with three snifters and a bottle of Spanish brandy.

Coralina pushed her chair to stand, but Jonas stopped her. "*Muñeca*, the kids will clean up. Come, sit by me." He dragged her chair next to his. "She's been working all day," he explained, holding up the bottle. "Brandy, Isabel?"

'Hmmm, I don't remember the last time... Maybe I shouldn't. What kind is it? It's very dark."

"It's *Cardenal Mendoza*, from our home town. It's delicious with dessert." Coralina smiled and pulled the cork. She poured a little in two snifters and then paused, staring at Isabel.

"Why not?" She watched, mesmerized, as Coralina decanted hers. Isabel held the snifter by the stem and waved it lightly under her nose. "It has a wonderful bouquet." She took a tentative sip. As the fiery liquid slipped down her throat, its aromatic vapors floated upward toward her nose and inward in a languorous heat wave throughout her body. Finally, it came to rest at the juncture of her thighs. *Oh, what a nice feeling.*

"Jonas, I would like to talk about the teaching position." Isabel broached the subject, though her heart was no longer in it. The flavorful liquid distracted her thoughts, and as it spread through her system, her limbs became spongy and soft.

"Of course. In fact, in advance of your arrival..." Jonas's baritone droned on. *What was it? Something about an interview...transportation...* Her mind had become slightly fuzzy, and his words floated playfully around her. She blinked. Jonas clicked his snifter against his wife's, and he now raised it toward Isabel. "*Salud.*"

She raised hers in response. "You are both so generous and helpful, I can't thank you enough." Isabel had the strangest impulse to giggle.

"No need. We are family, and we help each other, right, *Muñeca?*"

"Right," Coralina agreed. "I'll drive you to the interview."

Interview…when?

In the midst of her brain fuzz, dessert was duly dispatched. Soon after, Jonas pushed his chair back, and, bottle in hand, stood. "Let's move the conversation to the family room. Guys, take care of this," he said to Michael, waving at the empty plates.

***

"Your mom said I could use the ranch address. Is it still okay?"

"Absolutely. Come, I'll show you Dad's office."

They slipped through a long hallway. Lorrie opened a door and ushered her inside. It was an impressive den. Large bookcases stuffed with books and ledgers lined the walls. A massive desk and chair dominated the room. The graceful *bouillotte* table lamp sat on the left corner next to the phone, typewriter, and other office equipment. On the far wall, a paneled door served as a secondary entrance to the ranch. It had a metal opening midway, with two prongs hooked to the inside. Lorrie opened it for Raquelita, showing her a receptacle on the outside.

"Check it out. The mailman drops the incoming mail, Mom or Dad picks it up, and *voilà*, it's done. The office is rarely locked. If it is, let one of us know."

Raquelita lifted the two envelopes to her lips, kissed them lightly, and slipped them through. She turned to Lorrie and crossed her fingers.

"Let's go back to my bedroom. I want to know all about Matthew."

Huddled together, Raquelita spoke while Lorrie listened. Her mind filled with visions of tropical jungles, heavily armed men running, chopper blades thumping, thick clouds of dust lifting… *Stop living the future.* Matthew hadn't left the US yet, he needed her steadfast and focused.

***

Matthew checked his belongings again. They were mostly undergarments designed to keep him warm and dry. He'd live in fatigues from now on. His few civilian pieces would remain locked until he earned his airborne wings.

The military bunks were lined up in rows, with scant room for movement. A single locker served two bunks. At the trainee level, personal space and privacy were nonexistent. A man had to burrow deep to avoid hearing the next fellow's bodily noises. While a cloud of silent expectation hovered about the room, the men seemed relaxed as they went through their preparations. They had chosen this road and were mentally ready. It wasn't much different from the rigors of boot camp. Matthew expected the next three weeks to be identical, except for the added component of hurling his body out of a flying aircraft.

His neighbor, Brian MacKay, was a likable fellow Texan who hailed from nearby Pflugerville. After a few hours, they established an easy rapport, discussing similar goals with Special Forces. If they succeeded, they might conceivably maintain the friendship through the next round of challenges in their chosen specialty.

Matthew leaned his back against the metal rail of his bed. Taking slow deep breaths, he employed the method endorsed by Coach Brent in high school to relax. Coach Brent was an Eastern philosophy/martial arts guru who taught his players the benefits of mental introspection and body relaxation before a game, specifically a tough game. He taught the team how to meditate and quiet the mind, allowing the body's muscles, ligaments, and tendons to remain calm under stressful conditions. After an undefeated season, no one argued with the man.

He thought of his parents fondly and hoped he would do them proud. Then he let loose, and, gathering every bit of energy, he sent his thoughts to his angel: *My sweet girl, I miss you so. Tomorrow, training begins. Because you are with me, I'll dispatch every challenge with ease. You're my inspiration, my guide, and my strength.*

He reached inside the top pocket of his fatigues and pulled out the cherished poem. He read it again, and, closing his eyes, he pressed it above his heart and the medal. Peace fell upon him.

Chapter Eight

Ocala – June 4th 1967

With a light swirl of dark robes, the Ancients hovered, unseen.
The pieces were aligned on the board, the game slowly coming together.

"Timing is everything, Isabel. A ceaseless influx of Spanish-speaking exiles and immigrants has created the need for English teachers," Jonas explained. "Central Florida is also a magnet for Latin American migrant workers."

While Jonas detailed the plan, Isabel attempted to follow every word. Her fuzzy brain, however, missed one here and another there, all courtesy of the golden liquor in the bottle. Glancing at her empty glass, she snickered. She'd guzzled two full snifters. The delicious elixir generated a lovely floating sensation. Isabel couldn't remember when she'd been this relaxed, or in a better mood...ever.

She wanted to concentrate on his words, but for all her efforts, Jonas's deep voice waned and floated away. The chair Isabel lounged on heightened the soporific enchantment. Her limbs melted within the cushions, and her eyelids lowered.

A thunderous crash snapped Isabel out of a deep dreamless state. Daylight and shadows had entwined in a surreal gray light. The living room's panoramic windows displayed an apocalyptic scene. Thick black clouds barreled toward her, and lightning menaced distantly. A powerful gale rushed ahead of the storm, lifting roiling columns of dust and leaves. The huge live oak trees lining the driveway swayed humbly before Nature's formidable, fascinating, and fearsome display.

It was unnerving to wake up alone. She looked around the room, wondering how long she'd slept, but aware of one remarkable detail: she'd had no dreams.

She paused on the bright yellow label decorating the bottle of brandy. The lonely sentinel perched on the end table had watched over her. *Could the answer be this easy, this simple?* Isabel rolled the notion around. If brandy induced a dreamless sleep, perhaps…

"I hope this little beauty drops no hail," Coralina said, entering the room, her comment distracting Isabel's musings. She walked to the window as the storm unleashed its fury. Sheet upon dense sheet of water battered the glass. The world outside disappeared under the liquid attack.

"Do these happen often?"

"Almost every afternoon. It's the summer pattern for Central Florida. Hail is a concern. We're fortunate the ranch doesn't depend on crops." She returned her gaze to the windows. The storm was already moving onward. The initial fury had tapered.

"Did you have a nice nap? Jonas is still passed out, the poor dear. He had a really busy week."

"Yes, thank you. I slept soundly, and I needed it. I've not slept well lately. I believe your sweet potion was the culprit." She pointed to the brandy bottle.

"It did, really? Take the bottle home. Have some before bed."

"I can't. Isn't it expensive?"

"Nonsense. Jonas must have a case of the stuff. If it helps, take it. I insist." She picked up the bottle from the table, dropped it on Isabel's lap, and returned to the windows, bringing her face close to the glass. The breath from her lips steamed a small spot. "Great, the storm is winding down. This is the best part. The atmosphere almost crackles as the air cools and becomes cleaner, crisper." She peered out into the distance, arms folded over her chest.

"What would you like to do with the money Xavi sent?" Coralina asked without preamble. "He sent a thousand dollars and a note to let him know if you needed more. That's no small amount." She turned toward the sofa and sat facing a beet-red Isabel. Her hands smoothed her slacks absently.

"It's a lot, but I never asked Xavi for monetary help. If I accept… What would he ask in return?"

Coralina gave Isabel a long, thoughtful appraisal. "Are you aware Jonas and Xavi are close? They go way back, to the old days in Jerez… Anyway, regardless of their close friendship, I don't know Xavi as intimately as I would like. He's always kept some matters very private. But, he's never been an opportunistic heel either. My husband would never associate with such a man."

"I wasn't fully aware of the friendship," Isabel said. "I knew about Jonas and Emilio, of course." She paused as if weighing her words. "This is all new to me. A woman is told things. One can't help but wonder."

"For the record, Xavi and Jonas are closer than Emilio and Jonas. Xavi was offered the job in Texas through Jonas. He negotiated Emilio and you into the deal. He did the same with this teaching position. Xavi has paved your way twice and has been pivotal to the success and safety of both ventures. Has he asked you for anything yet?"

Isabel inhaled, preparing to answer, but Coralina cut her off. "Before you jump to the wrong conclusions, we're committed to ensuring your transition is smooth. We promised Xavi, and"—she paused—"we are delighted you and the girls are here.

"However, Emilio isn't thrilled with your move. Taking the girls out of the state without warning was wrong. Don't be surprised if he takes legal action. I'm not saying he will, simply warning you. Again, what would you like to do about the funds?" She slid to the edge of the sofa. "And, what's really going on between you two?"

"Nothing," she said a little too quickly. How else could she answer? Reveal her fantasies? Not a chance. Those were carefully guarded secrets. "There's nothing between us, other than friendship. And of course the obvious, that he's Raquelita's godfather."

Isabel stared nervously around the room, thinking of ways to change or deflect the subject. She wasn't ready to make a decision about the money, and she'd no intention of discussing Xavi with anyone, least of all Emilio's sister. Through the years, she'd become a master at escaping her demons and inner conflicts; today was not the day to stop. She jumped to her feet. "I didn't bring a watch. What time is it?"

"It's five thirty. In a hurry to go somewhere?"

"I should take the girls home. We've been here all day, wonderful as it has been."

"*Ay, por favor,* we love having you here," Coralina said. "It's still early. We could have a snack in a little while."

"It has been a beautiful Sunday afternoon. We should go home. Where is Marité? Last time I saw her, she was heading outside with Michael. What about Raquelita?"

"Michael brought Marité and the dogs inside, ahead of the storm. Lorrie and Raquelita were listening to music and have now joined them in the kitchen for a game of Monopoly."

"Music? What kind of music?"

"Sheesh, I don't know. The music kids listen to these days. I can't keep up with them."

"I don't want the girls exposed to the trash called music today. It's nothing but distorted sounds." Isabel walked toward the kitchen. "It isn't fit for decent ears."

Coralina stared silently as Isabel marched away.

***

The ring yanked Isabel out of her mystery novel. She glanced at the clock; it was 9:30 p.m. This time, she wouldn't dare ignore him.

"You didn't take my call earlier." Xavi's statement shook her to the core.

"I...well... Coralina invited us to the ranch for the day...and we must have been out." The stammer made her blush in embarrassment. No one, not even she, would believe the veracity of such an inane response.

"Isabel. Don't lie to me. Why don't you try again, this time with the truth?" He wasn't physically present, yet she could see his feline stare appraising her, studying her behavior, her blush, and her trembling hands. God, she was acting like a child again.

"Honestly, Xavi. We must have just left." Did that sound better?

"Really? The lie slinks through the mouthpiece. Sweetheart, I want the truth."

"I...I'm not certain." The unexpected endearment disarmed her, complicating her confusion. Isabel was drowning in a sea of Xavi's creation, and a lanyard was nowhere in sight.

"Let's start out slowly. Tell me *one* truth, sweetheart." Gently, he reeled her back. The sweet word carried a strong undercurrent of warmth and desire, and she no longer wanted to run away. If he were present, she would be on her knees, crawling to him, seeking to curl in his arms and bury her face in his chest.

"I'm afraid."

"Of me? Do I frighten you?"

Oh Lord, his sexually charged inflection was an irresistible enchantment; it nudged her soul open. A pulse of heat rushed from her core through her limbs. She shivered. "No, not you exactly. It's me, what I feel..."

"Let me help you, sweetheart," he said. "You stared at the phone until I hung up."

"Y-yes."

"About this fear, do you know I would hurt myself before I hurt you?"

"Yes. No. I'm nervous around you, and I don't understand myself."

"That was a lot. Saying it took some courage. What you feel unnerves you, perhaps?"

"It does."

"You have strong feelings for me, as I have for you. This confuses you. Please don't try to deny it. It would insult us both."

His declaration should have scared her witless, or at least irritated her, but it didn't. Xavi's confidence elicited a heady languor and peace. He handled her emotional labyrinth with such ease; she felt cosseted and treasured. That damned snare had reached her ankles.

"I want you to know the real me." He continued weaving his spell. "I wish I could be there tomorrow to guide you, but I can't. I must meet some obligations first. Sweetheart?"

"Yes, Xavi." Isabel trembled uncontrollably. *Guide me? How?*

"None of this can be discussed over the phone." He explained as if he'd heard her silent question. "I'll visit you very soon, and I'll show you then. Meanwhile, think of me as a good friend whose sole concern is your well-being. Is this easier, Isabel?"

"Yes. It's just...I get angry at times."

"Yes, sweetheart, you do. And I know why. Your feelings are new. I'll help you understand, when we are face-to-face. For now, don't concern yourself with any of it. What you need is rest. Allow my friends to assist you. They are good people."

"Thank you. Without your help, this trip would have been impossible."

"You're not alone. I'll take care of you." A long silence ensued. "What you will never do again is ignore any of my calls. Is that understood, Isabel?"

The command stunned her, and she trembled. In a heretofore untouched region of her soul, she accepted it without hesitation.

"Y-yes."

"That's my good girl," he said.

And now that same region was absolutely delighted with his approval.

"I'll call you tomorrow, before you start the day. Don't forget, and don't make me wait." The edge was back.

"I won't forget."

"Good night, Isabel. Hearing your voice pleases me no end."

Isabel smiled at the compliment, wished to return it, but was too shy to speak. A click followed, and the line went dead, and she felt immediately alone and, worse, abandoned.

***

I can't...I can't escape. She struggled. She couldn't see. She wanted to scream. Would anyone hear? The hideous breath rolled down her face. The despicable voice taunted: "No one can hear you. No one will help." The swirling dark void pulled her, down, down, down...

Isabel pushed herself out of the nightmare, slapping at her face and the diabolical blindfold. She sat up, staring into darkness. Nothing but the foggy tendrils of a torturing dream and the echoes of a horrid distant past remained.

She felt feverish yet chilled to the bone. Weary and exhausted, she crawled to the edge of the bed, thinking if she could only spend just one night without...she wanted to kick herself for not remembering. She marched to the kitchen and returned moments later armed with an empty glass and the bottle of brandy. She poured a generous amount.

The first sips conjured the elixir's magical embrace, and the comfortable lassitude rushed through her system. She liked this feeling. It wiped away everything and everyone who'd ever bothered or tormented her.

More relaxed, she returned to her discarded novel, but the warm, fuzzy sensations were too rich. She plunged head-on and poured another. The torpor deepened, and billowy clouds cradled her body, rocking her back and forth. And so, believing the mirage, the bottle's devious illusion of peace, she followed the path of countless deluded souls. Her lids gave up the fight, and at long last, she fell asleep.

Chapter Nine

Fort Benning – June 8th 1967

Matthew flopped on his bunk, exhausted. His thighs and calves must have been poleaxed along with the rest of his body. A week ago, he was foolishly certain he could meet the challenges of jump school; Ground Week had disabused him of such a notion. He shot a glance at his neighbor. His eyes were the sole body part to escape the jumpmasters' training torture. Sprawled on his back, Brian wasn't faring any better.

"Hey, pardner, how 'bout some chow?" Brian drawled with a dead-to-the-world expression. "I can't think or read till I eat." A hand clutching a few pamphlets waved weakly in the air.

"Yep, this is me rushing right up." Matthew winced. "Damn, it hurts to breathe."

"Help me up, an' I'll give you a boost." Brian laughed at his friend's grimace as he turned laboriously around. "Man up. Hold out yer hand." In an overly dramatic effort, Brian gripped Matthew's hand, flinched, and hefted his torso upright. They both sat up, panting with the effort.

"Mail call!" someone cried out, and an explosion of scuffling noises rushed out from every direction in the room. A group piled up at the doorway, jostling around two soldiers; one carried a large canvas bag bulging with envelopes.

"Buchanan."

Matthew stood, all aches and pains forgotten. As he approached the group, the ruckus faded. Sounds came from miles away. His footfalls thundered in his ears. He stared at the hand holding up two envelopes. He touched them, and the trance dissipated.

His fingers trembled. He hesitated. Finally he looked, there it was: *R. Muro c/o Reynolds*. She'd kept her promise. She was with him. All those nights of dreaming and sensing her with him hadn't been his imagination. He returned to his bunk with a sure step. Everything else could wait. Her words came first.

***

"*Muñeca*, why are you sitting in the dark?" What little light had been spilling inside the couple's bedroom was blocked by Jonas's large form at the doorway, and Coralina's body disappeared in the shadows. He reached for the wall switch and flicked it on. She squinted with the sudden wash of light, but her small smile remained. Jonas approached the bed and sat next to her, engulfing her hand in his. Although his curiosity was piqued, he remained silent.

"I had a long conversation with my brother. He's concerned about the girls, Raquelita most of all. She grew up like a serious little woman and has never enjoyed a normal childhood. It's so sad, Jonas."

Jonas grasped her hand and pressed a light kiss to her knuckles.

"I convinced him his daughters were well, and explained Lita's mood has been off, but it was to be expected. She's waiting for Matthew's response. As soon as his letters arrive, her funk will disappear."

Jonas repeated the caress.

"There's more," she said. "It's wonderful news. Emilio's marrying Julie next week, and they've retained an attorney to file a petition for shared custody." Coralina stared at her husband with a wondrous expression.

"It's fair. Emilio deserves equal time with his daughters. I'm glad he's fighting at last."

***

He loved Isabel's arrogance. Despite her supercilious attitude, Xavi longed to hear her. Her stubborn distance was a clarion call to every dominant cell in his body. He would enjoy blasting her defenses to fine sand. He looked forward to the day when she'd tremble in his arms, full of emotion and surrender. When he would touch her heart, reveal her strengths, guide her through her mysterious feminine ways. And in the process, he would unveil and eliminate the demon lurking in Isabel's spirit.

"We won't speak tonight, Isabel. I'll not allow you to take me for granted. Tonight, you'll enjoy the hollow pretense," he said. An old Purcell song floated out of his lips:

In vain we dissemble, in vain do we try,
To stifle our flame and check our desire,
In vain do our words our wishes deny...

He tried to relax on the lounge chair. Impossible. He missed her, and staying away was a challenge. But this ache in his heart was an ancient friend; he could handle it a little longer. Pushing Isabel's image aside, he picked up the phone and dialed. In two rings, a seductive voice answered.

"Hello."

He liked Julianna Black's husky contralto, and he openly admired it. "That sexy voice of yours, it always gets to me."

"Thank you, handsome. Wanna talk to your friend?"

"If I must. I'd much rather listen to you."

"Charmer, here's Emilio."

The conversation ended quickly. Xavi departed his little cottage for Emilio's place to finish the discussion over dinner—the date of the upcoming wedding and his surprise visit to Florida.

***

She hated him. Right when Isabel could discern a pattern, the evil man veered off course. It was infuriating, unsettling. She'd looked forward all day to talking about her tutoring job. Now, she would have to wait until tomorrow, unless she called Xavi tonight, which was totally out of the question.

Isabel ambled aimlessly about the living room. The routine had changed without warning, and she felt adrift. Fine, she could manage without him. She would search the TV for an interesting show. An hour later, Isabel realized she'd been staring at a blank screen.

Where is my mind?

It was focused on Xavi and his smoldering gaze. Her imagination suddenly revved up. Forbidden notions and suppressed desires exploded in colorful visions. Frenzied scenes and wild fantasies tortured and teased her mind. He demanded and commanded, and she obeyed, enthralled, following his lead to the edge of reason and beyond, to a world of conflicting pleasures.

"*No!*" she protested vehemently, pushing the disturbing vision away, far away. "*No!*"

Xavi's unexpected silence had loosened her precarious control over her thoughts. Without it, her traitorous mind released the tempting visions. She slammed her fists on the armchair and stood. The words of an ancient song mocked her:

> *In vain we dissemble, in vain do we try,*
> *To stifle our flame and check our desire,*
> *In vain do our words our wishes deny...*

She fled out the kitchen door into the night's stygian embrace. Isabel's shoeless feet plunged into the cool damp grass; hidden pebbles poked the sensitive soles. She faltered and stumbled. Her lungs labored and convulsed. The air, dense and laden with moisture, was impossible to inhale.

Her mouth gaped as she fought for oxygen. Panic throttled her when she failed to breathe. Wobbling precariously, she wrapped her arms around her torso and managed a precious lungful. It was followed by the inexplicable ordeal of exhaling. A sharp inhuman sound exploded. Her hand flew to her quivering lips. *Do I feel tears?*

Her control shattered. Her defensive barriers crashed. She fell to her knees, releasing all her pent-up sadness, frustration, and age-old fears. She wailed again, an uncontainable torrent as she released every tear within her slowly thawing soul.

***

An abrupt noise alarmed Raquelita out of bed. She'd been drifting in and out of sleep, enwrapped in sweet thoughts of Matthew. She fled past the living room, where her mother's lonely shoes were carelessly strewn on the floor. The kitchen's back door stood wide open. She hesitated at the threshold, but without the help of a bright moon, it was impossible to see. She waited until her sight adjusted, and it took her a moment to understand.

Her mother knelt with her forehead pressed to the ground as she contorted erratically. What were those strange sounds? Was she weeping? Raquelita scanned her memories as far back as she could. No, her mother didn't cry. Ever.

Instead of rushing out to help, Raquelita just stared, unmoved and empty, blank as a brand-new page of her diary. Had she lost her ability to care? Had she turned into her mother? *Nonsense.* Testing the possibility, she envisioned Matthew's face. Love, grand and energetic, rushed to life. She probed deeper, thinking of her father and her sister. Yes, love bloomed. But when she looked outside, nothing happened. Well, she could ponder this conundrum later. Now she had to retrieve the fallen woman from the damp grass and bring her to shelter.

Fighting her strange inertia, Raquelita reached her mother's trembling form and delicately held her. "Mom. Let's get you back inside."

Isabel's tear-streaked face looked up. "Raquelita?"

"Yes, it's me. Let me help you."

"Okay...okay," Isabel said.

With Raquelita's help, Isabel gained her feet. Laboriously, the women negotiated their way back to Isabel's bedroom. By now Isabel had calmed some, and her erratic breathing had eased. With infinite patience, Raquel removed the wet garments, ignoring Isabel's resistance, and in a few minutes, she had her dressed in a warm nightshirt.

"Mom, you need to rest. Come, lie down." She pushed Isabel gently upon the pillows, tucking the blankets around her. "Would you like some water?"

Isabel shook her head. "No. In the kitchen's left cupboard, you'll find a bottle of brandy. Please bring it with a glass. The warmth will be good. It'll help me sleep," she insisted.

Lita nodded and left the room. "Is this what you want?" she asked when she returned, showing the bottle and glass to her mother.

"*Si, Hija*. Thank you. Please, pour me some?"

Her mother rarely spoke to her in the old language, and never with the quality of an endearment. Raquelita's hand trembled, but she hid it, carefully decanting into the glass. "Here, Mom. Do you need anything else?"

Isabel gripped her wrist. "I want to know why you stopped calling me Mamá?"

The question was not a simple request, and she was not ready to answer. "I don't know, Mom. It just happened. If there's nothing else, I'll go back to bed. Good night." She kissed Isabel's forehead and walked out.

Isabel stared as the door closed; the ensuing click was her signal. She gulped the contents of the glass. It burned all the way down. She refilled the glass. It would take at least two more before she reached the state she desired. Tonight, she was going to numb out, no matter how many shots it would take to reach oblivion.

***

Late Saturday afternoon, Lorrie arrived at the Muro household, rapped a few times at the front door, jiggled the unlocked knob, and walked right in. "What a bummer, this house is a funeral home. Guys? Auntie," she called out. "Where's everybody? Hey…" A scowling Isabel stopped her next word.

"Lorrie. What's the reason for this racket?"

"Oh, hi, Auntie, I came to kidnap Raquelita, if you'll let me. My girlfriend Mandy is coming for dinner. She's a writer wannabe like Raquelita, and they liked each other's stuff. Would you let her have dinner with us? What do you say? Can she come, pretty please, with a cherry on top?"

Isabel stared at Lorrie like she'd lost her mind. "Hold your horses, young lady. Breathe."

"Sorry, I do get carried away. I know it's late notice, but we hatched this little get-together ten minutes ago. It would be great to have Raquelita join us. Please. I won't keep her out late. If you like, Marité can come."

"No, Marité is staying in. She's been playing all afternoon, and I want her settled down early." Against all her efforts, Isabel smiled. She liked Lorrie's humor. After the initial period of wariness, the girl had demolished Isabel's reticence.

"Go get your cousin. Don't keep her out late," Isabel said, detaining her by the shoulder. "Lorrie? Did you hear me?"

"Oh yeah, sure, Auntie. You're the best."

***

Lorrie approached Raquelita's room, and was surprised by the faint chords of a classical guitar composition. She tapped the door lightly.

"Yes? It's open, come in."

She found Raquelita lying on her stomach, writing in a notebook. "Hey, coz, writing in your diary?"

"No, this is where I write essays and foolish attempts at poetry," she said. "I only write in the diary late at night, when I know Mom is asleep and can't sneak up on me."

"Can't say I blame you." Lorrie turned to examine the old record player on the side table. "The sound's scratchy, but it's better than nothing. Every time I step foot in this house, it's silent as a tomb. Today, I find you listening to some moody piece instead of something cheerful. No wonder you're always gloomy. You need to lighten up. Wanna borrow some of my albums?"

Raquelita stopped writing and rolled to her side. "You're listening to the second movement of Rodrigo's Aranjuez concert. It's plaintive and beautiful. The first and third movements are livelier. It's my dad's favorite. When I miss him a lot, I play it, and it brings me closer to him."

"In that case, timing is everything. Get dressed. Mandy's coming over, and you're having dinner with us." She walked over to Raquelita, lowered her head, and whispered, "Your dad's calling around six. I hear he has good news and wishes to speak with you. Let's go."

***

Monday, June 12th – Ocala

My Father's Wedding

This night cannot pass without recording my thoughts on tomorrow's joyous event. Not many daughters experience their father's marriage.

I have beautiful images: exchanged vows, sweet kisses, and intimate glances. And so many questions: are they nervous, eager to join, accosted by misgivings? They might be. It is their second nuptials. It is also a second chance at happiness. And happy they will be. They have both suffered, paid their dues to karma, and are perfect for each other.

What about my feelings? In retrospect, my little-girl fantasies were amusing. All my knights resembled Papá, with the same dark good looks, all brave and affectionate. Is it possible to have a little-girl crush on your father? Or was he my marker for the future?

All has changed, childhood is over, and the little-girl crush has evolved. Julie, my father is wholly yours. I have found my grown-up love. Matthew Buchanan isn't a fantasy or a wish. He's real. He has imbued my childhood notions and fantasies with the complexities of adulthood: love, physical desire, and friendship.

On the eve of my father's future happiness, I cannot help but wonder: what will it be like for me, for us? How will it feel to give yourself to another? It must be blinding joy and overwhelming happiness to join body and soul with the one who completes you. I cannot wait for the day.

Raquelita put the pen down and closed the diary. She had been counting the days until her father and Julianna's wedding. She prayed nightly for their happiness. Interspersed with thoughts of the marriage were her own sweet anxieties regarding the mysterious nuances of romantic and physical love, nuances she was eager to explore with her grown-up love.

Chapter Ten

Ocala – June 13th 1967

Raquelita greeted a nebulous dawn bleary-eyed and exhausted. She'd given sleep a decent effort and failed. The few hours of pitiful slumber were taken by a strange dream. Not the classic nightmare of dark shadows or chases through endless alleys—it started out pretty, but the end was frightening. Every scene was still vivid.

She stood in a misty clearing, encircled by ancient olive trees, their twisted trunks and gnarled limbs revealing their age. Daylight, sheer as tissue, shimmered with golden hues. Her billowy white sundress fluttered about her ankles as she stepped barefoot on the dusty ground.

A small fountain, cracked and weathered with age, stood in the center of the clearing. Its tiny cherub spout ejected a thin trickle of water with soothing, bubbling sounds on descent. As she walked past the basin, she dipped her fingers through the crystalline water.

Several yards away, an ancient stone chapel beckoned. She entered and paused to examine the interior. Old pews distressed with the passage of time were strewn in disarray, as if giant hands or a violent storm had tossed them about the tiny nave. Only the three rows before the altar remained intact.

Remnants of stained glass windows illuminated the interior with unusual hues. She proceeded down the central aisle and stopped before a massive wooden cross and its simple altar underneath. She genuflected humbly, crossing her forehead and chest.

A sudden glow made her turn. Sitting on the front pew, a beautiful lady regarded her intently. An intricate white lace mantilla covered her hair, the excess draped around her arms. Her pale blue gown gleamed with an unearthly light. Her large, smiling eyes sparkled like black diamonds, and an aura of celestial peace surrounded her. Her hand rose in silent invitation.

Overcome by the presence, Raquelita approached slowly and sat. Love and tenderness filled the Madonna's gaze.

"I am the one you seek. I will grant your request. He will be protected."

She waved her fingers, and somehow Matthew appeared. Raquelita rushed to her beloved, reached out to him, but her fingers slipped through his insubstantial form. She called out, "Matthew." He didn't respond. His regard was cold, distant.

"What's wrong? Why can't he speak?" His silence frightened her.

"All will be well. It is my promise."

"Matthew. Speak to me, dear heart. Please don't leave me," she implored as he faded away. A pained gasp escaped her lips.

She awoke with a start. Reason came to the rescue, arguing it was only a dream. However, her face was sodden. So reason changed its tune. Perhaps it's a message, but what sort of message? Matthew didn't seem injured, but why couldn't he speak? The lady promised he'd be well. Still, something didn't feel entirely right. Why didn't he recognize her?

As the rising sunlight filtered into her room, the dream lost some of its potency. She curled into her favorite position, entertaining a hundred different thoughts. Even though the foreboding diminished, it refused to let go.

***

The morning dragged on despite her chores. The sense of dread was loath to depart. The next time Raquelita glanced at the clock, she sighed with relief. She called her sister out and, without any explanations, led her out of the house in the direction of the open fields. Marité followed without question.

"Can you keep a secret, Mari?"

"Of course I can, Lita." She almost sounded offended. Raquelita smiled.

"I have wonderful news for you. Well, for both of us. But we can't tell Mom, at least not for a while. Is that all right?"

"Yes, yes, I promise. Not a word."

"Remember Julie? The nice lady Papá has been seeing?"

"Yes. She's pretty and so nice."

Marité's candor never failed to affect Raquelita. The innocence and purity of her young spirit touched her deeply and made her want to embrace her forever. "Yes, sweetie, she's very pretty, and she loves Papá."

Lita paused, scanning their surroundings. "See that big live oak?" She pointed to a massive bent shape, its long limbs trailing above the ground. "Let's walk over. We can sit for a while. I have something to tell you."

The sisters reached the ancient denizen, chose an upraised twisted root, and sat under its cool shade. Leaning against its old trunk, Raquelita couldn't help but think about all the events it had witnessed through its long, long life. Today it would listen again while she gave her sister the happy news.

She'd barely finished when Marité's canine sentinels appeared, tails wagging, heads low to the ground, sniffing as they trotted through the grass. Once the usual greetings of happy licks and nudges were accomplished, they lay down calmly, flanking Marité on each side, heads propped on the little girl's lap.

Michael was not far behind. "Mom wants to see you, Raquelita."

"Now?"

"Yes, now."

She deliberated for a moment. It was too soon for Papá to call. What could her aunt want? "All right, let's go."

Michael extended his hand, giving her a boost. When he lifted Marité and held her small, thin body in his arms, a broad grin lighted his expression. She giggled as he whirled her around a few times before returning her to her feet. Playtime over, all three marched away, Sam and Nina in tow.

***

Lita followed Michael and Marité into the living room and stopped dead in her tracks. Her aunt and mother were engaged in animated conversation. *What the heck is she doing here?* She would ruin Papá's phone call. Then she remembered, it was her mother's first day at work, and Michael was driving her in.

Isabel saw Michael and stood. "Michael, are you ready?" she asked, picking up a satchel and slinging it around her shoulder.

"Yes." Michael's answer was short. In sharp contrast, he smiled at his cousin. "Hey, Mari, wanna keep me company?"

When Marité nodded, Raquelita gave her aunt a wary look.

"Go ahead, Marité. Michael loves company, but don't dawdle. Lunch is at twelve thirty sharp."

The moment the door closed behind the departing trio, Coralina pivoted and marched toward the office, index finger pointed up. "Young lady, you and I have some matters to discuss."

Lita swallowed hard. What had she done now? Resigned, she followed, expecting the worst.

Coralina went directly to her desk and opened a drawer. Her hand emerged, waving an envelope. "I believe you've been waiting for this?"

Raquelita stared. She wanted to take a step but couldn't. She could only extend a supplicant hand. Once the gift was given, she clasped it and pressed it to her chest, trying to keep her heart from jumping out of her chest.

"Well, aren't you going to read it?"

Half-paralyzed, she nodded once, holding the envelope against her chest, fearing if she moved it would disappear and turn into another frustrating dream. Her aunt smiled, coaxing her to sit. Coralina then removed the envelope from Raquelita's stiff fingers, made a slit along the top, and returned it to her trembling hand.

"Enjoy the moment," she said, walking out the door.

Alone with her letter, Raquelita stared at the envelope. With utmost care, she extracted the contents, struggling with clumsy fingers. She absorbed Matthew's masculine cursive.

June 8th, 1967

Angel,

How can I begin to explain the pleasure and joy of reading your letters? You've made me the happiest I've been since I held you in my arms and kissed your sweet lips. God, do you remember our last night together? I can't stop thinking about it, Raquelita. Your face has kept me sane through the past days and nights. You've become an intrinsic part of me. Without you, there is no Matthew. My soul needs you to be whole, to be well.

The enforced silence nearly drove me insane. I can't imagine your strain, sweetheart. You've endured it the longest. Once I devoured your letters, I sat down to write mine immediately. I couldn't let you wait one additional second. From now on, you can expect more, lots more. Writing to you is as essential as breathing.

Our hearts and spirits are one; I know it with full certainty. I sense when you come to me in the late hours of the night. When I'm overtaken by exhaustion, I feel your loving fingers running down my body and easing my aches, filling my spirit with life-giving energy. I love you, angel.

I have so many questions and concerns, sweet girl. I want to know everything. Is Momma behaving? I'm so relieved the Reynoldses turned out as wonderful as you hoped and I prayed for. If luck holds, I'll meet them (and your papa) soon. Before I forget, give Marité a kiss for me.

My life has been training, training, and more training. Luckily, I found a friend in the guy who bunks next to me. His name is Brian MacKay, a decent funny guy, also from Texas, who has entertained me many a night with his aches, gripes, and witty comments.

Which brings me to my next topic. Keep your fingers crossed—I can probably manage an escape to Ocala between orders. I'm not sure if it will work out or for how long. But I'll drive to hell and back to see you for a few hours. As soon as I know for sure, I'll let you know. Meanwhile, ask your family if I may visit you. Their approval is necessary.

I have to go now, angel, much as I hate it. They're calling chow time. As you know, the base runs on a schedule, and I need food in this very tired body. Brian is giving me dirty looks (he must be starved).

But tonight, when all are asleep, I'll be here, awaiting your arrival. I'll hold you in my arms, my hands will caress your silky skin, and your warmth will fill my senses. Do you feel me, angel? Do you feel my kiss upon your honeyed lips? If I may quote Arnold:

> *Come to me in my dreams, and then*
> *By day I shall be well again.*
> *For then the night will more than pay,*
> *The hopeless longing of the day.*

Until tonight,
Matthew

Oh, *my love*. Her hand fell on the desk. Her forehead followed. Scant hours ago, she'd awakened in abject dread. Now, exhilaration replaced it. Matthew had written a beautiful letter, a letter that had gone a long way to eradicate all doubt, all insecurities. She glanced up and down the letter again. She would never get enough.

Then it hit her. Matthew might come to see her after jump week. If her calculations were correct, he would be here in less than ten days. *Ten days.* She raced out of the office in search of her aunt and found her in the kitchen, engaged in the last touches for the noon meal.

"Aunt Coralina?"

"The young lady emerges. Was it everything you'd hoped for?" Coralina paused quartering the large, pointy leaves of romaine lettuce.

"Yes, it was."

"Why do I get the feeling there's more?"

Raquelita relaxed. She was not addressing her mother. This was her aunt, the fairy who performed miracles.

"The letter is beautiful, and yes, there's more." With hurried words, she explained Matthew's plans. "Do we have your permission? May he visit?"

"And, if we don't approve?"

"In that case, he'll go directly to Fort Bragg." She stared at the floor, fighting tears of disappointment. *Oh please, Aunt Coralina.* She wanted this so much. She already saw him and felt him.

Coralina wiped her hands, dropped the towel, and drew Raquelita into a soothing embrace.

"Darling, would I do that to you? If he can manage, of course he may visit. I love how he asks. He doesn't disappoint and remains polite and respectful. No one in this family will reject Matthew. I'll inform Jonas and the kids."

"Oh, thank you, Aunt Coralina. I don't know how to thank you." Raquelita tightened the hold around her aunt's middle.

"That's fine. Um... Sweetie, you're squeezing the air out of me. All right, *querida,* you have a few days to plan. Make sure you both coordinate this effort carefully, and don't forget about Isabel. Meanwhile, help me finish here. Michael and Marité will be coming through the door any minute. We'll have lunch before your father calls. Or, did you forget?"

With Matthew's letter she'd forgotten about her father's wedding. And wasn't her behavior normal? *"For this reason, man will leave his father and mother."* If she were to inject a good dose of the sixties attitude, the passage should include women, shouldn't it? For she would leave father and mother, and follow Matthew to the ends of the earth.

She stood next to her aunt, ready to assist with lunch or any other request, while her spirit rejoiced and celebrated Matthew's long-awaited words of love. Oh yes, their bond was very much alive, and tonight she would join him. With the boldness of youth, Raquelita judged herself ready to face any hindrance life hurled at her.

The Hags smiled at the foolish youth…

Chapter Eleven

Ocala – June 14th 1967

The Muro sisters returned to a silent, dark home. In Lita's opinion, the place grew creepier by the day. With hurried steps, they swept the house, turning on lights. Where in blazes was her mother? She went directly to her mother's bedroom. The door was slightly ajar, and she knocked lightly.

"Mom?"

Silence answered her, and she nudged the door. The light from the hallway sconce offered a sliver of light, enough to discern a body spread on the bed. A chill crept over Lita. "Mom?" This time she pushed the door open. The hallway light spilled inside her mother's bedroom. *What the hell?*

Isabel lay on the bed, her face to the side. The partially open robe revealed half a nude body. One foot rested on the floor, one arm dangled off the bed, the other was across her belly. Raquel was about to panic when the faint rise and fall of Isabel's chest stopped her.

Madame Perfection looked a mess. Her lids were not fully closed, a thin white line showed underneath, her slack jaw hung open, and a strange odor emanated with every breath. Madame Composed was undone. Raquelita touched Isabel's arm. "Mom?" She waited. "Mom, wake up." No reaction. Finally, she grasped her mother's shoulder and shook harder. To her dismay, her mother mumbled some unintelligible sounds and flipped on her side.

She stared unbelieving at her mother's semicomatose form. She lifted the loose end of the robe and covered her naked body; next she pulled the trapped bedspread from underneath, threw it over Isabel, and left the room. The image of her mother's state and awful smell were indelibly etched in her brain. Everything she'd heard or read about indicated a drug- or alcohol-induced sleep. Wouldn't it be rich, the Iron Lady drunk? It was almost impossible to believe, and yet…

"Let's get you ready for bed, Mari. Mom is out cold."

As she pulled out PJs and turned the bed down for her sister, she recalled her mother's implosion nights ago and her subsequent request for brandy. If she found her mother in this condition again, she would speak up.

***

The muted light from the TV bathed the bedroom and its occupants. "Johnny's Theme" announced the start of The Tonight Show. Tucked between her husband's sinewy chest and arms, Coralina smiled in utter contentment. She loved the feeling of his warm bare skin pressed against hers. They could spend hours in the sweet afterglow of lovemaking.

This had been an evening to be savored. As much as they would like to, they could no longer sustain the insatiable ardor of the first years, when they couldn't keep their hands off each other, before the responsibilities of business and children took a toll on their intimacy. After nineteen years together, the bonfire of their love had eased. Now their passion smoldered like superheated glowing embers in a hearth; add but one small log, and flames would burst.

The way it had exploded tonight. She wasn't sure who threw the log in, nor did she care. The lovemaking had been furious and wild, until they lay spent, exhausted, and sated. Jonas was a magnificent lover who knew how to make her vibrate in ecstasy. Not to be outdone, Coralina gave back to Jonas every sensation in kind until he came apart in her arms.

In moments like these, she got a unique thrill examining her big man. Especially when his lips curved in an absent smile or the corners of his bright blue eyes crinkled at the edges. Not only was she insanely attracted to him, she adored him more than life. She loved the rumble of his laugh, the rise and fall of his chest, and the steady beat of his heart, each one a powerful statement. He was here, healthy and very much alive.

Jonas's ebony hair was starting to show silver, though the thin pelt across his chest and the sensuous line extending past his abdomen toward his crotch remained solid black. Coralina loved to tangle her fingers with the crisp hairs while feeling the dense layer of muscles underneath. Ranch life was tough and demanding. It kept his body hard and looking prime. No one could guess he was turning forty in July.

She counted her gifts—the life and precious family she'd been granted—and sent a prayer of gratitude for all her blessings. Particularly now, surrounded as she was by the pain and anxiety with the split of Emilio's family, Isabel and her demons, her involvement with Xavi, and Raquelita with her Matthew.

Which reminded her, she had to discuss the visit. She pressed her hand against Jonas's breastbone, her fingertips making little tapping circles on his warm, dewy skin.

"Jonas?"

"*Sí, Muñeca.*" His deep baritone rumbled below her ear.

She turned liquid each time he used the Spanish endearment. It meant "doll," beloved, cherished, and beautiful, all rolled into one little word. Her husband used it with ease. Jonas had inherited from his father his love for Spanish horses. From a very young age and whenever possible, Jonas had accompanied his father on business trips to southern Spain. With each visit, he plunged deeper into the culture and customs, thus his exceptional understanding of the language, colloquial nuances, and, best of all, the endearments.

After a few seconds of silence, Jonas looked to his wife. "Cora, what is it, honey? You started to ask." He gave her a light squeeze.

"Well...I had a couple of thoughts swirling at once. I wanted to talk about the possible visit. It will be special for Raquelita."

"Sure, I remember. Matthew should be here in about ten days or so, right?"

Jonas slid down in the bed while lifting Coralina's body directly above his. They were face-to-face, body-to-body. His long legs tangled around hers, pulling them gently apart.

"Mmmm... Remember what it was like, *Muñeca?* Our excitement, the fever of first love?"

His breath was hot. His hands began a slow exploration down her back, squeezing her buttocks and searching lower still, toward the warmth of her sex. Arousal surged like wildfire. "I could never forget." She brushed and kissed his lips, enjoying the teasing pressure of his hard penis at her sheath.

The phone's unexpected ring was a jarring attack to the eardrums, freezing all activity and intentions. Jonas glared at the phone. "What the h...?"

Coralina sat up, looking at the clock on the nightstand. "It's late," she said. "God, I hope it's not bad news."

Jonas picked up. She heard a man speak, but the words were unintelligible. Jonas's expression went from irritation to surprise.

"Hey, my friend, are you all right?" A flurry of muffled words followed.

"Well, of course, you don't need reasons. You're never a problem. Everything's fine. The phone startled us, that's all. Coralina and the kids are well.

Yes. How should I say it to convince you? Same here, my man, drive safely. All right, see you then."

Jonas hung up. Bemused, he looked at his wife, and she returned the look expectantly. Jonas sat upright, raising Coralina's body with his. A slow snigger began, growing to a hearty laugh.

"*Muñeca*, things are going to get interesting. Xavi is on his way here." He roared now. "He should be arriving sometime tomorrow evening. We should warn the kids and fireproof the house. We're having Fourth of July fireworks in June." His laughter turned into something entirely different when he pulled her against him. "Now, where were we?"

Chapter Twelve

Ocala – June 15th 1967

"Come on, Raquelita. I only want to check a couple of stores," Lorrie begged. Raquelita's circling pace would soon dig a hole in her bedroom's carpeting. "It's only three thirty," she pleaded. "I'll bring you back soon, promise."

Raquelita gave her a slanted look. "Honest, coz. You know I hate shopping. I wanted the time to write my next letter."

"Please, I need a few toiletries. Maybe do a little window-shopping with my favorite cousin? I promise we'll be back before your mom comes home. The sooner we go, the faster we return." She smiled, seeing the grimace of capitulation. "Yes." She sped ahead of her cousin in search of her mother.

The young women peeked inside the kitchen, and their eyebrows shot up. Coralina rushed from one corner to the next like a small twister. Her face, tightly knit in concentration, glowed with perspiration. A haphazard ponytail and loose wisps of hair flew every which way. Cabinets slammed, doors thudded, pots banged, broom, mop, and pail were lined up in a corner. Lorrie raised a hesitant hand.

Coralina gasped. "*¡Señor del universo!* Don't sneak up on me." She pressed a hand on the kitchen island for support. "What is it?"

"I'm sorry, Mom," Lorrie said. "I didn't mean to startle you. Came to tell you I'm taking Lita into town for a couple of hours."

Coralina's grimace turned to a smile. "That's fine, sweetie. I'm a little pressed for time and didn't hear you." She pointed a thumb at the clock above the stove. "Have fun." With a dismissing wave, she resumed her frenzied chores.

"'Kay, Mom. See you later."

Bemused, Lorrie turned her attention to her cousin and shrugged. "Let's go." They reached the door and, without looking, Lorrie rushed outside slamming into a body, much harder and much taller than hers.

Startled, Lorrie looked up into a pair of tired hazel eyes. A lock of dark blond hair reposed lazily above the handsome man's forehead. Belatedly, she realized the stranger's hand had steadied her to keep her from falling on her butt. As she offered a smile of apology, Lita gasped behind her.

"Xavi."

"Hi, darling. It's good to see you. And you must be Lorrie, Jonas and Coralina's youngest?"

"Yes, that's me. And you are?" Lorrie took a backward step.

"I'm Xavier Repulles. My friends call me Xavi, and your parents are in that group. Raquelita is my goddaughter. You probably don't remember me. You were a little girl the last time I saw you." He propped his hands on his hips and looked around. "Is your mother home?"

"Oh crap, my mother will kill me for my lack of manners. Yes, she's home. I'll go get her." She bolted inside the house.

"¿*Padrino?*" Raquelita tapped his arm. "I didn't know you were coming."

"I decided the day of your father's wedding. And to answer your next question, Isabel doesn't know." Despite the weary lines, a distinct look of mischief danced on his face.

A whirlwind of commotion arrived. "Xavi, Xavi," Coralina exclaimed with Lorrie in close pursuit. She pulled him into her arms, speaking quickly. "Finally. You've stayed away much too long." She stepped away a little, fussing and examining him from head to toe "Jonas will be so pleased. I'll send word immediately. Come in. You look beat. Did you rest at all?"

"I stopped outside New Orleans, and have been driving since. Yeah, I could rest."

"Well, you can relax now. I'll make the call, and then I'll show you to your room." Coralina returned inside the house.

What Raquelita had never done before, she did now. She examined the man who had designs on her mother. He was handsome, serious, and often forbidding, but his smile was like Matthew's—it made the angels sing. Shorter than Jonas, taller than her dad, he was sinewy and elegant. He walked with a distinctive aura of authority and confidence. Strangest of all, he seemed to exist on an alternate dimension from most mortals. And didn't it all make sense?

Coralina reappeared, breaking the spell. "Jonas is on his way. Sit for a second. Goodness, you probably don't want to sit anymore. Give Jonas a chance to arrive before you rest. You will nap, of course. Let me get you something to drink..."

In silent resignation, the young women returned to Lorrie's bedroom, today's outing squashed. Raquelita quivered, thinking about later, and her mother. It was going to be an unforgettable evening.

***

Summer twilights linger in Florida. The afternoon's bright gold light was turning rosy with the sun's descent. The evening's purple mists approached. The breeze was warm; a touch of sultriness instilled a lazy indolence to their already easy pace. Jonas and Xavi reached the fence bordering a training track. Jonas leaned his broad shoulders against it, and his friend faced opposite. He restrained the desire to ask. Xavi would speak when ready.

Crossing his arms on the top rail, Xavi let his forehead fall forward. "Damn, Jonas, I'm exhausted."

"It's a long haul. Did you rest?"

"Not much. Tonight, I'll sleep like a rock."

"So certain, my friend?" Jonas smirked. "Sometimes plans don't turn out..."

"Quite often indeed," Xavi interrupted. He turned, imitating his friend's stance. As he stared out toward the shadows, the dim light etched his sharp profile. "The place looks remarkable. You've added a second track." Xavi scanned the large property. "Business must be good."

Jonas glanced at his stalling friend and almost scoffed aloud. If he did, Xavi would retreat further inside, and Jonas wanted him to lean on their friendship for support. Isabel was at the heart of the matter. Jonas had known for many years about his friend's silent obsession. With such an unstable woman, who knew how it would all work out? He took a deep breath, resolving to bide his time and follow Xavi's lead.

"We've done well. Breeding two champions made a difference."

"Always the modest rancher. You've worked your butt off. Your reputation as an ethical breeder and trainer precedes you. Word gets around."

"Really? My beautiful bride will be pleased when I tell her."

"Jonas, I'm not sure how to approach tonight." Without preamble, Xavi broached the topic Jonas had been expecting. "When is she due home?"

Patience rewarded. "You have until eight fifteen to decide. That's when Michael picks her up. She usually goes straight home, and one of us drives the girls over later."

"I want to pick her up myself. Maybe I could go with Michael. I want to surprise her, not scare her out of her wits. Any suggestions?"

Xavi at a loss? Jonas stared but couldn't read his expression. Xavi's face had melted into the shadows. "Too late now. She's going to get a jolt regardless. Going with Michael is a good idea. She'll be expecting him. We should ask Coralina."

Xavi's white teeth flashed in the dark. "I could use a woman's perspective." He straightened to his full height. "Hey, I'm getting hungry. Do you know what's for dinner?"

"It doesn't matter, I love everything Coralina cooks." Jonas slapped Xavi's back. "Let's go, I'm starved."

***

The approaching vehicle was not Michael's clanging heap. This engine purred. It had to be the Reynoldses' jeep. Poor Michael, Isabel thought, maybe his wreck had finally reached its end. Many a night she'd feared that the old clunker—miraculously held together by the hand of a favorable god—wouldn't make it. Heck, she was tired. As long as she had a ride home to her bedroom, her comfy slippers, and her private pleasures, all would be well.

Isabel's wonderings came to an abrupt halt, along with her heartbeat. Xavi sat at the wheel. She would recognize the dark blond hair anywhere. Her body exploded with a surge of adrenaline. His unexpected presence had her at a total disadvantage.

The jeep made a dizzying U-turn, stopping right before her in a soundless, easy-as-you-please maneuver exhibiting Xavi's expertise. Michael sat in the backseat with a smirk she wanted to smack right off his face. *Does he find Xavi's driving amusing?* The little creep.

A grinning Xavi pulled the parking brake and nimbly jumped out. He stopped a scant inch away, her personal space be damned. He was so close she felt the heat radiating off his body and his exhalations on her face. He stared intently with those cursed hazel eyes, and she thought she would faint.

"Isabel, I've missed you." Xavi's smile gleamed. His hand, calloused by years of training, grasped her upper arm and pulled her even closer.

She would never survive this. Phone conversations with miles of separation were a challenge. But now, he was here, pretense and acting were no longer possible. Worse, what coursed through her veins was no longer an adrenaline prickle. It was a hot and heady rush, urging Isabel to lean against his body and rub herself all over him like a feline in the midst of mating fever.

"Xavi. This is unexpected." Her voice trembled. Her lips parted, and a soft breath escaped. What was the matter with her?

That smile... The bastard knew her difficulties, she was certain. Perhaps he found them amusing. Internal sparks flew, and her anger exploded. She took a step back, trying to pull away and assert herself.

His expression changed. The mirth disappeared, and the hand became an iron shackle. *You are going nowhere*, his expression warned. He shook his head, lips pressed together.

"Oh no, you don't, Isabel. Don't start fighting me. We both know you want me." And the uppity little grin she loved to hate reappeared. She had to suppress the urge to scratch it away, when his lips brushed her ear. "Almost as much as I want you. Come. Let me take you home."

One moment she stood on the sidewalk, the next she was sitting inside the jeep, Xavi behind the wheel, key in the ignition. He turned it, and the engine roared to life, but he kept the vehicle idling. Hoping to regain her own control, Isabel pressed her back stiffly against the seat, refusing to look at him, although utterly aware of the traitorous dolt sitting in the backseat. The disconcerting caress came unexpectedly. The backs of his fingers stroked her cheek tenderly, diffusing her irritation with a silent message: *I want you.*

"Are you ready?"

"Mmhmm," she said.

"Michael. Are you okay back there?"

"Yep, Uncle Xavi. I'm set."

He released the parking brake, and the jeep rolled forward. Isabel shot him a furtive glance and regretted it. Xavi's confidence handling the vehicle disarmed her. He was so alluring she forgot her anger. Damn him a million times. Why had he come? The car hurtled into the dark, empty streets heading for the ranch. It was going to be a very long night.

***

Driving north on IH-75, Xavi marveled at his new reality. His fantasy, the happiness he once envisioned, was possible. Isabel was no longer his *princess lointaine*, forbidden and unattainable. He was free to claim and hold on to her. He would surround her with love and give wings to her sexuality. In turn, she would enhance and validate his. They perfected each other. The blissful tableau was clear in his mind, but selling it to Isabel was another matter.

Her beauty gave him a pang of need at the pit of his stomach. She was lovely and breathtaking, yet stubborn and skittish. Xavi loved the enticement. He would have to dig deep in his bag of taming tricks to ease her fractiousness. Nothing could stop him now. For all her efforts to hide her feelings, she desired him, and her body language betrayed her, which utterly pleased him.

He would push her no further tonight. For as much as he needed and wanted her underneath him, satisfying his natural desires, he adored her and would foremost be patient. It didn't mean he couldn't indulge, at least a little.

"Isabel, you work tomorrow. Don't you?"

"I do. Why?" Xavi felt her burning gaze on him. It was a pity he couldn't return it.

"I wanted to know." There was no why. He had to educate her in his ways.

"Michael, should I take the next exit?" At Michael's affirmative answer, they pulled off the highway toward the ranch. He turned into the Reynoldses' driveway and drove past the main house. In the rearview mirror, he saw Michael's surprised expression. However, as a true son of Jonas, he didn't ask. Xavi also felt Isabel's glance, knowing she'd expected the same. When would they all learn predictability was not in his vocabulary?

"Safely delivered," he said, pulling the brake. "Michael, wait here for me. Okay?"

"Yep."

Out of the corner of his eye, he saw Isabel start to descend without his assistance. "Isabel, stop." His tone immobilized her. Startled, she waited while Xavi came to her side, opened the door, and extended one hand, the other reaching for her waist.

"I'm here to take care of you," Xavi grumbled as her feet touched the ground. She seemed confused. "Isabel, are you listening?"

"Hmmmm...?"

"You need rest." He placed a hand on her lower back, leading her toward the door. She didn't resist.

He stopped under the entry light. He'd driven hundreds of miles to see the glorious sight of Isabel's sparkling whisky irises. She looked even lovelier with the new minute lines here and there. The hint of maturity enhanced rather than diminished her beauty.

Reluctantly, Xavi pulled out of the golden spell and silently extended his palm up to her. She looked at it curiously. He tilted his head, moving his hand a little closer to her purse. A sudden gleam of understanding lit her expression. She reached inside and pulled out a set of keys, and with tremulous fingers, she released them. Xavi smiled when they fell into his hand. "Good girl," he murmured in approval.

He unlocked the door and pulled her inside. An overwhelming sense of tenderness filled his soul as he admired her exquisite form. Lord, he'd missed her so much. He grasped the nape of her neck and gently pulled her close to him. When she acquiesced, his heart wanted to sing with joy.

"Give me your mouth, Isabel. I wish to taste you," he whispered, husky and rough. Her lips parted obediently, and her breath rushed out. Isabel's sweet scent intoxicated and dizzied him, and for the merest moment, he lost control. He paused, not wanting to maul her like a randy, inexperienced youth. Instead, he kissed her beautiful features in a languorous caress—the elegant nose, the sweeping eyelashes, the silky cheeks.

"Oh, Isabel." Years of starvation clamored, and his mouth covered hers. She responded tentatively, and his tongue invaded her mouth. *Give in. Release yourself to me.* His plea was loud, yet it remained unspoken. Her hands lifted to his chest and landed lightly. Xavi almost fell to his knees.

He pulled back a bit, not wanting to overwhelm her. He needed more, so much more of her. For the moment, this would have to do. So he took slow, tiny nips, enjoying her full lower lip, and let his arms drop to the side. Her lids opened slowly, reluctantly.

He kissed the tip of her nose. "Now close the door. I won't leave until I hear the lock." He nudged her farther in as she looked at him, flushed, misty eyed, her lips quivering. He almost changed his mind to leave.

"Sleep well. I'll see you tomorrow." His knuckles brushed her lip. "Go, lock the door."

"Xavi, I wanted…"

"Tomorrow. I'll answer all your questions tomorrow. I'm staying a few days. Okay?"

She nodded and closed the door. As soon as he heard the click, he returned to the jeep.

"Uncle Xavi?"

He'd completely forgotten Michael. "Yes?" Xavi threw the vehicle in gear.

"I want to be like you."

"Like me?" Xavi stopped, leaned an arm on the headrest, turning to look at the young man. "Your dad is a formidable man. Why would you want to be like me?"

"I like how you do things."

"How's that?"

"She's always so difficult. Aunt Isabel, I mean. How do you handle her?"

Xavi gave Michael a slow appraising look before returning to the business of driving. As he pulled away, he stared at his best friend's son through the rearview mirror. "None of your business, kid."

***

The door shut, and Isabel was plunged into darkness and silence, but the riveting sensations remained—a trail of heat on her skin, a hint of scent on her nose, a trace of passion in her mind. Disbelief mixed with awe. A scant hour ago, she'd waited, unsuspecting, unaware, and now...

She rushed through the house, turning lights on as she went in a futile effort to dispel the internal chaos. She reached her bedroom as her nerves began to fray. His unique signature fragrance lingered. It was all over her, even her clothing. Unable to manage its effect, she flew to the shower, stripped, and dove under the spray. What had he done to her? She couldn't process the wild surge of instincts she'd long suppressed, and others she'd never experienced—love, mating, and happiness. All brought to life by Xavi's seduction.

"He's not for me. I can't hold him. I'm not worthy." She repeated the mantra as she soaped and scrubbed her skin with furious intent. She rinsed until she was satisfied all physical reminders of Xavi had been purged. Now it was time to numb out and wipe away the mental reminders. Would he condemn her if he discovered her nightly habit? She stared at the amber liquid in the glass. Before the rite of inebriation began this night, she needed to make one last call.

Chapter Thirteen

Ocala – June 15th 1967

Jonas said good night to Isabel and hung up the phone. He looked at his wife in consternation. He wanted to elucidate, but not with this many young ears nearby. Coralina understood his husband-to-wife message and nodded. She would try to deflect. It might have worked had Raquelita not been present.

"Are we going now?"

"No, sweetheart. You and Marité are spending the night with us."

"We are? Why?"

"Your mom sounded really tired. She said you could both sleep over. She's going to bed now."

Raquelita flinched, and he knew she wasn't buying it. Just then, Xavi and Michael arrived. He hoped it would distract his niece.

Xavi was a different matter. "Okay, what's going on?"

"Not much." Coralina answered for Jonas.

"Mom doesn't want us home tonight. Don't you think it's weird?"

"I do, sweetheart. When I left her, she seemed all right. Maybe I should check on her. Cora, what do you think?"

"I say, let's not overreact. She's likely surprised with your unexpected visit and tired from work. Give her a night to gather her wits." She looked around the room, gauging everyone's expression. When everyone frowned back, she gave in. "Okay, I'll call."

Xavi watched her go. Why didn't she use the kitchen phone? He almost asked, but the strange undercurrent flowing in the room stopped him—eyes didn't meet, and faces were averted. He'd timed his arrival perfectly. In the next few days, he would learn what went unsaid. Pondering those thoughts, he went after Coralina.

"Well?" he asked the minute she hung up.

"She sounded normal. Tired and listless, more or less."

"Cora, I need a favor." He sat on a recliner and crossed his legs. The tips of his fingers played absently with his knee.

"Sure, what is it?"

"I've been thinking. Is Nieves friends with the widow Llorenz?"

"You mean the old biddy, Isabel's mother?"

"Yes. The very one."

"Gosh. Her name hasn't been mentioned in ages. What do you wish to know?"

"For starters, if she's alive. Alicia could answer some of my questions."

"Ah, you've noticed, haven't you? The inconsistencies in Isabel's behavior."

"Some. Hell, maybe Isabel's not aware of them. Either way, I'll find out. There's much at stake, and it's not only me. The daughters are affected."

"I couldn't agree more. Raquelita is already a woman. I doubt Isabel's prepared to handle that challenge. I remember a rumor about an old scandal, right after the Spanish Civil War, when Isabel was a child. Something about Alicia's brother, Iñigo. If the uncle was involved, I don't like what it suggests."

Xavi pressed his lips upon steepled fingers. "It's the worst-case scenario, but it would fit."

"I'll call Mother first thing tomorrow. Don't worry, she'll find Alicia."

"Thanks, Cora. Really." He came to his feet, and in two long strides reached her side and planted a noisy kiss on her cheek. "Hey, Jonas. I just kissed your wife," he yelled out, heading toward his bedroom.

"That makes sense. She's always liked you better," Jonas retorted.

***

It was not yet time for the game to be revealed,
sins confessed or wounds discovered.
Isabel escaped for a future reckoning...

***

A few nights later, Raquelita reached for her refuge in the pages of her journal. She had much on her mind.

June 20th, Ocala

A new letter has arrived full of hope. If the mercies of heaven allow, we will see each other in less than a week. A day to count for a thousand reunions, to live many lives in a few hours. Life is but a collection of moments and happy times. We will add this memory to the others and continue to thread our string of precious pearls.

It is strange. I've wondered if a phone call would be more gratifying. Letters don't satisfy the soul as much as the spoken word. Yet, while a live conversation sates the heart, it is ephemeral. Once it is finished, it can exist only as a memory, subject to fading with the passage of time. The letter remains. It is a palpable testament of undying love and devotion.

I have his letters to hold on to. His voice is ingrained in my heart.

I live for the day when he returns home to stay. We will live in each other's arms, free to create our small miracles, our extensions into immortality, our children, and our legacy.

As for the rest…

Padrino. With every passing second, a man of many facets unfolds. He's uncontainable, disdainful of limits, and prodigiously intuitive. Did I know him at all? He loves her; he lives for Isabel. Is she ready for it?

Abuse, I heard the whispers. Was this my mother's undoing? What sort of abuse, physical or mental? Would this knowledge change my emotions toward her? If so, what a tragic way to recapture lost tender feelings. So high the price!

***

The morning rays danced upon the young women in capricious angles, making whimsical shapes. Like long fingers, they reached past branches of live oak and magnolia trees and through the windows. One beam bounced and gleamed on Lorrie's long brown tresses and continued on its way to animate the pamphlets strewn over the kitchen table with shadows and patterns of light.

"What about this class? Intro to Creative Writing. It's made in heaven for you," Lorrie drawled. Her cheek rested on her wrists as a finger tapped on a brochure.

"I'm including it in my course list," Raquelita answered, jotting in her notebook.

Lorrie shifted her attention to her cousin, pinning her with her pretty blue gaze. "Don't keep me in suspense. Have you heard from Matthew yet? When is he coming?"

"I hope to get something in the mail soon."

"You seem rather confident for one who was a total wreck a week ago." She snickered.

"Well, it's more like my faith in him has been restored." Raquelita sat up, shaking her shoulders uncomfortably. "No, shame on me. I did it. I let fear take me. The day we met, I recognized the other half of my soul. That night on the bus, we became one. Our parting was more like a ripping. With a pain so sharp, I allowed my mother's attitude inside my heart." Raquelita waved a hand in the air, dispelling an unseen presence.

"I crumbled while Matthew stayed strong. He gave me his love and trust. He was taking a chance as well. I could've been some crazy chick ready to experiment with many guys, and quick to forget. Do I deserve him?"

"Take it easy," Lorrie protested. "Your meeting was short and unconventional. Was the relationship expert around to guide you? No, instead you had, good grief, your mom."

"Well, believing is easy now. His letter is physical evidence of our promises on a bus. Geez, coz, will I fall to pieces when he's sent overseas? That'll be the real test."

"Ah…sigh." Lorrie pressed a melodramatic hand to her forehead. "So pathetic, so romantic. I want my drama, soon." She threw her hands upwards in mock supplication. It broke the intensity, and both women chuckled.

They were still laughing when Coralina entered the kitchen. "Ladies, good morning."

"Good morning," they answered in unison.

Coralina placed a hand on Raquelita's shoulder. "A word, *querida*?"

"Of course."

"Not here—in the office."

"Is anything wrong?"

"Nothing's wrong. Lorrie, darling, she'll be right back."

"Sure thing, Mom." She watched them leave, and at the last minute, her mother turned and winked. Lorrie relaxed.

Coralina returned alone. "A letter," she answered before the question.

Just then, an excited squeal burst out of the office. Lorrie smiled. Matthew's arrival date was finally set.

***

Three male voices carried from the family gathering in the Reynoldses' living room: Jonas, Xavi, and Michael, each distinct, each powerful. And Matthew would make it a perfect quartet. *Oh Matthew.* Lita couldn't shake his worrisome words.

I grow angry and feel powerless with this separation. Countless nights I want to say the hell with it, drive down, whisk you away, and run together, somewhere far. Angel, I miss you so.

From here, what could she do to appease him?

We are completely isolated within these facilities...training for a dangerous future...while the US population drones on without a care or consideration.

Raquelita tightened her arms about herself, staring at her aunt and uncle. Their affection and deep regard was an aspect of married life she never saw growing up. They lived in a universe where love flourished and relationships lasted.

"How is my goddaughter doing this evening?" Xavi asked as he came around, an arm enclosing her affectionately.

Here was a man of many facets. With each passing second, she liked him better, discovering she could trust him. "I'm well, *Padrino*." She returned the pleasantry, keeping her thoughts to herself: *he is determined and focused; he knows what he wants and how he wants it.* "I'm surprised you're still here. I thought you'd be on your way to pick up Mom."

"In a minute. I know the way now. When are you meeting Matthew?" he whispered. She might have bolted were it not for Xavi's firm hold. Had he read Matthew's letter?

Saturday evening, right after the graduation ceremony, Brian and I will drive to Ocala, angel. Please remind your aunt. I'll call first thing, and if there are no objections, I'll hold you in my arms come Sunday morning.

"How?"

Xavi laughed. "I'm an old devil. I know people, and nothing escapes my attention. So, tell me, when?"

"It's only for a day. This coming Sunday."

"Let's see what we may do to help." He spoke to no one in particular and nudged her forward.

"Help whom?" Marité asked.

Michael stepped in to assist. "Your sister's been checking out some class schedules, sweetie."

Do they all know? She looked at the complicit, smiling faces: her aunt and uncle on the sofa, Lorrie leafing through a magazine, and Michael entertaining her sister. Was this what Matthew meant about family support and love? She felt a reassuring squeeze on her shoulders.

"It'll be fine, darling. Hey, everybody. I'm picking up Isabel. I'll be back in a few." Xavi released Raquelita and walked out the door. For long minutes, she stared after him, and it finally dawned on her: Xavi would make it happen.

***

"I want to take you away for the weekend." Xavi pulled Isabel's attention away from his maneuvering antics. The man drove the rented Mustang like his own Porsche back in San Antonio, ignoring the drastic differences between the two vehicles. As the car barreled through the night, buildings and homes became dark blurs along barely lit streets.

"Well?" Staring forward, he reached out to cup Isabel's cheek. "No answer?"

"What if I say I don't wish to go?"

"I'd say you are lying."

"I have no choice in this matter?"

The sudden sharp turn of the wheel unbalanced her. The car came to a dead stop against the curb. "Of course, you have a choice, an honest choice."

"You aren't asking. You're telling me."

"All right, I'll ask. Isabel, would you like to go to Destin for the weekend?"

In her silence, he pulled her toward him, almost daring her to refuse. They were face-to-face, so near she was certain they could taste each other's breaths. His was decisive and hot.

"I'm waiting." His lips brushed hers, and Isabel shivered. "Honesty, Isabel. Nothing else will do."

She dropped her lids as confusion reigned. She wanted to scream; she wanted to crush her lips and body against his. She wanted to escape the hot grip at her neck. Isabel inhaled, and the movement brought her even closer, making the decision for her—or so she would argue—and without thought, she pressed her lips against his.

Xavi released a deep-seated groan, slipped a hand behind her shoulder blades and pressed her tighter, fusing his lips with hers. Just as abruptly, he pulled away.

"You stubborn woman, will you answer me?"

"Yes, yes. I will."

"Ah, Isabel." He sighed, resting his forehead on hers. "You make me a happy man." He turned to face the steering wheel, and started the car. "Let's go home. They're holding dinner for us."

***

Even though she'd read them repeatedly, Matthew's words remained fresh, caressing her thoughts without pause.

> *I can't wait to hold you again…the words escape me…I'll love you slowly and thoroughly; by the end of the day, you'll know for certain.*

He elicited such daring images, such suggestive possibilities. Raquelita shivered and blushed, smiling at her shyness and excitement. How could she sleep in the next two nights? She curled into her favorite position, allowing her thoughts and questions to soar. Did she understand Matthew's words? Of course she did, and she shivered again. Was she ready? Yes, she was more than ready. She wanted to be his.

She stretched her body languorously, experimenting with her senses, setting out on a voyage of self-discovery. Her cotton gown rustled against her warm skin. She slipped her hands along the sides of her torso. Would he like her like this? Would he find her attractive?

Feeling awfully silly, she scoffed and halted her fledging explorations. What the hell did she know about this stuff? Frustrated, she abandoned her bed and stomped toward the window, when the memory of a cherished night resurfaced vividly. True, she didn't know about intimate matters, but on that night of first love, she'd followed Matthew's lead as far as they could go, without an iota of doubt or concern. Indeed, perfection existed within the arms of her beloved, and she had no need to scrutinize further. Whatever would develop between them in two days would be a divine and righteous act.

An inopportune knock interrupted her contemplations.

"Yes?"

"Raquelita?" her mother asked from the other side. "Are you awake?"

Her heart jolted with the unwelcome visit, but she collected herself as best she could.

"I am. Come in, Mom." She turned to the door as her mother entered.

"Lita, take a seat." Isabel signaled to the bed as she moved to a small armchair ensconced in a corner. "Tomorrow…" Isabel paused, fidgeting nervously with the edges of her sash. "As I was saying…"

Raquelita almost gawked. "Mom?" she asked, stupefied, as a deep scarlet flush covered Isabel from the neck to the roots of her hair.

Isabel made an odd sound, clearing her throat. "Tomorrow morning, Xavi is picking me up, and, we'll…" Isabel stood up, and headed for the door. Raquelita jumped out of bed and blocked her.

"What, Mom? Finish. You can tell me." She held her mother by the arms, attempting a conciliatory smile.

Isabel glanced down, first to her daughter's face, next to the arms curbing her escape. She exhaled. "We're going to Destin for the weekend."

A Cheshire cat smile began to appear on Lita's face; wisely, she held it in check. "With Xavi? That's…wonderful. It should be fun." She released her mother and slowly returned to her bed, camouflaging her excitement over the news.

"Well… It's highly irregular, and I'm not entirely convinced it's a good idea. But Xavi is a most exasperating, insistent man. So I've agreed. We're leaving tomorrow morning."

"When are you coming back?"

"I wanted to return Sunday, but Xavi complained about weekend traffic."

"Let's see what we may do to help."

Xavi's words rang out like a church bell urging the faithful to services on a Sunday morning. *Padrino*. A man of many unexpected moves had stepped in to help, and this new wondrous alliance felt really good in her soul.

"You'll spend the weekend at the Reynoldses'. They have agreed." Isabel was back to her stern demeanor. "Well. That's it. Good night, daughter." Isabel bent over, patted Raquelita's head, and walked out, leaving a bemused daughter behind.

Chapter Fourteen

Ocala – June 24th 1967

It's really happening. Raquelita pressed her palms against the window, watching her godfather load the last bag and close the trunk with a solid thud. The rented shiny black Ford Mustang convertible, confirmed Xavi's uncompromising sense of style. He wasn't a snob; to him, class was a simple matter of taste and preference, and he was casual about it. He knew his mind and rarely budged or compromised on anything. Lately, however, Lita was surprised to discover some matters and even some moods had changed. Like today, in sharp contrast to his chronic solemnity he looked positively resplendent and, dare she think it, happy.

Raquelita shot her mother a side-glance. If her godfather's attitude was an accurate meter, her mother was in over her head. She had to squelch an irresistible desire to laugh and was perversely and thoroughly delighted with Isabel Muro's obvious discomfiture. She'd stepped out of her bedroom with her sunglasses already perched on her pert nose, revealing an abundance of nerves and a restless night.

"Okay, girls. We're ready." Isabel shifted her purse from hand to hand. "Behave. Mind your aunt and uncle."

"Yes, Mom."

Xavi, with his happy smile and shiny aura, entered the house, hands on hips and car keys jingling from his fingers. He waited patiently for Isabel to finish her last-minute instructions. He flashed a knowing look toward Raquelita, and she ran to him, hugging him tightly. "Please, be careful driving, promise?"

"I promise. I have precious cargo with me." He tilted his head in the direction of her mother, and Isabel rolled her eyes dramatically.

"Thanks, *Padrino*."

"We'll never get started with these lengthy good-byes," Isabel huffed.

"You hear that? She can't wait to get me all alone. All right, let's start this expedition." In a blink, Xavi and Isabel were inside the car. The engine roared to life, and the Mustang took off.

***

"It's time." Coralina patted Raquelita on the shoulder, and with an upraised finger, she signaled her to follow.

"What?" Startled, she trailed behind her aunt. "Is it bad?"

Coralina spoke over her shoulder as they entered her atelier. "No, it isn't, although it's never a comfortable subject to discuss with a young one."

The dreaded talk approached. Raquelita was familiar with the birds and bees and should have stopped her, except her aunt's discomfort was so amusing, she didn't want to end it too quickly. *Tempus fugit*. If her aunt didn't start quickly, her opportunity would be lost. Lita had to suppress a laugh.

"Auntie, maybe I should tell you I know about the birds and the bees." Lita took a seat by the kitchen table.

Coralina released a deflating breath. "That's reassuring. Knowing how your mother operates, or doesn't, I wasn't sure how much information I'd have to cram into one speech."

She picked up a tray with sliced apples, offering some to Raquelita.

"I don't want to fail you, and I don't care if this is uncomfortable. I'm fairly ill at ease, yet I'm dealing with it, so I'll be blunt." Coralina looked around. Satisfied no indiscreet ears were nearby, she approached the table, set the tray down, and sat facing her niece. She reached across to Raquelita and held her hands. "Okay, here goes, woman to woman. Tomorrow, when you meet up with your young man, I want you to be careful. Use your head. Protect your future.

"I would urge you not to engage in premarital sex. However, I'm also a realist. I'd rather educate you. There's a lot of emotion between you two, with precious little time to assuage it, and so the deck is stacked. I recognize love when I see it. I won't limit your privacy. I also don't want you to get pregnant." Raquelita blushed lightly yet remained steady, appreciating these generous words of truth and experience. She'd be a fool not to listen.

"Maybe it sounds clinical and cold." Coralina shrugged. "I want you and Matthew to go to the nearest drugstore, buy condoms, and use them. Are you listening? You can love each other to exhaustion. Do it wisely. Wisdom doesn't arrest love, it enhances it."

Raquelita nodded and blushed but remained silent, eager to hear more. "If Matthew is the sort of young man I think he is, he will arrive prepared. Still, don't take it for granted. There's much at stake here. I hate to remind you where he's going. Heaven forbid, if the worst should happen, you'd remain a single mother. Raising a child without a father isn't romantic. It's a daily struggle." Coralina made a strange noise as if trying to swallow, and shuffled in her seat. "Do you have any questions? Any concerns?"

Not exactly what she'd expected. Coralina had gone to the heart of the matter: pregnancy. Raquelita had prepared for the interminable speech on purity, chastity, and morality. Instead, her aunt had addressed the stark realities and consequences. She trusted Matthew to think ahead. He cared deeply and wouldn't leave her pregnant.

Only one little question remained. And her cheeks began to burn.

"Aunt Coralina. Is it true the first time hurts?"

Her aunt turned beet red. "Well, it's become a cliché. It depends on the man, honestly. If the lover is skilled and gentle, it'll pass quickly. But if he's clumsy, or in a hurry…right… well, there's your answer. I have a feeling you'll be fine, *querida*." She patted her hand and offered the tray of apples again. "Have a slice. They're delicious."

***

Tucked away on a sandy road, the inn was charming, cozy, and surprisingly elegant. The lady who owned it guided them solicitously up the stairs to their bedroom. The door opened, and Isabel was rendered speechless. A grand, four-poster, king-size bed dominated the room. It faced a set of French doors opening to a patio with a breathtaking view of the beach and beyond.

"Will you be all right for a few minutes? I'm going to speak with the owner." He deposited her case on a valise stand. "Here's your bag, if you wish to freshen up. I'll return shortly with dinner arrangements." He gave her a quick peck on her hair and walked out.

The ride had been easy and beautiful in spite of its length and her misgivings. Isabel had visions of a wild, speeding maniac intent on getting her to a bedroom as quickly as possible. Not so. Xavi had been entertaining and thoughtful. She'd misjudged him terribly.

When they stopped for lunch outside Tallahassee, she realized he'd planned this excursion with care. Instead of taking I-10 he deviated to Route 61, taking several county roads, driving along the most breathtaking coastline she'd ever seen. The Apalachicola National Forest bordered one side. On the other, snow-white sand dunes highlighted the turquoise waters of the Florida Gulf.

She stepped out onto the patio, lured by the beginning stages of a summer sunset and the unimpeded view. Lost in the beautiful scene, her thoughts entered the perilous zone. What lurked in her future? Damaged and unstable as she was, what could she offer anyone? Least of all to a man like Xavi, who demanded perfection, who *was* perfect.

She took in a deep breath when his hands fell on her waist. His breath rolled down her neck as he murmured, "Isabel, you are overthinking. Don't worry so much."

"Always so sure."

"I am. Are you hungry yet?"

"A little," she admitted. "But it's such a beautiful sight, I hate to leave it."

"If we hurry, we'll enjoy the rest of the sunset from our table. The restaurant is but a couple of minutes away. Come, my lady."

***

"I wanna get there more than you. Will you slow down? If some dumbass MP stops us, we'll be delayed, and then I'll kill you, good friend or not," Matthew grumbled as Brian raced toward the checkpoint and the last gate out of the military grounds.

"Stop chewing your bit, Matt James. We'll get there. Chill." Brian smiled, his foot easing off the gas pedal.

It had been a frenzied day, culminating with the presentation ceremony. His only regret was Raquelita's absence. Now he raced to her with his airborne wings in his pocket. He would offer them to her with pride. He hoped she would keep them.

Matthew wanted to fly south, not waste precious time driving. He leaned back against the seat in a futile bid to relax. He couldn't, not until he had her in his arms, a few agonizing hours away. If it weren't for her mother, he would drive straight to the ranch and let the chips fall where they may. He peeked behind his seat to the makeshift vase holding the roses. They should last until tomorrow, he hoped.

"Matt, did you buy the rubbers?"

"What?"

"Aw, shoot. Please, tell me you remembered. I don't know of any drugstore on this road."

Matthew shrugged, feeling like a fifteen-year-old. Condoms hadn't been his first thought. Flowers, yes. *"What a sap,"* Brian had commented.

"Yes. I have them."

Once Brian brought up the matter, he'd remained conflicted. He was so eager to see her, he hadn't thought further. Certainly not to the conclusion Brian suggested. The image mortified him no end. *Hey, darling, here's a dozen roses, and a box of condoms.* He would look like a complete idiot.

He wanted to see her and be with her, touch her, smell her delicate scent, listen to her for hours without interruption and try to sate his soul within the allotted time. If anything else were to develop… Why didn't he think? Indelicate or not, thank goodness Brian was thinking. In reality, Matthew had no clue how this visit would work out. He'd suggested they meet at some park, an idea he hated already. In the end, she would dictate the conditions, depending on the situation at the ranch, and he would follow.

"Thanks, pardner, for reminding me. I'd not…"

"Yeah, yeah, I know. You bein' in love and all. My bud, Matthew, sharp as mashed potatoes and shit. I had to look out for both of you. The way you twirl her medal around, I know she's special. Gotta take care of the lady."

"Yeah, you're right. I could've been running around Ocala in the middle of a Sunday afternoon searching for the damned things, or worse, faced with the act and unable to stop. I'd never do that to her." He shook his head.

"Amen, pardner," Brian drawled, shooting him a quick glance. "Relax, will you? Turn on some tunes. Let me drive. You have a hard day ahead." Brian guffawed, and his fist connected with Matthew's shoulder.

Matthew didn't react but stared silently out at the road. Shadows took over as light waned, and just before he lost all discernible sight of the landscape, a sign gleamed as they passed: WELCOME TO FLORIDA.

Soon, he would soon be there.

***

A distant murmur of rushing waves tempted Isabel back to sleep, but the bright morning light streamed through the open doors. Thoughts slowly filtered in. Destin. She was at the beach with Xavi. What happened last night? Details were fuzzy: a lovely candlelight dinner, champagne, delicious and bubbly, and what else? Where was Xavi?

She stretched enjoying the silky, cool sheets. She wanted to linger, but a dangerous man and a gorgeous beach beckoned. Isabel pushed up and... Odd, she was wearing her nightgown but couldn't remember changing. She slipped her feet onto the tiled floor and stood, perhaps a little wobbly, but she gained her balance and headed for the toilet.

"Well, the queen finally awakens." He spoke from somewhere on the patio.

"Err...bathroom first."

"Better?" he asked when she exited after a necessary body relief and some hurried ablutions.

Holding a glass of juice, he stood by the French doors. Her mouth slackened at the sight. Clad in ordinary swimming trunks, a loose shirt, and a pair of flip-flops, the man was glorious. From the slightly rumpled hair to the extended fingers, to the long, well-muscled legs and amazingly sexy toes on his arched feet, his masculinity electrified every feminine nerve she owned.

How had she overlooked this? He'd always been Emilio's forbidding friend, aloof and castigating with a sharp word and manner. The universe had a sense of humor. The man who at times made her feel less than human was now displayed in his most human, splendid form, and she had no idea what to think or do.

Accept the juice, spoke the judicious side of her mind. *And take it from there.*

"Isabel. Come." He extended a hand, instilling direction and purpose to her addled mind. He held her hand, guiding her outside. Spread on the table was a tray with coffee service, assorted pastries, and sliced fruit.

"It awaits my lady's pleasure. Take a seat. Enjoy. Here, I believe you could use these." He presented her with sunglasses.

"Do you think of everything?"

"Always."

"Where did you find them?"

"In your purse."

"Xavi?"

"Yes?"

"H-how?"

"You wish to know about last night?" His smile—which could shame the sun's brightness—dazzled her. "In a few words, you found the champagne delicious, we returned from dinner and sat outside enjoying the night sky, and soon you were deeply asleep. I put you to bed."

"Did you?"

"Of course. How else?"

"I see." A sudden blush heated her cheeks. "Should I thank you?"

"No need. I assure you, the pleasure was mine. Go ahead. Eat." He pushed the plate of fruit at her. "We have big decisions—beach, or nude sunbathing on our private patio." He winked, and she knew he teased her.

"Coffee first."

"As you wish."

As the first delicious drops of juice burst upon her taste buds, she smiled. She was amazingly at ease. It would be a good day. The home front was taken care of, past troubles gone forever. No other worries or concerns, except for the formidable masculine challenge answering to the name of Xavier Manel Repulles.

Chapter Fifteen

Ocala – June 25th 1967

At the Reynoldses' bedroom, Jonas approached having a conniption. His wife stared in bewilderment. "*Muñeca*, I always side with you on everything. Not on this." He tried to ease the anger in his comment, but he envisioned the park scene, and it upset him all over again. "On this matter, I won't budge. There's no justification for it, not anymore." He riffled his hair again and again.

"Jonas, I…"

With a rare imperious wave, he silenced her. "No, I won't be swayed. She has a family. She's not a vagrant. Matthew met Lita traveling with her mother. Your sweet romantic heart wants to help them, and so do I. But as the head of this family and Emilio's agent, I insist Matthew will pick up Raquelita at the ranch. Damn it. The situation is unorthodox enough already. You are *not* delivering her to some park corner. No, I say again. Would you do it with Lorrie?"

"Of course not. But it's not the same."

"It is the same. Xavi fixed it, the sly devil. He knew about Matthew. It's the reason for the long weekend. He opened the door for Raquelita and us. And we're going to follow through with normal parameters."

Hell, they were in a pickle of a situation. He was not an unfeeling bastard and understood the young couple's need to spend time together, but his paternal instinct refused to disregard respect and protocol. He also understood subliminal messages. If he sanctioned this park meeting with a virtual stranger, what sort of message did it send? The thought pushed him right over the edge.

He walked over and sat next to a dumbstruck Coralina. Scant minutes ago, a frenzied giant exploded when she revealed the morning's plans. He cupped her cheek, his gaze mellowing at last.

"Will you trust me on this? He will suffer scrutiny, *Muñeca*. Raquelita lives under our roof, and I require it. Only then will I permit this visit."

"After they made you, they broke the mold. I can't believe I got you all to myself. I agree with your decision. Xavi did make it easier. Promise me one thing?"

"Anything."

"Don't scare Matthew away."

"If I scare him, he doesn't deserve Raquelita and has no business going into Special Forces. He *will* endure my chest-thumping bravado. If he loves her, he'll respect it as well. What time is he calling?"

"I believe around nine today."

"Good. Before he does, explain to Raquelita the change in plans. If you'd rather, I will handle the matter."

"No, my love, I'll do it. I can't wait to see my Jonas, all mighty and protective in action. Dear Lorrie, meet your real father. Come here, my fierce warrior, growl in my ear…"

***

Coralina marched into Lorrie's room with the new orders. There would be no special delivery to the park, and Matthew was to appear in person, present credentials, pass inspection, and receive approval for a special date. Curfew hours remained unspecified.

"Alone or accompanied, Raquelita, you better be on premises before your uncle awakes in the morning."

It would have been comical, except the heavy dose of nervous anticipation addled Lita's ability to appreciate humor. Lorrie's muffled snickers didn't help. Proclamation over, Coralina departed with an air of royal dignity and without a backward glance. Lorrie exploded in raucous laughter, holding her stomach as she rolled side to side.

"They're something, aren't they?" She flipped on her belly.

"Laugh it up, coz. Remember the saying: *Él que ríe último ríe mejor.*"

"Huh?"

"Pay attention. Translation: *He, who laughs last, laughs best.* Cousin dearest, this is your future." Raquelita waved her index finger, stressing the *your future* part.

***

Alone in the office, unable to relax, Raquelita waited for Matthew's phone call as butterflies rioted in her stomach. Would he agree? What if he didn't? With each apprehensive question, she would either soar in elation or plummet dejectedly.

A second past nine, the phone rang with military precision. Her heart somersaulted, and blood pounded in her ears. "Hello?" she whispered into the mouthpiece.

"Good morning, angel." Three words, and the madness, the grating sounds and noises of the world disappeared. His voice conjured serenity, certainty, and completeness. Peace enfolded her. What she had expressed to her cousin was the absolute truth: he was indeed the other half of her. If a doubt existed, it now ceased forever.

"Matthew."

"Angel, could we do this a different way?"

"What do you mean?"

"I'd much prefer to pick you up at the ranch instead of meeting at the park. I don't feel right about it."

Peals of laughter escaped her lips.

"Is everything okay, angel?"

"Yes, yes. Everything is fine. Wonderful, in fact."

***

Thirty minutes after Matthew's phone call, Jonas followed Coralina into the kitchen. Standing on tippy toes, she threw her arms around his neck as he kissed her forehead.

"Such a grouch," she said.

"Honestly, I'm not going to hurt him, it's my job."

"I get it. You're rehearsing for Lorrie's turn."

"Lorrie? Lorrie is too young for this kind of activity," Jonas snarled as he poured coffee into a mug. He needed caffeine desperately for his first beau inspection. And, Lord, he hoped to be up to the task.

"She's *only* six months behind Lita."

"Lorrie isn't ready yet. She hasn't dated anyone. She prefers the group thing." He wanted out of the subject. "Hey, do I smell bacon? Are you making breakfast?"

"I am. I doubt Matthew's had any food yet."

"Good idea, *Muñeca*. Without Isabel's interference, the kids can spend time in peace. The grounds are large, and we can make ourselves scarce. Our niece hasn't had any normalcy in Lord knows how long, if ever. It feels good to offer her some, at least for a day."

Coralina lifted her head, ignoring her husband's comments. Raquelita had passed by the kitchen's entryway; her lustrous dark locks bounced and gleamed in the morning light. Her attention was intent on the front door.

"He's here. Let's see," Coralina whispered.

Hand in hand, the couple approached the kitchen's threshold to observe the scene. In the middle of the room, Raquelita stared at the front door. Lorrie had followed silently and now stood a few paces away, next to Michael. The distinctive sound of tires crushing the gravel road reached their ears.

Raquelita uttered a slight whimper, bolted toward the door, opened it with a jerk, and stepped out into the sunlight. On the driveway, an ice-blue Pontiac GTO came to a full stop. Her niece stopped on the landing. The driver's side opened, and a young man unfolded his tall, lithe frame out of the car. His smile was resplendent.

A falling pin would have boomed in the silence as all four witnessed a rushing Raquelita disappear within Matthew's embrace.

"Oh, Mom." Her daughter's exclamation pulled Coralina out of the spell. Her husband's grip on her hand tightened, and she had to blink. Through her tears, the world had become a blur.

***

"Matthew." A sob escaped Raquelita's lips. She ran toward his beautiful eyes and his brilliant smile. His strong arms tightened about her waist and lifted her up in the air, light as an exquisite peacock feather.

"God, angel. You're in my arms again." He twirled her around, unable and unwilling to release her. "I have you. I have you."

"What's this?" He stopped abruptly, brought her slowly to her feet. "Tears? Not yet, angel, please."

"They're happy tears, Matthew. Give me a second."

"A second, two, three, however many you want. We're just beginning. The day is ahead of us. Let me look at you, my beautiful angel, my lovely girl with the caramel eyes. I've tried to explain their beauty to others. I always fall short."

"I've tried to explain yours too, and failed miserably."

"Wait. I have something for you." He turned to the vehicle, emerging with the roses he'd carried from Ft. Benning.

"Matthew, they're gorgeous." She immersed her face within the fragrant petals and inhaled deeply.

"I asked the lady at the flower shop to remove the thorns before she wrapped them."

"You did?"

"I didn't want anything that could hurt my angel."

"Matthew, you're really here."

"And you." A shuffling noise made him look forward. "Hmmm, an impatient group has formed at the front door. I should present myself formally."

"Yes, of course. Let's go."

Matthew turned back to the car. This time he held a box wrapped in colorful paper and ribbon. She eyed it curiously, and he shrugged.

"It's a little something for the lady of the house. I'm so relieved we didn't have to meet at the park." He ran a possessive arm around her shoulders and glanced around the property in obvious admiration. "The ranch is nice. It reminds me of my home in Texas."

"Do you miss it?"

"Never more than I miss you. I miss you above all else, more than anyone or anything in this life." He dropped a kiss on her hair. "All right, let's go pass inspection." And with her shoulders firmly under his arm, they went forward.

***

"Sweetheart, this is perfect."

"Yes, it is." She sighed, leaning deeper into his embrace.

The huge lawns and immaculate white fence sparkled under a splendid sunshine. The breeze had issued the invitation. She'd heard it and brought him to this cherished spot, where seclusion and peace abounded under the friendly shade of the majestic oak, old lord of the region.

"I've something for you."

Raquelita shifted in his arms, searching his beloved countenance. In this quietude, the changes were obvious. Training had been demanding. His closely shorn hair enhanced the sharp angles of his face. He'd lost weight. He looked tighter. But the bright emerald eyes, the dazzling smile, and the shy dimple were all him.

She watched him search inside a jean pocket, and moments later, he presented her with a small metal object in his palm. "Matthew? Is this your graduation insignia?"

"Raquelita, you guided me, you gave me fortitude, and inspired me with your poem, your letters, and your spirit, your presence in my lonely nights and in my dreams. I want you to keep the proof of your support, my honor, and my success.

"Will you accept this token as a reminder of my love? When my tour is over, I'll exchange it with a ring, if you'll still have me. Until then, know I love you with my heart and soul." Matthew placed the pin on her palm and closed her fingers over it.

"I'm so honored, Matthew. Of course I accept. Like you, it's very handsome. My aunt will help me make it into a charm. I'll keep it close to my heart."

"Same as I wear yours every day." As he spoke, he pulled out her medallion. "See? I'm never without it."

"*La Virgen del Pilar.* She's very powerful. Everyone in Spain says so. I've asked her to watch over you, always."

"If you bid her to protect me, I know she will."

Just then, a brief echo of a dream reverberated through her mind, and she shivered.

"Cold?"

"No, love, I couldn't be better."

"Do you wish to go somewhere? Maybe go see a movie this afternoon?"

"A movie sounds great. We could check the Sunday paper." She made a move to stand.

"Not just yet, angel, there's no rush. We have time, and I'm enjoying the divine pleasure of having you in my arms again." Matthew leaned against the tree, pulling Raquelita along with him. He enclosed her within his arms as his legs flanked her sides protectively.

They sat in silence, each immersed in the other. Words would only be superfluous. And as Raquelita and Matthew reposed, the wizened old oak, with its ancient, shading limbs, enclosed the lovers within its benevolent protection for a long, long while.

***

The newspaper spread over the kitchen table advertised all available selections. Everyone had an opinion about the movie offerings.

Matthew was pleased beyond measure. This organized chaos was the perfect nurturing environment for the Muro sisters, who had grown up with little familial warmth. When they'd parted in Tallahassee, he'd been sick with worry. No more. His angel would be well cared for. Regardless of the insanity of one parent, Raquelita had others to protect her. He could now do his duty with peace of mind, and focus on a single purpose: returning to her safe and sound.

"What do you say, angel? We could decide on the way to the theater."

In concert, the Reynoldses lifted their heads from the papers.

"What?" Michael burst in. "You're not going to tell us? Oh man, that's just not cool."

Coralina walked over to the side windows and peered out. "You should go soon. Clouds are starting to gather. An early afternoon storm is on the rise."

Marité appeared at his side and tugged a loop of his jeans. "You'll take care of my sister, won't you?"

"Always, I promise." He placed a quick kiss on her head.

"All right, that's it. We should let them go before the storm arrives," Jonas added.

Matthew looked to everyone in the family, pausing on each face as he expressed his gratitude. "Thank you. You've all been so welcoming. I've no words. This was a wonderful visit for many reasons. For a few hours, I felt like I was back at my parents' peaceful home. I'd like to take Raquelita out for dinner after the movie, if that's all right with y'all."

"Certainly, young man. Go, have fun. Don't forget." Jonas stared at Raquelita.

"Yes, I remember. Alone or accompanied, be on premises before his lordship wakes."

The mood shifted, and they shook hands gravely. "Take care of her and yourself, young man."

"I will, sir. Ma'am."

Matthew nodded, and Coralina reached out to him, planting a resounding kiss on each cheek. "Breakfast will be ready tomorrow morning." She ushered them out.

***

Matthew drove in silence. He couldn't speak. The feelings were too strong. He looked down. Lita's warm hand was secured inside his. He tugged gently, and she slid closer to him. He'd kissed her, though not properly. Not yet, not yet. He wanted her so much he ached. His heart was pleading. He longed to ask but didn't want to push. Matthew inhaled, shoving his need down. He lifted her hand to his lips and kissed it fervently.

He pulled to the side and stopped the car. He reached with both hands, holding her face tenderly. Bringing her mouth to his, he kissed her thoroughly. Savoring deeply, he relearned her taste and the full slope and curve of her moist lips. She placed her hands above his, acquiescing to his caress, melting into him and kissing him back, echoing his urgency.

Breathless and panting, he straightened, staring deep into the eyes he'd missed so much. He could no longer tame his need and desire.

"Raquelita, I need to be with you."

"I know. I need you too."

"Are you sure?"

"I am. Don't make me wait any longer."

He leaned his forehead on hers. "Okay, let's skip the movie."

"Yes, please."

***

In the stillness of Matthew's motel room, she stared at him. The significance of the moment was heavy upon her. She felt bashful and nervous until he smiled, and all her fears and hesitations disappeared. She rushed into the shelter of his arms, seeking his warmth, basking in his strength.

Matthew trembled as well, weakened by the force of real love. He raised her chin, and his mouth descended to meet hers. She sighed and lifted her arms around his neck. He touched her lightly, exploring her face delicately, fearing she would break. She sighed again, and a thousand emotions exploded inside his chest.

"I love you."

His embrace tightened, his mouth fell on hers again, and his tongue slipped inside, seeking hers. She mewled and stroked him back, dizzying him out of his mind. Need would singe him.

In a sensuous dance, Matthew stepped forward and Lita followed his lead. They fell upon the bed in a tangle of arms, unrelenting kisses, and desperate hands. Urgency gave way to a strange composure. He pulled a foil wrapper out of his back pocket and tossed it on the bed. In slow, determined movements, he peeled her clothes as she removed his. He enfolded her again, joining skin against skin, nude, feverish and with the immeasurable joy of their first union.

Tenderly, he nuzzled her neck, adding tiny licks in a teasing journey to her beautiful breasts and the pale-rose nipples. He nipped and nibbled, his tongue swirled around the crest, he blew lightly across, and it peaked to his satisfaction. He grazed the damp tip between thumb and forefinger, as his mouth dedicated the same attention to her other breast.

She moaned and Matthew smiled, sliding through the valley of her belly and beyond, toward her beckoning legs. His hands glided along her inner thighs gentling them apart, allowing his questing lips entrance to her virgin and most sensitive area. He deposited a long, thorough kiss between her inner folds, and his tongue began its search. When he found her precious pearl, he suckled and drew, pulling gently at her delicious nub until her moans turned to gasps and her musky aroma announced her excitement.

"Matthew?"

"Relax, angel, let me love you."

He settled between her legs, reached for the wrapper, opened it carefully, and rolled on the condom. His sweetheart would now be protected. Slowly he guided her thighs around his hips as his loving arms secured her. He nudged the entrance of her sheath and paused, waiting for her expressive eyes to signal her readiness. He bent over her face, kissed her, playing with her lips, distracting and relaxing her fledging tension. The moment he felt her ease, he locked onto her gaze and thrust past her membrane, filling her virgin channel deeply and completely.

Raquelita gasped.

"I'm sorry, angel. It won't hurt again."

He did not move or speak. He witnessed in tender awe the beautiful panoply of emotions on her face: her surprise with the initial prickle of pain and its curious evolution to an expression of delight, her wonderment as her body adapted and molded to him, and finally her amazement when the walls of her vagina tightened around him in her first contraction of pure pleasure.

"God. You feel… I have no words."

Her hips tilted toward him as tiny spasms enfolded his cock within tight, intimate embraces. Engaging all his control, Matthew kept his body still, allowing his manhood to speak for him. It thrummed and pulsed in response to her contractions. He shifted a little, going deeper. His shaft twitched again, and her expression changed. Her lids fluttered, her lips parted, her torso curved in a beautiful arch, and he knew she was close.

"Matthew?"

"Yes, sweet girl. I know."

Matthew retreated slowly, almost to the entrance of her sheath in search of that elusive, inner ridged area. He initiated a series of shallow thrusts, the tip of his cock stroking insistently the seat of her pleasure, while showering little kisses on her lips, cheeks, nose. Her eyelids flew open, and her legs tightened around his hips.

"Matthew, oh my God, Matthew."

They could no longer wait. He thrust all the way in, completing her, becoming one, returning to the source and relishing her precious offering, her physical tribute of love. Slow and tender, powerful and possessive, like unrelenting waves at high tide, he thrust and retreated until Raquelita understood what it meant to be his, body and soul, same as he was completely hers.

Matthew pumped, giving no quarter. He couldn't stop or retreat anymore. He could only go forward, seeking her apex, urging her to a place where she would have no choice but explode in his arms. Through their blistering release, his gaze never released hers. He waded through her caramel pools until he found what he desired most—to enter her soul and live within.

***

The patter of waning rain against the windows accompanied the soft sound of their breaths. Lightning dimmed, thunder grudgingly retreated, its hushed rumbles stubbornly refusing to give up their fearful dominion on the hearts of men.

Matthew couldn't speak. The only communication existed within their arms, and their rhythmic heartbeats. Slowly, realization descended. They were truly one and the same. They had entered the fiery forge together and emerged remade: one heart, one soul. Nothing could separate them, neither time nor distance, not even death. Wherever they went, whatever happened, they would be *one* for the rest of their lives and beyond.

Chapter Sixteen

Destin – June 25th 1967

Kicked-up sand, encroaching towels, screaming children, and frantic parents are synonymous with Florida's beaches. When Xavi and Isabel emerged, such was the panorama. The inn's tiny shoreline was insanely populated. Isabel turned to Xavi, a small moue on her lips. His answer was a quieting finger upon them.

"The hordes aren't our concern, Isabel," Xavi said with calm authority, handing her their beach accoutrements. "Wait here," he instructed and headed for the water's edge, where he approached a young man. They exchanged a few words, and, moments later, a single-mast skiff had been procured. Before she had a moment to debate, they were out on the clear azure waters of the Gulf.

Reading her trepidation, Xavi sailed within a placating distance to the shore, although far enough to maintain seclusion and silence. The day was beautiful and the temperature ideal, nothing but pleasure and serenity surrounded her. Isabel's spirit lolled gratefully in this beach haven. She had almost forgotten her tenacious struggle to resist Xavi's persuasive siege. Out here, only they existed. Rejecting this peace could be painful. She'd be a fool to refuse this paradise, this aquatic Eden.

Isabel spied him beneath hooded lids as he steered the tiny vessel. Was there anything he couldn't do? And not look magnificent in the process, so unreasonably attractive? Had it always been so? A year ago, she dared not look at him, convinced he detested her, certain she should keep a safe distance from him. However, that singeing kiss in Texas had upended all her assumptions.

Why would an unencumbered and handsome man want her? He could choose from an abundant pool of young, single, attractive women. She'd be thirty-eight in August, and her body showed the effects of carrying two daughters. Still, if she assessed herself against some of her peers, her shape had kept some of its original form. She had a few lines here, an assortment of smaller bumps there. Her nineteen-year-old figure was long gone, and yet the explicit, feral glances he sent her way burned her soul.

This untiring Xavi had been knocking at her emotional door since the kiss. Did she have the courage to trust him? What about her nightmares and the secret devil lying in wait? Xavi had no idea what he would tap into if he continued on this path. Isabel was weakening under his insistence, and soon her control would disappear, and then hell would smite them both.

"Are you hungry yet, my beauty, thirsty perhaps?"

The murmur interrupted her troubled thoughts with unearthly precision. Xavi peered at her with his steady gaze, assessing and divining.

"I'd forgotten. Since you ask, I could eat."

"If I made you forget, I have accomplished my task for today. It's past noon."

"Already? It is so beautiful, so peaceful. I hate to end it."

"The day isn't over yet, *Tesoro*. We could come back out later, if the elements cooperate." Xavi's gaze was fixed on a spot above and behind her. She turned to where he looked. Clouds gathered and darkened. A summer storm approached.

"Oh."

"Don't worry, beautiful. Sailing isn't the only pleasurable activity available. We will head back to shore for lunch and see what develops."

His detailed plan kept unfolding. Waiting for them was a basket filled with cold roast chicken, mustard dressing, leafy green salad, fruit, and Italian carbonated spring water. The perfect repast at the ideal location, tucked under a beach umbrella, next to a cluster of queen palms, shaded and very private.

"Did you have enough to eat?" he asked, offering a stem of luscious, bright red grapes.

Isabel reached for the proffered fruit, and his fingers enclosed her wrist. He turned it around, exposing the pale underside, and pressed his lips upon it. It wasn't a simple kiss. It was an erotic and lingering caress, the heat from his lips igniting a fiery, consuming rush. Isabel tried to dismiss it but could not. She was entranced.

"You are so beautiful..."

He released her wrist, seemingly unaffected, and resumed his previous activity. He picked up the delicious red gems and popped one at a time within his enticing, smiling lips.

"More?"

"No, thank you. I've had enough."

"Have you? Had enough, that is? I've not even started, *Tesoro*."

Damn the man, everything Xavi did was an adventure in sensuality. Isabel wanted to retort with a smart comeback, but had none. All intelligence and speech were muddled by the clash of conflicting emotions: excitement, anticipation, fear, and, yes, desire.

A sudden gust of wind snapped her out of her confusion, and they both turned toward the shore.

"It's early." Isabel stared at the dense, fast-moving gray wall of clouds. Wind picked up, and the once tranquil azure waves spiked with frothy peaks.

"Perhaps not, or maybe its timing is perfect."

The next gust attacked the umbrellas. Some tumbled. The storm seemed intent to raze everything and everyone in its path. Xavi gathered the lunch leftovers as if no impending maelstrom approached. "It's coming right for us. Let's go inside. It's angry enough."

Xavi picked up the basket and reached for her hand. Isabel held on obediently, following his stride. As they neared the building, the gusts strengthened, lifting painful waves of sand that struck everything on their path. Isabel's feet dug for purchase, but she could barely move as the wicked bursts tangled her sarong around her legs.

Xavi swung the basket on his shoulder, dropped one arm below her knees, slipped the other around her back, and lifted her in one single motion. "Put your arms around my neck. Turn your face to my chest, away from the sand," he yelled above the noise. He ran inside the little inn, carrying her all the way up the stairs. "Open the door for me. Here we are, *Tesoro*, safe in my arms and through the threshold."

He kicked the door closed, just as heavy drops of rain plopped on the patio tiles. An unmistakable scent of wet earth and grass wafted through the open doors. Gently, Xavi deposited Isabel on the floor.

Somehow, the storm had infected his features. He was back to the shuttered scowl. Isabel couldn't believe his earlier joviality had disappeared. She stepped away from him gingerly, hoping he wouldn't notice her retreat. She knew this man and dreaded that expression. It was a reminder of the past—his anger against her, his ugly remarks and punishing observations. His verbal lashings would begin any moment.

Unaware of her turmoil, Xavi stared at the patio and the rain's intent to douse everything in its path. Giant drops splashed, straining to reach their dry room.

"Are you cold? I could close the doors."

"Whatever, you decide."

Xavi snapped around. He frowned; his fists flew to his hips.

"No. Please, *Tesoro*. I don't want to go back to where we started. Don't hide from me."

"I...I'm not hiding." She took a step back. "But you're angry, why? What did I do this time?"

"Do? I don't understand."

"You are angry with me." She retreated again, to no avail. He pursued her, closing the gap with every determined step.

"I'm not angry. Why do you think so?" He gripped her bare arms, stopping her backward motion.

"Because you've always been angry with me, because I've always been the object of your contempt and displeasure."

"You? The object of my displeasure?"

His hands tightened. She cowered in response, and awareness struck like a bolt of lightning. Her instinctive gesture affirmed what he suspected and feared—his Isabel had been abused. A mishandled woman-child trembled and cringed in his hands. He eased his grip a little.

"Please, look at me? *Tesoro*, open your beautiful eyes. That's it. Let me see them. I'm not angry, and certainly not with you. My anger is directed at me. I'm a perfectionist bastard, and I keep myself on a pretty tight rein." He ran his hands gently up and down her arms.

"I live in a deep well of emotions. Few are gentle. All my life, I've kept them under control so as not to frighten folks. This effort to curtail them is what you perceive as anger. But never with you, beautiful. Never. You don't know, do you? I love you, with every desperate, lonely inch of my hard-assed heart and soul. I've loved you from the first day I saw your beautiful face. You were meant for me. You were supposed to be mine. But Emilio spoke first, and when he did, I was shut out."

He'd released the words slowly, as if each one hurt more than the next. She stood because he held her; otherwise, she would collapse. The strength of her legs had long ago deserted her. The raging storm outside was a mere weakling against the power of Xavi's confession. Every word spun around her, one truth followed another, linked in continua. Xavi loved her…always…from the start.

The truth was naked on his anguished features. As bare as she'd been on the day she took her first breath of life. He loved her. In the wake of his admission, the feelings she'd carefully suppressed came roaring to life, demanding to exist, clamoring to requite his.

She searched his face, seeing him as she'd never seen him before, discovering him anew. The firm, generous lips and defined cheekbones, the wide-set piercing eyes, and the rebellious curl, errant upon the elegant forehead creased with lines of concentration or frustration. This was honesty's moment, and she allowed her actions to do what they willed. She freed herself of his now tenuous hold, slipping her arms around his neck. His genuine flicker of surprise, the fugitive spark of uncertainty, amused and surprised her. But this was Xavi. His composure returned instantly.

"Isabel?"

"You've been honest. Now it's my turn. I feel for you, deeply. Please understand, I'm all mixed up. I have questions and need answers. I've lived years believing you hated me."

She dropped a hand to his chest and pressed her forehead upon it. "You've disapproved of me. I've feared you, even despised you at times. And yet, through it all, you've haunted my thoughts, my imagination, and my heart. It is bewildering."

"I understand your confusion." He pressed his lips to her hair. "I will show you the way, *Tesoro*. It's going to be my absolute pleasure, and yours."

The master was back. It must be thus between them. Isabel needed this from him; any deviation would drown them both. She was his beautiful vessel, and he would guide her expertly through the rough, uncharted waters set before her with his practiced eye and sure hand.

He disentangled himself from her arms, walked to the patio doors, and closed them, muting the sound of rain. He turned. His burning gaze began a circuitous route over her body, and even though she was dressed in full beach attire, she felt oddly disrobed.

"Your beauty leaves me speechless."

In two steps he returned to her, slid his fingers through her hair, and with a firm grip, tilted her head back, presenting her face and throat to his hunger and want. He started at the hollow of her throat, lining a trail of kisses, down, down, down, to her covered breast. She jerked under his lips.

"Don't move. Keep your arms where they are." The sharp, husky demand reached deep, stirring a corner of her soul, urging her to obey and surrender, to tilt her face farther back and give in to the lips singeing her skin.

"My God, Isabel, I've dreamed of this for so long."

He sounded almost strangled. But she abandoned the thought when his fingertip initiated a torturous journey from the nape of her neck down to her right breast. He teased the nipple until it pushed anxiously through her bathing suit.

"Yes, *Tesoro,* that's it. Come, reach for me." His mouth fell upon the daring peak. He lapped and suckled the material until it was thoroughly wet. The nipple spiked farther, his teeth clamped down, and Isabel gasped.

"You're mine now," he affirmed when he returned to her lips, mixing his breath with hers. It was a fierce onslaught, but he couldn't hold back. He wanted her to know and understand: she was his everything, all he ever wanted, needed, loved.

Quick as lightning, he tossed her sarong aside. He followed with the top of her bathing suit; a second later, the bottom piece fell when he ripped it at the hip. He kicked off his shorts, seeking the decadent sensation of her bare skin against his.

The man's heat overwhelmed her. She stood encased within his powerful thighs as his heavy ridge throbbed against her belly. His arms steadied her as she quivered, like a tree's last autumn leaf, stubbornly clinging to a branch in the midst of a winter's first gale. He was the wild whirlwind, instilling insane, mind-numbing pleasure to every bend and hollow.

Xavi nudged her mouth wide, wider, and his tongue shoved inside. Like a feral beast, he captured her breath, drawing and inhaling her essence into him, every last bit in exchange for all of his. He tightened the arm around her lower back, pressing her damp torso against his. He almost buckled at the erotic sensation of her breasts sliding on his chest. Drawing on his dominant control, he smiled at the beauty in his arms, slid the other arm under her buttocks, and lifted her to his waist. It pleased him when Isabel hooked her legs around him.

"Put your arms around my neck."

In two steps, he reached the bed, then gingerly sat at the edge, where his thighs would have full control. Isabel was perfectly ensconced upon his lap. Tilting the small of her back, he cradled his tumescent penis within her labia, seeking her delicious heat. He glided back and forth. Soon her splayed sex turned crimson, and drops of their mixed arousals gleamed on his cock. He reached for the discarded sarong on the bed, and tied her wrists behind her. He grasped her waist, flexed his hips back, and in a single thrust, took her. Xavier groaned. Isabel gasped.

With intent concentration, he slipped his hands under her buttocks and lifted her hips, releasing his cock from her liquid heat. He repeated the up-and-down motion between her moist folds, rubbing against her clit. Isabel moaned, and her head dropped back. Smiling, he plunged back in. Keeping an insane rhythm, Xavi's untiring hands lifted and brought her down, pumping hard, one deep stroke followed by another powerful stroke.

He was the master key maker. She was his precious, mistreated lock. He had her now, after many years of desperate waiting. He would repair every hurt, every abuse. With every twist, pull, and push, he would unwind another stubborn knot, untangle a twisted cog, and remove an offending bit. He would clean and polish with sweet oil, and she would be remade, new and sparkling. This he promised.

Isabel couldn't believe where he'd taken her. She had never… Only lately, in the early hours of the night, she'd fantasized how it might be. But her visions had been insignificant compared to the reality. Tension coiled, tighter and tighter, within her core, where he drove insistently. Would she lose her mind? No, she wanted this, exactly this, with no deviation.

She heard him speak her name. "Isabel." Sweetly. "Isabel." Gently. "Isabel." Rhythmically. "Isabel," he prayed.

She responded, enchanted by the ebb and flow of his possession. His name surged free: "Xavier." It was a husky chant, the quality and tone transformed by the call of the past, to the world of their ancestors, the old ways. "Xavier." She spoke in the ancient language suddenly remembered. "Xavier." It rolled off her tongue. "Xavier Manel." Breathless. "Xavier Manel." Frenzied, heated. "Xavier."

"Isabel," he groaned. "I'm yours. Take me. Take it now. Let go."

She climaxed as he ordered. Pride and satisfaction filled his spirit. He crushed her against his body, and, impaling himself deeper still, he declared his triumphant release.

"Yes, damn it. You belong to me. I'll never let you go."

**

When reason returned, Xavi stared at her in awe. Isabel was here, within his reach, real flesh and bone and not a frustrating fantasy. If he extended a finger, he could touch her. This was his prize, his woman.

Fulfillment, once a stranger to him, now delighted him. Circumstances had forced him to love her from afar, but that was the past. Now he had all the time in the world, and he would relish all of her: the classic lines of her face, her generous lower lip, and most of all, her bewitching gaze.

He extended a hand, brushing a mischievous curl out of her face. At his touch, her eyes opened, and liquid caramel peeked out from under half-opened lids, a smile tilting her lips, and his need renewed. He stirred with potent emotion and desire. He would never be sated. He'd spent too many years without her. It would take just as many to even out the debt.

He knelt between her legs, reached under her knees, and, with a swift tug, brought her hips to rest above his thighs. Imperiously, he pressed her silky thighs flat to the mattress. Now she was fully displayed, exactly the way he wanted—her beautiful face, golden skin, erect nipples and glistening sex, available and breathtaking.

"Again?" she gasped.

"Oh yes. Again and more." His lips traveled in exploration, found and captured an excited nipple. He bit; she inhaled sharply. They spoke no more.

Chapter Seventeen

Jerez de la Frontera – June 25th 1967

Doña Nieves Chavez de Muro, august mother of Coralina, Emilio, and Alejandro, stared at her husband, Enrique, the Muro patriarch, with a stony regard. One elegant knee was crossed over the other, and her impeccably manicured hands were folded on her lap, as the perfectly dressed and handsome woman waited for her husband's final opinion. However, don Enrique was not about to fall into the trap. The morning's expedition to the Llorenz household had been cooked up between his daughter and his wife. He shrugged noncommittally and returned to his morning paper. Hiding her frustration as best she could, Nieves stood and smoothed her skirt primly. With a swish of her snow-white, chin-length hair, she marched out the door.

The afternoon was auspiciously sunny, but not enough to cheer up Nieves. By the time she arrived at the address on avenida Alvaro Domecq, dots of perspiration speckled her upper lip, betraying her internal distress. Quizzing the formidable widow was going to be no easy task. The woman was cagey at her best, cuttingly rude at her worst.

She rang the doorbell, and, interminable minutes later, Alicia Llorenz, a diminutive woman with an intelligent regard, thin, paperlike complexion, and a deeply wrinkled smile slowly opened the door. To doña Nieves's relief a felicitous wave of fresh air rushed out from the interior of the home, cooling her flushed features, drying the telltale perspiration, and returning dignity to her appearance.

With a slight bow of the head and a sweeping hand gesture, Alicia invited Nieves into the ancestral residence. Swallowing hard, she stepped in. A few turns later, down hallways and rooms, Alicia halted next to a small café table set with a full coffee service and an assortment of rich pastries. Alicia appeared composed and calm, cool as the antique azulejos decorating the interior patio walls of her home. It vexed the heck out of Nieves.

They settled at their opposing corners, and the verbal warm-ups began, the widow expressing surprise at the visit, while doña Nieves protested disingenuously. Now properly limber, the opponents engaged in a verbal thrust and parry. The widow used a point to her advantage—their offspring were no longer married, and circumstances of the divorce had been unfriendly. Nieves protested a defense—they were family once; thus, they would always remain so.

No one could accuse doña Chavez de Muro of timidity. She daringly braved the spiny topics. Using the lightest touch, she broached the Llorenz marriage, Seve and his ill-timed passing, the Civil War, but when she reached the subject of Iñigo, her fact-finding mission came to an abrupt end. The instant her brother's name surfaced, Alicia stiffened, and a large DO NOT TRESPASS sign appeared. The conversation veered irrevocably away from the direction Nieves sought.

Nieves felt drained, highly overwrought and with an acute need to go home. On the way out, Alicia guided her through the spacious living room. A grouping of nostalgic family photographs decorated a buffet table. Nieves admired them, and Alicia paused, proudly describing the collection. One in particular, of Seve and Alicia, in an exquisite silver frame, grabbed her attention.

"Ah, Seve," Alicia uttered with pride and a tinge of melancholy. "This was our wedding day. He was a most dashing young man, so tall and handsome. Isabel took after him, except for his dazzling green eyes."

"And this one?" Nieves's fingers lightly touched the next frame.

"That's Iñigo after he joined the Navarran Carlist group. He looks grim, does he not?" Alicia laughed, perhaps too heartily. To Nieves's ears, it had a grating edge.

"Anyway, I'm glad you came. It's nice to be remembered. We could visit again soon." And with this declaration, the gracious lady was summarily dismissed.

***

Alicia had to control the urge to slam the door after Nieves's departure. What did she want? Why the sudden interest in Iñigo? She remembered the wagging tongues and the inceptive scandal she'd carefully squashed. Did Nieves think she could judge? The sordid business during and after the Civil War had to remain buried, along with the men involved. Those years of penury had challenged everyone, compelled folks to neglect ethics and morals. Like countless others, Alicia had done what she must to survive, and she was not one iota ashamed.

Those damned Muros, so successful and prosperous, a name synonymous with preeminent Jerez society through countless generations. They had been pivotal to the economy of the town and had managed through the worst of the Civil War and its aftermath without sacrificing anything, or losing men to the warring factions. Not her little Llorenz family. No, they did not share a similar fortune.

Alicia padded slowly through the empty house, returning absently to the spot where the afternoon had been spent. Overcome with the prospect of what could lie ahead, Alicia dropped her weight on the chair, resting her forehead against her fists. Evening was upon her, and as the shadows grew longer, a torrent of ancient memories began a rolling attack upon her mind. Thanks to Nieves Chavez de Muro and her prying. The Muros should all go to the devil!

***

1927 – Puente La Reina, Navarra

Severino Llorenz met pretty Alicia Saenz on a business trip to the province of Navarra. Her father was the official contact for the young pharmacist. One night, filled with compassion, Sr. Saenz invited the homesick young man for a home-cooked meal. Alicia and Seve fell in love. Seve was the handsomest, most interesting man Alicia had ever met. Not only was he intelligent and ambitious, he had a joyful sense of humor and was unabashedly affectionate.

Alicia's parents were thrilled with his suit. They approved of Seve's enterprising personality, particularly for one who was raised an orphan. He was a self-made man who loved Alicia dearly. After a proper proposal for her hand in marriage, they blessed the union.

It was a blissful first year. Love flourished, and Seve's new pharmacy was a success. An expert in his chosen field, Severino offered knowledgeable advice and comfort. The word spread, and a faithful clientele increased. They began plans to branch out when they learned the good news that Alicia was pregnant. Isabel was their joy, a healthy baby girl with intriguing topaz eyes and her father's good looks. She was the culmination of their dreams: a happy family and a thriving business.

Life was perfect, until it took a left turn.

Isabel was five years old when Alicia noticed Seve's cough. It was sporadic at first, and Seve attributed it to a sore throat. When it continued, he blamed a cold. Soon he started to disguise its frequency, hiding from Alicia when bouts of incessant coughing began. Seve was lanky, but he began losing weight at an alarming rate. Alicia became worried, really worried.

A year passed before Seve admitted the terminal diagnosis, bulldozing Alicia's world to the texture of smooth powder. The Fates had upended the hourglass of her happiness, and with a heavy heart, she watched the fine grains slip slowly through. Cruel and jealous, the Moirae wrested her happiness away, for their love was rare. While most couples around them barely suffered each other, Alicia and Seve remained deeply in love.

Resignation found a niche at the Llorenz home; the illness would consume her beloved's body within a year or two. As word spread around the neighborhood, a few erstwhile envious looks turned to distant pity, others to deserved comeuppance; they'd never approved of Seve's marriage to the woman from the north. Not one soul offered help. And folks wondered how she'd become cold and calculating. The infamous *Viuda Llorenz* rose out of the ashes of her blissful marriage bed after it was razed to the ground by the conflagration of disease and human indifference.

As Seve's body languished, her economic distress deepened. Seve's business was highly specialized, and while Alicia's education, typical of the era, was good for polite conversation and entertainment, it couldn't sustain the business. Taking care of Seve and her child took up most of her day. Expenses mounted, and her parents, sadly and apologetically, couldn't travel that far to help, and her brother, Iñigo, who had joined an extremist Carlist group, couldn't be found.

Several bids to buy the business were presented. Spiritually weakened, Alicia capitulated, accepting the highest offer. Fortunately, Seve had inherited the ancestral home without any debt. From the business sale, she saved a little money, and the rest went to satisfy Seve's and Isabel's needs. From then on, Alicia concentrated on what little time she had left with her husband.

In 1936, the military uprising against the Republic exploded throughout the country, while Seve, coughing up blood, labored in his last fight at the hospital. As Spain fell into the despair of civil war, Alicia, while holding the child of their love tight against her chest, watched impotently as half of her heart slipped quietly into the night and away from her forever. No man occupied Seve's space again.

The nation was at war. Information from outside Jerez was grim. Ultraconservative Nationalist forces rose against the elected leftist Republican government. Brother fought brother in the most brutal and destructive of wars, leaving permanent scars of rancor and mistrust within the hearts of its citizens. The population was frightened, confused, and became suspicious of each other, the authorities, and the politicians. The ongoing strife cut off roads, isolated towns, and interrupted communications. Supplies, if any, were found through word of mouth. Alicia's resources dwindled further; she might last six months before she was forced to use her emergency funds.

That was how the next year found her. Rumors of a major offensive were incessant, and Málaga, the neighboring port city, a likely target. Civilians in and around nearby towns panicked when word came that Italian and Moroccan troops, famous for leaving a trail of ruin, fought alongside Nationalist forces. By mid-February the campaign was over, and Málaga, barren and blackened by artillery fire, lay crumpled at the feet of the Nationalist forces.

Her little neighborhood escaped disaster, and the population breathed a selfish sigh of relief. The gossip machine stilled, but what couldn't be silenced were the hungry, growling stomachs. Food was scarce. Everyone was affected, as war never discriminates. Those were the bleak conditions when Alicia opened her front door to answer the loud knock. A gaunt and malnourished apparition in tattered clothing—barely passing for her brother—leaned against the body of a stranger.

Iñigo had lost one leg below the knee and gained a wooden stump for his Carlist's efforts. He was thin beyond reason, his skin stretched tautly over sharp bones. What he lacked in body mass, he made up for in long, matted hair and a scraggly beard.

"Iñigo?"

The wraith nodded. "This is my comrade, Alvaro. We were both injured at Málaga and have been released from duty as we are unable to help further in the effort to regain our country from the leftist dogs. We must come in."

Her mind worked quickly. Was this a blessing or a drain to her diminishing resources? "Come in, Iñigo. You look tired and hungry. I don't have much, but what I have, I'll share, so long as Isabel doesn't go hungry."

"Isabel?" The glacial blue stare sent uncomfortable shivers down her spine.

"Isabel is my daughter, and she comes first. There will be no compromise on this point." Courageously, Alicia volleyed the frigid look back with her own ice. She was no longer a passive girl.

"I see. You and the pharmacist have a brat? Where is the pacifist?"

"Careful, brother, be very careful. Seve lost his fight against consumption, but this is *his* home, and you've come seeking shelter. I won't tolerate disrespect."

Each man shot a knowing look to the other. Iñigo's face contorted in lieu of a smile. "I'm sorry for your loss and mean no offense. Truthfully, we were unsure how you'd receive us. We hope to stay and recover from our wounds here. If you and the child live alone, we could help in return."

"Help, how?"

"With chores, maintenance, and a man's presence. Our side will win the war. That is a fact. Morality and decency will return." He sneered. "You are a widow alone with a child. The presence of two Nationalist men, one of whom is your brother, living under your roof will help your situation. Am I wrong?"

Alicia examined her brother's weakened state, doubting their presence would be helpful. And yet, he might have a point. Was their arrival providential? Carefully, she worded her conditions for a tentative agreement.

"All right, brother. We'll start out slow, for now. After you both recover, we will reevaluate."

"Agreed." The shadow of a smile passed over his countenance, and the eerie chills returned.

Isabel turned eight in August, while the battle of Santander raged on. The civilian population in Madrid endured punishing German aerial bombardments, foreshadowing what would rain upon London scant years later. Despite the warring up north, life at the Llorenz household continued under the terms of the tentative pact. The men recovered slowly, although Iñigo, with the loss of his limb, would never heal completely. Cleaned and dressed in Seve's clothes, the wraiths began to look human again.

Iñigo proved true to his word. The men eased matters through negotiations and bartering. Both Alvaro and Iñigo offered all sorts of services to the neighbors, and life limped along. Alicia discovered Alvaro had a sense of humor and was rather amiable despite his radical Carlist views. She enjoyed his easy company. He was the polar opposite of her brother, which made her question the relationship between the two men. When the autumn of 1937 arrived, she extended the men's tenancy indefinitely.

Alvaro landed a job at a local bar. "People have to drink," he explained, and extra money flowed. Life began to stride.

Iñigo remained surly and silent. Initially, Alicia believed it was acceptance to his fate, but it turned out to be a seething, slow-cooking bitterness eating her brother from the inside. His curt manner became the norm. He chastised everyone except Isabel. Whenever he saw or spoke to the child, his demeanor became almost human. As for Isabel, the girl did not share her uncle's feelings. If he entered a room, she would exit in the opposite direction, wariness stamped on her face.

It irked Alicia. Why would the child not cooperate? Iñigo offered her little gifts—a ribbon, a sweet, hand-carved figurines—yet Isabel remained distant. Iñigo didn't complain; he simply continued to court his niece's affections in patient resignation. Alicia grilled Isabel repeatedly, but the child deflected the issue, fleeing whenever possible.

In town, life returned to a normal course. The old malicious rumors returned to her neighbors. Whenever she picked up Isabel at school, all conversation would cease. Once, at the neighborhood store, she caught the end of a loud whisper: *"A woman living with two men."* To her eternal frustration, everyone loved to hate her. Fed up with the gossip and trying to create a little distance from the other women, she occasionally asked her brother to pick up Isabel from school.

The change prompted a major tantrum in the child. Tired of Isabel's brattiness, she admonished and silenced her peremptorily. The child would abide by her orders, by the gods. And so the days passed in apparent peace, but the girl's silence and moroseness increased. Taking her brother aside, Alicia addressed the change with Iñigo. He seemed to be at a loss as well.

"You know how she is," he said. "She doesn't talk to me."

"You walk home in silence? With Isabel? Impossible."

"Yes, we do."

That very night at bath time, Alicia decided to emulate all her ancestors and take the proverbial bull by the horns. Lately, Isabel had taken to bathing alone, and Alicia barged in unannounced. She was unprepared for the sight. A profusion of dark welts marred Isabel's young back and buttocks. Alarmed, Alicia rushed to her daughter. Isabel yelped in surprise, attempting to cover her frail little body from her mother's examinations.

"What is this?"

Her daughter's belly, undeveloped breasts and nipples displayed innumerable bruises, some purplish and red, others fading to yellow and green. Alicia pushed Isabel's timid hands aside as revulsion and anger roiled in her stomach. The marks trailed toward what should rightfully be the innocent groin and thighs of her daughter, and stopped strategically above the knees.

"I'm so sorry, Mamá," Isabel pleaded amid sobs and tears. Alicia wiped her daughter's face dry and embraced her as her hands searched blindly for a towel to wrap around the thin body.

"Isabelita?" The bleak expression broke Alicia's heart. The crime had eradicated the natural radiance of innocence, childhood dreams, and happiness.

"Please don't be mad, Mamá. It's my fault."

"No, *hijita, no,* this isn't your fault. Mamá isn't angry. You are my sweet treasure." Her efficient moves to dry Isabel belied the wild anger in her soul. She wanted to leave this horrid chamber. She dressed her quickly, and, with the speed a mother will summon in protective mode, she picked up Isabel, kicked the door open, and carried her to the safety of her bedroom.

"From this night forward, Isabelita, you will sleep in my bed until Mamá can manage things. First, you must tell me everything. Mamá needs to know."

Everything Isabelita revealed left Alicia sleepless that night. Possibly, she would remain sleepless for countless others. It all made horrific sense: the silence, the haunted look, and the fight-or-flight reactions. The only saving grace of the night was the absolute certainty Isabel would never be molested again. Not while she lived. From now on, and every minute thereafter, Isabel would live under her constant watch. She wanted to strike out, thinking about the ignominy, the horrid violation under her roof, her home. Iñigo was fortunate she was not a man. Tearing her brother into thin strips would never quell her need for appropriate punishment.

What surprised her was the odd sobriety surfacing out of the chaotic anger. It cooled her emotions and filled her thoughts with calculating reason. It was imperative she examine the situation. Life in Spain was unstable, and much as she hated it, she had to measure her steps and play a delicate game of cat-and-mouse. Iñigo kept his connections with the government through his extreme-right-wing Carlist-Requeté associates. In life, Seve had supported the leftist Second Republic. As his widow, her political position was fragile; she could be arrested on a trumped-up charge and Isabel taken away from her.

Alicia needed an ally, one she could recruit quickly and who'd be unimpeachable. Ironically, Iñigo had brought one home. She smiled as ingenious tactics surfaced. War and need had taught her to keep her own counsel and to think before she spoke. She had learned the art of survival.

Alvaro had shown an interest in her, and she'd kept him at bay playing coy. Alicia congratulated herself; her discretion had averted an irremediable insult upon Alvaro's masculine sensibilities.

Iñigo's violence forced her hand. She had to study Alvaro, learn which way he leaned. Was he friend or foe? If Alvaro could be persuaded, her idea might work. The undertaking required a certain amount of finesse, and Alicia was up to the task.

Wherever Seve was, she prayed he would understand, as Isabelita's welfare was at stake.

Chapter Eighteen

Destin – June 26th 1967

Xavier gazed at Isabel's sleeping form, moved by a wondrous sense of tenderness. Only moments before, she'd cozied up in his arms, all supple and dewy with the heat of lovemaking, as if within this circle she would find utter safety and peace. Xavi could do nothing but hold on tight and enjoy. Every notion of happiness he'd ever conceived of slept in his embrace.

He watched her, the slow, even cadence of her respiration, the intermittent flutter of her lids, the elegant cheekbones, and her lips both generous and determined now relaxed. Xavi shifted her weight a little, cradling her against his chest and shoulder. He smiled; her leg had trapped his hips in a quest to snuggle.

She jerked. Was it a cramp? Should he move her? The next jolt was stronger. He frowned when she began to pant, and her mouth opened slightly, seeking air. She twitched again. Her body stiffened, and now he could barely hold her. Isabel's head shook violently from side to side.

She uttered a strangled "No." Her arms pushed rigidly against him as the nightmare became a frenzied struggle.

"Isabel," Xavi called, noticing the sheen of perspiration on her features. He nudged her, trying to break the connection in her mind. The dream refused to let go.

When the next "No" ejected and a distinct plea for "Mamá" ensued, Xavi had enough. He jumped out of bed and ran to the bathroom in search of a damp towel. When he returned, the terror on her face startled him. Kneeling next to her, he pulled up her shoulders, shook hard, and yelled her name.

Isabel awoke frightened and disoriented, her whisky irises translucent with tears. Slowly, he leaned her against the headboard and placed the towel on her forehead.

"Nightmare's over, you're safe," Xavi said, smoothing her damp hair, stroking her face until he saw a glimmer of understanding. She was back. The episode was over. "Do you wish to talk about it?"

Isabel's thought processes went into overdrive. If she acknowledged the nightmare, he would want an explanation, and she was not ready for a Xavi inquisition. She took the easiest road out.

"Hmmm, what do you mean?" she asked, sounding rather innocent and sincere. "Talk about what?"

Xavi frowned. There was such a thing as not recalling dreams upon waking. He also knew Isabel's penchant for hiding. He wondered if this was not one of those secret moments. "It was strong, Isabel. Don't you remember anything, anything at all?"

She shook her head, deep in the act and forsaking a golden opportunity to gain Xavi's aid. Skepticism still shone in the man's perceptive eyes. She had to give him something. "Well, I think I was restrained and unable to move. It was dark and so confusing." She blinked.

"All right. If you don't remember the dream, maybe it's just as well." He would cede this battle for another in the future. Right then he changed plans. He'd stay one more night in Florida. If she had another dream, he would pursue the matter.

He finished wiping her face, returned her to the shelter of his arms, and she sighed contentedly. Xavi took a deep, calming breath as his body reacted to Isabel's warmth. He kissed her hair, and she wiggled closer to him. He swallowed. Why was he holding back? He stared at her luscious body. What better way to erase nightmares? She must have guessed his thoughts, because she looked up at him with wide, expectant eyes. He reached down and grazed a nipple with his fingertips. Isabel gasped, and his hungry lips devoured hers.

***

They entered the empty kitchen with soft footsteps. With a few remaining minutes of privacy, Raquelita sat on Matthew's lap as his arms encircled her. In silence, she leaned against him while he slowly caressed her back. The moment was fleeting, soon reality arrived with the sound of approaching footfalls. Lita looked intently into Matthew's tranquil green eyes. His smile was resigned. "They're coming. I should leave now."

"No, please. Not yet." Lita buried her face against his chest, gathering his T-shirt tightly within her fists. "Stay, at least for breakfast."

"Of course, my angel. I bow to your pleasure, although soon I must take my leave." He kissed her hair.

Sounds got closer. Raquelita jumped out of his lap but held on to his hand like a drowning swimmer would a lifeline. Her grip was strong but cold. "Are you nervous? So am I." Matthew tightened the hold, instilling warmth and reassurance.

"Good morning, dears." Coralina chirped.

"Good morning," Jonas rumbled and turned to examine the percolator. "No one's made coffee yet."

"Sorry, Uncle. We forgot."

"Ah, youth. There was a time when I didn't need caffeine either. It's a necessity these days. Matthew? Interested?"

"Yes, sir. Thank you, may I help?"

"Oh no, you don't," Coralina said. "Stay right there, young man, next to your sweetheart. Mine and I will do the honors."

And soon the beguiling aroma of coffee permeated the kitchen, and the sweet scent of warmed maple syrup and spicy grilled breakfast meats enticed the hungry senses. Breakfast came and went. Time passed through the indifferent hands of Chronos, denying Lita's prayers for a temporary stay. The ancient being, donning its spectral gray robes, pointed at the door, cruel and unrelenting.

"Another separation, it's our history," she murmured.

"We will change it, I promise," Matthew whispered. He raised her hand to his lips and pressed a warm kiss. She nodded.

He lifted her chin and smiled. *I love you.* He mouthed. Suspect moisture gleamed in his gaze.

I love you, she returned, closing her lids, stamping his image indelibly on her mind. Departure could be delayed no longer. Matthew stood and faced the Reynoldses.

"Thank you." He extended a hand to Jonas. "For the hospitality and the care." He spoke with a slight quiver, staring meaningfully at Raquelita. "She's everything to me."

"Go in peace," Jonas said. "We'll watch over her."

Matthew turned to Coralina, who stood behind her husband's shielding body. She smiled shyly.

"Ma'am." He tapped his forehead. "It's been a pleasure meeting you."

Impulsively, she came around Jonas and hugged Matthew, then planted a kiss on each cheek before releasing him to Raquelita.

"Take care, young man."

Matthew tugged; Raquelita followed. Once outside, he opened the car door and turned to face her. His fingers threaded through her hair, tilting her face and lips up for a last desperate kiss. A kiss to embed in his soul, a kiss to draw upon its healing sweetness later, when the nights of loneliness blinded his sight and the bile of separation embittered his lips. She nestled her body against his, her salty tears flavoring the farewell.

"I must go." He brushed her lips. "Do you give me leave? I've no strength to depart, not unless you release me."

"Go. I know you must. But first I need your promise we'll meet again, before you deploy overseas. Swear it to me, or else I'll keep you here, tied to my angry arms. I won't release you otherwise."

"I promise. I couldn't depart without seeing you, and on that day, I will love you in every way a man can possibly love a woman. Don't you understand? I need you too. Damn it, I miss you already."

"Matthew?"

"I know. We always know, don't we?"

"I'll come to you tonight, in our dreams."

"I'll be waiting. Kiss me again, angel, and then I'll depart to keep my oath of service."

"Yes." Blinking her tears away, she threw her arms around his neck.

Imperturbable, time fled. The tire marks on the empty driveway announced his departure. The grip of a small hand offered solace once more. Marité's voice promised, "If you need me, I'm here."

***

Softly tanned and eyes glowing with private secrets, Xavi and Isabel entered the Reynoldses' living room. Amid happy greetings, they settled in and, with careful circumvention, spoke about their weekend. Isabel's relaxed demeanor was a revelation. A critical evolution had transpired; her normally cutting speech was flowing and dulcet.

Even more surprising was the couple's behavior. Cool and assured, Xavi sat on the armrest of Isabel's chair and leaned indolently against her, two fingers lightly caressing between her shoulder blades. The familiarity of the gesture and Isabel's easy acceptance were startlingly intimate.

Raquelita stared at her mother with skeptical regard, wondering from past wisdom how long this contentment would last. Her uncle remained impassive, but Coralina could barely conceal her curiosity. "I think I'll make munchies for all of us." She fled toward the kitchen.

"I'll give you a hand." Abandoning his perch, Xavi gave Isabel a light peck on the head and followed Coralina. Isabel frowned, bothered by his action. She focused her attention to listen in.

"Did you speak to Nieves?"

"Tomorrow, I promise."

What was happening with Nieves? Why was the question so hushed? An uncomfortable pang hit Isabel's chest, her face flushed, and she dropped her gaze.

"I would like to stay with Lorrie tonight."

Raquelita's question pulled her out of her thoughts. Isabel stared from her to Jonas.

"It's okay with us, Isabel."

She nodded silently. She had other matters to consider.

***

"What was that all about?" Isabel whirled about the house, turning on lights and fiddling with the A/C unit in the window.

Xavi followed her. "What do you mean?"

"The hushed conversation about my ex-mother-in-law."

"Of course, it would pique your curiosity. I need a favor from Nieves."

"What kind of favor?"

"No, *Tesoro*. I don't like that tone, it doesn't suit you."

"What? You are trying to sidetrack me, Xavi!"

"I'm not, my love. Not at all."

He turned her gently around. A finger traced the side of her face; her expression mellowed when it paused on her lower lip. "That's it, much better. I love looking into your eyes, Isabel. They're breathtaking."

Isabel locked her brows and shut her lids, cutting off his source of pleasure. "You're doing it again. Will you tell me, or do I ask Coralina tomorrow?"

"Woman, you are so stubborn, I'm trying to seduce you, and you wish to talk. Fine. Nieves is doing a little research for me regarding two men from our town who died after the Civil War."

He released her and turned to the kitchen. "What do you have to drink?" He began rummaging through the cupboards, and Isabel jumped into action.

"I'm sorry, Xavi. Let me." Abandoning the topic of Nieves, she hurried after him, closing the doors he opened and diverting him from her stash. "What do you wish to drink? I have juice or mineral water."

Xavi stared. "What are you up to, Isabel?"

"Nothing. W-why?"

His voice dropped an octave. "Soon, you'll realize there is little you can keep from me. If I don't pursue the matter, it's because I'm either tired or temporarily letting you off the hook." He stepped close, grasped her wrist, and brought it up to his lips for a lingering kiss.

"I hear every word, notice every nuance when you speak, every hitch in your breath, any change in your pulse. You have this little vessel, right here." He pressed the base of her neck. "It pumps faster when you lie. Did you know that?" His smile was beatific as he lowered his lips to her pulse point and nipped it lightly.

"You are brewing trouble. I know it, so don't attempt to beguile me, woman. It doesn't work. Don't push me. I won't allow it. Don't lie to me. I won't tolerate it. Do you understand?"

He smiled, and yet the steely warning scared her for the first time since she'd met him. A terrible premonition of pain, loss, and abandonment descended upon her. Isabel shivered.

"Whatever you're presently hiding, I will find out in due time. Tonight, I'm watching out for dreams. On a different day, I'll handle other matters, one repair at a time."

Her heart jumped. God, if he only knew how intricately knit those issues were for her, how close he was to the bottom of the chasm. Even Isabel couldn't fathom the full accumulation of toxic debris. Surely he would run if he ever found out.

"Hmmm, I've hit a sensitive topic. There's wildness in your face. Don't worry so much, *Tesoro*. I told you I love you, and I meant it. In spite of all your perceived sins, I don't scare easily. I'm here to stay. Now, where were we? You were offering something to drink."

***

The silvery light of the full moon bathed Lorrie's bedroom with eerie shadows, making the psychedelic posters in the room come to life. Colorful waves and shapes conceived during a drug-induced fantasy undulated, same as in the artist's vision. Raquelita watched the magic in awe.

"Do you wish to talk?"

Raquelita turned toward her cousin's indistinct shape. Lorrie's face and body were hidden in the shadows. Did she wish to talk? Could she? The unrelenting fist squeezing her chest made it difficult.

"I don't know." She opted for the truth. "I want to escape to him in my dreams. I wish to protest, and I wish to cry. I wish to just sit here until Matthew returns. Could I do it, Lorrie? Time is my enemy."

"Then dream, Lita. Dream into his arms." Lorrie's disembodied voice floated across the room. "The magic is powerful tonight. Do you feel it? Release your spirit," her hypnotic intonation continued, weaving Raquelita's aching soul into her trance, coaxing her lids to relax and close.

"You are a princess of the night. Don your magic slippers, step onto the moonbeam spilling through the window, and soar. Yes, that's the way. It will carry you, if you believe. Matthew awaits, dear cousin. Go to him. Fly, princess. Unfurl your gossamer wings and fly."

A benevolent fairy godmother this night, Lorrie continued her soft incantations until Selene's glittering threads, conveyed her cousin into the arms of her lover.

***

The nightmare did not materialize, not even a ripple, and waiting for it had afforded little rest. Instead, in each wakeful moment, he found Isabel's legs and arms wound around him. He turned to the clock on her nightstand and sighed. It was already seven thirty. Tired or not, he had to go. With great care, he extricated himself from her arms, hoping she wouldn't wake. He hated good-byes. Still, he couldn't leave without saying he was coming back as soon as possible, that he loved her and would miss her. He'd leave a note and call her from the first rest stop.

With clumsy fingers, he dressed in silence. His heart tumbled, overcome by the impending separation. In the past, he'd known how to exist without her. Now it would be an ordeal. It was a humbling experience indeed, tight as his soul was wrapped around her. He found paper and pen, and jotted down his farewell, an uncomfortable knot gripping his throat. He left the note where she would see it upon rising. Picking up his keys and bag, he opened the front door and closed it behind him, avoiding any sound that might wake her.

The cold bed awoke her. Isabel twisted and reached for him, but his side was hollow, empty, abandoned. A stab to the chest brought her to full awareness. *Xavi?* The front door's soft click answered.

Isabel jumped out of bed and grabbed her robe on the run. She flew through the empty home and despaired, his absence palpable. Tears blinded her. How could he do this to her? She jerked the front door open. She found him, in the car, the engine roaring to life.

"No, no, no!" She ran out to the driveway, reached his car and pounded her fists against the hood.

"Isabel, what's wrong?"

"How could you? How could you leave me like this?" Her tear-streaked face contorted.

He rushed to her, and now she pummeled his chest.

"You said you loved me."

"I thought it would be easier this way, without a long good-bye. I'm sorry, *Tesoro*, please forgive me. I love you. I do. I'm sorry."

She tucked her arms against her chest, protecting the aching heart within. It broke his heart to see her like this. And yet, she never looked more beautiful. He caressed her hair, swaying her gently in his arms. When the frenzy abated, he tilted her face up. "I honestly thought it would be easier. I left you a note. I'd planned to call you tonight, tomorrow, and every night thereafter. I'm new at this sort of thing, my love."

"Xavier Manel, never leave me like this, please. Not without a good-bye word or a kiss."

"I promise, *Tesoro*. Never again."

The Ancients were amused. They had other ideas...

Chapter Nineteen

Fort Bragg – November 4th 1967

Matthew finished reading his treasured missive just before lights-out. With exquisite care, he folded the sheet of paper and tucked it inside its envelope. The three precious letters, tethers to his sanity, had arrived while he was deep in the North Carolina woods, engaged in heavy ops training. He'd read them with the need of a mendicant; every word was a coin or a meal.

The young man turned on his bunk, stretching his long, tired legs inch by inch, and leaned against the cold, metal headboard without a sound. He tilted his head back and inhaled. In his mind, the dates on the letters flashed like neon signs. Four months of excruciating training and hardship had passed; another two loomed.

In this hellish outfit, humanity and the needs of the soul were forcibly tamped down, buried, and extirpated whenever possible. They nurtured expediency, ingenuity, adaptability, and above all, endurance against all odds. Within the cradle of the Special Forces' unconventional philosophy, a man was torn apart at the seams, molded, and reforged into a perfectly honed warrior, a force of one, able to overcome insurmountable odds. Matthew's instructors even had the indelicacy of introducing him to a stubborn, tenacious streak in his personality, heretofore unknown to him. They had presented it Special Forces style, on a sweaty and very painful platter.

Tonight, however, his aches and pains meant nothing, he was troubled for her, and sleep refused to come. He reached for the thin gold chain and the tiny medal around his neck as he peeked at Brian. No counsel there. Brian slept soundly. Raquelita's letter gnawed at him, and this on the eve of his most demanding training yet. Tomorrow, he would need all his mental capabilities free and clear.

Matthew had a much-desired talent—he was fluent in French and had been picked for intelligence training. In 1967, the availability of Vietnamese speakers in the Special Forces' home front was limited. Such deficiency was compensated with their Luc Luong Dat Biet counterparts, the Vietnamese Special Forces. France had left a legacy in its ex-colony, and the language was still commonly used. Any member of the Special Forces who spoke or understood French was deemed an asset. Matthew could do both very well. Two weeks ago, he'd begun immersion training. Soon he would think, breathe, and *be* French. His assignment to the 5th Special Forces Group stationed at Nha Trang was a certainty.

His mind returned to Lita's letter:

I started working at a cute coffee shop just outside campus. It gives me extra money, and it's fun. I meet lots of different and unusual people, a marked contrast to the life we were forced to live in Texas. I'm surprised Mom hasn't banned me from the job yet. But she has been distracted lately, and when she arrives from work, she locks herself in her bedroom.

What was happening with Isabel? He'd believed Xavi was on top of this matter and the lady had become manageable.

Mom is either drinking or taking some kind of illegal drug to help her sleep. I know she hasn't been to the doctor since we arrived.

The assorted sleeping noises in the darkness of the room crazed him. He wanted to yell at the rows of slumbering shadows. Shake them to awareness. *How can you sleep? Why are we here? Who are we really fighting for? Do you know what's going on at home, what's happening to your loved ones?* Not that any of them could change their circumstances. They might have chosen the color and metal of their cage more to their liking, but it did not change their reality. Gilded or not, the essence remained. They were all trapped.

School is wonderful; I adore my writing and art classes. I have two new friends, coworkers at the coffee shop, Dalia and Linda. New Yorkers, both of them, they're nice and listen to my griping with patience; they don't mind my Texas naïveté. But some of their friends are a little strange, same as their conversations. They talk about balling and taking trips, but never go anywhere...

Shit, shit, shit! *Balling and taking trips?* These girls seemed nice to Lita, and perhaps he was overreacting, but he knew what those words meant, and in this age of drug experimentation, free love, and antiestablishment attitudes, anyone from a big city, especially New York, worried the crap out of him. Why didn't Raquelita seek her aunt's help? Should he call the ranch? Maybe if he spoke to Coralina, alerted her...

Out of the darkness, Brian's sleepy comment reached out to him. "Matthew James, that brain of yers. List'n, turn down the volume, yer thoughts're keepin' me awake."

He turned with a start. "I'm sorry, I thought I was being quiet. You were out cold."

"Yer mouth may be shut, but all yer rustlin' around is making one hell of a rattle. Wanna tell me what's goin' on? Sure has to be that gal of yers. What else'd keep you up? After the last three days, you should be as wiped out as I am."

Matthew was so grateful his friend had awakened and wanted to listen. In a hushed voice, he unloaded his misgivings while Brian listened.

"Are you aware we're getting a leave?" Brian asked.

"We are?"

"Yep, just before Thanksgivin', our last holiday in good ole USA, 'cause I'm sure we'll be gone before Christmas."

At Matthew's silence, he continued, "The head honchos are under scrutiny, you see. Before they send our sorry asses to our intended hellhole in Vietnam, they're bein' real nice like. Don't wanna rile up the population too much against them, now do they?"

"You've a point, my friend. Who knows what the powers have in mind?"

"Well, for one thing our favorite Texas son, Johnson, hasn't escalated this military conflict to a full-blown war. We're all still blissfully livin' in the guns-and-butter era." Brian snickered.

"Indeed, especially after the fiasco and embarrassment of Tong Le Chon back in August. That backstabbing business with the cut perimeter wires, white rag markers, and fake bandaging... One has to wonder who we're really fighting for and against whom?"

"Dang it, pard'ner, I love when the outstandin' Buchanan brain goes into action. Case in point: look at the developin' situation near Dak To camp. In June, a civilian unit abandoned their positions when the North Vietnamese Army attacked. Leavin' everyone behin' holdin' their dicks in one hand and an M16 in the other.

"From what I've studied, it's standard Civilian Irregular Defense Group behavior. Their philosophy is entirely different from ours. In my less than expert opinion, they're simply not reliable. Though for diplomacy's sake we must invite them to play. Don't it beat all? You saw how the 173rd Airborne Brigade had to come in and assist. Braddock just took over, tryin' to hold it together, but without regular line battalions, it don't appear he can."

"I agree. The entire area has been a continuous struggle for us. We've already lost a few of our own. The NVA refuse to give up, and I fear the fighting will intensify. It wouldn't surprise me if an infantry brigade isn't brought in for additional support."

"It's inevitable. Our good ol' Texas boy will have to escalate, and when he does, the nation's gonna blow. Mark my words, it's already startin', with protests here and there. By the time the party gets started, you and I'll be swimmin' deep in hell's shit."

Matthew chuckled at Brian's caustic comment. "We'll remember these moments as the days of 'Sunshine, Lollipops, and Rainbows,' won't we?"

"Yep, think of it, pardner. The government's been involved in this crap, while the population's been watchin' inane movies the likes of *Ski Party*. Yet, here we are, learnin' how to don a fireproof life vest in a hurry. Maybe we should've been mice instead of men. Is anyone awake in the nation, listenin' at all, I wonder?"

One, two, three comments in rapid-fire succession. Matthew stared at his friend's shadow with newfound respect. "Damn it. Get out of my head, the same thoughts have been hounding me all night."

"I do use the gray matter from time to time, son. I ain't jest a purdy face with a hot bod. Now, on to yer li'l gal's situation." Brian turned all business. "We need to plant a seed, bro. So we can both get some rest, preferably tonight."

"A seed?"

"Yep, call the ranch ASAP. Ask Raquelita to spend Thanksgivin' with her father, tell her to speak to the Pope if she has to, 'cause we know her momma's really weird. Bring her sister too. We have our own plans to make. We're goin' home, pardner. It ain't like we have an abundance of time. The leave's round the corner, they're grantin' it, and we're takin' it.

"We can fine-tune details later. Now please relax, Matt James. Git some sleep." Releasing a long sleepy yawn, Brian rolled around.

Matthew smiled at Brian's shadow. He was right, of course. He needed to rest. And Brian had just gifted him with a much-needed sleeping pill. He'd be making a few phone calls tomorrow.

***

"We're going to San Antonio for Thanksgiving." Raquelita's announcement got everyone's attention at Rosie's. It even stopped the conversation between Dalia and Linda.

"I want details. Let me get your apron." Dalia pulled one out from some mysterious spot behind the counter drew it into a ball and threw it at Lita.

Linda waved at Lita to come closer. "Definitely. Spill it, girl."

"Two days ago, I asked Papá if we could go home for Thanksgiving. It was almost a lark, really. I was sure Mom wouldn't approve," she explained while wrapping her waist with the apron's ties. "Today, surprise of all surprises, Mom said we could go. It's a miracle." She whispered with a note of reverence, "I think my godfather helped."

"Is this your mom's boyfriend?" Dalia asked.

"I think he is." Raquelita frowned and walked toward the edge of the countertop, riffling the stack of menus. What else could she call her mother and Xavi's relationship?

"Oh, who cares how it happened," Linda interjected. "It's the visit that's important."

"Yes." Raquelita sighed wistfully.

It didn't escape Dalia. "Wait. There's something else here? Where does Matthew fit in?"

It was an astute question. Shrewd and raised in tough South Bronx neighborhoods, Dalia could never be described as naïve. Raquelita blushed and averted her gaze. Dalia had successfully read the subtext of her happiness. "Not far from San Antonio." Raquelita's concession was barely audible.

"Nice move." Dalia's white teeth sparkled against her warm café-au-lait complexion. "I'm proud of you. If it all works out, you'll get some action."

"Action?" Raquelita frowned.

"Action? Did I miss something?"

"Will you please try to keep up?" Dalia tapped her fingers on the countertop. "I swear, Linda, sometimes I don't know if anything happens inside your brain."

"Oops…" Linda's jerky laughter turned harsh. It grated on Raquelita's ears. "Dalia, I'm sorry. I started early today. I saw Ricky and…"

"Shush, girl. What's the matter with you? Get it together before patrons arrive. Straighten out, stat. Eat something." Dalia pulled Linda by her shoulders from the stool and onto her feet. The censure was harsh but quiet enough to stay within their little group.

Bemused, Raquelita followed the exchange. She'd never seen the usually amiable New Yorker display such irritation. Dalia glared at Linda's contrite expression.

"You're following your brother's path. Is that what you want?" Dalia whispered. Linda stared at the floor, a curtain of silky blue-black hair blocking her expression.

"Yes, you're right, of course. Ricky…"

"Ricky-schmicky. This isn't the time to indulge, get it? Do it later, after work." Throwing her arms up in the air, Dalia turned and walked away from her friend.

Linda looked at Raquelita and offered a small apologetic smile. "That's my hotheaded friend. She has a loud bark but means well. It's her Latin roots that make her so excitable."

"I understand. I have Latin roots as well. Who's this guy Ricky?"

"Just a friend. Well, more like an acquaintance, really. We connected when we arrived in town. He's an odd little fellow, eccentric but nice. He's in college. I understand he's rather popular. I'm surprised you haven't heard of him."

"I can't say I've met or heard of him. What do you mean by a connection, to what?"

"Ah…well, I'm sure you'll meet him. Lita, excuse me, doll. I need to prep my station before this place turns into a zoo. We'll talk later, okay?"

"Sure, I need to prep as well." Raquelita walked away, wondering what the heck had just transpired. What had she missed? At times she didn't understand them at all.

Thirty minutes later, Rosie's started to fill with the usual crowd of college students. Everyone's station filled quickly, but for some quirky reason, Raquelita's tables had only a handful of customers. She dispatched their orders quickly, and as she waited for more to arrive, she chatted with Meg, who waited on the counter patrons.

The bell at the front door jingled, announcing a new arrival, and a rather peculiar character walked in. He was short, tiny, in fact, with mussed, longish black hair, a hooknose, and shifting, sharp beady eyes. His moustache—longer than Frank Zappa's—drooped over effeminate, pursed lips. Faded jeans, strappy earthy sandals, a flowery shirt, and a bandana tied around his neck completed what this personage must have believed was a "cool" outfit.

Raquelita followed his progress while he prowled the establishment in search of an empty spot. As if by design, he chose her station. Instead of rushing to a client in her usual manner, she held back. Something about him wasn't quite right. Not a single piece of clothing seemed to fit his awkward body. This individual—unlike her Matthew, who embodied masculine flair—exhibited no such trait. His look was forced. Meg muttered something close to her.

"What did you say, Meg?"

"Ricky Lopez. Just look at his pompous strut," Meg insisted. "He's a rabid Beatles fan. It's all he ever talks about. I think he's boring. He's tolerated because he does special favors for people and has the connections to get things done. Do yourself a favor and stay away from him."

Without further explanation, Meg turned away to take an order. It was the second time today Raquelita had heard connections attached to this guy. And exactly what did that mean? He piqued her curiosity. She could give the table to someone else. But would a little conversation hurt? This man had such an interesting air about him. A bit sad, absurdly proud, and looking awkward in his skin, he was the polar opposite of the men she knew.

Ignoring Meg's warning, she made up her mind to wait on his table. Not knowing why, she searched around the room, looking for an absent Dalia, as if she needed her approval. Menu in hand, she approached the man everyone had talked about today.

"Welcome. My name is Raquelita, and I'll be your server this afternoon." She handed him a menu.

The man stared at her, eyebrows to his hairline and chin pointed up in a blatant examination. His lips puckered even tighter, highlighting the quirkiness of his features.

"I'm Ricky," he said in a strong Latin accent. "You're beautiful. I'd love it if you served me." One edge of his lips lifted.

Out of nowhere, Linda barged in. "Ricky." She touched his forearm as her full Black Irish figure swayed in concert with her long, glossy tresses.

Ricky turned to look at Linda, not without some surprise. "Linda, sweetness, didn't I take care of you? Need anything else?" he asked solicitously.

"Yes, you…did. I came to say thanks." She twirled the edge of his bandana. "Be a dear, Lita. I'd like to take care of this table. You can have any of mine."

"Why, sure, Linda."

Swift as a raptor swooping onto its prey, Dalia reached for Raquelita and pulled her away by the elbow. "Come, darling. Let Linda take care of her friend."

***

Later that night, Raquelita revisited the strange events of the afternoon—the puzzling conversation between Dalia and Linda, the hidden messages, Ricky's odd comment about serving him, and, at the last, Linda's interference.

A saying her mother used frequently came to mind: *Camisa de once varas*. It meant in over your head, or biting off more than one could chew. She couldn't help an uncomfortable prickle, a sense of forewarning. Lita rubbed her arms, quickly shaking it off. Geez, her imagination was running wild. She should concentrate on happier thoughts. Composing a letter to Matthew was definitely in that category.

Chapter Twenty

San Antonio – November 18th 1967

The winged behemoth hit the ground hard and bounced. Lita's stomach rolled, and her hands tightened on the armrests. The monster slammed the ground again, and the engines screeched. The plane jerked rudely side to side, and the forward motion stopped with a lurch.

"We're home, Mari."

A cheerful, disembodied announcement came over the public address. Passengers could now stand and deplane. The forward door opened, and a pool of light illuminated the cabin. They picked up their small bags and ran toward a beautiful Texas day, to a cloudless cerulean sky and the undimmed salutation of a glorious sun. *Welcome! Welcome!* it proclaimed. With great care, Raquelita held her sister's hand and stepped down the airstairs.

Suddenly, the powerful arms of the man they had known since birth encircled them in a tight embrace. His scent enveloped them in primal comfort. His voice and resonant laughter, intimately familiar, thrilled their hearts. As one, the sisters responded, holding him tight.

"My girls, my girls." Soon, the emotions became too much. Emilio kept one arm wrapped around each daughter, fearful this was a devil's trick or a momentary apparition. They had changed so much, he felt resentful of Isabel. He'd been robbed of unrecoverable moments. *Time, because it is so fleeting. Time, because it is beyond recall.* Julianna touched his shoulder, and he remembered there was no room for anger today.

"You've become a woman, Raquelita." His little girl was no more. Still the same beauty, but with a new light in her face. Womanhood cloaked his daughter with a breathtaking gown of mystery and allure. A tug between pride and dejection warred in him. He didn't have much time left to enjoy his baby. Another man had a claim on her.

He turned his attention to Marité. She'd also grown, though childhood still had a strong hold on her. "My, you've gotten taller," he murmured tenderly, placing two fingers on her cheek. She nodded sweetly, and the need to squeeze her in a tight embrace became unbearable.

"Girls, your father is thrilled to see you." Julianna's opportune comment dissolved the knot of anguish squeezing his heart. Among the thousand things he loved about Julianna, he loved most her intuition and wisdom to act in concert with him. Emilio sighed, loosening his hold, though not quite ready to release them. His heart was reluctant, and it issued a pang of complaint. The past five months of separation hurt deeply, and it clamored for changes. Yes, Emilio was determined changes would be made.

"Okay, enough mush. Let's go get your bags." Hand in hand, the happy foursome entered the terminal.

***

Julianna's jet-black Chrysler New Yorker merged onto US281 heading south. Soon a distant line of buildings spurred an avalanche of not so unpleasant remembrances. This was home, Raquelita's place of childhood, and she'd really missed it. Raquelita had supposed one day she would return, if not to San Antonio, then somewhere close. With Matthew in her life, supposition would become reality. Florida had been forced upon her. It was only a way station for her next phase. She knew this with dead certainty, and the moment approached quickly. Her time in Ocala was coming to a close.

"We'll go visit the ranch tomorrow," her father murmured. He must have sensed her longing. Raquel leaned her head on his shoulder and nodded a silent agreement.

Moments later, the Muro sisters were ushered inside their father and Julianna's brand-new home. It was as comfortable as Raquelita had imagined and more. A sense of lightness permeated their abode. The cool November breeze flowed through wide-open windows, enhancing the sensation of optimism and cheerfulness.

Gone were the dark shadows under her father's eyes. Shadows Raquelita had assumed, during her childhood years, were natural. He looked younger and healthier. Ah, separation most cruel, she mused. It throws changes into sharp relief. It shreds complacency.

The small group followed Julianna as she led them through the hallway. "Since we had ample warning of your arrival, we converted the office into a proper bedroom. Marité, will you be comfortable here?" She pushed the door open and stepped aside, signaling for the sisters to enter.

The sisters gasped. A lovely day bed was the focal point. An array of pink and yellow cushions contrasted with the white frame and matched the pastel colors in the room. Photos of Emilio, Marité, and Raquelita set in whimsical frames hung on the walls. An oversized twine basket filled with huge, stuffed animals took up a corner.

Marité clapped with pleasure. "Pretty."

Julianna moved to another door and opened it. "The bathroom opens to both rooms."

They followed Julianna through the bathroom into the next bedroom. This was a woman's retreat, as indicated by the color and style. Black-and-white photos of orchids in several stages of bloom decorated the pale blue-gray walls in careful arrangements. The crisp and smooth mahogany furnishings added a modern contrast, while the billowy sheers on the windows added luminosity.

"I wish I had pictures of Matthew, though I hope by the end of this week, we'll have lots to play with." Julie winked.

"What a gorgeous room," Raquelita whispered.

"You're both home. We want you to be comfortable."

The crunch in Lita's heart became unbearable, and she rushed into Julianna's surprised arms. An unbidden thought surfaced: this was Matthew's doing. On her own, she might never have asked for, nor been granted, this happy reunion.

***

"Raquelita, honey?"

"Hmmm...?"

"Wake up, darling."

"Papá?" She rubbed her face.

"Yes, sweetie, you're home, and you have a phone call."

Home—what a glorious concept. She blinked, getting her bearings. The lovely room brought it all back. *Texas.* She was at her father's home. "What time is it?"

"It is eight thirty, and your young man is searching anxiously for you."

"Matthew?"

"Yes."

"Oh." Matthew was on the phone? Of course he could call. This was her Papá's home, where life was normal, where she didn't have to hide. "I'm sorry, Papá. Did he wake you?"

Emilio placed two fingers on Lita's lips, silencing her. "Everything is fine, darling, don't apologize. Go, quickly. He's going on maneuvers or something. You and I have all day."

She picked up her robe and shot out of the bedroom like a missile. Standing at the entrance to the living room, Julianna held up the phone's handset and base. Raquelita careened around the corner, barely staying on her feet. Julianna planted both pieces firmly in her open palms, and the women exchanged places. Julianna headed for the kitchen as Raquelita, like a faery princess in a swirl of robes, flew inside the living room.

Bemused and amused, Emilio watched the riot of mahogany curls that was his daughter vanish from sight. It was all so strange, and he had to adapt in a hurry. Six months ago, he was the sole male interest in Raquelita's heart. He was still important, but he now shared that space with a new tenant. Could a father ever get used to this and not be jealous?

Emilio looked to his wife. Sitting next to Marité, she crooked a forefinger in a-come-here-and-sit-next-to-me motion. "What?" The mild irritation in his voice surprised him.

"Come on." Undeterred by his scowl, she insisted, pointing to the empty chair.

"Okay, I'm here."

"Get ready for the invitation."

"*¿Qué diablos,* Julie, what invitation?"

"Gosh. Men can be so obtuse, even the smartest. An invitation for Thanksgiving dinner," she said pointedly, but smiled when he grasped her hand and entwined his fingers with hers.

"How do you know?"

"It's logical. If he doesn't invite all of us, I'll be disappointed. He asked Raquelita to join him in Texas. If he's the sort of man we'd hoped for, an invitation to his father's ranch is a given. I would dare say he truly loves her and has the best intentions. He may be young, but he's not a kid. Consider the military outfit he's chosen. Special Forces isn't for the weakhearted. I'm convinced he's a good guy. You should be pleased. Raquelita has chosen well. He's not into the 'turn on, tune in, drop out' philosophy so many profess nowadays."

Julianna's hand fell on Marité's hair and began to caress her tresses absently. "I'll make another pronouncement, my love. The next few days will be an adjustment for you. Your oldest daughter is in love. You'll have to share her attention with another man and accept it. Gracefully, as best you can. And now I'm going to check my baking supplies for the party. I know you'll consent." Julianna disengaged her hand from his and winked. With a solid push from the table, she stood and marched to the pantry.

Emilio let her go, deep in thought. He wanted to be supportive, not an encumbrance to his daughter. She had enough with Isabel. He suspected there was more to Julianna's observation that his oldest daughter was in love. Tonight, in the privacy of their bedroom they would have a private tête-à-tête.

***

"Bri, it's gonna work out fine." Pleasure and relief rang in Matthew's voice as he gathered his pack and gear. "Her dad has agreed. Our families are going to meet."

"I knew it, pardner," Brian drawled, his slow grin widening. He was not far behind in his own preparations.

"I owe you, man. You're the architect here. I might never've thought about this."

"Oh, I don't know, Matt James. You can be pretty ingenious. Some unusual interference had you a li'l jammed. I hope you'll address yer worries back home. Don't let the lovey stuff distract you."

"I won't. I can't ignore it." He shoved his backpack aside and sat down with a low thud. "This feeling I have, it's a warning I can't shake." He found a pair of socks and began to twist and roll them into a tight ball.

"Heed the warnin'." Brian's expression turned odd, then pointed two fingers meaningfully at his friend. "I know about those feelin's. Dang, all this love talk and yer puppy-dog eyes are makin' me ill. I've been thinkin', if love makes smart people like you this silly and happy, I may have to give it a go."

"You, settle down with one girl? Heck, that would be the day." Roaring with laughter, Matthew threw the ball of socks at his friend and slapped him on the back as he walked past.

The Ancient, hovering above, regarded the unsuspecting men with a keen eye.
Her words were inaudible to human ears.
"So intuitive, Matthew Buchanan. The effort will be useless."
And she vanished.

Chapter Twenty-One

San Antonio – November 19th 1967

The glow of the hallway sconces cast ethereal shadows upon the bed. The faint light enhanced Emilio's tactile feast as Julianna's silky tresses slipped through his fingers. The couple thrived on these moments of intimacy. Some nights they would converse for hours, some not at all, enjoying the warmth, the proximity and feel of the other.

Tonight was different. Emilio had a pressing agenda. "I need your wisdom. Please, help me see the way?"

"Hmmm... so serious," Julianna said.

"Raquelita concerns me deeply. I want to remain optimistic, for her sake, but she and Matthew are facing so many obstacles." Emilio's chest rose and fell in mild agitation. "This afternoon, I took the girls to the ranch, and while they rode, Xavi and I had a long conversation. Coralina and Jonas speak highly of Matthew. Jonas is strict, and he set up parameters for his visit. Matthew kept them, well within expectations. They were impressed with his maturity and the depth of his feelings for Raquelita. He specifically addressed the discord between Lita and Isabel. Matthew thanked them for their care, would you believe?"

"Will you listen, husband? You might not like my opinion."

"Yes," he said after a long pause. "I'll heed your words, and I hope you'll remind me should I blunder. This is all so new to me."

"Emilio, Parenting 101 isn't yet in print." Her laughter sounded like a bubbling stream. "Everyone makes mistakes. The overriding facts are that you love your daughters above all else, and you are willing to try. Raquelita knows this, I promise you."

"I'm listening."

Julie shifted under his arms. "You'll meet your biggest challenge in the next few days."

"Expound, please."

"Matthew arrives on Tuesday. Raquelita will want to spend time with him, alone." Julianna paused, allowing her words to sink in. "Remember, their time together is precious. I'm certain this is Matthew's last holiday on US soil."

"I see. Now I understand Jonas's dilemma."

"What will you do, when confronted with the issue?"

"Damn, do I need to answer right away?"

"No, but you must think about it. May I speak freely?"

The hand on her hair stilled. "*Joder*, I don't want the image of my little girl in the arms of a man, regardless of how wonderful he is."

"I understand." She stroked his chest, easing his tension. "Try to see it as a gift. Give them time alone, allow them to go see a movie, or go on a picnic. Decide after you speak with Matthew. Raquelita isn't frivolous. She's constant and serious, and she loves this young man. We've not met Matthew, though his actions speak for him. He's going through a lot of trouble and planning to enjoy a few days with her. Now, close your eyes," Julianna whispered, pressing lightly on his lids.

"Imagine, look into the future, when Matthew's in Vietnam. Try to see Raquelita's long days and nights, missing him, and worrying about him. Each time a *World News* segment airs, her little heart will shrink with concern. With each bold headline of horrid battles and death tolls, think of her and what she'll go through. If you doubt my words, wait until six o'clock tomorrow evening and remember, Raquelita is listening." Julianna abandoned his arms and leaned on her elbow. He couldn't see her, but he could feel the heat of her gaze.

"In those moments of anguish and uncertainty, she will think of these days you gave her. These happy hours spent with Matthew, carefree and lighthearted, celebrating love and life, under the benevolent yet watchful eye of her father." Julianna's tone turned urgent. "I wish Raquelita lived with us. I have a bad feeling she's going to need support, and Isabel isn't fit."

Emilio reached out and returned her to his chest. His hand resumed caressing her hair. He felt relieved, despite the hard truths spelled out. War and its harsh realities challenged everything: norms, morality, habits, beliefs, and people. Nothing and no one remained unscathed, his daughter's happiness least of all.

"May third," he said. "In six months, she'll be eighteen. I'll bring her home to us. I saw her in the future, and it broke my heart. You're very good at this. Before I release control, I'll wait until I converse with the young man."

"Wise choice."

"It's all moving so fast. I need to spend time with Raquelita and meet the woman she's today, instead of holding on to the girl who left six months ago. I have a few days to adjust before Matthew arrives. I only see the baby." He stiffened again. "She'll always be my baby. But I won't do her any favors if I don't change my views. She's in the world of adults now. Her upcoming dilemmas will be challenging."

"I agree, love. Don't waste a moment."

"I won't, count on it. There's been too much of that already."

***

Raquelita stood before the mirror and gave her reflection one last inspection. She was fairly pleased with her appearance. She'd opted for a tweed miniskirt—Julianna's gift—rather than jeans, enhancing her slender legs and femininity. The light beige turtleneck did wonders for her topaz eyes, and the makeup looked good. She'd applied just enough to accentuate her features. Matthew, she hoped, would approve. *Oh Matthew.* Her chest rose and fell with a sigh. After months of separation, he was on his way over for dinner. Any minute, he would knock at her father's door.

She stepped right up to the mirror, peered closely into her eyes, and frowned. Would she find answers to her confusion in the golden depths? Earlier today she'd almost run out the door, abandoning Matthew, family, and loved ones forever. Was it so much to wish for a normal life and normal relationships? A life in which boyfriends were received openly, or girlfriends didn't spend sleepless nights fearing the god of war? A life in which parents respected one another and mothers loved and supported their daughters unconditionally?

In the end, Julianna added the right note of perspective. Her words still rang in her ears: *"Mortals may never glean the celestial purpose or the karmic lessons behind the cards we are dealt. Either way, play them we must, it's the only hand we get. Understand this—had you lived a normal life, Matthew might not be here. Forget your doubts. Would you give him up for the sake of an illusion? Because, sweetie, normalcy is another word for illusion. You'll figure it out eventually. I lost my first husband living a normal life."*

***

Julianna was right. The doorbell rang, and her heart jumped. It almost floated out of her chest when the door opened and his tall form stepped through. *Matthew.* She exhaled and the world faded.

Matthew walked to Raquelita, taking all of her in, silently restating his claim and rightful place. He stopped inches from her and raised both hands, cupping her face reverently. She was his holy, precious chalice. At long last, his lips descended on hers, tenderly partaking of the love exchange. Love, the breath and water of life, mingled in their glorious kiss. They were one.

"Would you give him up for the sake of an illusion?" Never. She might as well stop living.

Matthew pulled slowly away. He searched her features, exploring every line, every minute detail. His head tilted, his finger traced her cheek, forehead, and lips. Finally, he slipped his arms around her in a tight embrace.

"Oh, angel, I've missed you so much."

Nestled in his arms, Raquel pressed her cheek against his chest, listening to the comforting, steady beats of his heart, smiling at the familiar rhythm. She reached around his waist tightening the embrace. "Matthew. My Matthew," she avowed. All earlier doubts unraveled and evanesced in the air.

"Aren't they pretty together?" Marité said, breaking the spell. "I want a boyfriend like Matthew when I grow up."

Matthew loosened his hold on Raquelita. Tucking her to his side, he extended an arm for Marité. "Come here and give me a hug," he said, kneeling to her height, and Marité rushed into his arms. "My little flower. Your boyfriend will be much better than me, I promise."

Emilio appraised the sweet relationship between Matthew and his youngest daughter. It was so genuine, it shattered his resistance. He liked Matthew on the spot, despite every defense he'd built. For he had prepared to resist—Lord knew he'd dug moats and ditches, erected fences and walls—all to reject Matthew at the slightest sign of misconduct. The genuine emotions in this reunion awed him. This was no youthful whim or fancy, it was love, authentic and real. Raquelita was happy, and to a father, it was everything.

Emilio Muro had been thoroughly disarmed. And not a shot had been fired.

Raquelita pressed a hand on Matthew's shoulder. He stood in answer to her urging. "Papá, Julie, meet my Matthew. Matthew, this is my father, Emilio and Julianna, his wife, my stepmom and my friend."

Matthew's remarkable smile beamed. He approached Julianna and, with typical Southern charm, raised her hand for a whispered kiss on her knuckles. "Ma'am, it's a pleasure." He turned to Emilio. "Sir, it is an honor to meet you." Matthew extended his hand to the progenitor of his love on earth.

And as the afternoon passed, Emilio's opinions evolved. Throughout dinner and after-dinner conversations, Matthew was polite and respectful. He spied an occasional touch, a look, a light kiss to Raquelita's palm, but other than the initial tenderness at the front door, Matthew kept himself within the strictest guidelines of polite behavior.

When Matthew asked permission to take Raquelita to meet his parents, the request sounded proper and logical. Not only did Emilio consent, he suggested they should spend the day at Round Rock. Later, he would convince himself it had been an acceptable risk to hand Matthew a long rope. What better way to learn his true nature? Julianna sent him an approving glance. He believed he acted appropriately, he mused, as he saw them walk out the door.

***

Out in the portico, the crisp evening breeze enfolded them. Lita's fragrance mingled with the night air, and the need to possess her exploded in his soul. Impulsively, Matthew reached for her yielding body, enfolding her in his arms, in her rightful place. "My dream has come true. You replenish my soul, sweet girl." He shifted, tightening his hold. "You restore my humanity."

"I restore nothing. You have boundless humanity. I understand your challenges from your letters, and I've researched the military outfit you joined. Your undertaking has demands most men could never meet. Despite what you may believe, you're still my Matthew, kind, loving, and brave."

"Angel, you're much too generous."

"It's the truth. You complete me. You give me strength. When I look at the road ahead, sometimes I weaken. Then your letters arrive, and I grow strong again." She snuggled deeper. "I've read them dozens of times. They're so beautiful and full of love. If we're ever blessed with a daughter, I may show her some. It'll teach her the nature of real love."

"Learn from my letters? I'm not sure I'll want our daughter reading my intimacies to her mother."

"Not all of them. But you write beautiful letters. At the proper age, I'd be proud to share a few."

"You're determined to put me on the spot, aren't you?"

"No, that's not my intention."

"You know what the truth is?" he whispered. His lips dropped to her cheek, and his arms tightened. Succumbing to desire, his body stirred and the evidence of his need pressed hard against her. Raquelita looked up at him with parted lips. A faint frown appeared on her lovely features as her own passion soared. His lips hovered above hers, barely touching them. "I need your lips." His delicious breath teased as he descended for a slow, scorching kiss.

Desire became unbearable, cracking the weakened dam. Days, weeks, months of denial and bitter separation piled upon them, demanding reparation, urging satisfaction. She molded her body against his in full abandon, deepening the kiss. Her tongue joined his, begging, asking, wanting. This sweet idyll wasn't enough. They needed more. They needed their bodies knit tightly together in a loving tapestry of intimate caresses.

"Matthew. My Matthew."

"We'll meet tomorrow." As Matthew pulled back, his lips nuzzled her cheek.

"Yes, I must have you then, please?"

"My greedy angel, we're still at your father's door. If I don't stop, he'll never let me near you again."

"Letting you go feels like my arm is being ripped out."

He cupped her cheek, running a thumb over the crease of her lips. Difficult or not, he needed to soothe her. Leaving her in this state of excitement would be cruel. He had a long drive; she only had a few minutes to compose herself.

"I understand." He took a half step back. "Tomorrow. I'll keep all my promises." He released her with a peck on the lips, giving her a little push toward the door. "It's cold out. Go back inside," he urged with mock impatience. She gave a little salute, entered the house, and closed the door without looking back.

Chapter Twenty-Two

Round Rock – November 22nd 1967

"Matthew James Buchanan, bless my stars. So the rumor is true. Goodness, handsome, you sure are a sight for sore eyes."

Kathy? Matthew froze, curbing the impulse to bolt like one of his father's wild broncos out in the corral, or simply march inside the house without answering. He shut the door to the shed slowly, delaying his actions to gain composure. He tugged, ensuring the lock held, and turned to face his ex-girlfriend.

Her appearance stunned him as he recalled her fastidious preoccupation with fashion and styles. Her long blonde tresses were angle-cut above her earlobes. A thick lock dangled over her eyes. Her feminine softness had been sacrificed in favor of the starved angularity of some European models. A silvery plume of smoke wafted from a cigarette held by an indolent hand resting on her tilted hip. Oh man, when had she picked up the habit?

"Kathy Miles, this is a surprise." He meant it. Shock was closer to the truth. "It's been a while."

She approached him slowly, swaying her gaunt frame. "Yes, maybe two years, or one and a half? Who remembers, and really, who cares?" She raised her shoulders dismissively, halting scant inches from him. A wave of stale cigarette odor entwined with her sickly sweet perfume. He almost gagged.

Matthew was trained to observe details and minutiae, and Kathy did not escape his attention. Despite a carefully applied layer of makeup, the harsh lines and dark shadows on her face couldn't be camouflaged. A twinge of pity hit him; life was not treating her well. And wasn't it amazing? Life had pitched him a fastball as well. Looking at Kathy, he realized he'd never really loved her. Rather, it had been youthful infatuation and an acute attack of hormones. Still, just because their relationship had ended on a bad note and his ego had been bruised, it didn't mean he wished her any ill fortune.

"Your hair. The army, of course, but it suits you. Who would've guessed such a pedestrian style might be appealing. You look good." Her gaze traveled up and down his body. "Very nice, if I may say so. You're slimmer, more sinewy, and quite sexy."

He didn't care for the observations, wishing to squirm away when vapors of morning-after alcohol assailed his nose. She must have been partying hard last night. The impulse to climb in his car and drive to Raquelita almost overtook him. The urgent need to dwell and be cleansed in her pure essence called to him. *God, please don't ever let anything destroy that in Raquelita.*

He stepped back as if Kathy were a source of contagious infelicity. With a few inches of separation, the discomfort began to dissipate, and he relaxed. "Thank you." He accepted the compliment carefully. "The last six months have been demanding with lots of physical activity. It's the army," he finished lamely. He had absolutely nothing to say.

"Whoo, big boy, aren't you being modest? You excelled at sports, I remember. I hear you'll be around this weekend."

"I'm on leave for the Thanksgiving holiday. Training is almost o—"

"If you're free," Kathy interrupted, "we could get together, for old time's sake?"

"Uh…thanks. I can't, my time is limited and accounted for. In fact, I'm heading for San Antonio within the hour."

"What ever for?"

"To pick up my girlfriend. We're having dinner with my parents." He almost winced. Hurting Kathy was not his intent, but neither was hiding Raquelita.

"Girlfriend? Pity. Oh well, tell you what, if things don't pan out, give me a call when you return, if I'm still around."

Matthew relaxed. However, her comment achieved the desired effect. He bit. "Are you leaving?"

"California's calling my name, and I must go before I lose my girlish charms. And Matt…good luck over there. I mean it sincerely."

"Thank you. I know you do. California is you. You've always wanted more than this old town could offer."

"You know it, big boy. Too small for the likes of me." She laughed. "See ya around." With a slow saunter, she returned to her car, climbed aboard and drove out of the ranch. Matthew watched until the car disappeared.

***

When Matthew picked up Lita in San Antonio, he was all smiles and affectionate kisses. But as he drove, he became increasingly silent, words turned to monosyllables, and the smile tightened into a frown. By the time he opened the door to the inn's room, the scowl wouldn't leave.

Raquel examined the dubious décor. It was simple and clean, perhaps a bit tired but certainly not seamy. She turned to him. He stood at the door, looking stiff and pale.

"Angel, I…I want so much more for you."

His usually bright eyes were dark and cloudy. Shame, she realized with a stab to her heart. Matthew was ashamed. She stepped right under his chin and her fingers brushed his cheek. "Don't do this. Everything is perfect." She reached past him and closed the door.

"No, it's not. You don't deserve this small, bare room." He spun on his feet, pointing in agitation to the lackluster accommodations. "But"—he pivoted, his gaze smoldering as he held her shoulders firmly—"I wanted to be with you so badly. I still brought you here, because I can't afford a better place."

His expression turned determined. He grasped her forearm and tugged lightly. "Come on, I can't do this. We're leaving." He turned to the door handle, but she dug her feet in, resisting.

"All right, darling," Raquelita murmured, "but before we go, may I show you?" She pulled him to the center of the room.

"Those"—she pointed to the plastic wall fixtures—"are gorgeous crystal sconces, and look"—she waved at a pair of worn armchairs next to an ancient dresser—"they're brand-new. The cushions match the pretty bedspread. The rugs are silky and spotless." She turned back to him. Holding his large hands within hers, she pressed them together against her chest.

His mellowing expression and the deepening dimple encouraged her. "Do you see it? We're in a palace bedroom, beautifully decorated, filled with magic and love, because *you* are here. I don't care where we are." She shook his tightly clasped hands for emphasis. "I only see you. I only want you. And if you don't hold me and love me as you promised, I'm just going to die."

The vision took shape. He was in her world, surrounded with beauty, riches, and color. Submitting to the fantasy, he lifted her body within the cradle of his arms and brought his face to hers. "Yes, my angel, please forgive me. I've delayed your pleasure, and you shall wait no more."

He pulled the bedspread back, gently lowering her to the sheets. He sat on the edge, admiring her beauty. "I want your eyes locked on mine, nowhere else." The order was both gentle and strong, and Raquelita's breath hitched. Her hands fluttered toward him, and he grasped them midflight and pressed them to his chest. With the contact, her long restrained passion burst in a thousand sparks. *Now. Union. Fulfillment.* She held his shirt, and his fingers moved to her buttons. As one, they removed hindering garments in a frantic search for the bare lover, the mate, the sustenance and balm to their souls. *Hunger. Need.* Hours upon lonely hours of denial clamored for satisfaction.

Matthew stood abruptly. "Forgive my urgency," he pleaded. Shedding his remaining clothes, he revealed his glorious body for her. He took her breath away.

And she took his breath away. She had quickly followed suit, revealing her glorious body for him. Matthew returned to the bed, and like a predator, he advanced until his large frame hovered above hers. "Put your arms around my neck, angel." Slowly, he descended.

"Aaah…" Hot naked skin upon delicious, hot naked skin elicited the joint exclamation. The relief was supreme and scalding at once. His lips possessed her; his tongue tangled with hers in preparation for his urgent invasion. Later…later he would play, tease, and taste at his leisure.

All of it later…

Now he kissed her, everywhere, murmuring sweet endearments, "Love you…missed you…want you." He reached down to her sex, where he played, aroused, and tested.

"Baby, you're ready. I need to be in you. I can't wait."

Holding on to his powerful neck, she urged, "Take me, please." Raquelita declared her desire to Matthew's probing eyes, the visual connection riveting them both. He donned a condom, pushed her legs apart, and breached her moist threshold. Raquelita, a prisoner of his gaze, thought she would lose her mind.

"Matthew."

He drove his erection deep.

Raquelita gasped, and Matthew paused. He smiled, allowing her to ease and adjust. Her legs clamped around his buttocks, and Matthew's arms locked her in.

"At last, look at us. Look how I take you." She followed his direction, staring at the point where they joined. The breath escaped her as his cock, slick, and bright crimson, stretched and possessed her, instilling ineffable pleasure.

He slid his palms underneath, and, grasping her buttocks, he lifted her hips, pressing her firmly against him. He angled and twisted his hips, his erection seeking and searching for her sweet spot, for her pleasure, her climax and his. Her eyes widened, her pupils dilated. There…there it was.

"Ah, sweetheart, I want it." Holding her like a man possessed, Matthew bent his knees and climbed wildly after her orgasm. He pushed and drove until she exploded. His torso arched as he roared his release to the skies.

***

"We've spent the better part of the day inside your palace chamber." With her cheek pressed against his chest, his voice was a satisfying, deep rumble. "We should leave soon. My parents can't wait to meet you. Unless, you're not satisfied."

"Oh," she mumbled against his chest, "I am. We should go." But she burrowed farther in his arms. "So lazy."

"All right, if you don't wish to move, we'll talk."

"It's amazing. I've dreamed of talking to you for months, and now the need to have you overrides all else."

"When this is over, we'll have time for love and intellectual discussions…maybe. In the meantime, how are things with Momma?" If she bolted like a filly with her first saddle, she'd throw him off. Well, he started it, and now he braced for her reaction.

She stared at him. "Does it matter?"

Oh, it mattered all right, because she'd become defensive. "I'd like to know, sweetheart."

"What could you possibly do about her?"

"Hmm…" Matthew tried to stay loose. If he antagonized her further, he would get nowhere. "I could desert and take you away…"

Raquelita opened her mouth. He placed a finger on her lips. "Angel, what affects you affects me. While I'm away, I may not be able to help directly, but I can ask folks who love you and have committed to help."

"I'm sorry. I overreacted."

"Dang, I thought we were going to have our first fight." He repositioned her in his arms, purposely entwining a long leg around hers, securing her in place. He sensed something else. Trouble lurked in the background.

She scoffed. "Not on account of my mother. I wouldn't allow her to ruin the precious time I have with you. She's done enough damage already."

"What is it, baby? You can tell me anything."

"I'm a terrible person. How can you love me?"

"How can I not? You are my soul, and there's nothing terrible about you. Talk to me."

"I don't know if I love her. I don't wish her any ill, but when things don't turn out well for her, it feels gratifying, like justice is being served. I've told no one, only you."

Oh hell, Matthew knew about the years her mother had oppressed her, the sudden uprooting and separation from a parent Lita adored. All summed up to throw her in chaos. "Breathe, honey, please?" He touched her face, and she nodded. Still, an ancient sadness twisted her lovely features.

"There are so many valid reasons why you feel this way. We discussed them on our first night together. The divorce and then the move, remember? Either situation independently would be difficult. Together, they're intolerable.

"With so much disruption, a little irritation is natural. Besides, she's exerted the tightest control and demanded perfect behavior. If she's drinking or taking drugs, the contradiction should shatter your respect. When you need a mother's stability the most, it's absent. You do love her, but you can't trust her. Am I making sense?"

He tightened his hold, hoping to instill comfort in her. "I wish I could take this away. While I'm overseas, remember you're not alone. I'll always be with you. Your aunt and uncle will help and support you. Your father is but a phone call away."

He couldn't evade it any longer. They had arrived at the crossroads, and he had to ask the question. He took a lungful of air. When he exhaled, it whistled softly through his lips. He went for it. "Tell me, Raquelita. Are you close with your new friends, the ladies from New York, Dalia and Linda?"

"You remember them?"

"I remember everything you write."

"I like them well enough, though we're very different. Out of the two, Dalia is the serious one, levelheaded, more focused, perhaps. Linda's a bit ditzy and absentminded." She shook her head. "They use odd words, I don't quite understand how they communicate."

And he hoped she never would. From the first letter she wrote about them, he had the sickening sensation of his first jump out of an aircraft, waiting for his turn, just before the big drop, blind to what lay ahead. He didn't know the friends, he shouldn't make assumptions, but he couldn't help himself. The contrast between them troubled him—big-city women, experienced, mingling with a naïve small-town girl. This friendship was ill timed. The strife between mother and daughter could make Raquelita vulnerable. Kathy's ruined image reappeared, and he shuddered.

However, her thoughtful explanation was encouraging. She wasn't totally taken by the new friends and had noticed key differences. It gave him a measure of peace, but still he pressed his point. "You'll talk to your aunt as soon as you return to Ocala. Promise?"

"I will."

"While I'm away, please take of yourself, for me, for us. I promise to do the same."

She nodded and pressed her cheek against his chest. He felt tears, but didn't hinder the release.

***

Isabel slid out of bed, and the usual nausea after a night of heavy drinking pounced on her. Today, however, a new emotion made its presence known: she missed her daughters.

"Isn't this a kicker?" She spoke aloud. "They're with their father and I miss them. Well, let them enjoy him, he's the only man in life who won't break their hearts."

Pushing all other thoughts aside, she focused on her projects. First order of business was returning sanity to Marité's room. She was the messiest. Once finished with that particular little chaos, she would proceed to Raquelita's room. There, she would likely spend little time; Lita was neat to a fault.

Soon, *Marité's* collection of *cachivaches* was organized and the clothes for Goodwill separated. She was folding the bundle when the doorbell rang.

Likely Coralina again. The woman pestered without pity. *"Spending the holidays alone is not healthy."* She could go jabber somewhere else. Isabel wanted her privacy. With her daughters away, her numbing project was in full throttle. She'd erred with Xavi, opening up and becoming vulnerable, and for what? Sure, he called. She also hadn't seen him in five months. Didn't matter, she'd regained control.

The doorbell insisted. The Reynoldses would drive her loony today. Isabel rehearsed a bored expression in the hall mirror when she passed by. Satisfied, she reached for the knob. "What could you possibly want now?" She swung the door open. The foyer light blinded her.

"I want you."

Xavi. Could a man be loved and resented in one breath? Isabel did. She'd likely hate him when he returned to Texas. Yet here she stood, loving the possessive fingers at her neck and his ferocious kiss. He offered no quarter and demanded unconditional capitulation, terms her body and heart accepted. He'd come, he wanted, and she would cede. Simple.

Chapter Twenty-Three

Round Rock – November 23rd 1967

On Thanksgiving Day, Matthew's parents received the Muro family with the same genuine affection offered to age-old friends. Emilio was so impressed, he stared quizzically at his daughter. She wasn't surprised and returned his look with a smug smile. Last night Raquelita had met the Buchanans, and the loving couple had received her as a daughter on sight.

Handsome and of easy manner, Jonathan Buchanan was Matthew twenty years hence. He greeted Raquelita and her family with sincere warmth, and Ernestine—the endower of Matthew's beautiful green eyes and dimpled smile—welcomed her again with a feast of motherly kisses and hugs.

As soon as all introductions and pleasantries were accomplished, Matthew pulled Emilio aside, asking for a private audience. Emilio shrugged at Juliana and, looking bewildered, followed the young man out of the receiving parlor. Jonathan and Ernestine must have expected this development. Once the men departed, the Buchanans smiled and whisked the Muro ladies to the bustling festivities outdoors.

Word had gone out: Matthew was home. Relatives and friends from all over had come to celebrate. People, food, and drink abounded, as no expense had been spared. The patio was an explosion of color. Tents with matching tables crowded the space, arrangements of Mexican paper flowers—an orgy of blues, reds, teals, and yellows—served as centerpieces; votives and *chimeneas* added luminosity and warmth, while a mix of country and rock music piped out of unseen speakers. At the far end was a well-tended, though very busy, bar, and on either side of the patio, two huge barbecue pits churned out heavenly aromas.

"Follow me, ladies. Would you like somethin' to drink?" Jonathan said amiably, ushering the women through the crowd. "Look, there's Brian MacKay and his parents let's join them. Matthew and Emilio won't be long." He smiled at Raquelita.

When Lita saw her papá again, he had a wistful expression. Matthew, looking pleased, followed close behind. "Did you know what Matthew wanted to discuss?" Emilio threw his arms around her. "My little girl is all grown up, all grown up."

Matthew had surprised and delighted Emilio's conventional Spanish soul when he'd requested Raquelita's hand in marriage upon his return. He hadn't expected old-fashioned protocols, not with the changing trends in behavior. The end of 1967 approached. It had been a year of turmoil and conflict. A stunned nation had watched the riots of the long hot summer and, with raised eyebrows, Haight-Ashbury's Summer of Love. Everywhere, traditions collapsed.

Tonight, Matthew reigned over the celebration, with his queen Raquelita. He couldn't abide her distance. In and out of the long procession of introductions, greetings, and well-wishes, Matthew kept her close, tightly held under his arm. By the end of the night, all present knew Raquel María Muro owned his heart.

The party raged on throughout the night in a whirlwind of laughter and song. Toasts were raised among speeches of pride, remembrance, and hope. No one whispered or hinted about the war. Why give incertitude authority over the present when it already had a firm hold on the future?

***

The plethora of green vegetation at Austin's Zilker Park sparkled in the morning sunlight. It was a beautiful Saturday, clear and cool. Hardly a soul was around, ideal for lovers seeking privacy, or couples who needed to forget the passing of each second toward the dreaded tomorrow, when their time together would end. Matthew pointed toward a small copse of trees, and Lita nodded. Hand in hand, they reached the secluded spot. In minutes, they had spread the picnic accoutrements generously supplied by Julianna and Ernestine.

Using the tree trunk for support, Matthew pulled Raquelita until she was settled between his raised thighs and torso. He played with her tresses, twirling them between his fingers. Raquelita closed her lids, enjoying the moment.

"No," he protested, "look at me. They're so beautiful."

In the jungle, the memory of her face would be his compass to sanity in the midst of chaos. So he trailed every inch and every beautiful line to remember and call upon later, on demand, just in case.

"God, I love you so much, I can hardly speak it." His fingers continued their journey down her graceful neck, enjoying the supple skin, pressing lightly over her tiny pulse. Did he count the beats? He splayed his hand, and his long, possessive fingers spanned the breadth of her throat.

She stammered, "I...ah."

"Don't try, angel. I understand."

He shifted her onto the blanket, aligning his body next to hers. His face hovered above. After the slowest, most maddening descent, his lips held hers in a languorous, wet kiss. When he pulled back, his bright emerald eyes contained a wealth of unspoken words.

"I need to feel you. May I touch you? Look there's no one around. I wouldn't do anything to make you uncomfortable. It's such a beautiful day, and I'd like to stay in the park a little longer"—Matthew's lips feathered above hers—"lounging under this warm sun, with my gorgeous angel, building memories to last us a lifetime, to tell our grandchildren. We'll seek your palace bedroom soon, if you'd like."

"Promise?"

"Yes, ma'am."

With trembling fingers, he opened the top button of her blouse, and her scent dizzied him. His hand fell to the side as he tried to regain control. "I don't know, angel. This may be a futile attempt. We may have to leave if I can't control myself."

Breathless herself, she nodded. "Anything you wish, Matthew."

"Thank you for your trust, sweet girl." He kissed her lightly, returning his attention to the buttons. The underside of his fingers brushed the swell of her breasts, becoming a lingering, intimate caress. "I can't stop kissing you," he protested between playful nips. "I have to see you. I need your beauty in my soul."

He was overcome and humbled by her mirroring desire. Her breaths quickened, and her pink nipples spiked through her lacy bra, asking for attention. Perversely, he delayed their mutual satisfaction. He grasped her palm and placed it on his cheek, infusing her warmth on his face.

Raquelita quivered. He dropped his hand, brushing one excited peak, then the other. They rose farther in response to his touch. It was her body's silent proclamation of love and desire. She gasped, and he smiled, fighting the ache in his throat.

It was all too much, yet not nearly enough, and getting away from him. The unbearable need to be sheathed within her dizzied him. With a supreme effort, he moved to the curve of her waist. A moan of protest escaped her lips. To expiate this offense, he pressed yet another kiss to her lips, soothing her complaint.

"Sweetheart, if I don't stop, in my need I may end up behaving inappropriately. I don't want to embarrass you."

"Matthew, you'd never do anything to hurt or embarrass me. But…I'm no longer hungry. Not for food, anyway."

"I love when you blush. Are you sure you aren't hungry?"

"Only for you, my love. Will you feed me?"

"Right away, angel."

***

"Do you have everything? Did you check the bathroom?" Isabel asked. She fidgeted, watching Xavi pack his belongings.

"I didn't bring that many clothes." He smiled. With a fist on a hip and the other riffling through his hair, Xavier completed the visual check around his suitcase. "I think I have everything. Oh hell, whatever I forget, you can hold it for me. Won't you?"

"I suppose."

He frowned, dropped his hands, and walked slowly to her. "What's going on in that complicated, lovely head of yours?" He held her by the waist when she attempted to turn away from him. "Stop. Look at me, Isabel."

"Nothing, it's just, I…"

He lifted Isabel's chin, forcing her to look up. "Let me guess. You're thinking I won't return."

She blinked and he released her chin. "Yes, that's better. Will you listen?" She relented at last with a nod.

"Good. Isabel, I'm coming back for Christmas in less than a month. You know I'm working things out at the ranch. When I return, we will make permanent plans. Give us a chance. Trust me."

Inside Isabel, a pugnacious spirit rose from the depths where old wounds and past damages lived, and lashed out. "I believe you are sincere. Only, people change, and men forget their promises."

"And we reach the heart of the matter. You're so convinced I'll forget you. Don't you know I love you?"

Isabel couldn't tell if he was angry or stunned. She almost didn't care. She knew men, what they did and how they hurt. They couldn't be trusted. He'd left her once before, after Destin, after he'd pushed her emotions to the brink of sanity. "So you say…"

"Why don't you lay it all out? Have a little courage."

"Men make promises, but don't keep them. Men speak of love, but don't mean it. They don't care what women feel. They only want physical gratification, and when they're finished, so is the woman. They swear to protect, yet they leave, abandon us, die." She swayed, and Xavi grasped her arms to steady her.

"Easy, *Tesoro*, I have you."

"They come in the night and…hurt."

Xavi took her in his arms and sat on the bed, tucking her on his lap. He had to wait until she calmed, especially now, after she'd revealed her fears, even if he missed his flight.

"They swear to protect, yet they leave, abandon us, die." Her words ricocheted through his mind. *"They come in the night and…hurt."*

He knew a little of the Llorenz history and her father's untimely passing. In small towns, everyone's business was everyone else's. To a young girl, it must have been traumatic. But what did the other part mean? If Nieves did not make progress, doña Alicia would not escape him.

"Better?" he asked when her breaths eased. She nodded. He lifted her from his lap and stretched her on the bed. He walked over to the bathroom, returning a few moments later with tissues in hand and a gentle smile.

"Take these." He sat next to her while she dried her tears and wiped her blotchy cheeks. When she finished, he reached for her hand and clasped it between his.

"You've been hurt before, and I wish I could undo the damage, but I can't. I also know trust doesn't grow in a vacuum. It must be earned. The onus is on me. One or two visits aren't going to convince you. Time will prove my feelings.

"I don't know when I'll die. Life is fragile, but my love isn't. I loved you at the beginning, and I always will. If I should leave tomorrow, my love would remain with you until it's your turn to go, because at the other end, *Tesoro*, I will claim you again. I'll do my best to last to a ripe old age with you. Okay?"

"Yes, Xavier Manel. I get lost sometimes." She sniffled.

"I love when you say my name. It will take time, but we'll get through this." He cupped her cheek. "*Tesoro*, I need to get ready. Jonas is arriving any minute. I'll call you tonight. I'm not abandoning you. How can I abandon my soul? When I return in December, we'll plan for our future. Now, if I leave my favorite slacks"—he smiled—"will you trust I'm coming back?" When Isabel returned the smile, he knew she would be fine, for now. Xavi would not delude himself.

***

The spectral Ancients floated about.
A thin predatory smile danced on eidolic features.
All was in place.
The weak mortal was a malleable puppet.
Let the fun begin.

Isabel waved one last good-bye in Xavi's direction. She entered the kitchen, pulled out the coffee percolator, and prepped it for another brew. Bemused, she stared around. She'd performed all actions without a single conscious thought. Her mind had been entirely absorbed in Xavi's words:

"I'm not abandoning you. How can I abandon my soul?"

He asked for trust. He deserved it, didn't he? Xavi had managed to calm her with his declarations, but as the scope of his influence dissipated, a fearful shiver grew. If she were going to accept him, she would have to relearn how to live. Start from the beginning? No, that would be a dire mistake. Her secrets had to remain shrouded. She could begin from the weekend in Destin. She shivered, this time from sheer pleasure, recalling the afternoon and evening.

Xavier was her awakening and revelation. Would she dare admit it? Yes, she loved him. Of course, she would give him a chance. Feeling restored and reassured, Isabel filled her coffee mug. What was she doing before Xavi had arrived last Wednesday? Ah yes. Straightening Raquelita's room.

She gave her daughter's closet a quick overview. Not much laboring here. She continued surveying, then stopped. On the top shelf, an oblong box decorated in gift paper and gold ribbon glinted in the dim light. She touched it. Later, she would remember the cautionary tingle in her fingers, the eerie warning: *Stop, Isabel.* She had no reason to peek, none, other than her motherly and feminine curiosity prodding her. She plunged ahead. Picked up the box and sat on Lita's bed.

For many years, Isabel would recollect with regret the unheeded karmic remonstration to stop and the eerie cackle echoing throughout the house. The image rushed unbidden: a mythical clay woman, deceitful, curious, and stubborn,

Pandora with a *pithos* of terrible gifts. Isabel untied the gold ribbon and lifted the cover. Several envelopes addressed to Raquelita lay stored among flower petals. She focused on the return address. *Matthew?* It couldn't be.

Ire exploded with the energy of a summer fire in the Rockies. Like dry brush, she erupted in flames of anger. *How? When?* She wanted to stomp on the box, strew the petals, and shred the contents. Raquelita had duped her ignominiously. Comprehension descended like a sheet of ice. It hadn't been just Raquelita. The letter was addressed to the ranch. They were all in on it. She blinked, holding back a new surge of anger as curiosity won over reason. She had to examine the evidence.

Gritting her teeth, she opened the first envelope and lifted the paper. *Leave the letters unread.* She paused as Karma appealed one last time. An odd pang hit her as she envisioned the hurt in her daughter's face at the invasive betrayal. What about *her* betrayal, the lies and disrespect? So she waved her motherly banner. Raquelita was a minor. Isabel had the authority, if not the moral imperative, to investigate. Filled with such resolve, she proceeded.

You've made me the happiest I have been, since I held you in my arms and kissed your sweet lips...

He kissed her on the bus ride? All her efforts to keep her daughter pure and unsullied, trounced in a few hours. With shaking hands, Isabel lowered the letter to her lap in one last effort to exercise control. But control was gone. The fascination of his words urged her on.

I can't imagine your strain, sweetheart. You've endured it the longest...

In spite of her fury, his caring words softened her spirit.

From now on, you can expect more, lots more. Writing to you is as essential as breathing...

The level of duplicity was staggering, and she hardened again. Why did they lie? *Because they knew you would stop them,* said a little voice. Raquelita should have come to her. *You would have berated her,* it continued.

Isabel put the letter down again. The more she read, the worse she felt. The pervasive sense of wrongness surprised her. Why did she feel like a voyeur when she'd acted correctly? Did she regret opening the box? She might have been happier not knowing.

The discovery eroded the happy balance she'd reached before Xavi left. *Diosito*, did he know about this unsuitable, ill-fated affair? For doomed it was. The casualty list grew daily, so the newspapers said. And there was her answer on how to proceed. She'd return everything to its original place and say nothing. If Matthew hadn't left already, he would soon.

He'd forget Raquelita. With the abundance of brothels and prostitutes, how could a seventeen-year-old ingénue compete? Isabel smirked. She could play the game. Raquelita was her daughter, and she wasn't going to allow some good-for-nothing country boy to touch her again. She'd always been right. *Trust no one.*

***

December 8, 1967 – fifteen days later.

"Raquelita, thank God you're here."

She almost jumped out of her skin. She'd just arrived from Rosie's and was removing her shoes when her cousin barged in.

"Lorrie?"

"It's Matthew. He's being deployed. He's calling back in ten minutes. Hurry."

Virgencita, por favor... Her stomach lurched. Since her return, she'd been living at the edge, waiting for the inevitable. At least she was home to take the call.

"Okay. Let's go." She pushed her cousin ahead and fled after her. A weird clamminess and a sense of disconnect surrounded her, and the world started to tilt. *This is it.* Her brain pounded the thought. *This is it.* She ran with her cousin, and the ground sped by, faster and faster, as she rushed to the Reynoldses' to meet her fate and to hear his voice. *This is it!*

They entered the ranch at full speed. Coralina watched them impassively, leafing through a magazine, preparing for the fallout.

Once inside the office, Raquelita paced. Lorrie's pretty eyes followed her agitated behavior. Minutes passed. Lita started to fantasize it was a crazy dream. The jangling phone shattered the illusion. She picked up on the first ring. Lorrie disappeared.

"H-hello."

"Angel."

Peace. Even in the midst of insanity, Matthew had the power to calm and reassure her. "I'm here."

"I wish I could tell you more, sweet girl."

"I understand, my love. I do. Please stay safe."

"I love you. I can say that, I love you."

"I love you, with all my heart."

"Angel, I have to go. Others need the phone. Write to me."

"I will. I'll come to you in our dreams, tonight, wherever you are. Look for me. I'll find you."

"I'll be waiting, always."

Raquelita returned the receiver to the cradle. Her head fell forward. "Oh, Chaos, leviathan of the deep, have you broken free? You rule my life now." The dreaded vigil had begun.

PART TWO

Chapter Twenty-Four

Ocala, December 15, 1967

News has finally arrived through Mr. Buchanan, bless his soul. Matthew is in a small camp, Lang Vei something or other, near the Marine base in Khe Sanh.

I miss him so much. He warned me about the hardship of silence in time of war, but I didn't quite understand. My mind is my worst enemy. It plays and replays images of the jungle, the camp, the enemies, day and night. Worry is my constant companion, as I search through news articles and war reports, my daily obsession. Will this vigil seem shorter if I learn more about our cause, the reason for our involvement in Vietnam? Will it pass faster if I learn about the land and the enemy? Will the knowledge help me grow stronger, feel closer to him? Is fortitude nurtured by familiarity?

I don't know.

Meanwhile, Padrino is returning for the holidays, and the interaction between him and Mom is fascinating. The man calms her mercurial moods with a look. How did they evolve from enemies to lovers? Was true love their "Beast in the Jungle," waiting patiently to change their lives forever?

Life's most interesting lessons will never be taught in school.

***

Raquelita wondered if this holiday party at Dalia's would be worth her titanic negotiations with the Iron Lady. She'd almost given up, but attending the party had become a symbol of a new, determined Raquelita, and she had insisted. The evening was perfect, cool and crisp. Lorrie had pulled the top down for the drive, reviving Raquelita's spirits, until its chilly embrace reminded her of a night in San Antonio, when she spent precious moments in the arms of her beloved. Sweet,

sweet memories and the loneliness of Matthew's absence crushed her soul again. She'd gone full circle.

"Crap, not a space." Lorrie's grumble intruded into her thoughts. This fête was busy. Cars lined up back to back. Lorrie must've had great parking karma, for less than a block away, a car pulled out. As she slipped right in, a frisson of anticipation ran through Raquelita. It was her first party among her peers.

The young women stepped out of the car and stood on the sidewalk, taking in the scene. Groups of revelers dotted the grounds surrounding the cottage. Voices, gyrating shadows, and flickering lights spilled through gargantuan front windows with a spectral, dreamlike quality. Staccato riffs of "You Really Got Me" boomed across the lawn.

"Someone is heavy into The Kinks. Is there a pun somewhere?" Lorrie smirked.

Raquelita nodded and sniffed at the peculiar smell wafting through the air. Initially, she thought it was the uncomfortable odor of clove cigarettes preferred by the self-appointed intellectual snobs in school. On occasion, the spicy aroma wafted through corridors, the student cafeteria, and even at Rosie's. This was different, and it smelled dangerous, triggering a silent warning in her gut.

"I don't know about this." Lorrie echoed her thoughts, tugging at her wrist.

"I hear you," Raquelita whispered as her mind warred between the desire to leave and the curiosity urging her to stay.

"What a surprise. It's the Texas chickie. Darling, come to join the dark side?" The comment, oozing with sarcasm, killed Raquelita's urge to go home. Ricky emerged out of the shadows, wearing a pair of tired jeans and a dark shirt. The top three buttons had been left open to exhibit a pale, concave chest. His beady black leer examined Raquelita from her new boots to her face.

"And who's this beauty?" He turned his lascivious perusal toward a frowning Lorrie. She scowled down at him in Jonas-like fashion. Ricky had never looked shorter.

Trying to ease the tension, Raquelita introduced the ungracious man to her cousin, before Lorrie stepped on the creature beneath her nose. Undaunted, Ricky reached out for Lorrie's hand and, to Raquelita's surprise, brought it up to his lips for a brief kiss.

"*Encantado,*" he said with an odd smirk.

If he hoped to impress her cousin, he failed miserably, because Lorrie snatched her hand away to wipe it on her jeans. Raquelita winced at the gesture. Ricky, however, seemed to ignore the snub He focused his attention on Raquelita, grasped her elbow and, with a firm tug, ushered her toward the party, squashing all notions of escape. Raquelita shrugged in resignation, as Lorrie had to follow. When she came within earshot, Lita whispered, "We'll say hello, and at the first opportunity, we split."

Aretha sang "Respect" when their little group ran into a swaying Linda. "Raquelita, you made it," she exclaimed, managing to plant a kiss on her cheek. "And who's this?" she asked, doing another circular sway and flicking back the curtain of hair that now covered her eyes. Linda and Lorrie assessed each other. Lorrie appeared miffed by the entire situation. Her pugnacious expression threatened combat. One wrong comment would set her off. But Linda, perhaps more experienced, and thus far managing her altered state, laughed, easing some of Lorrie's animosity.

"You must be Lorrie, Lita's cousin?"

"And she's smart." An arched brow accompanied Lorrie's sarcastic retort.

Rolling her bloodshot eyes, Linda pondered the remark for a moment, pressed a finger on the doorframe, and slurred, "Oooh, she bites."

Raquelita shook off Ricky's hold and fired a warning look to her cousin in conjunction with Dalia's arrival. Quickly, she introduced Dalia and Lorrie, and sent a pleading glance to her cousin for civility. In turn, Dalia offered Lorrie a disarming smile, and her cousin's expression softened.

Explosion averted.

Raquelita regarded her friend with new appreciation. Cool and serene, Dalia moved with genuine ease, unaffected by the outrageous ruckus. Her youthful, placid looks were deceiving, though. One had to look closely, as Raquelita did now, to discover the faint traces of a hard life and hints of a weathered soul. Dalia stepped to the side and, with a gracious wave, invited them in.

In the background, "Respect" faded, overcome by the mysterious chords of "I Am the Walrus," and Ricky tipped his head back in a gesture of delight. "Ah, yes… This is more like it," he exclaimed.

Ricky shoved Linda aside, who again fought bravely to stay on her feet, and headed in the direction of the dance floor. He affected an absurd swagger he might've deemed hip, although it did nothing but enhance his piano legs, short torso, and caved-in chest. He disappeared the same way he'd appeared, into the dark.

Just then, an attractive man with long dark hair, wearing a teal Nehru jacket, happened to walk past. With precise timing, Dalia thrust Linda, with her rhinestone hoops and black lamé dress, into his surprised hands, pointing to the grounds outside. Smiling, she turned her attention to Raquelita and Lorrie.

"Any refreshments, ladies? Liquor is not available. Beer is for those over twenty-one only. So don't ask." She winked and, with the air of a regal queen, flicked two fingers in a come-after-me sign, gliding gracefully away. Raquelita and Lorrie followed, squeezing their bodies against the wall, navigating as best they could past the dancers. At the back of the room, Dalia waited next to a table with an assortment of drinks and snacks.

"Help yourselves to the munchies," she said loudly enough to be heard, then pivoted and vanished into the crowd, leaving Raquelita and Lorrie to plan a dignified escape.

The living room had been cleared of furniture. In the far corner, a disc-jockey station had been set up. A skillful young man with a fall of straight blue-black hair jostled LPs between turntables. The scent of musk and perfumed oils wafted from the dancers' heated bodies, along with incense and cigarette smoke in a heady, intoxicating attack against the senses.

"One drink and we leave," Raquelita yelled at her cousin, and Lorrie nodded.

"No, don't leave yet." Out of nowhere, a young man with a genial smile reached out to Lorrie. "Dance with me, please?" The polite request in the midst of this bedlam was a breath of fresh air. "Come on," he insisted, his blond mane swaying.

Raquelita nudged Lorrie, urging her forward. "Go. Dance. It's a party. I'll wait for you right here."

Lorrie placed tentative fingers on the young man's palm, and his gray irises flickered in gratitude at Raquelita. He gave a light tug, and the vortex of convulsive humanity swallowed the couple.

Raquelita stared at the commotion and sighed, then sipped her soda and leaned against the table for support. She felt Matthew's summons. Even in the midst of this riotous scene, if he called, she would answer. Visions of him filled her mind and heart, demanding she reenter that separate space that was uniquely theirs.

Raquelita blinked.

***

Over nine thousand miles away, Matthew, Brian, and four Bru Montagnards slinked through dense mountain vegetation, their moves economical and watchful, past copses of Khasi pines, bamboo thickets, and glossy giant ferns. Heavy condensation fell upon them in huge drops, splotching their uniforms. A dense canopy of trees hid their progress from possible spies above. In stealth, they looked out for traps, mines, and deadly punji sticks. They wove through massive foliage, avoiding the footpath created by a complacent adversary.

On this clandestine mission, the men donned the enemy's tired green garb, floppy jungle hats, and weapons. The US government didn't acknowledge their presence in Laos; only a select group in the CIA knew. So they carried absolutely nothing to officially link them to America. If captured, they'd claim mercenary status, thus relieving the US from any wrongdoing.

Acknowledged or not, recon missions on the Ho Chi Minh trail were critical. Rumor on the mountain spread as it did at a social gathering—fast. The friendly locals whispered of underwater bridges, enemy concentrations, and heavy equipment advancing south. The patrol came to verify and collect the necessary proof for the naysayers in Saigon.

They progressed with guarded ease, following the forest's natural sounds: bird calls, animal groans, and insect chirps, rather than the unnatural silence that warned of man's heavy presence. A day later, they returned, frustrated with the lack of intel.

Once he crossed the perimeter wire and entered camp, Matthew took a deep breath. This was his third such patrol, and he wondered if the tension cramping his shoulders would ever ease. Raquelita's beloved face appeared in his mind, and he relished it before it floated away. These transitory visions and her letters were the few pleasures he allowed himself.

***

The jungle vision dissipated, and she was back at the party, staring at a surreal mass of arms, legs, and outlandish clothing. Guided by the expert hands of the DJ, the dark intro and heavy bass of "I'm a Man" reverberated through the floor. Drums initiated their tribal summons electrifying the dancers. When the organ flourished, the mood turned feral. Steve Winwood clamored his masculine needs, and a bestial roar sprang from the heart of the crowd.

Dalia danced in the center. She swayed in wild abandon, intimately tangled with her dance partner. A few feet away, Linda bumped her hips against her dark-haired rescuer. Entwined between two women, Ricky flashed a smile of satisfaction as they explored his body, seeking his illegal treasures. Lorrie held on to the neck of her blond friend, appearing enraptured by the energy pulsing throughout the room.

Couples, trios, foursomes—the melee had reached bacchanalian proportions. The disc jockey mixed "Gimme Some Lovin'" with the last chords of "I'm A Man," and the dancers went wild.

If she lived to be a hundred, Raquelita would never forget this evening, wishing she could have been on the dance floor with Matthew, enjoying the fun in his strong arms, partaking in the youthful insanity she witnessed. Soon the music turned plaintive, as "Try a Little Tenderness" softened the mood. Lorrie emerged from the dance floor, smiling and a little flushed.

"Did you have fun?"

"Yes, but it's time to go home." When Lita remained silent, she explained, "His name is Steve. He has my phone number."

"Cool. Are you sure you're ready?"

"Yes. It's enough for one night. If he's really interested, he'll call."

***

Ocala – December 22nd 1967

Matthew's first letter arrived, a little crumpled, and half the contents are blacked out. I should be furious with this violation of our privacy. But we're at war, and I'm reminded that personal rights disappear for the good of the nation. So unfair.

Still, happiness overrides the irritation. He's with me again. My cup runneth over. I didn't realize the emptiness until I read the first line. I'll read and soak up his words until I am full, replenished, and fortified to face tomorrow, when Xavi arrives.

Mom has been driving us crazy with preparations. With Padrino in town, anything is possible. It may be the start of many interesting days.

***

Raquelita walked through the door and froze. A stately Fraser fir and a multitude of boxes, replete with sparkling decorations, confirmed Xavi's return. This happy bedlam could never be Isabel's creation, and Raquelita's hungry gaze devoured the lovely clutter in awed silence. Obviously, Xavi had decided to bypass her mother's Scrooge-like behavior, in his usual take-no-prisoners style. Raquelita approved of his coup.

Padrino was an ongoing revelation. For years, the horse trainer had presented to the world a core of steel, a gruff mien, and a commanding personality. And yet, he'd also revealed a loving heart, solely devoted to her mother. He would need every ounce of that steel. Isabel embodied "difficult." If he didn't keep his seat, she'd buck him off out of pride and stubbornness. In the meantime, Raquelita thoroughly enjoyed the spectacle of Xavi maneuvering and outflanking her irascible mother.

Like today—*Padrino* stood in the middle of the room holding up two strings of multicolored lights with a befuddled expression. He heard Lita and Marité's arrival, and his head snapped up with a brilliant smile.

"Ladies, perfect timing. I need assistance," he said, extending a string toward Marité. "Don't you have a step stool in the house?"

Lita rushed through the kitchen toward the back door. "I'm on it," she called out and disappeared.

***

Xavi had to suppress a laugh as moments later his goddaughter returned, struggling with a six-foot ladder, bumping the heavy legs against corners and walls. "Thanks, let me help you." Xavi relieved Lita of the ladder and proceeded to climb, light strand in hand. "Mari, honey, come closer. Start circling the tree as I set the lights on the upper branches."

He glanced at Isabel, controlling his urge to snicker. At the moment, she sat frowning, lips pressed, refusing to look at him. Yeah, she had reason. He'd become a tornado in her house. She'd picked him up at the airport and driven back with light conversation. Once inside the house, he'd regarded her Spartan décor, snatched her car keys, and disappeared. He returned dragging a fir tree and decorations. In a matter of hours, her home was being converted into a Christmas wonderland.

"Come here, *Tesoro*. Join the party," he called from his perch. "This is for you too, my lovely *bah-humbug* grouch."

They finished placing the strands and tested the lights. None failed, and Marité applauded in childlike approval, gladdening his heart. Decorations were not up yet, but oh, the lights… Their twinkling beauty foreshadowed magical splendor. The Christmas spirit would come to this home, as was proper, along with the intent of the season: love, good will, and gifts. It would be a fine holiday if he had anything to say about it.

Three hours later, every box had been depleted, outdoor garlands pinned; a colossal red bow and matching ribbon circled the front door. They finished just in time for twilight. Lita and Marité sat on the floor, waiting in hushed expectation. Isabel remained on the sofa. As director, Xavi stood next to the light switch, strand plug in hand. The suspense rose.

He flicked the switch, the room plunged into darkness, and Xavi connected the lights. Christmas exploded around them in a spectacle of multicolored light beams, glittering balls, stars, and angels. Sheer ribbons cascaded in wondrous streams of red and gold. The scene rivaled any of the imaginative stories of Hans Christian Andersen.

"Ahh," they exclaimed in unison.

Satisfied with the results and his cohort's happy reaction, Xavi turned to Isabel. Her mouth had opened just a little, and he couldn't resist the desire to touch her. He stepped close and brushed a fingertip along her lip as he said, "You're welcome." Isabel shivered; their gazes locked.

"I wanna see what the tree looks like through the window." Marité breezed past, opened the door, and ran out.

"We should all go. Isabel?" Xavi extended a hand.

"Yes, let's take a look. I'm sure it's beautiful."

"You bet. But we're not done yet."

"We're not?"

"Uh…some last-minute shopping and a few boxes need to be wrapped."

"Which boxes? I didn't see anything when I picked you up."

"They arrived a few days ago, *Tesoro*. Jonas and Coralina were kind enough to hold them for me. It's Christmas. Did you think I'd arrive empty-handed?" He smiled, squeezing her hand. "Let's go. The girls are waiting."

Chapter Twenty-Five

Lang Vei – December 24th 1967

Man's creativity is limitless. Matthew pondered that while tying his boots and half listening to Brian's singing in the outdoor shower. *Imagination emerges when it's needed the most, during war or extreme conditions.* The men of Special Forces were credited for amazing improvisational skills, but the Marines were no slackers. He recalled again the story he'd heard from another team member. The old Route 9, a primary road used long ago by the French as a passing air-post road, had successfully connected the men of Lang Vei and Khe Sanh to transport the precious cargo of beer for this event.

As long as the nearby section of the Laos border and the DMZ remained quiet, Captain Willoughby had agreed to a private—emphasis on unobtrusive—Christmas gathering at the TOC. May of 1967 had proved spies were everywhere. Enemy infiltrators within the CIDG betrayed Special Forces at the old Lang Vei camp. The resulting Vietcong night assault wiped out the command group in one bunker. Trust was an expensive commodity. Precautions were never redundant.

"Hey, Bri. Does Cap'n know about the beer? I heard getting in and out of Khe Sanh unseen was an ordeal. I hope this is worth it."

"Fuck, yeah." Back from the outdoor showers, Brian answered from underneath a towel as he rubbed his lengthening reddish-blond hair. He stopped his drying efforts and hooked the towel around the back of his neck. "The officers are hip to the transaction. But no one wants the convenient li'l gig denounced, especially when both camps enjoy the perks. The Marine has a sweet deal goin'. I hear he gave us a special price, bein' Christmas and all. Men with generous spirits durin' tryin' times are gifts from Sanna. I ain't expectin' Bud 'r Miller. We can't be too picky out here in the wilderness. 'Sides, we can't git wasted either. Shit, can you see it if we're attacked? Them li'l Montagnards in camp, scurrying round, rallyin' up a group of big, drunk Americans." He sniggered and resumed his drying.

"Well...our Bru CIDG despise the North Vietnamese. They may not understand or care about Christmas, but we can trust their hatred. They'll watch our backs for a few hours."

Brian pulled the towel away and hung it on a multipurpose contraption he'd rigged on a corner beam.

"Always so neat," Matthew muttered. "I'm glad you are."

Brian shrugged. "It's my thing, it keeps our sanity intact. In this crazy place a man can forgit himself, his identity and humanity. Become a savage. The routine grounds me, I feel connected to my home. After this experience I can face anythin' life throws my way...that is if I survive—" Brian stopped, picked up a folded T-shirt from his cot and threw it on.

Matthew hadn't quite listened to his friend. His thoughts were miles away as he tapped a finger on his wristwatch.

"Shouldn't you tone down the cheery attitude?" Brian asked, tucking in his T-shirt.

Matthew looked up. "Sorry, bro. I was thinking of Raquelita and my parents. Maybe that's why Cap'n doesn't allow free time. It gives a man a chance to think. It feels like an eternity since we got here. Whenever I look ahead... Crap, don't listen to me."

"Maybe we should hang out here instead of the TOC. Yer rosy outlook could overwhelm the guys."

"Nah, I'll get it together. It's the solitude and remoteness of the mountains. The Bru nice as they are, bring it on. When we interact, I feel like an intruder. I can't seem to find a comfortable spot on my skin to lean on." Matthew rubbed both palms over his face and hair. "I looked at the time and wondered what they were doing. I miss them." He gazed up and around the hut, inhaled, and his cheeks puffed. With a soft pop of his lips, he released the air. "Listen, I'm cool. Once I step out, I'll be myself again."

"You're allowed, Matt James. Fuck, we're all allowed this feelin'. It's our first Christmas away from everyone we love. It's easier for me. I've only got my parents to worry about. Some say it's best to have single men in Special Forces. Who knows fer sure? Look, we were lassoed, branded, trained, and shipped by dear Uncle Sam to this godforsaken shithole."

Brian sat at the edge of his cot across from Matthew and pointed two fingers in his direction. "We were given a choice of which poison to drink. That's it. I know it's distant up here, but the guys sent south and at the Delta are fighting a fucking inferno, a true Gehenna, as my Bible-reading momma would say. Don't forget, you hadn't met Raquelita when you signed on. Do you know Ashley? He's married with a kid."

"Not yet."

"It's time you two met. He's been here longer. You could talk 'bout stuff."

"Brian...I'll be fine. I won't freeze when the time comes."

"Matthew James Buchanan, there is no one I trust more than you. Now please, let's go before the beer's gone. 'Sides, I can't handle any more sentimentality." Brian jumped to his feet, slapped Matthew's shoulder, and turned to the door. "You comin'?" he demanded.

"Yep, right behind you."

***

Raquelita should be proud of her efforts. She'd pinned evergreen branches tied with a satin red bow on every corner of the crown molding. Pale green Bordallo Pinheiro majolica plates, heirloom silverware, crystal goblets, and the exquisite linen tablecloth finished the décor. She walked around admiring the pieces. Pity it would be decimated by ravenous beasts in minutes. She almost laughed aloud at the thought.

Job completed, she entered the kitchen. It was redolent with the delicious aroma of a slow-roasting leg of pork cooking in garlic, rosemary, and red wine.

"Thanks for your help, Lita," Coralina said. "I always feel better once the dining room is done. When's Xavi picking you up?"

"Any minute."

Coralina stepped close and touched her cheek. "I see anguish in your face. Pain's darkening your pretty eyes, *querida*. Is it Matthew?"

Raquelita huffed. Since early morning, her emotions had been a nest of angry wasps. "I can't stop thinking about him. Look at that beautiful room. Tonight we'll chat about meaningless topics without a thought for anything else." She took two steps back, extending an accusatory finger at the dining room.

"We won't discuss touchy subjects, especially *Vietnam*, because it'll ruin dinner. Despite our indifference, Matthew and his fellow soldiers are still out there, in harm's way, fighting for us. What about their Christmas dinner? Will anyone, other than their families, pray for them? I want him here, next to me. Safe. Like Steven and Lorrie," she whispered, lowering her gaze.

Coralina closed the distance and gripped her arm. With a sudden snap, Lita looked up. "I can't even express my feelings aloud for fear of my mother. I'm such a coward."

"*Querida,* how can I help you?"

"Can you bring him home?"

Raquelita wrenched her body away from her aunt's hold and rushed out of the house. By the time she stopped, she stood under the canopy of the giant oak tree, beneath which she and Matthew had once spent time together. She pressed a hand on the gnarled trunk and sat on an ancient root, directing her gaze skyward.

"Just a prayer, dear Lord, for my Matthew, Brian, and every man serving our nation. Keep them safe, in the hollow of thy hands. May the prayers of family and loved ones comfort them today, and every day thereafter, until they are safely returned."

***

Late Christmas night, Isabel waited on her sofa, mentally preparing for Xavi's arrival and their one night together. All other nights he'd slept at the ranch for propriety's sake. So she'd followed his instructions, her girls would spend the night at the Reynoldses, she wore her robe, and she'd left the front door unlocked. They'd been intimate before, yet tonight felt different. To suppress her nerves, she let her thoughts drift to Christmas morning.

Marité had received a shiny red bicycle. She'd spent all morning with Xavi and Michael until she pedaled away, Sam and Nina trailing, delighted, after her. Lita unwrapped a superb collection of leather-bound books. The complete works of John Donne, Emily Dickinson, and ee cummings, along with a set of journals for her personal writings.

She trembled, remembering her turn. Xavi had presented her with two boxes. She'd hesitated.

"Try one at least," he encouraged.

Isabel opted for the larger of the two. *He knows everything about me,* she thought as she removed the wrapper. *Fleur de Rocaille,* Rock Flowers by Caron, her signature perfume. Emilio used to comment—with great derision—that it personified her. She stared at Xavi. He smiled blandly.

"Open the other box, *Tesoro.*"

Her fingers shook. What else would he surprise her with? The black velvet box snapped open, displaying a set of Asian pearl drop earrings. Their rose luster glinted mysteriously in the light.

"Xavi."

"Hmmm, don't start, Isabel. I wish to see them on you."

It took an eternity to lift her clumsy fingers and remove her plain hoops. He took the box from her, picked up an earring, and held it up against her cheek.

"Yes, women should wear pearls often. They heighten the feminine aura." His smile was as enigmatic as the pearls.

She inserted and clasped one earring; the next followed. Xavi touched the tip of her lobe and smiled.

"Perfect."

Isabel heard a muted click, and her heart jumped. A frisson of panic rushed her. Could it be an intruder? No, it had to be Xavi. Then her thoughts froze. Xavi standing at the threshold cut a mystifying figure, a Michelangelo sculpture, perfect in form and shape. The Christmas tree lights dappled his black slacks and muscled, naked torso with a vivid, multicolored swirl. He carried a gift box under one arm, a rolled bundle under the other, and an arresting smile on his lips.

"Merry Christmas, *Tesoro*." Xavi presented the large box. Her childlike smile and eagerness to take the box surprised him. Moved by her reaction, he sat next to her and let the bundle drop.

"Xavi."

"No," he interrupted. "Tonight I'm Xavier. That's the name I wish to hear."

Oh, his damned imperiousness. He'd come to her with every intention of being gentle. He wanted to show her the other Xavier—the man he rarely revealed—the man she might learn to trust. The master, the controlling horse trainer, had to take a step back tonight.

He smiled at her fumbling attempts to open the large box. "May I?"

"Yes, please."

Xavier removed the ribbon, gift-wrapping, and tissue paper and tossed the box away. He stood holding the thin straps of a lustrous, dusty-rose French silk peignoir. An ethereal strip of beaded lace adorned the top.

"It's a nice contrast with your golden skin. Do you like it?"

"It's gorgeous." Isabel said, running a finger down the length of the gown.

"No, it's only the framework. You are beautiful." He extended a hand to her, and she stood. He released the sash of her robe and reached through. The robe slipped open, affording him a glance of her curves, plateaus and a hint of her enticing scent. With gentle touches, he moved along the continent of her body until he reached her shoulders. He flicked his fingers, and the garment floated behind her. He saw her tremble, yet she remained steady, brave in her nudity.

"Raise your arms for me." As the negligee slid down, her nipples puckered and tiny goose bumps appeared. Xavi had to inhale for control.

"Now for the final touch," he said, holding a thin, black velvet box. When he opened it, the matching necklace to her pearl earrings gleamed in the dim light.

"I've had this fantasy for days, you wearing the pearls. Will you?"

"Y-yes."

In swift movements, Xavier clasped the necklace around her neck and stepped back for a look. She took his breath away. The necklace resting on her golden skin enhanced the beauty of her shoulders and arms. The cascade of mahogany locks framed her graceful neck and lovely face. The gown delineated her peaked nipples and the contour of her curves.

"My God, Isabel."

The air around them had thickened and heated. Xavier breathed in. The headiness of the moment threatened his control. Isabel's allure and the desire to be inside her conspired against it. With great difficulty, he returned to the next part of his plan. A moment later, he reached down and unrolled the bundle on the floor, alongside the sofa.

"I found this quilt. It's thick and soft. I think you'll find it very comfortable."

Xavi straightened and with much grace and little effort, he lifted and delicately deposited Isabel on the plush surface. Her scent reached his nostrils, and he wavered. If he wanted to last the night, make it special and memorable, he needed a distraction. So he set up the last details of their lounging area, pulling the sofa cushions down, one to pillow her head and shoulders. The remaining cushions he placed carefully around her.

"Comfortable? Good, I'll be right back."

He stepped out of the room and returned with a dark bundle, knelt before the fireplace, and, in minutes had a fire going. "Do you like it?" he asked as he returned to her side and placed a soft kiss on her lips. "Did you have a good Christmas?"

Isabel nodded.

"Your face is full of questions. I promised I would take care of you, and I will. Tonight I have your pleasure in mind. I've not disappointed you yet, have I?"

With Isabel's less than forthcoming personality, he knew there'd be no quick answer. He positioned himself at her feet, brought them to his lap, and began a deep-kneading massage. He could feel her relax, and the conversation flowed. She explained about work, and he told her about the past months, the ranch in Texas, future projects, and most of all, how much he missed her. As he spoke, he traveled gently up the underside of her calf, caressing her skin, cupping and working the feminine muscle. The gown slipped down her thigh, exposing both legs. The dancing light from the fire enhanced the image. He swallowed, and finally articulated the question he could no longer hold back.

"I love you, *Tesoro*. Will you marry me?"

Everything stopped. Panic flooded Isabel, and pleasure made a speedy egress. The warm lassitude he'd infused turned cold. Of all the questions, he had to ask this one. A question to remind her of reality, a question she'd no right to answer. She was already given to another, his best friend. How could he forget?

She tensed and jerked her legs. Xavier, quick as lightning, pinned her ankles to the floor. Reflexes honed by years of horse training responded on the spot. With thunderous expression, Xavier from the past had returned.

"Where do you think you're going?"

"I have to get away. I can't stay with you." Isabel shifted, still trying to squirm away.

"Why? Am I not good enough for you anymore? Last time, you didn't want me to leave. What's your game?" The steel in his voice joined the grip on her ankles. He shifted and knelt between her legs. Pain, raw and stark, hardened his features. She had to explain.

"No, Xavi. I mean, Xavier. I can't. We can't, don't you see?"

Why couldn't he comprehend the impossibility of their situation? Of course, she wanted him. Hell, she loved him, but it made no difference. By Spanish law, Emilio was her husband. What would they do? What *could* they do? "Please try to understand," she murmured.

"Why don't you enlighten me? Before I lose my temper."

His face was a mask, and his fury came out in short pants. The pressure on her ankles increased. His hands were steel manacles. She should be frightened, concerned, irked even, and yet, a discordant thought sliced through the fog in her brain. She wasn't frightened at all. His display of power sent bewildering pleasure pulses to all corners of her mind and body.

"I, we... Emilio's still my husband."

"What are you saying? I was there, at the—" A burst of illumination blazed over his features. "Spain. This is all about those archaic, repressive Spanish laws. Am I right?"

"Y-yes."

"I see."

He pulled at her ankles, dragging her away from the pillows and settling her hips against his knees. The sudden change in position left her arms trailing behind and the gown gathered around her waist, baring her lower half to him. She tried to avert her face but the pull of his gaze wouldn't let her.

He bent over. One hand pinned her shoulder, and the other slid under her, holding her still. His face fell close to hers. "Why would I pursue you if I didn't have the right?"

Xavier breathed to collect himself. He stood at the edge of despair. The notion of losing Isabel again stabbed his heart "If your first marriage failed, do we forfeit happiness? You should never've married Emilio. Wonderful as he is, he was never the right mate for you. You were induced into making a bad decision. Are you that rigid? You better tell me what you think, woman. Do you love me? Damn you, tell me the truth. If nothing else, give me that answer."

"I do," she whimpered. "I love you, Xavier."

He had her admission at last. He sat on his heels studying her for a long time. Then moved forward, crawling over her, reached past her shoulders, and stopped. His face was scant inches from hers.

"Good," he murmured brushing his lips over hers. "You're mine, *Tesoro*. I'm not letting go, and I'm not allowing anything or anyone to pull you away from me, not even you. Forget the stupid Spanish laws. We don't live in Spain, we live in the States, and your divorce is very legal. The rest will be worked out later."

He slid to the edge of her mouth and nibbled. "Are you mine? Tell me, are you?"

"Y-yes."

He lowered the straps of the gown past her shoulders, below her breasts. She tried to arch toward him, but her arms were trapped. Instead, her nipples pebbled, speaking for her, and he smiled. He sat back again, pulling the straps along, and freeing her arms. Isabel had the most delicious sensation of decadence come upon her. She'd become an uninhibited pagan goddess, brazen and nude except for a brief strip of silk around her waist.

"You're so beautiful." Releasing her gown, Xavi reached up to her tresses, spreading the mass of locks like a dark halo around her face.

His actions were slow and determined, yet the bulge straining against his slacks belied his patience. It seemed Xavier wasn't ready to indulge his desire just yet. He bent to her breasts, swirled a nipple with his tongue as he plucked and pinched the other between thumb and forefinger. She arched toward him, and he replaced the tongue with his teeth. He scraped, bit, and pulled. The tip spiked up, and she gasped, surprised by the pained pleasure. Xavier suckled over the bite, and a rush of arousal slammed between her legs.

"Enjoy, *Tesoro*. You love erotic pain," he murmured after releasing her throbbing tip.

He played with her, knowing her confusion over the stimuli he delivered. The full spectrum of emotions showed in her face: surprise, pain, and delight. He knew her desires, intuited her hidden wishes. Tonight they'd become reality in his arms. He looked forward to teaching her the finer points of his brand of lovemaking.

He moved her arms upwards, setting her wrists above her head. A length of dusty-rose silk appeared, and he bound her wrists together. Next he tied them to the leg of the sofa. Isabel searched his face, but he ignored the wildness in her eyes. He focused instead on the binding ensuring it wasn't tight. Task accomplished, he retraced his movements along her body. Xavi dragged her hips until her buttocks pressed on his need, held her in place, and slowly rubbed his shaft against her. Even through his slacks, the pleasure was intense.

"You're going to enjoy this."

Yes, she would. They'd made love several times since the afternoon in Destin, but tonight he enacted her secret dreams of surrender. She arched again, hoping to be consumed in a fire she desired more than life. "I want," she whispered.

He slipped his palms to her lower back, lifted her belly to his lips, and took a small bite, then placed a kiss where he bit, gentling the prickle of pain. "I can see your want."

At his unhurried pace, he lowered her body, reached for her knees, and, holding the underside, he planted her feet wide apart on the quilt. He leaned close, examining her slit with a fingertip. Isabel flinched. Xavi looked up, and she stopped. "No. This is mine, and I'm going to enjoy every gorgeous fold. I want to see them damp, flushed with excitement. This is how I want you. Your hair floating above you, wrists bound, legs open."

He began a slow, maddening caress with his elegant fingers, up and down, teasing and burrowing through her intimate lips. He bent down again. Using the flat of his tongue, he licked up her sex, reached her tiny hood, and flicked. Now he employed both thumbs to spread her, still urging her sweet pearl to rise. The moment it emerged, Xavi pressed his knuckles to the sensitive flesh surrounding the nub, clamped them together, and tugged. Isabel bucked.

"Oh…oh…that feels—"

"Beautiful. I love how you respond. It makes me crazy. Look." He lifted his wet fingers to show her. She blushed when he slipped them in and out of his mouth. "Ambrosia. I love your scent and taste. It drives me mad. Your body pays me the greatest compliment."

He stood slowly, gaze locked on the beautiful woman before him—the love of his life. Overcome with emotion and need, he reached for the clasp of his slacks. They dropped, and he exhaled with relief.

The virile god before her took her breath away. Xavier's cock jutted out, thick and demanding. Every inch of him was the ideal of masculine beauty at the peak of desire, flexing anxious fingers, tense forearms, taut muscles, chest, legs, and buttocks. He pulsed with energy, and she could see every vein, every sinew standing at attention, ready to take over, and take her onward.

"Do you want me?"

"Y-yes."

He returned to his place between her legs, hooked her knees on his arms, and inched forward until the tip of his penis touched the portal of her sheath. Drops of intimate dew eased his path and invited him in. He moved in a little, making his presence known, and then paused, eyes ablaze.

Isabel wiggled her hips, attempting to urge him inside. He smiled and shook his head.

"What's wrong?"

"Nothing's wrong, *Tesoro*."

"Then why… What are you doing?"

"I'm teasing the hell out of us. I want us to lose our minds. That's what I'm doing. I can barely hold on, but I'm not taking you yet, not until you tremble and beg for it." He shifted forward and raised her legs higher, focusing on her glistening petals now spread by his cock. The sight made him dizzy with want. He pushed, entering halfway.

"Please, Xavier." She stared at the sheen of perspiration covering his muscled chest; his face was locked in sheer concentration. Need crashed through her core. Internal contractions begged for his presence.

"Ah, sweetheart, don't do that."

"I can't help it. I'm burning!".

"Isabel," he groaned. He hooked her legs on his shoulders, leaned on his hands, and, with a hushed grunt, buried his shaft to the hilt. "Give me your mouth," he demanded, "I want to show you what possession really means." She opened her lips as he thrust his tongue like his cock, filling all the warm spaces inside. Her tongue tangled back, and he moaned in delight.

He wrapped his arms around her, pulling her as close as the bindings would allow. "We're both going to burn tonight." He slid almost out, then drove back in. He sought to plunder every opening in her body. In this position, he had access to all of Isabel. He searched gently between her buttocks. Upon reaching the oft-forgotten pleasure passage, he began a slow, insane invasion. Isabel squirmed.

He released her mouth, whispering close to her ear, "Shhh, easy, *Tesoro*, trust me." He dropped a quick kiss and returned to his coaching. "I'm taking all of you. Breathe, sweetheart. Now push, baby. There, against my fingers. Yes, that's my girl," he encouraged heatedly. "This is it. You're all mine. Give me one deep exhale." Isabel obeyed, and the last barrier opened for him, two long fingers sliding well within her heat.

"Yes," he exclaimed, losing himself in the world that was Isabel, his Isabel.

"Xavier Manel." She gasped at the double penetration.

He claimed her mouth again, crushing it against his, and silencing her words. Xavier pumped stroke after stroke, deeper and deeper, twisting his hips and rubbing her clit, plunging his fingers in a counterbeat, pounding his presence, embedding himself in her body, mind, and psyche. "Now, Isabel. Let it go. Now," he urged. He pushed her onward with every beautiful movement, over the edge, to a blissful explosion of joint ecstasy.

Hours later, while Isabel slept in his arms, a sting of warning pricked him. A discomforting sense of foreboding took over. He loved her with all his soul, had given every ounce of himself. She had released her body to him. But would she trust him? Would she cede her spirit?

Chapter Twenty-Six

Ocala – December 27th 1967

The perfect piece had been placed on the board.
Nothing could stop the chain of events...
There would be no escape now.

Marité awoke to Isabel's pained call. Startled, she threw the covers off and stood in fright. "Mamá?" she asked, as if the air around her could answer her question.

When she heard the next round of wails, she bolted out of her bedroom. A blur of pink pj's with little white stars and baby unicorns rushed through the night-darkened hallway, following the trail of her mother's exclamations, seeking to wrest her away from whichever peril besieged her.

With a mix of trepidation and relief, Marité reached the door to her mother's bedroom and wrenched the knob, expecting it to yield. It didn't. The door stood like a giant, huge and forbidding, a solid rampart between her and Mamá. She called out, kicked and pushed, pummeled with her small fists, ignoring the pain. When Marité's ear-rending barrage ended, not the tiniest sound returned to her. It was eerily quiet.

This is bad, her brain warned. She pressed her forehead against the inflexible door. What should she do? Isabel's choked complaints had stopped. However, in Marité's opinion, silence was not a confirmation of her mother's good health. She pivoted and sped down the hallway again, this time in search of her sister.

"Lita, Lita," she called, shaking her sister awake. "Wake up, wake up."

"W-what, what is it Mari?" Raquelita rolled on her side as she pushed her mussed hair away from her face.

"Mamá, she was screaming," Marité said, pulling at her hand. "I tried to open the door, but it's locked. Hurry, Mamá needs help. We've got to call Aunt Coralina." Marité released Raquelita's hand and rushed out of the room.

Raquelita bolted to her feet. "Wait, Marité, wait. Let me check on her door first, then I'll call Aunt Coralina."

***

Morning light tickled her eyelids, coaxing her brain into a state of semiconsciousness. At a snail's pace, her senses awoke. Taste was first. She ran her tongue along her teeth, feeling a disagreeable coating. Her mouth felt thick. Not good. These were signs of heavy drinking.

She rubbed her eyebrows. Recollections of the previous night were rather hazy. No, she didn't drink. She hadn't picked up a bottle since Xavi's arrival. She didn't need it. Nights had been peaceful, some beautiful. With the memory, a flicker of a smile appeared.

Wait! Thoughts and scenes started to take shape as the mists dissipated. Memories piled up, one on top of the other. She did have an episode. Now it came to her—the dream had been monstrously bad. The hands were invasive, repulsive, and hurtful. A rag had been shoved inside her mouth with harsh warnings of dire consequences if she told. Worse, last night she had seen an outline, a profile, however indistinct. The first time she had almost discerned the face of her attacker.

Isabel turned on her stomach, hoping to escape daylight. More memories surfaced. She did drink. Something had interrupted the nightmare. She'd awakened in the dark, had reached for the stash in her closet. She emptied the first bottle and half of the second before she felt sleepy again.

She rolled faceup, the first pound of a...

"Headache?"

Her lids flew open as her hand went to her forehead in an automatic gesture to ease the pain. The question startled her. No intimacy or pleasantness warmed it. Why was Xavi here, in her bedroom, sitting across from her, on this of all mornings? She looked up as her focus improved, but the Ice Man staring at her paralyzed her.

"Xavi?" she rasped out. Her throat hurt.

"Thirsty? Do you need water?"

She saw the full glass in his hand, the rumpled clothes, tired face, and disheveled hair. The unwavering chill in his tone terrified her. Her soul fled her body. Panic filled its place.

"Yes, please," she managed. Xavi approached the bed, offering the glass. Impassivity and remoteness ruled his features. He gathered the pillows strewn about the bed, piled them behind her, and propped her up so she could drink. His actions were competent and unsettling.

Isabel sought his gaze with an urgency she didn't recognize in herself. It's a marvel how the human heart and mind achieve enlightenment. It took seconds of Xavi's distance to awaken her from self-deception. The love of this man, naked and raw, unapologetic and honest, was as necessary as food. She could no longer live without his fire.

With a shaky hand, she reached for the glass he offered. He misunderstood and cocked an eyebrow. "DTs already?"

Isabel raised the other hand to assist, embarrassed and confused by the mocking tone. "Xavi, I don't understand any of this."

"Whatever." He shrugged. "Drink. The water will help. Would you like some aspirin?"

She shook her head, and the renewed hammering in her temples reminded her not to do it again. "No, thank you. I'll be all right in a few minutes."

Hands on hips, he peered at her. "Good. Why don't you get cleaned up, change, and come to the kitchen? Coralina is making breakfast for the girls. Marité had a frightful night and needs her mother." Without his customary light kiss or caress, Xavi turned and headed toward her door. "We'll talk about this later."

For long seconds, she stared at the door. Coralina was here? Marité needed her? Last night must have been bad if it brought out Coralina and Xavi. She examined her bedroom. It was a bit messy, a few clothes thrown around...then she homed in on the empty bottle on the floor. A half-full bottle stood on the nightstand, along with a glass cloudy with finger smudges. A sudden retching wave assaulted her. She gripped the sheets, hoping it would pass, but when the next surge hit, she clenched her teeth and, despite the pounding headache, stumbled toward the bathroom before she humiliated herself any further.

She finished spilling her guts, leaned against the sink, and looked in the mirror. Her disheveled appearance explained Xavi's reaction. She turned the shower on, stepped under the torrent of water, and within moments, her spirits improved. She dried off, finished dressing, glanced at the mirror, giving herself a passing grade, and walked out. Her mind was a beehive of questions. How to rekindle Xavi's fire? Would a few sincere words of apology soothe her beastie man?

Hushed sounds from the kitchen and the scent of warmed maple syrup reached her nostrils and led her in. *Nothing like a good morning meal to revive the spirits*, she thought, rather upbeat.

"Good morning," Isabel said as her youngest stood, looking ghostly pale.

"Mamá?" Marité asked coming closer. "Are you okay?"

"Of course. Why, sweetie?"

"I couldn't get to you. The door was locked. Was it the nightmare? Did the bad man hurt you? I was so scared."

Isabel saw Xavi's expression change and both eyebrows rise. For a second, the ice melted, only to slam quickly down upon his countenance. A look passed between him and Coralina, along with an unspoken question. Isabel was at a loss.

"Silly Marité. I don't know what you mean, sweetie. I am fine, darling, see?"

"But Mamá—"

"Hush, everything's fine. Did you have breakfast yet?" Isabel asked, assessing the situation. Coralina stood next to the stove. Xavi watched from the kitchen table, a mug of steaming coffee in hand. Raquelita sat next to him, her expression unreadable.

Isabel addressed Coralina. "Thank you for coming. I'm not sure what impelled Marité to act this way."

"But, Mamá—"

"Mari, I'm fine." Isabel bent over Marité's head and, with uncharacteristic affection, deposited a soft kiss on her head.

"It's no trouble at all, Isabel. The locked door frightened Marité, and she called for help."

"I must have locked it by accident." Marité quieted, and Coralina seemed to accept her excuse, but the other two people did not. Lita knew, and a little smirk appeared on her face. Xavi wasn't buying any of her acting. She would have to work a lot harder with him.

With a deep sigh, Isabel ran an arm around the girl, took a seat next to the table, and sat Marité on the chair next to hers. Isabel stroked her shoulders in a soothing up-and-down motion.

Xavi watched.

Raquelita watched too.

"Well, now that the crisis is over. May I borrow the car?" Raquelita's timing was horrid, but she didn't care. She wasn't jealous of Marité. She was angry at the injustice. She'd been the dutiful caretaker of her mother's thrashings and had never received a word of gratitude or an explanation, much less an affectionate gesture. Not a single one throughout her eighteen winters. Now her mother's secret was out, and Xavi didn't look happy. If heads were to roll, Lita was stepping away from the beheading stone.

Her mother stared, and Raquelita fidgeted. "School starts in a few days, and I need supplies. It's just for a little while. I'd ask Lorrie, but she's busy with Steven, and—"

Isabel interrupted her inane chatter. "Lita, take my car. You know where the keys are."

"Thanks, Mom." She went around, kissing everyone, and left before her mother changed her mind, or the bomb's wick burned out and the house exploded with her in it. She hopped inside her mother's black Falcon and backed out. With a swift turn, she took the access road leading to IH-75 and to the only place—apart from her father's home—where she could be herself: at Dalia's.

Raquelita knew this was the calm before a very nasty storm. She'd seen the faces in the room, all three adults avoiding the huge elephant that had appeared in the early morning hours. Well, the game was up, and *Padrino* looked pissed off. If the conversation she'd overheard between her aunt and Xavi was true—Xavi's father had been an alcoholic? Would her stubborn, obstinate mother reveal her troubles? What if she didn't? Would he leave? No, she didn't want Xavi to leave. It would send her mother into a tailspin, a spin so terrible it would drag everyone down.

***

"Come in, let's discuss this calmly," Dalia said as Lita entered her living room. "You're afraid Xavi will break up with your mom, right?"

Raquelita nodded.

"Was he angry before you left the house?"

She nodded again.

"Okay, here's my expert two-cents assessment." Dalia plopped down and the beige tufted sofa creaked under her weight. Her laughter rippled at the sound, narrowing her dark-chocolate eyes. "It's my New Year's gift to you and your family, and I hope you listen. I'll bet you anything your mom's suppressed the memory of her abuse for years, but now it surfaces through nightmares. I've seen the same in others, my friend. It happens much too often."

"Really?"

"Likely. I wish you had more information. Apparently she's picked up drinking to fight the dreams. It's her palliative, her drug of choice. The trauma is spiritual. Look, I'm not one of those new-fangled hippies, a good-vibrations kind of chick. I know reality. I live it, and I've seen what happens to people when wounds remain unhealed." Dalia's expression filled with distaste. "Abuse attacks the soul, and it's a devil to heal. It happens in the nicest families. It's ordinary and common, and it doesn't discriminate. Children are the usual prey."

Dalia regarded Raquelita, her expression ancient as she stood, then knelt before her friend, and grasped her hands.

"I don't mean to scare you, but if your momma's got that shit, it'll be a while before you guys see the light of day. Like all addicts, alcoholics manipulate, and lie like the government. Your momma's challenge and blessing is her Mr. Xavi, who apparently knows the way. He may not accept her excuses. In turn, it may save her." Dalia shook Raquelita's hands. "I'm here. If you need to get away or if it gets to be too much, come. Don't even bother to call first."

"Who are we calling, or not calling, as the case may be?" Ricky. Oily, slimy, and leaning on the doorjamb, made an impromptu appearance. "Raquelita. Darling. It's the Texas chickie, gracing us with her untainted presence."

"Listen, badass." Dalia slowly came to her feet. "If you're here to start trouble, you can march on out the same way you came in. Raquelita needs a friend. Behave."

"A million pardons, dear girl. I came to inquire about the New Year's Eve bash. After your last successful fête, many of us would love an encore." His unctuous smile glided down his face to his moustache and past his nonexistent jaw.

Dalia frowned, pressing a hand to her jean-clad, curvy hip. "It all depends on Skip."

"Skip?" Ricky and Raquelita asked in unison.

"Yes, Skippy. My old man. He arrives tomorrow."

"Now there's a New York expression for you." Ricky laughed, dropping his less than spectacular frame on one of Dalia's deep chairs as he waved a thin white cigarette like a wand. "You don't mind if I do, darling?" He placed it at the edge of his lips, lit the end, inhaled and held his breath. The acrid smoke made its way to Raquelita's nostrils. She gave an indelicate sneeze.

Dalia frowned. "I can't protect you or keep you away from these activities, Raquelita. It's out there. Everyone smokes pot these days. You might as well get used to it, unless you wish to live under a rock."

"I don't expect you to protect me, Dalia. Do I have to smoke as well?"

"Not at all. It's strictly your choice, my friend. In my house, you'll be respected. Right, Ricky?"

"*Absolutamente.* However, I'll wager you'll join our ranks soon enough, my dear, soon enough." He returned the joint to his lips.

***

Isabel waited in the company of her thoughts. If only he would come. Xavi had breathed life into her. No one had ever reached inside her the way he did. Yet she had no illusions about this meeting, it would be the last one. Distressed, disheartened, desolate. Three words to describe her abysmal emptiness, and everything she was about to become. What happened to the woman who encircled herself in self-sufficiency, isolation, and detachment?

The consequences of her silence. Would she have the courage to speak? Could she reveal everything he wanted to know? How? Some events were so mired in the past, she couldn't straighten them out anymore. She'd buried the ugliness and had done a marvelous job, until last night.

She heard a soft knock at her door. *It begins now.*

He stood at the threshold, handsome, the same man of a few nights ago, who stole her heart and soul forever. She stepped aside, and as he passed, his scent reached out to her in a diabolical wave, a torturous reminder of her upcoming renunciation. What she would no longer have, and would forever regret. Her hands clenched into tight fists.

"May I offer you something to drink?"

"No. Thank you."

She pointed at the sofa. He waited for her. When had they become so strained, so alien, so separate? Just a few nights ago, they trembled in each other's arms. In the closest of intimacies, in the pleasure of each other's thrumming bodies. Was her sin so terrible? She wanted to scream her pain to the four corners of the world.

"Xavi, I—"

"Why?"

They spoke in unison, the words bouncing off each other.

"Tell me, what makes you drink to total insensibility?"

"I've had difficulty sleeping."

"What about the effect on your daughters? Marité was terrified. She didn't know what was wrong. You'd been screaming when she called us for help."

"I...I don't know. Sometimes I have dreams, bad dreams."

"What are the dreams about?"

His expression was hopeful. Would she trust her burden to him? No, she had to deflect his questions, change the focus. "I don't remember."

Diosito. Her answer made him angry; it was all over his face. In anger, he always saw too much. Isabel lowered her gaze.

"No, no, no. I'm not doing this again. Tell me the truth. Stop hiding."

"I'm not."

"If you were any other woman, I would already have left. My father was an alcoholic, and I refuse to endure such hell again. I'm here because I love you, and I need to understand. I want to help you. What are these dreams about?" He stood abruptly and, with urgent steps, reached her. Bending over, he grasped her shoulders, almost cajoling, urging her to trust him. "Marité asked about the man who hurts you. Who hurts you? If you need help, let me, Isabel. Trust me. Haven't I proven myself to you?"

Oh, she wanted to give in. He was using the voice, the one with the power to evaporate her toxic ice. Xavi stood at the door to her stronghold, where she hid her dirtiest secrets, her stained core. And now he was pounding on it with all his strength. But how could she open the door? How did one change the habit of a lifetime overnight?

Isabel allowed shame to weigh heavier than hope, convinced he was lost to her whether she told him the truth or not. She'd rather let him think she was an incurable dependent. She'd tell him anything but her soiled truth. Thus, intractable in her resolution, she closed her arms to Xavi and happiness, and refused to answer further.

"No one hurt me. I don't remember. It was a dream, Marité exaggerated her tale."

"And the empty bottle of liquor on the floor? Was that an exaggeration too? How long have you been drinking to sleep? What would Raquelita answer if I asked her?"

Isabel shrugged with an insouciance she didn't feel. "There's nothing to tell."

"There is nothing to tell, or are you unwilling to tell?"

Distance had returned. The impending separation initiated the crack, shook her foundation, and weakened the mortar. An aching stab pierced her chest. She needed to beg him to stay. She wanted to get on her knees. Do anything he wanted, anything. And yet, in a last stubborn effort, she retorted, "What is the difference?"

"As you wish." He stood and, without a single glance, walked out the door.

She stared at the closed door for minutes, hours, seconds; she lost track of time. Something stirred in the inner reaches of her mind, a sound, a tiny voice.

He loves you, and he wants to help you. You're losing him.

It began as a small quiver and grew into an all-out tremor. The finality of the thought barged in forcefully. *You fool, he's leaving.* And Isabel took flight. Mindless, she ran out of the house, down the long driveway, past the fields to the ranch house. Could she be in time to stop his departure? She swung the door open. Xavi and Jonas were engaged in a heated discussion. Xavier had a rictus across his face. Jonas scowled. Coralina clasped her hands together.

"Are you sure?" Coralina asked.

"It's the only way. I've no other choice."

Xavi picked up his large bag and turned to the door. A twitch of surprise flashed when he saw Isabel blocking his exit.

"Xavi, I…" She paced toward him, hands outstretched. All the wonderful words she was going to say disappeared. Panic disabled her brain, and she couldn't think past his departure. Forever. This time he would leave forever.

He stood, implacable and unmoved, his brow knit together. "Yes?"

"Please."

"Please, what?" He advanced until he stood in front of her. "For the love of God, Isabel, talk to me."

Here it was, her chance when she would tell him everything. Spew all of it, the years of darkness, of torturing dreams, of half-remembered thoughts, of deep pain. Out of nowhere, the spectral hand pressed her lips, and the nightmare came alive. She froze.

"I c-can't."

He made a move to go past her. Pain stabbed her chest and doubled her over. Isabel hunched and embraced him at the waist, burying her face against his torso. "I can't, I can't." The scared, abused little girl of yore pleaded for an empathy that would not arrive.

Blinded by disappointment, Xavier failed to see the frightened child. Instead, he lifted her hand and kissed the palm. "I've got to go." He unwrapped her arms from around his waist. "I'll call as soon as I arrive." He spoke to Coralina, then walked out behind Jonas.

***

The two men drove in silence. Clutching the steering wheel, Jonas shot occasional glances at his friend. Xavi stared out the front window, a man of stone. Only a sporadic twitch, a flare in his nostrils, a quick contraction of muscles, indicated life.

Jonas's mind felt like a revolving door. Thoughts and memories flashed in and out of his brain, dropped off their contribution, and sped quickly out. How many years of friendship had they shared? Twenty? Twenty-five? Longer?

Jonas knew about the Repulleses' battle with alcohol. The years of hardship as Xavi's father fell off the wagon repeatedly, the toll it had taken on Maura, and the end... After several frustrating attempts, Jordi conquered his addiction only to discover his liver had given out. It was no accident Xavi had turned out to be such a controlling hard-ass. He had powerful reasons.

Jonas also knew Xavi's life-long obsession with Isabel. When he saw them together, he was thrilled. He'd never seen his friend happier. And now this... The trip Xavi was about to embark on made sense. Jonas would move heaven and earth, he would seek the pope or resurrect a dead relative for Coralina, but he wouldn't have left her in a state of such grief and confusion.

"Jonas, you don't have to speak. Your thoughts are killing me."

"I've never doubted or questioned any of your decisions. You've always been judicious and wise. But tonight—"

"What kind of monster would leave the woman he claims to love in such a terrible state?"

"Well, to some you may be a monster, but I know you better than most. I prefer son of a bitch instead." Jonas's laughter vibrated inside the car, easing some of the tension. "In answer to your question, yes, I do wonder. Why?"

"I know this looks bad. I can't explain how much this hurt, but I had to leave while frustration strengthened my resolve. Tomorrow might've been different. I was a step away from stumbling inside the trap with her. It was the overwhelming desire to stay, to comfort and dry her tears that scared me to death. I saw my mother's face. For years, I couldn't understand her devotion to my father. Tonight I did, because it's what I feel for Isabel. I also know more than my mother did years ago. Isabel is an addict. I can't be weak for her sake. If I relent, we're both doomed. Hell, we're all doomed, the daughters included."

Xavi turned to the window again. "I know she loves me. But instead of trusting me with her secrets, she let me go. Alcohol magnifies her confusion and shame. I can't wrestle against shadows at sunset. I need light. I need to know what I'm fighting. Isabel won't truly be mine unless she's healed. Anything else is a pretense."

"Doña Alicia is in for a heck of a ride, isn't she?"

"If I have to hold the woman by the toes until she speaks, I will. I'm not leaving Spain without learning every detail Isabel is so ashamed about. She will be my wife. I want her right next to me, happy and healed, without fucking nightmares or alcohol."

"Well, you're cursing. You must mean business. When are you going?"

"As soon as I buy the tickets, in a day or two."

Chapter Twenty-Seven

Ocala – December 31st 1967

Raquelita couldn't believe it, 4:00 p.m. and Rosie's was a ghost town. Everyone was either home watching the football game between Dallas and Green Bay or making preparations for a New Year's Eve celebration. She had volunteered to pick up shifts for Dalia and Linda, knowing they had their own preparations to make. She glanced down at the table. *Some people should not eat in public.* She pointed the bottle of ammonia like a six-shooter, pumped several sprays, and wiped the greasy tabletop. If she could only do the same with Ricky's ominous words.

"You'll join our ranks soon enough, my dear, soon enough."

He'd managed to scare her, as if her fortunes were set. A destiny he'd seen and she couldn't evade; a destiny she didn't want.

She'd seen his lifestyle, and on both occasions, she'd felt uncomfortable and out of place. The behavior of Ricky and his friends had turned weird. Often she couldn't follow their conversation or thought processes. Drugs transported them to a world apart, and she'd been left behind.

She could *almost* understand why folks like her mother—beleaguered by spiritual wounds—would seek oblivion. She'd witnessed the devastating nightmares, and the need to escape made sense, in some skewed way. But drug use for fun was a different animal. She'd seen the ritual—cop, roll, light up, smoke—to indulge in a taboo pleasure. It was the old biblical theme. Forbidden fruit always tasted sweeter. It was not a good equation.

Her thoughts took a sharp left turn. *How could you leave, Padrino?* Fine, so now he knew her mother was drinking, but Isabel needed help, not anger. None of it made sense. Xavi loved her mother, and he was not a quitter, so why? Where had he gone? In a few hours, her mother had deteriorated, and it gave Lita the willies. Yes, she could definitely kill him.

"Raquelita."

She looked up. Meg waved at the spray bottle.

"Raquelita, you're done. I'll lock up. Lorrie called. She wants you to stop by the ranch on your way home."

"Sure, Meg." She gave the empty room another glance. "I don't think we can squeeze another customer into this place today. Thanks for the message."

Not one for many words, Meg took both towel and bottle of cleanser away from her hands and pointed to the door. "Happy New Year, Raquelita."

***

"Hi, coz. You left a message with Meg," Raquelita said as she entered Lorrie's bedroom.

"Look what I have here," Lorrie exclaimed in response. A crumpled envelope danced between her fingers.

"How? There's no mail delivery on Sunday."

"It got mixed up with other correspondence. Dad found it after you'd left for Rosie's."

Raquelita opened the stained envelope and scanned it quickly. Forgetting her previous moodiness, she imbibed the lines like a thirsty woman in the desert.

Dec 24th 1967

> *My darling angel,*
>
> *Merry Christmas, sweetheart! Tonight, I'll celebrate Christmas holding you in my heart. You're the light guiding my step, the energy behind my actions. If you think of nothing else, remember this: my love for you will last forever. Until this struggle is over, we'll have to exist in our own universe, where time does not follow the rhythm of the world. I have adopted a new rule: the holidays arrive with your letters. You are my Christmas, New Years, and Fourth of July.*
>
> *We've been so busy, the schedule is hard and hectic. Our efforts to XXXXXX and XXXXXXXX are nonstop. By the time our shifts are over, we have just enough energy to drop in our bunks, much less hold a pen. That's when I remember you need to hear from me; same as I need to read your words and I regain new energy. I wish I*

could give you more details about XXXXXXXX, but I know they will block them out. I won't waste my time or energy...

She stopped reading and pressed the sheet of paper against her chest. *No, no, my love. Don't apologize. I love you too.* She wished she could tell him, hold him, reassure him. He was her sanity and her drug of life, mightier than anything offered in Ricky's world. His precious words conjured real magic. They had the power to dissipate the gloomiest thoughts.

She looked at her cousin. "Thank you, Lorrie. You've no idea how much I needed his letter, today of all days."

"I can only imagine, coz. I am sure it'll help start the year on a good note. Go home and enjoy it. Don't forget, tonight it's the family's yearly countdown. Try to convince your mom to come. It might be good for her." Lorrie looked at her with compassion. Compassion and commiseration, the pathetic looks everyone offered ever since Xavi left.

"I'll do my best." She whirled on her heels and bounced out the door. Why had she not noticed the gorgeous evening? The sky was a limpid darkening blue. The temperature was perfect. She felt all knowing and all-powerful. She might even convince her mother to come out and greet the New Year. Matthew's words coursed through her heart and soul, and she was whole again.

***

The aircraft touched down on Spanish soil, and damn if it didn't feel odd. Xavi had vowed he'd never return unless it was absolutely necessary. Well, he had come, and, yes, the need was extreme. His future and Isabel's depended on his discoveries.

His plans to depart immediately had been stymied, and Xavi was starting to think some force was throwing obstacles his way. Ferguson had scheduled a huge delivery for the first of the year, and even though Emilio could handle the colts, the boss man had *hoped* Xavi would assist. Skirting Emilio's curiosity had been an acrobatic act. Xavi had concocted a convoluted story about Jonas, a Spanish breeder, and Xavi's much-needed personal involvement. Finally, ten days behind schedule, he'd flown out, when he should've been on his way back to the States.

Despite his citizen status, a stern face and an intrusive Q&A session greeted him at passport control. Gathering patience, Xavi focused on his goal and answered all the indiscreet questions. A qualified *bienvenido* and a loud stamp on his passport released him to collect his luggage. The customs officer dismissed him toward the sliding glass doors.

The hall outside customs was packed. Over the throngs of greeters and past the panoramic glass windows, he could see the hustling pickup and drop-off traffic at Barajas, the gateway to Madrid. Xavier breathed in a mix of cigarette smoke and a familiar scent, *café con leche,* espresso coffee and hot milk, riveted every synapse in his brain. Strange how some aromas are ingrained in the soul. He remembered it from his youth. It wafted out of homes and corner bars. An aching pang stabbed his soul, a unique feeling, a melancholy, and a longing. Maybe after all this nasty business was settled, he would bring Isabel for a visit. Later, he mused, he would examine his surprising feelings. Now he had four more hurdles to clear: rush over to the domestic terminal, catch the flight to Sevilla, meet up with Alejandro, and drive south.

***

In the grand Muro estate, a grandfather clock marked 1:00 a.m. with a sonorous *dong*. The sound reverberated through empty hallways and reached Xavi's bedroom. It didn't matter. He was wide awake. With arms crossed behind his head, he stared up at the ceiling. His mind swam with scenes of the evening and the purpose of his visit.

Earlier in the day, the Muro-Chavez and Romero clans received him as one of their own, a cherished son rather than a close acquaintance. The night had been spent in conversation. Nieves, always the perfect hostess, had prepared and served a sumptuous dinner with the typical dishes Xavi might have yearned for. Most significant had been the relatives' need to hear about the next generation, the American children none had met, their heritage, and the continuation of the bloodline. In that moment, Xavi renewed his vow. Somehow he would bring them all together soon. He returned to the purpose of this visit. His love wasn't frivolous. He cherished a small group of people. In that select group, two suffered the same affliction, one in the past, another in the present. He'd lost the first; he never had the power to save him. He would die before the same happened to Isabel.

***

Xavi entered the living room, and Nieves almost jumped out of her chair. Just yesterday she had admired his handsome, still youthful appearance. Life in the States agreed with him. A few silver threads sparkled in his dark blond hair, adding to his allure. His expression had mellowed. But he'd returned from this meeting a man plagued, a deep line carved his forehead. She recalled her visit and shivered.

"What in the world... Xavi?"

He flopped on the large sofa, lifted a trembling hand, threaded his hair back, and let it fall again. Nieves sat next to him, time passed, and he didn't move nor speak. Enrique arrived, sending a questioning look to his wife as he sat in his favorite wing chair. They both waited.

Xavi slapped the cushion and, shoving hard, sat straight up. "I don't even know where to begin."

"My dear, take your time," Nieves said. "Let me bring you something to drink. Would you like water, juice, perhaps some wine?"

"If it's not too much trouble, I'd love a glass of water. Thank you."

The august lady nodded and quickly left for the kitchen. Xavi and Enrique stared at each other. "I'll wait for Nieves to return. I don't think I can tell the story twice."

Enrique nodded. "If it involves Alicia, it'll be complicated"

Nieves returned holding a large bottle of carbonated water and three glasses. She passed the glasses around, filled them quickly, and reclaimed her seat as Xavi began to speak.

"Doña Alicia acted as if she'd been expecting a visit, from Emilio, I presumed. Although she was surprised to see me, she didn't hesitate. She conversed with ease, as if we'd seen each other yesterday. I didn't have to wrestle her for the information. She almost seemed relieved. What she revealed went further back and uncovered more hardship than I ever imagined. Everything people gossiped about... It's not true."

Xavi sipped again and continued. Word by painful word, he took the Muros back in time. To the happy wedding, the joyous birth, and Seve's tragic loss. He spoke of the lean years during and after the war, the struggle of a young widow with a child. He related the hopeful arrival of her brother and his comrade. And the worst, the unthinkable betrayal against her baby had come from her own kin. Xavi trembled, remembering the words.

"Please don't be mad, Mamá. It's my fault."

His initial reaction had been visceral and violent. He wanted to scream or break something. He envisioned the terrible scene and despaired.

"Alicia was trapped, you see. Iñigo returned a war hero with the Nationalist forces. Severino had sympathized with the Republican side. In those turbulent years, she had to walk a thin line."

"So, what happened?" Nieves asked, visibly disturbed. "How did she manage? I can't help but feel guilty. My family remained intact. We had each other; she was alone."

"She didn't finish the story. We were both exhausted. We agreed to meet tomorrow. She hinted at some resolution but didn't explain. If she told me she'd burnt the man alive, I would approve." Xavi flopped against the sofa. "She's given me the help I need. If it's all right with you both, I'd like to call Ocala. I need to speak with Coralina right away."

"Of course, my dear. This is your home. Do as you must."

Nieves watched him go and turned to her husband. "The town shunned Alicia and her daughter when they needed help the most. We were part of the town. I am full of shame."

***

Xavi returned to his room with a fresh sense of urgency. He had to conclude his business in Jerez, speak to Alicia, get the last details, then go. Coralina's report was worrisome.

She looks sickly. She's lost weight. Lita says she stopped drinking on her own. But without it, she gets the nightmares. It's a crazy cycle. Xavi, she needs you. When are you coming back?

Damn it all to hell. A bad feeling twisted Xavi's stomach. He could call Isabel, but he wasn't ready to speak to her just yet.

Indeed something was brewing.
A maelstrom of gigantic proportions was poised
to swallow everyone and everything within its reach.

Chapter Twenty-Eight

Ocala – January 11th 1968

Isabel stared out the huge window. As evening approached, an array of dusky shades—fuchsia, deep cobalt, and violet—colored the world, muting lawns and landscapes. Darkness would soon rule. She pressed a trembling hand on the breakfast nook table and stood shakily, her heartbeat accelerating with the effort. She felt ancient. With tentative steps, she reached the window and pressed her forehead on the cool glass. Maybe she should listen to Coralina and seek professional help.

Her stubbornness had compelled her to quit alcohol on her own. After Xavi stormed out, she hadn't picked up a bottle, but she hadn't been able to sleep either. As soon as her lids closed, the nightmare slid in, and she would wake up again. She hadn't considered the symptoms of alcohol withdrawal, the sleepless hours, and the exhausting bouts of retching. Lack of appetite sapped what little energy she had left. Isabel had become a prisoner of the waking horror.

Xavier. His name popped in her mind, and pain slammed into her solar plexus. She bent over, forcing a few breaths out, letting the pain pass unimpeded. She'd learned not to stiffen when his image appeared. The trick helped her cope.

Could she blame him for leaving? She'd given him no option. He had asked her to explain, almost pleaded with her, but she would rather he left before he learned the extent of her shame. If he looked disappointed when he found her drunk, the truth would have blasted him. *Truth,* an interesting concept. Everyone demanded it, but no one really accepted it.

So she let him go. And when Xavi walked, what little happiness she had regained in his company flew away—like a tiny, scared bird—right alongside him. Nothing remained except her duty to Raquelita and Marité. Where were they? Yes, dinner at the Reynoldses. Distancing themselves, especially Raquelita.

God, Raquelita was lost to her. It had begun on the ride to Ocala, when she'd met that soldier, and degenerated during her trip to Texas. In that visit Isabel had discovered not only Lita's lies but also everyone's perfidy, including the plot to cover up the correspondence between her daughter and that country boy.

Just like that, it slipped in, without effort, collateral damage of her explosive thoughts. For a second, Isabel coaxed herself, *stay in the kitchen, far from Lita's room*. But an insistent ghostly hand reached out to her and pulled lightly at her robe. Isabel followed as it guided her toward her daughter's bedroom.

Did she really see spectral hands guiding her way? Hear voices? Could she blame alcohol? Sure, alcohol withdrawal provoked visions, minimized good judgment and maximized depression. But would she have the courage to be honest? Admit to a sliver of irrational jealousy, a need to destroy her daughter's fragile happiness?

She headed straight for the box. Sat on the bed, picked up the first envelope, and read.

> *That's when I remember you need to hear from me; same as I need to read your words and I regain new energy. I wish...*

"Ha! So sweet, so sincere. Liar. All men are liars."

She spit at the vision in the room, or was it the man in her brain? Somewhere between picking up the envelope and reading the letter, Isabel made a tragic transfer. Matthew became Xavi. Anger escalated and wiped reason, fully committed, she held envelope and letter, and ripped them both to tiny pieces.

"Liar." She stared as the pieces fell slowly to the floor. "I can see through you. I will teach you to con my daughter."

The next letter suffered the same fate. On and on she went, rending and ripping, yelling at the imaginary man in her mind. Not yet satisfied, she stripped the wrappings and tore the box, as huge, angry teardrops ran down her face. She stepped on the pile until it became a pulpy mass on the floor.

"Why, why, why?" she asked the image in her mind. She slumped on the corner of the bed and slowly slid to the floor, ending amid the mess she'd created. "Why did you leave me?" She slapped the floor. "You promised." She slapped again. "You promised."

When no one answered, Isabel jumped up and ran out of her daughter's bedroom leaving behind a small mound of woe. A sad trail of tiny pieces of paper marked her path of fury. In each one, the fragment of a loving word valiantly hung on.

Out of control, Isabel reached her bedroom. One last bottle remained. She pulled it out and proceeded to drink every last drop. Damn Xavi, damn her mother, damn all of them.

Tonight she would sleep.

***

Raquelita opened the door to dead silence. Mindful of the bowl of leftover *fabada* in her hands, she stepped back. Something was wrong. A light breeze blew on her face, and she had an eerie vision, Xavi, next to the Christmas tree, staring at her. She almost dropped the bowl. *What, Padrino?* Her skin rose in goose bumps as sudden panic overwhelmed her, tears welled up in her eyes.

"Lita…?" Her sister could sense it too. The hideous odor of violence permeated the home.

"Shhh…. Stay right here, and leave the door open. I'll take a look." She walked through the foyer and past the living room, entered the kitchen, switched on a light, placed the bowl on the table, and took a deep breath. Goodness, she needed to relax. She had been so jumpy lately.

"Everything's fine. We got spooked for nothing. Come in, sweetie. I think Mom's sleeping. Maybe tonight she finally conked out or, well…you know." Yes, everyone knew.

Marité met up with her midway toward the hallway, and she turned on the sconces. The soft light washed the passage. Her mother's door was closed, not a good sign. She looked at the scattered white pieces on the hallway floor and pressed her lips together. Something niggled at her.

"Are you tired?" She slipped an arm around her sister, heading to the kitchen. "Do you want something to drink?" She looked back. Something about… She opened the refrigerator door and placed the bowl inside. "What about some milk, or juice maybe?" It hit her then.

She fled to the hallway, to the torn pieces. Had Isabel read her journals? She stopped, picked one up, held it to the light, and the world spun. "No." An inhuman sound ripped out of her and took her heart along with it. "No, no, no."

Marité's arms held her from behind, tight around the waist. "Lita, please, what's wrong? You're scaring me."

She bent to the floor, picking up the cherished remains, the treasured scraps treated with less respect than trash. She didn't have to see her bedroom to know the debacle. She knew Matthew's handwriting. In a malicious act, his loving words had been ripped to shreds. She stiffened, turned around, and extended her open palm.

"What is it?" Marité squinted.

"The remains of Matthew's letter."

"No."

"Yes...well." Exhaling a fortifying breath, Lita entered her bedroom.

There it was, next to her bed. The calamitous pile, her link to Matthew, to love, sanity, and fortitude, destroyed. All but one had escaped, his last letter in her purse. She winced at the box, the shiny paper, and the matching ribbon, everything she'd picked out with so much love, ruined.

"Because you hurt, you must hurt me. Because you never knew love, you must destroy mine. We end here, you and I. No more, no more."

She then remembered Marité. At the edge of tears, Lita reached for her sister and sat her on the bed while she collected her hidden journals, gathered any remaining pieces from the floor, and placed them with great care inside a plastic box. She found a surviving length of ribbon and tied it around the box. She pulled a shoulder bag from the closet, picked out a few items of clothing, and packed everything inside.

"These can't remain here. Come. It's time for bed," she said, pointing to the hallway.

"Lita?"

"I'm fine, honey. Let's get you into your pj's. You need sleep." She had to stay cool. Little sisters frightened so easily.

From the small dresser, she dug out a set of bright yellow pj's, very much like her sister's sunny disposition. "Brush your teeth, darling." She directed her as she would her own child during her evening ablutions. Marité jumped into bed, and Raquelita sat next to her, caressing her hair and forehead, soothing her to sleep, waiting until her breath slowed.

A few more minutes of acting, and then she could fall apart. When Marité breathed her first raspy snore, Raquelita kissed her sister's forehead and left the bedroom. She passed her mother's door and gave it a cursory look. *The bitch is drunk again.* Despite the commotion, Isabel hadn't awakened. Raquelita returned to her bedroom, picked up her bag, and left the house. She stepped outside and ran, focusing on the sound of her boots pounding the gravel road and nothing else…nothing else…least of all the memory of her torn letters.

It didn't take long to reach her cousin's bedroom window. She tapped the glass, and a sleepy Lorrie—her light brown hair tousled every which way—peeked out, saw her, and flung the panel open.

"Raquelita, what the heck? Do you—"

"Yes. I know it's late. I wouldn't be here if I didn't need help."

"What can I do?"

"That's what I love about you—straight to the point. I need a ride to Dalia's."

"Are you crazy?"

"Shhh—you're going to wake up your parents. Come on, I'll explain on the way."

"Dalia's? Gee, I don't know. Why don't you stay with me?"

"It's too close to my mother. I don't want her to know where I am either. Please, I need the favor. Just drop me off, and you'll be back before your warm bed cools."

Lorrie tried to read her expression. Lita waited in silence. Finally Lorrie nodded. "Okay, I'll get dressed, and you'll tell me everything. Otherwise, I'll blow the whistle on you."

"No problem. I'll answer all your questions and more."

"I hope I'm doing the right thing. I wish you'd stay here."

Raquelita didn't speak, but her expression must've been enough. Lorrie stopped arguing and ducked back in to get dressed. As she waited, Raquelita pressed her forehead against the side of the house, the rough stucco abraded her skin, but she pressed harder. This pain was preferable to the one squeezing her heart.

***

"I'm so sorry. It's late, I know. You told me I could come."

"It's cool." Dalia smiled and turned to Skippy.

"Baby, go back to bed. Us girls need to talk for a little while."

The imposing man who answered to Skippy grunted, touched Dalia's hair, and pivoted away. Tall and sinewy, he didn't have an ounce of superfluous fat. His skin color was slightly darker than Dalia's lovely café au lait. The shaved head accentuated dark-as-coal, wide-set eyes and pronounced cheekbones. The tiny hoop on his earlobe might look effeminate on a different man. Not on Skippy. He could take a woman's breath away.

"Does he mind I'm here?"

"No, sweetie, he's a teddy bear. He's cranky now 'cause he's sleepy. Tomorrow you'll get to know him better. Now, tell me, what happened?"

Raquelita pulled out the box with its precious contents. The first words came out slowly. The rest picked up speed. In the comfort of Dalia's home, Raquelita accepted the shock, dismay, and anger she had suppressed for Marité's sake.

"You'll stay in the guest bedroom. Tomorrow we'll talk, after we get some rest. Come, follow me."

She followed Dalia into a pleasant-looking guest room. While she sorted out her things, Dalia returned with a set of towels.

"Do you wish to shower now?" she asked. Lita shook her head. "Do you think you can sleep? Do you need help?"

"What do you mean, help?"

"I've got some sleeping pills. They're harmless. You could do a half."

Raquelita was about to say no and then rethought the idea. "If they're harmless, I'll take a half, but only a half."

"Of course. I'll be right back."

"You will join our ranks soon enough, my dear, soon enough."

No, this was temporary. She was not committing to any change in life. She was here to escape, seek clarity, and grieve the loss of Matthew's letters. The letters she'd planned to reread as time went by, now all of them gone.

Dalia returned with a glass of water and a halved yellow capsule, and Raquelita pushed her troublesome thoughts away. It couldn't hurt much, could it? She swallowed it in one gulp.

"You're gonna sleep like a rock."

"Thanks."

Raquelita dressed for bed, started to turn the bed down and a pleasant drowsiness took over. She climbed into bed and enjoyed the slow descent. Her muscles eased, same as her mind. Oh yes, she'd sleep tonight. She might even forget her troubles for a little while, and thought no more.

Chapter Twenty-Nine

Ocala – January 12th 1968

Raquelita awoke in a shadowy, unfamiliar room. Where was this place? The black mass ruling her cognitive processes didn't loosen its hold. She scrunched her lids, urging her still-slumbering mind to work. How did she get here? The response was a cautionary stab at her temples. Ignoring it, Raquelita gritted her teeth and tried again. At last her mind acquiesced.

As you wish.

She was hurled into a roiling torrent. Thoughts, memories, words, and feelings ripped at her from every angle like hungry wolves, rending and shredding her skin. Her hands rose in defense. Wildly, she brushed—arms, torso, legs—fending off the feeding frenzy.

She jumped to her feet. A rush of sparks blinded her, and she pressed her hands to her face. As the starbursts slowly dispersed, light overcame the dark, and Dalia's guest room came into focus. Chaos was still present, however, so she replayed everything her mother had taken from her last night. In her usual style, Isabel had destroyed something very precious without a single regard.

Since early childhood, Raquelita had wished for a nurturing, supportive mother. Instead she'd lived with a woman who answered to the name of Mother but didn't know how to be one. Last night, Isabel had proved it, and Raquelita had finally accepted the futility and end of her old wish.

***

"Here, cold orange juice. Nothing better first thing in the morning." Dalia held up a glass full of golden liquid. "Go sit at the counter, coffee is on the way. Sleep okay?"

"Yep, I don't even remember dreaming. What did you give me?"

"Half a Nembutal. Did the job, yes? They're wonderful. Morning hangover is mild and short."

"A hangover? Isn't that with alcohol?"

"It used to be. It has since crossed over to other stuff."

"I see," Raquelita said. "I was a little disoriented when I woke up."

"Soon enough, my dear, soon enough."

Indeed, in her need to forget, she had accepted the pills without a second thought. It had been so easy, so like her mother.

"That's normal," Dalia said. "Have some coffee. Caffeine will take care of you, baby." She smiled and offered a steaming mug. "All right, let's get into it. Hit me with the sordid details," she said, peering above her mug.

It felt worse in daylight. Matthew's letters were really gone; only one remained. This was a happy thought, a gleam of silver to line her dark clouds. Matthew would write again, and until then, she would read and reread the one she had. In the future, she would keep her letters far, far away from her mother.

***

The headache threatened to kill Isabel. The nausea assured it. After almost two weeks on dry land, she'd consumed a full bottle, and her body wasn't nice about it. Anger exploded when she discovered Lita's absence. In her fury, she'd tried to awaken Marité.

"She's not home?" the girl murmured and rolled back on her belly, fast asleep.

Where are the damned letters? Isabel had wanted to make a point, but she had nothing to make a point with. Her intention to assert her authority had been stymied. Didn't matter; there'd be no more correspondence between Lita and that boy.

***

"Where are you hiding her?" Isabel's irate question snapped Coralina's attention and the peace in the kitchen, her head popped up from behind her newspaper. "Excuse me?"

Hands on hips, Isabel's eyes shifted furiously from Coralina to Lorrie next to her.

"My daughter, Raquelita. Where are you keeping her?"

"Keeping her? I'm sure I've no idea. And I don't appreciate the accusation," Coralina volleyed back.

"Guess what? I appreciate even less your meddling in my family affairs. Let's see if we can respect our territories. And your sneaky daughter knows something."

"Why don't you sit? We can figure this thing out together." Evidently, Isabel had lost her mind. Coralina motioned to the empty chair next to hers. "Lita's missing?"

"Yes, her bed wasn't slept in. She's not at Rosie's either. I called." Isabel plopped down. "I know Lorrie knows something."

"Lorrie?"

"Yes, Mom?"

"What do you know about this?"

"Nothing, Mom. I'm as confused as you are."

Coralina's mouth slackened. The lie had slinked through Lorrie's perfect teeth. Later she would extract every ounce of truth. For now, she turned to Isabel, deflecting further attention from Lorrie. "Why don't you explain from the beginning, Isabel?"

A simple notion in Isabel's afflicted mind had mushroomed to disaster. Coralina gasped when Isabel finished with a smirk. The woman was proud of her actions. Well, if she expected remorse or shame from any of the Reynoldses for their part in the so-called conspiracy, she'd be disappointed.

"You did what? Do you realize Matthew may never return?"

"I don't want my daughter involved with a damned soldier. And that's not the point." Pushing her hands on the table, Isabel met Coralina's challenging stare. "Raquelita lied to me. You all lied to me. She's a minor and has to obey me. And I say: No. More. Letters."

"You crazy woman, you've destroyed your daughter's sole consolation. You don't know the meaning of compassion."

"Ladies." Jonas appeared out of nowhere. "I can hear you from the last paddock. Now, will someone—"

Coralina started to speak, and Isabel jumped right in.

"Stop, you two," Jonas said and turned to Lorrie. "Daughter, do you know where Raquelita is right now?"

"No, Dad. I've no clue where she is."

Jonas turned to Isabel. "Apparently, you feel betrayed. I will remind you, you're *not* the only parent. If you object to the letters, take it up with Emilio. You've questioned our integrity, and I will not abide such disrespect."

Isabel opened and closed her lips in quick succession. If Emilio had given permission, she had little to stand on.

"Raquelita will not receive any more letters."

"Done. No future letters. Now it's my turn. In this family, we discuss matters civilly. We do not yell like banshees. You should decide if you wish to remain under those conditions. I know you're going through difficult times, and you have my support and friendship. If you stay, you will respect our ways. Understood?"

"Perfectly. I'll respect your rules, so long as you honor mine. I need to address matters with Emilio." Without another word, Isabel turned on her heel and exited the house.

The front door clicked, and Jonas peeked into the hallway ensuring she'd departed. Satisfied, he closed the distance to Lorrie, grasped her upper arm, and pulled her to her feet.

"Lorrie, go get Raquelita."

"But Dad, I'm not sure where she is."

"Don't play games with me. I'm in no mood. You will find her, and if you run into difficulties, call me."

"Yes, Dad." Lorrie took off in an instant.

"Jonas, what are we going to do?"

"We'll proceed as one of Raquelita's parents demanded. She'll no longer receive Matthew's letters." Jonas winked. "I will. It's all about semantics, *Muñeca*. Matthew and Lita are good together, and I mean to help. Besides, Xavi is due back any day, and when he returns, Isabel will forget the letters. What a shame. Raquelita must be brokenhearted."

"Lita has to be devastated and furious. This breach may be irreparable." Coralina sighed. "Xavi needs to return soon."

***

Xavi relaxed against the counter, despite the tension or the fact that his gut kept screaming: *go home…go home*. For two critical days, the elusive widow had given him the slip, so he took up this sentinel position at the coffee bar across the street. Today, she wouldn't escape.

The picture was not complete, and he wasn't leaving with half an image. Not after he dared his rival on the first day. Xavi had felt an eerie chill with Iñigo's photograph in Alicia's living room. The monster glared as if he knew Xavi's purpose. Two warriors, engaged in mystic combat for the same woman, one in this plane, the other beyond the grave. *You are right, old man, I'm setting her free,* Xavi had challenged.

A slight movement on the wrought iron gate caught his attention, and he smiled. The little woman had opened the gate just enough to slip out. Oh, she was crafty, departing early in the morning, before most men awoke after the usual late night, and returning after tapas when dinner was well underway. She'd also forgotten that after twenty years, Xavi no longer followed those habits.

In a few powerful strides, Xavi reached the widow. "Good morning, dear lady. You've kept me waiting." Gently, he detained doña Alicia by the forearm.

"I have. I see you are a man of serious intent."

"My intent is that you keep your promise. Where should we go? Your home, a café…"

"It's a beautiful day. Let's speak the truth in daylight. There's been enough darkness in our lives, Isabel's and mine. Should we head toward Plaza de la Asunción? You could buy me lunch."

"It'll be my pleasure." He offered his arm for support. The plaza wasn't close, but she seemed to be up for the walk and ready to talk.

"Not one of my proudest moments," she stated without preamble and an air of defiance. "I had to act. The circumstances forced me to seek help where I could."

Xavi nodded. He was a little older than Isabel and had vague memories of the Civil War. Life had been difficult. His heart went out to this woman, widowed and alone, forced to act against her moral grain in order to protect her child. He folded her hand on his forearm and patted it gently. Alicia smiled in appreciation.

***

Alicia Saenz de Llorenz needed an ally. She had no other way out of her dilemma. Alone, she could keep Iñigo away from her baby for a short while. Soon he would force her to admit she knew of his hideous deed and propel a confrontation that could wrest her child away. Alicia had sworn Iñigo would never touch Isabelita again. If she couldn't stop him, she'd take care of her child and then herself. Simple.

The opportunity appeared when the antiquated electrical system at the bar malfunctioned and Alvaro came home early. While Alicia offered him supper, she captured his admiring glance. Thus far she had played dumb. In turn, he allowed her evasion. It was an unspoken agreement to dance around each other and avoid his loss of face.

On this night, Alicia took her first step toward her daughter's salvation and returned the look. His deep blue irises offered warmth and affection. She'd never noticed their color. Their game didn't allow it. Tonight she saw the kind smile and the intelligent gaze that read through her soul and her pretense. He understood her devotion and knew she could love only one man in life. Because he loved her, he'd accept anything she offered freely.

In her next spiritual conversation with Seve, she explained the need to protect their child. Alvaro could save them. Nothing else would compel her to betray her vows or his memory. Moments later, a strange sense of comfort washed over her, and she knew Seve approved. Alicia plunged into a full relationship with Alvaro. Routines changed. Alicia walked Isabelita to and from school. Instead of going home, mother and daughter would head for Alvaro's bar. At the end of his shift, they'd all go home together. As a result, her daughter's demeanor brightened with renewed vitality, justifying Alicia's choices. But the strain on her brother was obvious. The lines on his face deepened. An explosion seemed imminent. Alicia's concerns escalated.

Iñigo had to die. While the notion brought horror to her soul, they couldn't live with a viper in the home. Iñigo had assumed that role. How did one go about disposing of a life and still remain sane? It wasn't a question of *how* specifically—she knew enough about poisons to kill a man in seconds—it was a question of morals, scruples. In the wild, she could protect her young by any means without condemnation. The cold analysis challenged her values, and the struggle kept her awake for hours. Then she'd look at her daughter, slowly returning to the world of the living, and Alicia's hesitations dissolved.

Isabelita had a right to live, to thrive in this world and one day have a family of her own. Whatever revulsion Alicia harbored against fratricide, she pushed it away. It would be a simple exchange, a deviant for an innocent—a good trade. For the sake of her daughter, Alicia would accept the mark of capital sin on her soul.

One evening, a desperate Iñigo hurled inquiries about Alicia's absences and whereabouts. He questioned her habits, her closeness with Alvaro. Alicia retorted it was none of his concern, and he was pushed beyond his limits. He accused her of wantonness, and his fist connected squarely with her face. The swollen eye and massive bruise left a vivid testament, infuriating Alvaro beyond measure. While he tended her injury, a wordless Alicia waited for his anger and promises of retribution to subside. Then she spoke the truth.

"He's abused Isabelita."

"What are you saying? Are you out of your mind?"

But Alicia's soft words and steady demeanor were more telling than any crazed accusation.

"*Santo cielo*, how could he? Isabel is only a child. He would have to be sick."

"Yes, he has. And yes, he is."

Alicia's calm shook him to the core. Alvaro and Iñigo had joined the Requetés to fight for a common cause, to defend the church and the true faith, for God, Spain, and decency. They fought the Republicans for their supposed atheism. And now, his ex-partner was a child molester? The knowledge crushed Alvaro's beliefs to a pulp.

"Alicia?" What he found in her face dismayed him, yet he accepted it. "All right, we'll do something about it."

Perhaps it was for services to be rendered, or the need to seek comfort in stressful times, or possibly to offer a measure of tenderness. Alicia went to Alvaro's bed that night. Leaving Isabel safely locked in her bedroom, she stole away to offer the fulfillment he sought and deserved. In turn, he gave her every bit of love in his soul.

Generous and unselfish, he surprised her—it wasn't the passion she'd shared with Seve—Alvaro's tenderness won her over. Alicia unfolded her heart, and they loved each other into the morning hours. She decided then, she'd be Alvaro's woman for as long as fate allowed.

Either Destiny or an even mightier hand took the hard decision away. A few weeks later, an irate Iñigo met the small group of Alvaro, Alicia, and Isabelita as they returned from a stroll. He paced anxiously at the front gate. He approached them with a pronounced limp, his balance precariously tested by his temper and the wooden stump. Instinctively, Isabelita hid behind Alvaro's tall frame. If he had any remaining doubts, the girl's behavior erased them. Alcohol breath and spittle spewed at them as Iñigo bellowed expletives and demands.

"She is mine!" he screamed.

Alicia could never recall the order of events. A struggle between the two men ensued. One reached for the girl, the other shoved away. In the tussle, Iñigo fell on the street as traffic approached. She heard screams and curses, and before she could understand what had happened, Iñigo's body lay inert near the curb, hit by an oncoming vehicle. She stared at her brother in stunned silence while the child sobbed in her arms.

Alvaro's large hand pressed on her shoulder. "It's over, Alicia."

***

Back in the midday sunlight, Alicia's dark eyes sparkled. "Now you know everything."

"What happened after?"

"A quick investigation. Iñigo was drunk. Folks witnessed his behavior. The findings were clear, accidental death. He made it easy for us."

"And you never had to go through with what you'd planned."

She nodded.

"You were protecting your daughter."

"Thank you. It helps to ease some of the guilt. I've chastised myself for many years after. Fortuitous events don't diminish the intent."

"What happened with Alvaro?"

"We lived together until his death, though we never married. It made the town crazy. He didn't mind as long as I was with him. He was a gift from above. I hope I made him happy. I'll ask him when we meet again."

"I'm glad he stayed with you. May I buy you lunch now?"

"Oh yes, in the plaza, please. After these past decades, it'll be lovely to sit outside and enjoy lunch with a handsome man."

A smile appeared, and Alicia Saenz, *la Viuda,* Llorenz, looked ten years younger.

Chapter Thirty

Ocala – January 14th 1968

Standing on her mother's driveway, Lita waved until Dalia's powder-blue Beetle dipped down a gentle slope and disappeared within a bank of purple shadows. Threads of nostalgia gripped her throat. She had gained so much peace and illumination during her three days of separation that she contemplated hiding out with Dalia until Matthew returned. A fantasy she discarded in a day. She had to return for her sister and for the Reynoldses, who deserved an explanation. Poor Lorrie had stopped by every day asking for Lita. Somehow, Raquelita was never in when Lorrie came.

She sighed, picked up her small bag from the gravel road, and scrunched her lips as she regarded her mother's house. Her mother. Two meaningless words describing an empty relationship. Isabel would misconstrue the reasons for her return. Did she care? Let her think what she would, Raquelita hadn't come back like a submissive sheep to the slaughter. She had a definite plan. In four months, she would claim her independence and move to her father's home, where she would live, study, and wait for Matthew's return.

She entered the house as a wave of nausea surged, remembering Dalia's earlier words. *"Skippy wants to take me back home."* It had been an unexpected blow. Her friend was leaving.

With a heavy heart, she passed through the gloomy hallway, touched her door, and froze. The image of her shredded letters exploded in her mind. She fled to Marité's bedroom, collapsing on her little sister's bed as Dalia's words crept back. *"It'd be great if you came along. We could show you the city."*

Dalia was leaving. Unique, clever Dalia, a friend who had been like an older sister, who, true to her word, had opened her home and offered three days of peace and healing. Including the last generous offer, a plastic vial filled with yellow capsules. *"Just in case..."* Dalia had suggested without conditions or judgment.

Raquelita refused. She would manage on her own, she hoped.

"Lita, don't forget, if you need anything, you know where I am."

She'd be miles away, somewhere in New York.

***

Lita entered the Reynoldses' home without hesitation, certain the family would receive her despite her unexplained absence. Their love was not a quid pro quo affair. Muffled sounds came from the kitchen. Her dear aunt toiled about, humming a soft tune. She cleared her throat.

"Aunt Coralina?"

"¡Dios del universo!"

In seconds, Coralina had Lita enfolded in her arms, and ushered her to the living room.

"Raquelita's home. Come, everyone. Raquelita's back."

They did; they all rushed out. And she was surrounded with hugs, kisses, and a million questions. Uncle Jonas, however, stated his disappointment.

"Why didn't you seek my help? Didn't I promise Matthew?"

"I don't know what happened to me that night. I wasn't thinking right. Please forgive me."

Uncle Jonas didn't berate forever. He opened his arms, and she rushed into his embrace, still murmuring apologies.

"Shhh, it's all right, darling. A lot's happened while you were gone," Jonas said, releasing her and nudging her to Coralina. "In a few words, Isabel called Emilio, and they quarreled over the letters. They came to an agreement when your father threatened to intervene. Xavi's in Jerez, talking to Alicia..."

Lita stopped listening. She had been so wrong. *Padrino* taught her a lesson again: never pass judgment, lest you be judged harshly. She owed him an apology.

"When is he returning?"

"In a day or so."

"I see. When will you call Mom?"

"Are you ready? How about now?"

"Sure." She leaned her head on her aunt's shoulder. "I'm as ready as I'll ever be." And prepared for her arrival.

***

The room turned frigid. Her mother's determination clashed with hers. They were antagonists without common ground, steadfast in their beliefs. She'd never apologize. Neither would her mother. An abyss yawned between them.

"I'm here as a courtesy. You should have gone straight home." Isabel's cold gaze swept over Jonas and Coralina. "Thanks for the call." She turned to Raquelita. "Do you have anything to say?"

Lita stared in silence.

"Don't you have anything to say for yourself?" Isabel stepped close. Raquelita's insolent silence irked her beyond measure. She was ready to push; she had to dislodge Lita from her righteous stance. Her daughter was not the aggrieved party.

"We're going home." Isabel grasped her arm and pulled.

Lita didn't budge. Isabel glared at her once meek daughter. "You dare provoke me?" She raised her hand to strike her. A hairbreadth before contact, Lita swung and gripped her mother's wrist.

"I'm not being disrespectful, *Mother*." She released Isabel's wrist. "But I will not allow you to hit me."

"You impudent—" Isabel growled and lifted her hand again.

Jonas moved. He reached and, using his full body weight, pulled Isabel back. He steadied her as he spoke. "Forgive me. I must interfere, Isabel. There's too much pent-up emotion between you two." He maneuvered her toward a chair.

"Why don't we keep Raquelita for the night, hmm? A few hours to calm down. You were so worried about her. I'm sure you want to throttle her. I would if it were Lorrie. You can discuss this in the morning. Don't you think that's wise?"

Isabel pressed her face against her palms, fingertips curving in. "It's such a mess. I don't know what's wrong. I've never been so angry. I'm losing control of my life, my daughter…" The words faded within her sobs.

Jonas sat on the armrest and stroked Isabel's hair. "Feeling better?" he asked, signaling to Coralina, who whisked Lita away.

"Yes, thank you."

"Good, good." Jonas patted her hand while sending a prayer for Xavi's immediate return. "Kids can really test our patience. I'll keep Raquelita for the night. Tomorrow I'll send her home. What do you say?"

"Thank you, Jonas. I'll leave now."

"I'll take you, Isabel. Raquelita can drive your car in the morning."

"You'll take care of the car?"

"Count on me."

***

Isabel's house was usually silent. Today, however, a muted chattering came from the kitchen. As Raquelita got closer, she realized it was a radio program. She found her mother leaning against the counter, still in her pajamas, her mussed mahogany locks falling down past her shoulders, and listening intently to the radio. Where had Madame Perfection gone?

"Good morning, Mother."

"Good morning, daughter."

The response was so bland it gave her pause. "Are you feeling all right? Can I get you anything?"

"No, I'm feeling a better. Maybe the poison is leaving my system."

"I hope so. Mother?"

"Raquelita?"

They had spoken in unison, and on her mother's pale face, a smile appeared. *What?*

"*Hija*, I was thinking, maybe we could discuss what happened later? Tomorrow might be better. Let's give each other more space and time."

"Ah, sure. Tomorrow's good."

"Good, we'll speak then. Meanwhile, do you mind if I lie down for a while? I'm still not feeling well."

"Did you sleep all right last night? Did you drink?" There, she finally had the courage to say it aloud.

"No, *hija*. I'm just so tired."

Such gentility unbalanced Lita. She had been expecting an epic battle, and now? "Mother, try to rest. Are you working tonight?"

"I called in sick. I need to rest. Raquelita, I'm sorry."

Just like that, her mother left like a wavering shadow.

Raquelita tried to smile but couldn't. She had stepped into her old caretaker role easy as you please. Granted, Isabel had expressed some sort of apology, but for what, Raquelita wasn't exactly sure. But, she was *not* resuming those duties. She would pass the baton to Xavi, and in four months she'd go home. She started for her room and stopped dead. The image of torn letters returned. Isabel's direct strike to her heart would never mend. She was definitely not picking up where she left off, and sleeping in this hateful room was impossible. From now on, she would bunk with her sister.

***

The warm hand felt uniquely familiar. Every nerve in her body tingled with the touch. This wasn't the dreadful hand of her nightmares. This hand she loved. It belonged to a man she missed, a man whose name she didn't dare speak—for if she dared, she might shatter to pieces.

"Isabel. Wake up, *Tesoro*."

Damn, she'd gone from nightmares to masochistic dreams.

"Isabel. You're not wearing your pearls. Why not?"

"B-because you left. It hurts to wear them."

"Well, I'm back, and I will not tolerate disobedience."

Isabel's lids flew open. Hazel eyes peered at her.

"It can't be."

"It's no dream, *Tesoro*," he whispered, cupping her cheek. "I know your torturer, the monster who's hunted you. I also know why shame silenced your lips. But this stigma was never yours. It was inflicted upon you, a helpless, beautiful child, by a twisted, evil mind."

Her lips parted, and he shook his head. "Let me finish. I've learned much. He will never soil your dreams with his foul presence again. I'll be with you, and he can't get past me. Your dreams and your waking hours are mine. I protect whom I love and what belongs to me. I love you, Isabel, more than my life. If needed, I'll march into hell and battle this specter." A hint of a smile eased his features.

"But words won't solve this problem. We'll get you professional help and work together. I already have the name of a specialist. I promise, we'll banish this demon forever. What do you say?"

"Embrace me with your warmth, Xavier Manel. Make it real for my disbelieving heart," Isabel whimpered. Overcome with emotion, she reached out to him with trembling hands. "Please, please don't leave me again."

"I had to leave to save you, *Tesoro*. I'll never do it again."

***

Matthew had heard the word. Informants north and to the west had confirmed that heavy equipment approached down the Ho Chi Minh trail. But Saigon refused to accept the reports. The enemy hadn't used tanks before. Why now? In their expert opinion, the pitch of the road south was too steep. It made such an advance difficult, impossible to hide. His captain was not so skeptical. The time he'd spent out here had eradicated his complacency. The enemy was determined and never followed a pattern. That was why the Special Forces were here, to anticipate such moves. It would be utter stupidity to ignore training, experience, or gut feelings.

Damn their bureaucratic souls. Matthew could've throttled every straight-leg, deskbound officer if he could. True, Lang Vei had been promised assistance from Khe Sanh if needed. However, if tanks attacked the camp, the Marines would be foolhardy to come out and expose themselves to such a deadly force. In the meantime, they had worked day and night to finish the last details of the fortifications and bring the camp up to specs. They still needed good intel, though. The last two patrols hadn't returned. Matthew's group was next.

"We have a briefing." Matthew had been looking for Brian around camp; he found him polishing his boots.

"We do? I reckon we better go." Brian had the *look*.

"What is it?" Matthew's stomach lurched. Brian *sensed* events. His weird vibes always came true. Initially, he called them uncanny coincidences. But after some close calls, Matthew took them seriously. More than once, Brian's feelings had saved them.

"Shit, ya know I can't explain. It's a feelin'."

"Bad?"

"Yep, it's gonna be touch 'n' go."

"Okay, let's get it over with."

***

Matthew and Brian had specifically chosen these four Bru Montagnards He'd fought with them in the past, and Matthew trusted their ferocity and dedication. Out of the four, two stood out. Dac Kien and Lanh. In Vietnamese, their names were auspicious: Acquired View and Quick Minded, respectively.

"We're doing this one by the numbers. No slipups, no laziness, a sharp eye out there," Matthew said. "Dac Kien, you know Brian, he's got a feeling." The man grunted. "Good. We'll be on our guard."

He inspected his men and was satisfied. They'd outfitted themselves with AK-47s instead of M16s or CAR-15s. Had donned the same load-bearing vest of the enemy. From a distance and for a brief moment, they might pass for Vietcong. It was what they hoped for in case of discovery. By the time the enemy approached to verify their identity, they would have vanished into the jungle.

The mission should take only a couple of days, though Matthew felt comfortable staying out longer. They carried enough supplies, and the Yards could extract sustenance from the jungle. Matthew shifted his shoulder, adjusting the strap of the one unconventional weapon in his personal arsenal, his crossbow. Others in camp jeered at their adopted tactics of using sticks and stones to fight the war. Let them laugh. He'd seen the efficacy of the weapon, especially in the hands of Dac Kien and Lanh. He'd adopted their art on the spot.

"Let's go. Lanh, you're on point."

Matthew made a mental note of the date. January fifteenth, he and his men crossed Lang Vei's perimeter wire.

Chapter Thirty-One

Ocala – January 22nd 1968

"This damned paperwork must be sorted, recorded, and...arrgh." Jonas's complaint cannonaded out the office past the hallway and into his daughter's room, silencing Lorrie and Lita's discussion over the Moody Blues' debut album.

"I need an assistant. Where are my children?"

Lorrie's mouth fell open. Her father was known for a phlegmatic temperament.

Raquelita's thumb pointed in the direction of her uncle's office. "What's the matter with Uncle Jonas?"

"I don't know," she answered, mystified. "It's not like him."

"Really, what gave it away?" Lita snickered.

"Go ahead and laugh," Lorrie said in mock indignation. "For your information, my dad does weird when necessary. Say...hurricanes and tornadoes, real cataclysmic events. Unlike your mom, who flips when the humidity is high." She twisted her head, and the end of her ponytail flicked against her cheek.

"Pfft... All right, don't get so huffy. Should we find out what's bothering him?"

"We should."

The office door was wide open. Holding on to the doorframe, they peeked in. Jonas was the image of concentration. Bent over his desk, he focused on a stack of papers between his elbows. "I really need some help with that mess," he murmured. "The pile of correspondence in the corner," he continued, two fingers pointing absently to the side. "The sorry envelope on top must have battled its way here."

Raquelita jumped, following the direction of his fingers. The referenced envelope stood out in all its filthy magnificence, and her heart melted in gratitude.

Her uncle had found a way to help without betraying his word. She picked up the precious item, then pivoted back to Jonas. She rewarded him with a tight embrace and a kiss on his whiskered cheek.

"I love you, Uncle Jonas."

***

Matthew's letter *almost* returned life to its proper course. She needed privacy to enjoy his words, and found it in the empty living room. Choosing a wide armchair, she nestled in and resumed her reading.

I can't believe it, angel. It's a new year...

Her joy was boundless. But as she continued, her smile waned.

I have to keep the letters simple and without details. Sorry, my love. I wish I had interesting topics to write about, topics worthy of my beautiful and creative angel...

Why did he trouble his heart? Matthew could write a dissertation about the average rainfall in South Vietnam, and she'd be enthralled. She needed his words, not a topic. She frowned.

Your letters are my tethers to sanity. I have kept every one and memorized the words; they inspire hope and ground me. It's difficult to remain focused on a necessary endeavor when rumors arrive. In this remote location, news of discontent at home erodes our resolve and conviction. But you, my love, strengthen me. I'm so blessed.

I dream of the day when this tour is over and I have you back in my arms. I pray every night for time to pass quickly, but I fear this war still has years ahead.

Her frown deepened.

I wish I could speak to you plainly, Angel, tell you more. Dear God, I hope you understand. We are constantly XXXXXXXXX. I have to finish this letter quickly before duties pull me away from you.

Raquelita, no matter what happens, I'll always love you. We've never discussed it, but should the worst happen, know this: my heart is yours; my love is everlasting, through time and distance. If I should leave first, do not fret. Live instead. I want you to live for both of us. Promise me you will, and your heart will be my home until we meet again.

"Matthew, what's wrong?" Was it the camp, an approaching threat? A foreboding tremor traveled through their connection. Raquelita, his soul mate, sensed it across the miles.

When their eyes met on the bus, their bond had grown vibrant and strong. The night of love confirmed their link. And now his message was plain. If the worst happened, they would meet in the next life. But if Matthew left, she had made up her mind to follow him somehow, regardless of his request. With a heavy heart and mind, she left the peace of the living room for the support of her cousin's bedroom, and flopped on the bed.

"Lorrie, what can I do?"

Lorrie tightened her face in her usual I'm-thinking scrunch. "Well, not much, coz. Knowing your letters are censored is a real bummer. But to Matthew, any encouragement would be like drinking ice water in hell." A mischievous smile replaced the scrunch. "I say to hell with the censors. Let it rip. Give it to him. Write it all down. Your wishes, your fantasies. Flip Matthew's head with desire and melt his heart with love. Give him something else to focus on. It can't hurt."

She blushed, entertaining the possibilities. "You're right, cousin. Screw the censors. Thank you."

"I've been spared. I could be on the same path you and countless other women walk every day. I can't even imagine how you manage." Lorrie glanced at her open palms and clenched her hands closed. "Offering a shoulder is the least I can do. I love you. I wish I could do more for you both."

***

Lita watched Dalia's every move. Gosh, she missed her friend. Their shifts hadn't coincided in almost ten days. While they enjoyed Rosie's complimentary lunch of grilled Reuben sandwiches and fries, Raquelita had brought her up-to-date.

"Told you, abuse is nasty stuff," Dalia said, and with an air of dignity, she dabbed her napkin at the corner of her lips.

"How did you know?" Lita asked.

"The big city's a good teacher, and your mom's a lucky woman. Xavi went through a lot to help. That's love." She took another bite and held up a finger until she finished chewing. "Have they decided on a treatment plan?"

"Not yet. Maybe they will tonight, after her follow-up visit. Her doctor wants to discuss test results and her constant nausea."

"Constant nausea, hmmm. Are you sure everything's okay?"

"Xavi doesn't look worried."

Raquelita took a bite and joined Dalia in the task of finishing their meals. The coffee shop was deserted and would remain quiet until the early evening crowd showed up. Occasional soft clinks of dishes and glasses and the far-off chatter from the kitchen interrupted the silence. The TV volume turned louder, and Dalia's head snapped up. Raquelita stared as her friend's expression evolved from placid to curious to outright serious. Dalia glanced behind her as a pair of hands pressed Raquelita's shoulders. Lita looked around. She didn't like Meg's expression.

"Raquelita, sugar, have you watched the news at all?" The edge in Meg's voice, initiated a rush of pins and needles throughout Raquelita's system.

"Meg? What is it?" Raquelita asked. Why was she so afraid? Her belly churned. Her heart threatened to jump out of her chest.

"Listen, hon, it's likely nothing. The media loves to sensationalize war reports."

"Oh God." Raquelita's voice trembled. Dalia's hands shot out and grasped hers.

"They're reporting heavy shelling at an airfield near the Marine base in Khe Sanh. So far there's no word about any Special Forces camps. Do you know Matthew's location?"

He was in the north, wasn't he? Khe Sanh sounded familiar. Her brain worked to clear the sudden invasive fog. "I think I could find out. Mr. Buchanan, he knows someone."

"That's not a bad idea. It's probably nothing. Like I said, reporters love to exaggerate. Stay calm, think good thoughts."

Raquelita stared down at her hands as if they belonged to someone else. Dalia must've tightened her grip, for her knuckles were white. And yet, Lita felt no discomfort, no pain, only the chaos in her mind. *Matthew, Matthew, Matthew!*

***

Isabel was shown Dr. Samuelson's examination room and instructed to wait. She smiled at Xavi, grateful for his presence. Since his return, he'd become her bastion of courage and support. Like now, intuiting her angst, he caressed her lower back, her shoulders, and the nape of her neck with his warm palm.

For over a week she had lived in a state of semi disbelief. If asked, she could never explain her joy. Of course, in typical Xavi fashion, his return had been full of bravura. *"We're going to fight this…we'll banish this demon forever."* He could rail all he wanted, as long as he didn't leave again. She was in love, and as the Universe—with its unique humor—would have it, she had fallen for the grouchiest, most demanding and domineering man in the world. She couldn't live a day without him. Of the Iron Lady, not a trace remained.

With Xavi back in her life, what she desired most was a new opportunity to mend the broken relationships, wipe clean the sins of disaffection and distance with Raquelita and others. She might have been outraged at the letters, but her reaction was inexcusable, alcohol or not. She had torn her daughter's dearest possessions, and along with them their tenuous relationship.

The plans were all in place. With Xavi's help, she would dry out, heal her spirit, and begin the long path to recovery. But with the specialist's second call, a new concern arose. Perhaps she might not get a second chance to atone. Why else would she be called back in unless she was terminally ill?

Her thoughts ended with the arrival of Francis Samuelson, MD, and his assistant. Dr. Samuelson's intelligent regard did not miss a detail. He watched as Xavi came around to stand protectively behind Isabel.

"How are you feeling, my dear? How's the nausea? I'm sure you're wondering why I called you back."

Isabel nodded. Xavi squeezed her hand.

"I called you in because your blood tests showed unexpected results. I asked the lab to run them twice to be sure. Both times the result was positive."

"I can handle the news. How long do I have?" Isabel asked holding back the tears.

"My initial estimate is seven and a half months." With a smile, he approached the table and held her wrist, taking her pulse. "Isabel, such agitation. You must calm down."

"How can I? I have seven months."

"Dear lady, it's not that long. You'll need to take care of yourself, follow a diet, and take vitamins."

"Vitamins, diet? What?"

"Yes, until you're examined by an obstetrician. Do you know one, or do you need a referral?" Dr. Samuelson maintained a straight face while he auscultated and tapped her chest lightly. He stepped back, moved the stethoscope from her chest, and placed it between her shoulder blades. "Two deep breaths, please."

"An obstetrician? Why?"

"Because you're pregnant, my dear. Should I congratulate you both?"

Chapter Thirty-Two

Ocala – January 22nd 1968

Pregnant? Dr. Samuelson's words ricocheted like stray bullets inside her brain. Isabel stared at Xavi. She couldn't catch a full glimpse of his face, yet the emotions reflected from this view surprised her. He seemed elated.

It's a mistake. She must have said the words aloud, because Xavi groaned, and Dr. Samuelson answered, "No mistake. As I said, we ran the test twice."

"How?"

Xavi huffed, and the physician looked to the floor.

"Surely, Mrs. Muro, you do remember the birds and the bees, don't you? You are, how old?" He paused, leafing through her chart, his attitude all business. "Not yet forty. Splendid. Other than the brief alcohol matter, you are healthy. I'm sure the baby's fine." He closed and dropped the file in his assistant's hands. "There's no reason why you couldn't have a successful pregnancy. One good reason to kick the habit." He cleared his throat and addressed Xavi. "Sorry, I should say two."

Through the examination, Xavi had been silent. The slight tremor to his hand helping her off the examination table and the singeing kiss on her forehead articulated one message. He wanted this child. They drove home in a silence full of stages. Passionate when he crushed her hand in his. Tender when he brought the punished fingers to his lips. Peaceful when he ran his fingers through her hair. He pulled into her driveway, and before she touched the car door, he was at her side, lifting her out like a doll. In a breath's span, he had her in the living room cradled in his lap and held within his arms.

"Are you thirsty? You must drink lots of fluids. Eat well. We'll get you on a program right away. I will care for you, both of you."

"You're not unhappy?"

"I'm not. I am—" He looked at her, seemingly puzzled. "It's not one emotion. It's a multitude. I have no words. I'm a sinful man. I don't deserve miracles. The joy is ineffable. *Joy is my name, Sweet joy befall thee!* Our child... I have no words."

Isabel watched the afternoon light slip, bright and playful through the windows, a symbol of the happy news. She returned to that moment when she thought her second chances were over. She understood Xavi's feelings. She'd been blessed with three miracles. Was she worthy?

"I am ready to start a program. I'm scared, but I will face him."

"*Tesoro*, I told you, never again will you face him alone. We'll defeat him together—"

An abrupt noise from the front door interrupted him. A dull thud hit the wall, followed by a slam. A human shadow slithered past the hallway, and Xavi stiffened in alarm.

"What a lovely scene." Raquelita materialized out of the shadows. A single clap of her hands punctuated each word.

Despite earlier resolutions, some habits were entrenched. Disregarding Xavi's cautionary touch, Isabel's riposte was instant. "Where are your manners, Raquelita? This is no way to enter a home."

***

Raquelita never begrudged. The word was not in her vocabulary. Still, the amorous tableau between Isabel and Xavi was the final stroke in a devastating day. The architect of her woes lounged in the tender arms of her beloved. Justice was a fantasy. No such thing existed in the universe. How could a woman who'd destroyed everything that mattered skate by without a single consequence? She remembered the loss inflicted upon her... and the thin tie to sanity snapped.

Her godfather's wise gaze was upon her. He knew she was ready to pounce, and yet he waited to see what she would do, what she would say.

"The merry disciplinarian speaks. Was the doctor nice? Tell me, Mother, did he explain? No? Because I wish to know what made you such a bitter, vindictive woman?" She spat every word. Raquelita reeled in the aftermath of the earlier news, her thin body vibrating in the grip of anxiety and terrible fear.

Isabel stood and took two steps forward. Raquelita jumped back. "Do not touch me, Mother. If you do, I will not be held responsible for my reaction."

"Raquelita, I'm your mother."

"Indeed, you delivered me into this world. How much do I owe for the unsolicited favor, Mother? Let's have the final tally for that dubious honor, shall we?"

"Raquelita, what's all this about?"

"Raquelita, Raquelita, Raquelita. I'm sick of the name. How long before everyone understands Raquelita's gone. Do you hear me? There's no more *ita*. My name is Raquel, Raquel María, the woman, with a woman's feelings, a woman's heart, and a woman's pain."

Astounded by her daughter's torrential anger, Isabel looked to Xavi for inspiration. He stood but didn't speak. She turned back to Raquel and stubbornly took a step forward. Steely fingers around her forearm arrested her progress. Confused, she looked to Xavi again; this time he shook his head. "Don't."

Raquel read his expression. Somehow he had gained insight into her despair. Could he see her chaos? For she was a boiling cauldron, and the need to scream churned. Did he think her dangerous? She wanted to hit and break something, do anything that might ease the ugliness inside.

"*¿Ahijada?*" That stopped her, the term becoming a magical endearment. Unafraid of her aggressive stance, he walked briskly around Isabel and held Raquel in a soothing embrace, restoring some sanity. The cold impersonality of the TV reports had tripped her, slamming the reality of war home, lucidity overcome by the madness of Vietnam.

"Is it Matthew?" he asked, rocking her back and forth.

"I d-didn't know, I didn't know. I thought I was prepared… It's worse than I imagined."

"Shhh… I've got you."

Her father's comforting spirit filtered through Xavi's arms. Was this the magic given to godparents? Were they anointed? In the ensuing peace, she pondered the thought abstractedly. It must be so, for as time passed, a marvelous sense of serenity filled her spirit.

"Come, sweetheart," he said, guiding her to the sofa.

Isabel was confounded and, in these days of sobriety, gaining wisdom fast. Her calamitous sin with Matthew's letters would haunt her to the end of her days. If the news her daughter mentioned were so bad… Well, she had ripped her daughter's source of solace, hadn't she?

This was all twisted around. Her firstborn ached. She should be consoling her. Instead, the job had been handed to the father of the child she carried. What a mess. She could make it messier; she only had to tell Raquel about their happy news. And so, with newfound discretion, Isabel sat at a prudent distance while Lita finished her story.

"Raquelita." Xavi lifted her chin, forcing her to look up. "Yes, you are still my Raquelita." He winked at her frown. "I am too old to change, and I hope you'll indulge me. We're going to call Emilio. I'm sure he's already heard from Jonathan. Are you listening? We will deal with this as it comes. I don't know what's up ahead. But you won't face it alone."

***

Xavi hung up the phone, his mind working at lightning speed. Emilio's report was worrisome but not dire. Not yet, anyway. Later, and from another location, he would call his friend and grill the details out of him. In the meantime, the real need was to inject peace in this unsettled home, try to build a new road between these two women, and ease Raquel's angst.

He slapped his thighs and extended a hand to Raquel. She took a few hesitant steps forward and held on tight. "Sweetheart, it sounds worse than it probably is. Communications are likely messed up. The military has to keep their movements and counteroffensives secret. Can you stay positive for a little while? Emilio said Jonathan sounded confident, same as his contact. They trust Matthew's abilities and training. I think you should too."

"*Padrino,* you may not believe this. Matthew and I… We have a connection. I feel when he's sad, worried, or happy. I do, honest." She disengaged her hands and fluttered her fingertips like butterflies in flight. "When you were talking, I stretched out my senses. I called out to Matthew, and he answered. He's alive. He's in a tight spot, but I know he's alive."

To her surprise, Xavi smiled and nodded. Isabel frowned.

"Matthew, I'm with you," Raquelita whispered. In her thoughts, a favorite canticle arose. *The voice of my beloved! Behold, he cometh leaping upon the mountains, skipping upon the hills…*

***

Lack of evidence stretched Matthew's mission well beyond the initial projection. Relying on natural resources and their expertise, they agreed to continue on a westward path, into Laotian territory. As the days progressed, the routing arced from a westerly direction to a southerly course, along the Laos-

Vietnam border, skimming the Ho Chi Minh trail. That was when they hit pay dirt and began to encounter telltale tracks.

They followed the route Dac Kien had set—when by luck, they forded a creek and literally stepped onto an otherwise undetectable submerged bridge. He gave the order to rush back to base. Tanks advanced south. They had what they needed. On January twenty-second, they had set on a direct easterly course, when a vicious mortar barrage to the Kha tribal 33rd Volunteer Battalion camp halted their progress. In utter dismay, Matthew and his men, obeying strict do-not-engage orders, could do nothing but watch in horror as the Laotian camp was overrun. Even worse, their path to Lang Vei was blocked. Tired and bedraggled, they would have to go home the same way they came.

***

Raquel arrived at Rosie's with a single purpose in mind. Find Dalia, who could give her Nembutals. She sat at the counter, tapping her fingers and attracting Meg's attention away from her cleaning duties.

"Hey, girl. What's up? You don't work today."

"Nope, I'm looking for Dalia. I saw Skippy's car pull away."

"She's out back. I'll let her know you're here." Meg turned and headed for the kitchen, humming gently. Nice tune. It was familiar… She resumed her tapping. Last night had been a doozy. Xavi had left town on a quick business trip. In his absence, Isabel had visited Raquel every night, seeking emotional support as if nothing had happened between them. The woman embodied self-absorption. She hadn't realized Raquel no longer slept in her old room.

"Dalia's changing. She'll be right over." Meg pointed her thumb toward the kitchen's swinging doors. Resuming her chores, she picked up her tune.

Yes, the words, something about the words, or was it the melody perhaps?

"Hey, surprise, surprise. Wanna take over my shift?" Dalia came out tying her apron. "If you need the extra dough, you can, I'll be happy to go home early."

"Ah, no. I came to find out if your offer still stands."

Dalia looked puzzled when Raquel pulled her to the middle of the empty dining room, away from Meg. "Which offer?"

"You know, my yellow friends," Raquel whispered. "Are they still available?"

"Of course."

"It's only for a few days, until Xavi returns and Mom stops hounding me."

"That mom of yours… Hang on, I may have some in my purse." Dalia pivoted and marched back to the kitchen, the apron's bow resting on her derriere dancing merrily with her steps.

I can stop whenever I want, whenever I want, Raquel droned to herself.

So easy…

It wasn't just the nights. The days were unbearable now. Other than the ongoing struggle at Khe Sanh, the Annamese range area had been engulfed by silence. Jonathan hadn't been able to extract further information. Matthew's dad stayed upbeat, saying no news was good news. Dalia came out of the kitchen with a triumphant smile, a hand waving a small vial.

Meg kept singing. The floor swayed. Raquel covered her ears to drown out the voice. Of course it was familiar. The singer promised an eternal love, a love that would last through time and distance… His words… Matthew's words. "Matthew!" Did she scream?

***

On the morning of January thirty-first, Emilio watched as a special news report flashed across his TV screen. Tet Offensive. In a surprise breach to the announced ceasefire—to celebrate Tet, the Vietnamese Lunar New Year—a combined force of North Vietnamese Army and Vietcong guerillas had launched a coordinated series of attacks against over one hundred cities and villages, including the former imperial capital, Hué City.

Emilio slumped on his chair, recalling Julie's prophetic words. *"With each bold headline…remember, Raquelita is listening."*

Chapter Thirty-Three

Ocala – February 3rd 1968

Rosie's was packed. Raquel panted as she cleared a table; behind her, Dalia set up just as fast, while a pair of annoying patrons breathed down their necks. Once the table was done, they shot the impatient couple irate stares, threw menus down, and left them to stew in their juices for a while.

The coffee shop's reputation for good food had grown, and the crowds had increased appreciably. It was always busy, and Raquel liked it. The busier the better. She didn't care about the tips. Activity was distraction, as a great deal of uncertainty remained in her life. Soon after January thirty-first, the news spigot for the northern region had thinned to a trickle, and Mr. Buchanan's inside man had gone underground. The yellow capsules had saved her sanity. The moment she received news from Matthew, she would stop, Raquel vowed.

A sudden commotion announced that Ricky and his entourage had arrived and taken possession of a table. Raquel clenched her fists, and stared at Dalia. She had nothing against those boys; they were average college guys she saw around campus. But whenever they hung out with Ricky, they turned into laughing hyenas.

"It's Ricky. Please, would you take that table?"

"That's your station," Dalia said.

"I know. They're just loud, silly, and batty."

"That's because they're high," Dalia whispered. Although she could have screamed and not been heard, such was the noise level.

"What?"

"You heard me. Make peace with Ricky."

"I don't follow—"

"They've been smoking, ergo their silliness. Who do you think supplies the campus, everyone around, and yours truly with drugs? What, no guesses?"

"Ricky," Raquel said.

"Yes, Ricky, local entrepreneur and supplier of your yellow friends. He'll be your contact when we return to New York."

"When?" Raquel dropped her hands, the linen she'd held floated to the floor.

"Sorry, girl. Skip wants to leave by mid-February. I was going to tell you. Can you imagine? In the middle of winter. He is such a meanie."

"So soon," Raquel muttered as her stomach tightened into a ball. With a sudden snap, she snatched the menus from Dalia's hand and turned to face the table hosting odd little Ricky and his merry band of friends.

A few minutes later, a speeding Raquel almost bumped into Dalia as her friend exited the kitchen, a large serving tray propped on her shoulder teetering precariously.

"Well, operation friendship has begun."

"Oh." Dalia halted and carefully rebalanced the plates. "That was quick."

"Just following orders, ma'am. By the way, I've been invited to your party."

"What? Which party, when?"

"Friday night. Skippy is throwing a little bash, and Ricky invited me. Didn't he tell you?" Raquel snickered as she breezed past her friend, pushing the swinging doors inward.

***

"Let me help you."

Matthew nodded gratefully at Brian. He could barely see his reflection in the metal of his canteen. Signaling mirrors were kept in their packs. Shaving was a routine they established two days out, and a difficult task to perform one-handed. Especially when the early morning light filtered anemically through a profusion of branches, leaves, and needles. Helping each other was a must, as nicks and cuts in this environment were guaranteed infections.

"Sure thin', bro. You seemed distracted. I didn't want you to bleed all over your pristine outfit." Brian chuckled. "Should I guess?"

"It's Raquelita, Brian. You know. She's always with me."

"And here I thought you were distracted by yesterday's fun. Charmed by one of the lovely specimens the chief so generously offered."

"Shit, if you don't stop, I'm going to slash my face. Maybe one of the lovelies got your attention."

"Right now, my friend, a stick wearing a skirt would git my attention. It was mighty difficult to reject them beauties."

"I get it. The missing teeth were deal breakers." They both chortled.

Two nights ago, they had chanced upon a tiny village on the Vietnam side of the border. Initially, the chief hesitated to receive them. But Lanh and Dac Kien managed to convince the old man using a few trinkets and promising to leave within a day. In return, they got some needed rest, food, water to bathe, offers of the gentle persuasion, and a lot of information. *"Many attacks, many attacks,"* Lanh translated. His people had witnessed multiple NVA battalions traveling south on the Trail for at least one moon cycle. *"No good, North Vietnamese."* Lanh spat on the dust.

Yesterday, as Matthew's patrol had begun the laborious ascent back to camp, they encountered some well-used trails. They maintained a concealed parallel course. In his estimation, they were about day and a half out.

An almost imperceptible rustle alerted him. Matthew froze and looked up. He lifted his SOG knife to hip level ready to throw it in an instant. With his back to the forest, Brian did not breathe, did not move. Out of the thicket, Dac Kien materialized, crossbow in one hand. With the other hand, he signaled in sequence: one finger to lips, two to the eyes, thumb to his back. *Silence, look, behind me.* When he saw Matthew understood, he disappeared again.

As one, they sterilized the resting area, picked up their gear, and followed in Dac Kien's direction. As he got closer to the line of trees, a rhythmic noise became clear. Just ahead, tucked behind a line of pines, Dac watched an NVA battalion on the march.

Looking to his men, Matthew circled his index finger in the air and pointed in the direction they came. A few meters away, they conferred. They could follow the battalion distantly, riding their coattails as long as they continued south. Once they got closer to camp, they would drop off.

Did it sound like a plan? No one objected. No one had a better idea.

It might have worked. A few clicks later, it went awry when Bao stepped on a punji stake trap. He was stoic. In fact, his groan could be considered silent. The noise traveled, Matthew was certain. He rushed to his wounded man and began to stanch the flow of blood, praying the tips had not been dipped in excrement. No way to tell; they needed to get Bao out of there in a hurry. God, they were so far away from camp. A rush of air flew past his shoulder, then another. He heard groans and a thud. One of his men with his crossbow had dispatched two approaching NVA in deadly silence. They couldn't stay quiet for long. As soon as the fallen North Vietnamese were missed, more would follow.

Brian ran to him, slipped an arm under Bao's body and swung him over his shoulder. "Let's go," he whispered.

They sought the forest, the thickness of trees. Matthew ran ahead guarding their front. His senses turned hypersensitive. He heard every sound and rustle, captured the slightest movement. Rivulets of perspiration ran down his back, and his hands became slippery. Brian's labored breathing was loud in his ears. Matthew tightened the grip on his weapon and looked quickly behind, Bao remained silent. Heavy footfalls thumped to his right. Lanh, guarding their flank, flew over obstacles, a wild gazelle fleeting and agile. A wet patch on his left shoulder darkened his shirt. Blood. Lanh was hurt.

A rat-a-tat-tat staccato rippled through the air, and bursts of dirt peppered his feet. Brian cursed. Matthew heard a body fall, and panicked. Brian was down and had dumped Bao's body. *No.* Matthew choked on the scream. Not Brian. Not his brother.

Off to his right, Lanh still ran with him. Matthew whirled back, lifted Bao, and in a superhuman effort hurled him toward Lanh. He didn't wait to see if Lanh caught him. He pivoted back. Ten yards away the NVA rushing for Brian's prostrate body held a round object in his hand. Recognizing the fragmentation grenade, Matthew ran—faster than he ever had in any game or life—for Brian.

It happened in slow motion—hands gathered, pulled the pin, prepared to throw. A hiss flew past Matthew's ear. The crossbow's bolt pierced the NVA's hand and blood spurt in the air when Matthew slung his knife deep into the NVA's throat. The man fell, uttering a low gurgle. The grenade rolled. A few feet from Brian, the ground exploded. The displacement lifted his body. *No, no, Brian!*

Matthew rushed to Brian, slid to his knees, and shoved his left hand against his neck seeking a pulse. In the periphery of his vision, an NVA appeared through the line of trees. The man aimed on the run. Matthew didn't have time to fire back. *This is it.* He bared his teeth. Jonathan Buchanan's son would not cower before death. His sole regret was leaving Raquelita alone. "R-Raq." He began to send his farewell when several dull clicks silenced him. The AK-47 misfired.

Maddened with fury, Matthew pounced on the man's knees, tackling him to the ground. They rolled and thrashed in mortal hand-to-hand combat, fists hitting flesh, boots meeting bone. In the end, Matthew glared at the limp body of his enemy, clenching bloody hands, poised to strike again. The expression of surprise waned as death's pallor took over the NVA's features, a pool of dark blood gathering around his fractured skull.

Matthew turned, heaved Brian's inert form over his shoulder, and ran toward the trees. A percussive blow like the impact of a thousand doors slammed his back and propelled him to the ground. "Raquelita, I'm sorry." This time, his farewell took flight.

The world went black.

***

The message traveled through their still-unbroken link, over miles of terrain and water, reaching the heart of a young woman, in a small town, at a party. A percussive blow like the impact of a thousand doors slammed Raquel's back and propelled her to the floor.

"Matthew."

The party came to a silent halt. Everyone stared. Skippy lifted Raquel and deposited her on the sofa next to Dalia.

"What is it?" Dalia asked.

"Matthew. He's in trouble."

"They're all in trouble. Uh…what I mean is, war is hell for everyone."

"This is different. I heard him. And that pain in the middle of my back." She pressed her forehead against her friend's shoulder.

"*I* believe you, even if no one else does." Ricky said, sauntering toward her.

"You do?"

"Sure, in my country we believe people who truly love each other have a bond. They sense each other, know when there's trouble. Is that what you mean?" He knelt before her, offering a tiny pipe. "Here, take a hit. It'll help."

"Hashish, Ricky? You better have nothing else in that pipe," Dalia protested.

Ricky made a dismissive gesture. "What's the problem? She's upset. This could relax her. It might even make her forget her troubles."

"Is that the truth? Will it make me forget?"

"Look, if it doesn't, nothing's lost, right?" Ricky leered, holding the mouthpiece up close. "Ignore her, just put your lips around it and suck."

It was sexually suggestive, but in her acute distress, Raquel let it pass. Instead, she looked to Dalia and Skippy. Dalia frowned, but Skip shrugged.

Feeling very alone amid a sea of staring faces, Raquel accepted the pipe. She inhaled once, deeply…and coughed.

Moments later, she was in a dream. Somewhere her father recited an old poem, and Raquel followed his voice into the world of Spanish legend, El Cid Campeador and Ximena, of Caliphates and Sultanates, the three Princesses of the Alhambra and their daring Christian Knights. As the bizarre dream continued, Matthew's message echoed, *"I'm sorry."*

***

Raquel woke up slowly and for a few seconds she was completely disoriented. The thin slivers of daylight filtering through the shades helped her place herself. She remembered the dresser and simple chairs, the single bed with its flowery comforter in Dalia's guest room. But how…why was she here?

The memory returned in slow drips, then faster—a sharp pain, an apology, and silence, Matthew's terrible silence. She had stretched, reached and invoked, called and called again…. and nothing. The way had been shut. The connection was silent. Matthew Buchannan was gone, as he had feared in his letter.

And she'd been left behind.

***

The abandoned newspaper stared at her, someone's trash. The headline called her name. In the midst of Rosie's lunch rush, Raquel paused, picked up the paper and read.

VIOLENCE IN VIETNAM ESCALATES: On February 6th, 1968, a combined infantry-tank NVA force overran the Special Forces camp at Lang Vei. Captain Willoughby and the men of Detachment A-101, outnumbered and inadequately armed, distinguished themselves with valor and determination. The bulk of untested, light antitank weapons misfired, and the rest bounced off tank hulls without exploding. Lang Vei is gone.

They'd taken Matthew from her. But, she'd find a way to follow.

And the hag above smiled…

Chapter Thirty-Four

San Antonio – February 8th 1968

"Dalia, she belongs with her family." Skippy's tone was firm. His wide stance meant business.

Dalia had just arrived from Rosie's. She kicked off her shoes and collapsed on the sofa. Undaunted by his forbidding expression, she massaged her macerated feet. "God, they are tired today." She wiggled her toes. "Baby, can I talk you into a little rub?"

"Sure, but no more talk of Raquelita." Skippy sat next to her and lifted her legs to his lap. His large hands picked up one foot and began to knead her grateful, wriggling toes.

"Mmmm…such hands you have," she said, evaluating Skip's expression. "You haven't seen her since the news about Lang Vei. I'm worried about her. Let's invite her up for a few weeks. You know, help her pass the worst of this."

"Raquelita has a mother, a father, and a family to help her through this. She's a minor. Can't you get that through your head?"

"Granted, but only for three more months. Her mom is unreliable. She may have stopped drinking, but she's still loony. If only Isabel would change. Lita needs her."

Dalia remembered when she'd met Raquelita. She was a lively girl, creative and sweet, full of questions and wonder. Being around her was like breathing fresh, clean air. No more—her friend's spirit had diminished to a tiny flame. What happened to her backbone? Raquelita wouldn't be the first woman or the last to lose a lover, and in worse conditions.

Dalia had seen it, in the forgotten corners of the city—gangs, drugs, crime took men away, to prison or death. Her Skippy had been one. She glanced at him, full of tenderness. She'd met him after his stint in juvie. Young enough to have the records sealed, old enough to remember the hard lessons.

Lita should be comforted knowing Matthew died with honor, fighting for his nation. He'd be remembered with pride, his remains interred with dignity amongst his fallen comrades, rather than trashed in an abandoned building or a filthy gutter, desecrated by a forgotten needle in a vein, riddled with bullet holes or knife wounds.

Dalia let it all go for now. She leaned back on the sofa and allowed Skippy's hands to knead away the concerns.

***

Ocala, February 8th, 1968

> *Much time has passed since I wrote on these pages. I return for our farewell. On this night, our journey together ends, I'm out of words. He filled me with joy, laughter, and love. He's left, and I must follow. My energy is spent. My light has dimmed.*
>
> > *Puedo escribir los versos más tristes esta noche...*
> > *I can write the saddest lines tonight...*
>
> *Oh Neruda, you speak for my lonely heart. Matthew bid me to live. Without him, I cannot.*
> *I go now, to the cold world of men, seeking my way out. I must hurry.*
> *Matthew, my love, you won't wait long. I'm coming.*

***

"What do we know about him?"

Dr. Holloway pulled a chart from the unconscious man's cot, leafing through it. He'd arrived in Saigon days after Tet; already it felt like a lifetime. Minimally staffed, his crew at the 8th field hospital in Nah Trang was worn out. It was impossible to catch up. The wounded kept coming, and still the nurses and doctors struggled to keep up.

He lifted his gaze from the clipboard and looked to the right. Fighting for his life, a heavily bandaged man moaned in restless pain. He was one of three men medevacked from the north. The Montagnard could return to action after the puncture wounds healed. With the two Americans, only time would tell.

Nurse Bradshaw took the chart from the young physician and scanned it quickly.

"I spoke to one of the pilots. These guys are Special Forces and were trying to get back to camp. They encountered NVA somewhere north of Khe Sanh. The Marines can't figure out how three tiny Bru Yards dragged their wounded through an impossible terrain, riddled with enemy forces, and in the middle of constant bombardment. *Puros cojones,* my boyfriend would say." She smiled and tipped her chin toward the moaning soldier.

"We had a devil of a time stabilizing him. I can't believe he's still with us. Tough kid." She turned her attention to the other. "We suspect he suffered severe head trauma. They need full attention. Our facility can't handle it."

"Germany?" Dr. Holloway asked in a low voice. She nodded back.

"Dr. Richards approved the move. Germany will sort it all out. These two are done. They're going home." She shook her head. "They were out, you know, when Lang Vei was taken. Are they lucky?" She pushed through the double doors and stopped. "Doc, I hear incoming Hueys. I'll be ready for you in a sec."

***

Late afternoon, Dalia marched through her front door, almost screaming. "You can start getting mad at me. Protest all you like. For all the good it'll do. I've decided."

"Okay, I think I've just lost a battle. Which one? What have you decided?" Skippy said, extending a hand and bringing her close. He grasped her by the waist and sat her on his lap, his large hand softly massaging her back. Dalia began to relax until she realized the direction of Skippy's thoughts. Alerted by his maneuverings, she frowned.

"Oh no, you don't. You're not going to butter me up and distract me again. Really, Skip, this is important."

"Okay, I give. What is it?"

"We're taking her with us," Dalia said.

"Who, where?"

"She needs three months. We can give them to her, until she turns eighteen."

"Raquelita again? I'm tempted to let you slide to the floor and leave you there. We had this discussion, why are you being contrary? This isn't like you, what has changed?"

"It's a disaster, baby. I blame myself. I should've seen it."

He raised a palm to her cheek, forcing Dalia to look at him. "Lady, don't do this. Tell me what happened."

"All right. Isabel returned from rehab gentle as a lamb, ostensibly adapted to a sober life. But Xavi had to leave on a quick business trip. Every time he does, Isabel falls apart."

"Go on…"

"Isabel hasn't apologized for tearing up Matthew's letters, and Raquel hasn't forgiven her. So they avoid each other. It works when Xavi is in town. But when he's away, Isabel uses Lita. Last night, Isabel told her she's pregnant, and Raquel saw it as gloating. The explosion was huge.

"Enter Dalia. I wanted to set her up with a reliable contact for sleeping pills. I didn't catch Ricky's interest in Raquelita. She's always been uneasy around him. Instead I pushed her, ignored her hesitation like an overbearing parent, just like Isabel."

Dalia slipped out of Skippy's lap and turned to face him. "I saw it today. He's a snake. He weaved his greasy body around her like a python ready to squeeze and swallow its victim." Wringing her hands, Dalia flopped on the chair opposite Skip. "I used to think of him as harmless, a quirky guy. He's a stinking drug pusher. And I did this to her. Well, I'm not leaving her alone at the mercy of this fucker."

"And you propose…?" Skippy raised an eyebrow.

"Three months, baby, in three months she'll be free. We're taking her away from this mess to New York," Dalia said with an expression of defiance. Silence descended between them as they waited for the other to speak.

A knock at the door reverberated throughout the house almost like a sonic boom. Dalia's gaze remained fixed on Skippy's as she yelled, "Door's open."

The door opened and a pale Raquel stood at the threshold.

Skippy spoke first. "Come in, darling."

With hesitant steps, Raquel entered and closed the door. She seemed uncertain. "I don't want to interrupt anything."

"Nah. Come on in, girl. You've never been shy with us before." He waved toward the sofa. "Can I get you anything to drink?"

"No, thank you. I'm fine. I came to ask you both a question."

"Dalia will speak for me. I'll be in the back," Skippy said and left the room.

***

Five nights later, alone in her room, Raquel made a last attempt. She breathed in, using a rhythm adopted long ago, a pattern that always yielded results. It wasn't a halfhearted effort. She concentrated to rally all her senses into one single point, focusing on the man who was the world to her. She swirled her forces around, faster and faster until they were ready to burst, and then let go.

With the speed of a slingshot, her spirit soared and flew above oceans, mountains, and rivers, seeking Matthew's, hoping it would answer. Straight ahead, she saw a glow. Matthew? She persevered at full speed. The impact against an unexpected wall almost sundered her to pieces.

Raquel lost consciousness.

***

A voice called out urgently, and Matthew awoke to a world of amorphous shapes and shadows. He blinked to clear his vision without results. He tried to lift a hand, but a hammering headache stopped him. Darkness overtook him.

***

When Raquel came to, the stab to her temple reminded her of her failed attempt. Her desolation was unbearable. Only the plan remained. With great care, she moved through the dark hallway and entered her sister's bedroom. She stood next to Marité's sleeping form. "Good-bye, sweetie. Be happy, always." She kissed her forehead and walked out the door.

***

"How do you feel?" a gray shadow asked in a woman's voice as fingers pressed against his wrist. He wanted to answer, but his throat was so dry he made noises instead. A small object was placed against his lips.

"It's a straw. Take a tiny sip. Too much will make you sick."

He sipped with difficulty. "Where am I?"

"What do you remember?" The shadow leaned closer.

"It, it hurts… I was on a bus. What happened?" He tried to wade through the dense mire in his brain.

"How's the pain?"

He gritted his teeth against the pounding headache and clamped the fingers holding his wrist.

"Where am I? What happened? Why can't I see?"

"Easy now. You received a blow to the head. Your vision will clear in a few days. We can talk later. Rest, get some sleep."

Fingers caressed his forehead, and he loosened his grip. He leaned against the pillows, allowing the unfamiliar hand to lull him back to sleep. Hovering in the dark, a pair of topaz irises stared at him.

***

Outside the college library, Lorrie waited for Steve on the usual bench. She leafed absently through the pages of a text, enjoying the shade of a magnolia tree. They met here on Fridays, but this Wednesday, Valentine's Day, he was making a special trip and she couldn't wait to see him.

"Lorrie." Raquel approached quickly.

Lorrie waved. "Hey, coz. Come here, sit."

"Lorrie, I don't have much time." Raquel, cheeks drawn and pale, sat at the edge of the bench. Her gestures were jerky, eyes shifty, an abused animal looking to run. During the past months she'd seen her sweet cousin become increasingly grim but today…

"Hey, what's with the face? You're scaring—"

"I love you, your parents, your brother, but I can't stay here. I have to go."

"What? No."

"I'm leaving. I'll call you when I get there."

"Don't do this. God, I was afraid of this. Where are you going? What about your sister, your dad, Xavi? What about us? We love you, we can help."

"No one can. It's too late. I can't explain, just…can I call you?"

"Yes, yes. Why? Oh God, don't go. Let me help you."

Raquel embraced Lorrie, kissed her cheek, and stood. "I love you, cousin. You were always so kind. Pray for me." She pivoted and sped away.

"Wait, wait." Lorrie stood. The book on her lap flopped to the ground as Raquel disappeared like a phantom between the trees.

Chapter Thirty-Five

Manhattan – February 14th 1968

The aircraft circled and banked, its wings tilted, and the Manhattan skyline appeared, a mass of imposing, intimidating, and impersonal monoliths pushing up against a layer of leaden winter clouds. A frisson of anticipation rushed through Raquel as she stared at the magnificent concrete display. When the baggage claim's massive doors slid open, a blast of icy wind buffeted her body. In all her eighteen winters, she had never felt such cold. This was true winter. This was New York.

Raquel and her companions walked out to the curb, and a shiny red Camaro came to a full stop. Skippy opened the passenger door and motioned for the three women to clamber inside. He threw the luggage in the trunk, slammed it shut, and sat up front. The vehicle exited La Guardia airport, merging onto Grand Central Parkway, where it began a laborious snail's pace all the way to and across the Triborough Bridge.

Someone said "Rush hour" as an explanation, which sounded ridiculous to Raquel. Buried between a mute Dalia and a chattering Linda, blasted by the car's heating system, and unnerved by the stop-and-go motion, she was past nauseated. After what seemed an eternity, the car exited the bridge, entered some expressway—Bruckner something or other—and traffic eased. The vehicle ran at an even pace, and her dizziness improved.

But something was amiss. The Manhattan skyline was no longer visible. What happened to the glittering city, the glamorous stores, or the brightly lit avenues with throngs of shoppers? This neighborhood looked like a war zone. The buildings' weathered façades resembled grotesque human faces caught in rictuses of surprise. Paneless windows looked like empty eye sockets, and the street-level doors their toothless, gaping mouths. A new concern bit at her. What did she really know about these people in the car? What the hell was she doing here? Nausea returned with a vengeance.

"Could you open the window a little?"

"We'll freeze, Raquel."

"What's the matter, kid?" The driver's gaze gleamed through the rearview mirror. "Too much heat?"

She stared back and nodded.

"This is all new for you, isn't it? I'll turn it off." The eyes crinkled with amusement, and he reached for the heating controls. "Skip, man, light up a joint. She'll feel better."

"It's okay, I don't need it."

"It's good for the nausea." The smile lines deepened.

"Is it really? Do we have a long way to go?"

"We're in the South Bronx. We've a ways to go before Mt. Vernon." Linda laughed. "You might as well smoke. At least you won't care. If she doesn't want it, I'll take hers." Linda leaned forward. "Come on, Skip." She slapped her hands at Skippy's headrest.

"Fire it up. Give the kid a hit. She's green and I just refinished the leather."

When the joint reached her, Raquel acquiesced. This was her plan, her exit strategy. Might as well dive in.

***

"Hey girl, we're here." Dalia shoved her shoulder. In the steel-gray light of this February winter afternoon, Raquel took a full measure of her surroundings. A continuous row of ancient tenements—a dismal brick canyon—lined both sides of the streets. Linda rushed toward the sole house on the block, lifted a chain-link gate, and entered, yelling indistinct words.

The vehicle's front seat was pushed forward, and the driver reached in for her. Her gaze locked with his dark stare, and she stepped out. His attractive face sported a thick Vandyke, giving him a slight rakish air. "Little girl, you should go back home. This city will eat you alive."

Was she so transparent? Could a stranger read her inexperience? Feigning nonchalance, Raquel shrugged. "If it does, it's my karma," she retorted and turned on her heel.

Her act ended when she entered Mary Callahan's house, Linda's house, the devil's own house. The gloom inside this place rivaled the one in her soul. Her desire to flee was overwhelming. Only, where could she go? Her sight adjusted, and she froze. A woman, tall and massive, dressed in a dingy housecoat, enfolded Linda within huge, ham-like arms.

Raquel made the mistake of examining her surroundings. A flower-print sofa, encased in heavy clear plastic, dominated the décor, and that was *the* nicest-looking piece. Under a thick layer of dust, everything else was in shambles. The blinds had missing slats, and the curtains were torn or shredded at the hems. She feared looking at the floor. Off to one side, an ill-patched purple recliner housed a body—she thought it was a body—thin and frail in direct contrast to the large woman hugging Linda.

"Dalia?"

"This is only temporary." Dalia grasped her wrist.

Then it hit her, the only suitcases on the sidewalk had been Linda's and hers. Her stomach vaulted.

"Don't worry, you'll stay here two days…max. Dickey's almost moved out."

Don't worry? Her descent to hell accelerated when the gigantic woman turned to her.

"Is this the little spic?" A smile missing a tooth crept between heavy jowls. The childlike voice was eerie.

Spic? Unsure, Raquel Muro extended a hand, which Mary Callahan ignored. Instead, Raquel was swathed within an overlarge embrace and overcome by a rancid smell. Just as quickly, the large woman released her.

"Shut up," Mary screamed at the human on the large purple disaster. "I told you to shut up."

The wraith mumbled in a beautiful deep voice. Golden hair swayed in concert with his gestures. Dirty, long fingernails scratched the face almost tenderly. He might have been angelic were it not for the drooping lids and the emaciated face. Through his thin lips, sibilant sounds escaped, unintelligible to her but not to the lady of the house.

"That's Gerard. Linda's brother, a hopeless dope fiend," Dalia whispered. "They've tried to clean him up. He stays straight for two or three days, cops another fix, and the cycle goes on."

Damn her naïve soul. She had envisioned following Matthew in a romantic, tragic ending, something out of the pages of a Shakespearean play. There wasn't a trace of beauty or romance in this hellhole. She was an idiot entrusting her exit strategy to strangers.

Why the hell hadn't Dalia warned her? She panicked when Skippy dropped her bag on the dusty floor.

"I can't stay here."

"I'll be back as soon as I unpack. We'll go out dancing later."

"I can't stomach this place for very long. And I promised Lorrie I would call."

"You can call from our apartment. Be ready."

Minutes later, she sat on her flimsy cot, staring at the filth around her. She was afraid to open her suitcase, lay out her clothes, bathe, or even breathe. "Oh Matthew, I'm so sorry."

***

Raquel followed Dalia through a short hallway and into a small living room. She caught the end of the conversation between Skippy and the driver of the red Camaro.

"Gerard, he's a poor devil," Skippy said.

"He's past the point of no return. Hello again," Mr. Red Camaro said when he saw them. He was dressed in faded jeans and a white T-shirt. His hair hung loose and damp, indicating a recent shower. "Are you ready for a night out on the town?" The dark gaze had softened.

"Lita," Skippy interrupted. "Meet my best friend and business partner, Dickey."

"Richard Winters's the name. My friends call me Dickey."

"I like Richard better." She was still smarting from his earlier words, but extended her hand politely. "It's nice to meet you. I hope I'm not putting you out."

"Not at all. The move was already in the works. You have pretty eyes, little girl." The rakish smile returned. He grasped her hand within both of his. "How did you get mixed up with these two?"

"Well…Dalia and I worked in the same coffee shop in Florida." His touch felt warm and intimate, she almost pulled her hand away.

"That was a rhetorical question. He doesn't really care," Dalia said, pushing her toward the kitchen.

"That's not true, I am very interested. Where are you taking her?"

"To the kitchen. She has to make a call, you goofball."

***

"She hung up without saying where she is." Coralina peered at her daughter, and Lorrie jumped.

"Mom, I don't know for sure, honest. I could guess, though."

"Well, tell us," Jonas grumbled.

"After the library, I went to Rosie's. Dalia and Linda had given notice, but from Lita not a word. I suspect she went to New York with them."

"This is my fault." A whimpering Isabel fisted Xavi's shirt tightly against her face. "I did this to her."

"No, *Tesoro*. We all share the blame. When the news from Vietnam got worse, we should've rallied around her. Please calm down. It's not good for the baby. We know where to look, and we're going to find her. I promise."

***

The car hustled past plumes of steam rising out of drains and bumped over potholes and metal street plates. "It's faster on FDR Drive, Raquel. I think you'll enjoy this better," Skippy explained.

At last, the bright lights appeared, chic storefronts and restaurants gleamed, theatres' neon signs flashed, and activity and people abounded. Everything she had imagined New York to be. Skippy took Fifth Avenue, cut across Park to Columbus Avenue, and headed toward the Circle, drove around it, crossed back to Fifth and continued south in a rush.

"You guys get out, and I'll go park. Wait for me outside the club." Skip had come to a full stop at the corner of Christopher Street and 7th.

Raquel stepped down, and her jaw slackened. Sheridan Square in the Village was busting at the edges with a mass of humanity. Every group representing the groundbreaking sixties milled around, impervious to the cold weather. The trendsetting youth of New York and the surrounding boroughs—elitists and fashion profilers, misfits, hitters, and hippies, wearing unique, colorful outfits—had answered the summons of the night. The Haven welcomed and sheltered all kinds. The image would forever remain in Raquel's mind.

Skip met up with the women, waved at the head bouncer, and the red stanchions were moved aside. The huge bouncer gave Raquel a cursory look, but a request for ID never materialized. As they entered, Skip held her hand and led her down the steps into the stygian depths. Dalia and Linda followed close behind.

As she descended, a powerful vibration snaked through the floor, up her feet, and gaining strength with every step. Monstrous amplifiers throughout the cavernous dance floor thrummed with the beat of "Time Has Come Today."

Raquel stopped on the last step, looking at a real-life image of *The Snake Pit*. From wall to wall, humans writhed and groaned, body to body and skin to skin. Skippy tugged at her hand. "Coming?"

Dalia nudged from behind. She took one step down, and the sea of humanity swallowed her, body and soul.

***

Matthew's sight had recovered, but the mallet pounding his temples refused to ease up. The staff's evasiveness worried him. Judging by the occasional uniforms he saw, he was in a military hospital. Still, if there had been an accident on the road, his father should be here. Details in his dreams bothered him too, the strange sounds and faces, the quick snippets and the mysterious whisky-colored stare. He was determined to get answers the next time anyone came near him. His target arrived sooner than expected. Armed with a blood pressure wrap, a nurse walked toward his bed. When she took his pulse, he reached for her wrist and grasped it tightly. "Where am I?"

She was startled, though not scared. "We must be feeling better."

"Yes, we are, and we need answers."

"What do you remember?"

He was sick of the question. "I told you and everyone else. I was traveling to Ft. Benning. I woke up here. I'm tired of the evasions. What is this place?"

"I'll take it from here, Nurse Edmonds. Thank you." A man in a white lab coat, stethoscope around his neck interrupted. "Please, don't harass Miss Edmonds. She's taken good care of you. I'll be happy to answer as many questions as I can." The man leaned over and pressed the diaphragm piece to Matthew's chest.

He was exhausted again. "I only want the truth."

"I'll tell you what I know. First tell me your name."

"My name? God, okay. Matthew, Matthew Buchanan."

"Good, Matthew Buchanan. Ask away."

"Are my parents all right?"

"Your family is fine in Texas. You, however, are in Germany. You were sent to us a week ago from Vietnam after suffering severe head trauma. As a result, you have a form of partial amnesia. You remember up to a certain point, this bus ride you speak about."

"W-what? I served in Vietnam?"

The physician nodded.

"I made it to Ft. Benning? What about Ft. Bragg?"

"You went through it all and served in Vietnam. We know it's confusing. Since you've recovered enough, you're entitled to know."

He listened grimly as the physician chronicled the past nine months of his life. He took it in, even when his mind denied it. He tried to push against the black wall, but the mallet speeded in tempo, and he was forced to stop.

"You remember a part of your life. Everything else is locked temporarily. You might remember on your own, or a strong stimuli could trigger the memories." The physician patted him on the arm. "Does the name Brian MacKay mean anything to you?"

"No. Is he important?"

"He is, or rather was, your partner. You went through training together and were stationed in the same camp. He's in a different wing and remains in critical condition. You should be proud. From what we learned, he owes you his life."

"I'm sorry, Doctor, I feel really tired."

"It's understandable. You've heard a lot in a short while. We can talk tomorrow. Maybe we can help unravel some of the puzzle. In the meantime, look at the bright side. You'll be going home soon."

Going home? Damn. He didn't remember leaving home. He collapsed against the pillows, feeling the sleeping pills' effect. What about Kathy? Could he work things out with her? And, why did the idea of talking to Kathy feel so...repugnant? Whenever he fell asleep, Kathy's blue-eyed stare didn't soothe him. Instead, that golden gaze imbued his soul with peace.

***

"Emilio, you have a visitor."

"What?" Emilio straightened in his chair. Behind Julianna stood the last man he expected to see: Jonathan Buchanan.

"Jonathan. Please, come in. How are you? Have a seat. May we offer you some refreshments?"

A smiling Jonathan stepped inside the office and sat across Emilio's desk. "Thank you, no. Julie already asked. I'm not staying long. I came to San Antonio on business. I should've called ahead."

"Nonsense. You're always welcome."

With all his mental processes back in order, Emilio steepled his fingers and stared at the man. Although he dreaded the answer, Emilio had to ask.

"Do you have any news from Matthew?"

Jonathan nodded. "We got word last night. He's in a German facility. Matthew and Brian were wounded in battle. They're still undergoing treatment."

"God, that child of mine." Emilio slapped the desk. "Kids today have such strange ideas."

"I'm sorry. I don't follow."

"Of course, you don't. Lita was convinced Matthew had died. Two days ago, she left Ocala, and we don't know where she's gone."

"That's terrible. Why would she believe that? We had no confirmation, only that he'd not returned to base."

"Lita insisted she had bond with Matthew and the connection had gone silent. Now she's disappeared because of a foolish notion."

"I've not told you everythin'. Matthew is sufferin' a type of dissociative amnesia. He remembers arrivin' at Houston's Greyhound station, nothin' else." Jonathan paused. "I'm a simple man with simple beliefs. I served in the Pacific and witnessed events that could never be explained by men of the cloth or science. If Lita claimed a spiritual link with my son, I believe her. She couldn't hear Matthew because he doesn't remember her."

Emilio felt a stack of bricks fall upon him. "What's the prognosis, Jonathan?"

"His condition could last hours, or the rest of his life. My visit has selfish reasons. I'd hoped Raquelita would help in the endeavor. Matthew loves her so much. I didn't know. You must be goin' out of your mind."

"We are, but Xavi and I have a plan to find her. When is he coming home?"

"In two or three weeks. He's recovering faster than Brian, poor kid. They removed his spleen. They're not sure if he'll keep his right leg. It's all so terrible." Jonathan's voice cracked. "War. A terrible transaction, and the children of our nation pay the price."

"When we find her, Lita could help with Matthew."

"No, first find your li'l girl, and when you do, keep her real close. She's suffered enough believin' my son's gone. It would be terrible if Matthew failed to remember her. If he improves, I'll contact you."

Emilio stood, came around the corner of the desk and shook Jonathan's hand. "I understand. I really like Matthew. I once thought he'd be my son."

"That's how I feel about Raquelita. Good luck findin' her. I'll pray for all of us. We need it."

Emilio watched Jonathan depart. He sank back into his chair mulling over Jonathan's words. *"If Lita claimed a spiritual link with my son..."* Son of a bitch, she believed Matthew was dead. She'd practically told him. They had to find her, quickly.

The Moirae's fun project came to full fruition.
The young lovers had been set apart.
And now, the thread, which should have remained intact, was severed.
An evil star rose upon Matthew and Raquel's sky,
and no human under its influence would escape.

Chapter Thirty-Six

Manhattan – February 15th 1968

Music stopped, lights blinded the dancers, and ear-rending whistles sparked the human stampede. The violence of the tumult separated Raquel from Dalia and Skip and thrust her instead with Linda, who led her out of the club undetected by the authorities. This was a raid? Raquel María Muro, naïve Texas girl, embroiled in an event worthy of Al Capone. Outside was bedlam. Men and women zigzagged through traffic on West 4th Street, while police officers brandished batons in pursuit. A young man's plight would forever remain in her mind. She stared morbidly as he resisted the assault, only to be beaten unconscious and dragged away. Raquel shut her eyes, sickened by the brutality.

"He's queer," Linda whispered.

"Queer, how?"

"Lord, you've lived a sheltered life. It means he likes men. Cops love to harass queers, PRs, and blacks. They constantly raid the Stonewall Inn, a popular homosexual hangout up the block." Linda kept nudging her away from the subsiding riot.

"Mark my words, one day the situation at Stonewall will turn ugly. Tonight was The Haven's turn, though the club's mixed crowd is tricky. If the cops aren't careful, they'll end up arresting some congressman's son or daughter."

Raquel's curiosity won. "What are PRs?"

"Damn, girl. PR's short for Puerto Rican. Like Dalia."

"But, she's not—"

"No, she wasn't born in Puerto Rico, but her parents were. It doesn't matter. To the cops, she's a PR. Hurry. I know some people. It'll be warm inside, and we can stay until the streets calm down."

The little apartment on Barrow Street was packed. A cross section from Sanctuary had taken refuge here. Applause and loud whistles erupted at Linda's arrival. A joint made a quick appearance on her lips. Raquel stared, unbelieving. She had fled Florida and had landed in Oz. Who was the real Linda? Back in Ocala, she was Dalia's shadow, silly, inane, and unable to function without her friend. Not only had Linda spirited her safely away, she was received as a star. This was her milieu.

Music blared; the ambient air was thick with incense and pot. Joints and tiny glass vials filled with white powder traveled from hand to hand. Some poured a small mound over mirrors, separated it into thin lines, and sniffed voraciously through cut straws. Others, as if it were communion at church, went around with little spoons, feeding the supplicants' needy nostrils.

Yes, she was in Oz. Spoon in hand, Linda materialized at her side. "Hold one side of your nose, inhale, now the other. Good girl." Linda pivoted as two guys trailed her. The trio disappeared behind closed doors.

The rush of energy startled her. Minutes ago, she'd been tired. Now she was wide-awake. Her temples pounded, her jaw clenched and released incessantly. She couldn't stop her thoughts. The feeling was hateful. Every emotion she'd tried to suppress surfaced: Matthew, her family, home. She was an unhappy stranger in a bizarre land, riding a hellish merry-go-round.

She shook and tingled. Her nose, teeth, and upper lip were numb. Repulsed by encroaching, sweaty bodies, Raquel dodged the slithering hands and nonsensical chatter. Somehow—God, her brain was so fuzzy—she found a deck of cards, then huddled in a corner and played an obsessive game of solitaire until the sun peeked out and a smiling and obviously sated Linda reappeared.

***

After a long train ride, Raquel and Linda returned to Mount Vernon and Mary's exasperated demands. *She has reason*, Raquel thought. They'd been out all night. Impervious to her mother's shrill voice, Linda disappeared as the wailing continued, grating on Raquel's nerves. Lack of sleep and the residual effects of the night augmented her irritation. An odd prickle crawled on her skin, and stars dotted her vision. The house's interior overwhelmed her anew. The overall disarray increased her discomfort. She would kill for one of her yellow friends to ease her frayed nerves. No, not frayed. Her synapses were fried.

"You are so lost," Gerard slurred, yet she understood him. Less than twenty-four hours ago, the man had uttered gibberish. The implication terrified her.

"I could send you to heaven. You'd sleep like the angels. I know why you hurt. I can take the pain away." Raquel stared at Gerard. His knowing look frightened her.

"Sure, after you hurl your guts out." Linda reappeared wearing a terry robe and a nasty look. "He is a fucking junkie. Once you start down that path, there ain't no going back. Do you know what he's offering?"

"No, I don't, any more than I knew what you gave me last night. What the hell was that stuff? I thought I'd lose my mind."

"Coke. We had to stay awake until the cops were gone. I thought it would help," Linda explained a little more quietly.

"Awake? I couldn't stop thinking. I came to New York to forget about Matthew's death, not to spend nights thinking about it. For that, I would have stayed in Ocala."

"How dare you keep my little girl out all night?' Mary Callahan's large presence entered the fray. She stared coldly at Raquel.

"*I* kept her out? Lady, I don't know this city."

"Please, don't listen," Linda whispered. "Mom, I was invited to a party."

Mary Callahan's grotesque smile reappeared. "My baby at a party. Did you see any cute boys?" Her beefy hand caressed Linda's hair.

Linda shook loose and pulled Raquel to her bedroom. "Please don't pay attention to my mother. She's not well. I didn't realize coke would make you hyper. Let me make it up to you." She opened her palm with two red-and-baby-blue capsules. In the other hand, she held a glass of water.

"I should've known you're a down-head. These rainbow beauties will do the trick. One will put you to sleep. Two will give you a down rush. What's your pleasure?"

As Raquel stared at the capsules, the avenue to her plan opened wide. "Maybe a down rush." She dropped the caps in her mouth, gave a little cough, and took a sip of water. One, however, found its way to her pocket. Why not? Linda was a walking drugstore. With a little patience, Raquel would soon collect enough pills to execute the plan.

In a moment, despite what Linda said, Raquel surfed through her first down rush, warm, seductive, and, above all, silent. The wave overtook her mind. She lost all cares and fell into a dreamless sleep.

***

As promised, two days later, she was rescued out of the Callahan home and brought to Dalia's. With only a few belongings to her name, she soon settled in Dickey's old bedroom. His scent lingered. Although it wasn't familiar, its intrinsic masculinity was a reminder of another. She sat at the edge of the bed, remembering loving memories, thoughts of what could've been. Nostalgia ached in her throat. Those hits of cocaine had disarmed her control. Emotions she had caged flew about like birds. The task to rebuild her defenses seemed Herculean, and this man's scent didn't help.

"May I come in?" Dalia rapped gently against the door.

"Door's open."

"Let's go out. It's cold but sunny. We could check out 5th Avenue, maybe Saks?" She smiled, entering the room. "Window shopping's fun."

Raquel nodded. "I think you're right."

***

As forecasted, it was a beautiful day sans the usual bluster of winter. The sky shimmered an unblemished blue. They arrived at 5th Avenue, and Raquel was enthralled. She laughed playfully, dodging the throngs along the sidewalks. She leaned over the railing at the Rockefeller ice-skating rink, crowded with pirouetting, leaping skaters. Marité would've loved this. One day Raquel might try to learn. *One day?* She didn't have many left.

Unaware of Raquel's thoughts, Dalia was pleased. The window-shopping expedition was a stroke of genius. Signs of sweet Lita, the friend she'd dearly missed, were making a comeback. They made it to the corner of 50th and 5th, and Raquel gawked at the pointed spires and gothic façade of St. Patrick's Cathedral.

"Oh, let's go inside. I've read it has beautiful stained glass windows."

"Okay," Dalia agreed, hopping lightly on her feet, waiting for the light to change. Despite her thick boots, the cold from the cement seeped to her toes. "From there we can go to a coffee shop I know. Have some lunch and hot chocolate. Afterwards, we can check out Saks."

"Yum." Raquel rubbed her belly with a big smile.

They'd reached the left side of the Cathedral steps when Dalia saw them. She tried to distract Raquel, but it was too late. The two men in full Army uniform had caught Raquel's attention. Dalia swallowed hard and crossed her fingers.

Mass had finished, and the servicemen—along with the regular parishioners—exited through the massive bronze doors. On the right side of the steps, a group of young folks loitered on the sidewalk. They noticed the uniforms, and a taunting murmur began. Like wolves with their prey, the crowd gathered around the soldiers in a threatening circle. They remained stoic as the voices grew louder and insults and jeers increased. It didn't take long before someone's hand shot out to shove. A young woman stepped up and spit next to their shoes.

"Assassins," a man yelled.

"Baby killers," another shrieked.

The circle tightened, and still they stood their ground.

"What are they doing?"

"War protestors. We don't want to be here." Dalia grabbed Raquel's hand, just as she lunged forward.

"Lita, no." She moved quickly behind Raquel, restraining her arms.

"Someone must help them," Raquel protested, shaking and struggling against Dalia's hold.

"They're not Matthew."

"I know." She stopped struggling and looked over her shoulder. Tears coursed down her face.

"Halt. Disperse. Now." The commands boomed over the crowd. From the south side of 5th Avenue, two mounted police officers approached. The group disbanded, leaving the soldiers rattled but unharmed after a brief conversation and a respectful salute. The servicemen waved and disappeared within the now indifferent throngs.

With the commotion over, Dalia hustled an unresisting Raquel to her favorite haunt and sat them at a corner booth. Soon, two generous mugs of hot chocolate topped with whipped cream were placed before them, rivulets of melted cream trailing down the sides.

"Mmmm." Dalia took a sip. The tip of her tongue darted out and touched her lip. She smiled, licking the thin line of sweet cream.

"I've been in this city less than a week. I've seen and experienced more in these few days than in my entire lifetime. How have you managed?" Still shaken, Raquel used both hands to steady her mug.

"I was born here, and like most New Yorkers, we're used to a little insanity. This is the center of the world. We have it all, from the very best to the very worst, and every level in between. Not every day's full of action. But when it happens, it's big. The city prepares us for everything. It makes us stronger, as famed Nietzsche would explain. You'll be fine, I promise."

"Will I?"

"Of course, this is an adventure, a little taste. Come May, you're going home."

Raquel didn't answer.

***

At first, the muffled whimpers took part in Skippy's dreams, but when sobs and mutterings got louder, he jumped up, fully awake.

"Baby," he whispered.

"Hmmm?"

"Do you hear that?"

"What?"

"That sound. Is it Lita?"

"Yes. By the time she starts sobbing, you're already in zombie land. I don't hear her anymore."

He nudged Dalia's shoulder. "Honey?"

"Yes, sweetie?"

"I've got an idea. Should we get Dickey and Lita together? He's a good guy, and ever since Vivian, he's dated no one. He's shown an interest in Lita. Maybe they could help each other."

"Raquel's not staying in New York. Not if I can help it. She's going home soon."

"Okay, okay. Maybe they could entertain each other, and who knows? She might pull him away too. He doesn't belong here either." Skippy thought he made lots of sense. He'd noticed the gleam in his friend's eye, and the girl seemed to be fond of him.

"Let's talk about this in the morning, when we're both awake."

"Oh, I'm awake, baby, wide awake." He smiled. Dalia flipped around. His lips captured hers, and her clothing began to disappear.

***

On the other side of the wall, Raquel stopped tossing. She opened the small drawer of her night table and searched beneath a stack of papers. She pulled out a plastic vial and counted. One, two, three...seven in total. A few more rainbows and her departure after Matthew was a certainty.

***

March comes in like a lion and goes out like a lamb. Raquel had heard the saying, and this beautiful Sunday afternoon was proof. She opened the living room window and stuck her head out, enjoying the spring-like air. Someone rang the doorbell, and Dalia yelled from the kitchen, "Lita, please answer that."

"Be right there." She rushed to the door and swung it open. A frowning Dickey stood on the other side. He had a helmet tucked under one arm, another dangling from his fingers.

"Richard." She stared at his frown. "Is something wrong?"

"Haven't these two knuckleheads taught you anything? Never open the door without checking first."

"Gosh, you're right. Come in, please."

"Hey there, what a surprise." Dalia emerged with a smiling Skip in tow. "What's going on?"

"I thought our friend would like to go out." He spoke to them but smiled at Raquel. "What do you say? It's a perfect day for a ride."

"A bike ride?"

"What a great idea." Skippy intervened, shooting a meaningful look at Dalia. "The day is warm, and Dalia can lend you one of her jackets. What about a hel— Oh, I see, you came prepared."

Dickey smirked, lifting the second helmet. "Have you ever been on a motorcycle, little girl?" he asked gently.

"Ah... No, can't say I have." She blushed at his intense gaze.

"A virgin," Richard exclaimed. "Say yes. I promise to be gentle. You'll really enjoy it. I don't race, nor do I take foolish chances. I like to take my time." He pressed a hand against his chest and smiled.

"S-should I...?" Raquel stammered, still blushing at his innuendoes.

"Definitely," Dalia said.

Dressed in Dalia's leather jacket, a scarf, and gloves, Raquel stood next to Richard's touring Shovelhead. He tinkered with the helmet, secured the strap around her jaw, then shoved his down. Swinging a long leg over the seat, Richard pulled the bike upright and signaled for her to approach.

"Step on the foot stand and climb over. Same as mounting a horse, Texas girl." His wicked little smile reappeared, and she felt the heat on her face again. "When you sit, you'll slide down. Put your arms around my waist and hold on."

Once she was settled, he turned to her. "Ready?" She nodded. The bike rumbled.

"Here we go." They took off into the wind.

***

On Sunday, March 3rd, Matthew Buchanan arrived in Texas. His overjoyed parents kissed, hugged, passed him from arms to arms, and then back around.

"My boy.... m-my boy." Jonathan struggled with the words.

"Oh, you've lost so much weight," Ernestine whimpered.

"He's fine, Mother. He's tight and looks real healthy." Jonathan patted Matthew's cheek.

Time hadn't passed for Matthew, and the emotional reception dizzied him. Everything looked the same. He'd seen his parents scant hours before he woke up. Though he'd been warned in Germany, it didn't change his reaction.

"Dad. I don't mean to be...but...I just saw you both," he tried to explain, feeling miserable, not wanting to disappoint them.

"Don't worry. It's been explained to us at length. Just indulge your old folks' exuberance for a minute, and allow us to enjoy your return."

"Dad, I'm a fortunate man, from what I've seen and heard. I love you both more than anything or anyone in the world." When he spoke, he felt a strange tightening in his stomach, but let it pass. "It's just incomprehensible. I've lost a year of my life."

"We understand, and you need time to adapt. When it's right, everythin' will fall into place. You'll see." He threw an arm around Matthew's shoulders and smiled at Ernestine. "Mother, our beloved son is back."

Chapter Thirty-Seven

Round Rock – March 7th 1968

"This has to stop." Grumbling under his breath, Jonathan marched to the barn. It was time to tackle and tie-down Mathew—metaphorically speaking, of course. His son wasn't a hermit, damn it. Jonathan followed the rustle of tossed hay and found him at the back of the barn. Matthew toiled, pitchfork in hand, his old chambray shirt dark with perspiration down to the waist of his faded jeans. And yet, it was a cool morning for early March. Matthew must've started at the break of dawn.

"May I have a word?" Jonathan asked.

Matthew thrust the pitchfork into the hay and stared silently.

"I truly appreciate yer efforts round the ranch. You've been a tremendous help."

"But?"

"Well, Mother and I... We've noticed. You've not called any of yer friends or gone out. Five solid days, Matthew, you've done nothin' but ranch work. It's not healthy. You're young and you need distraction, social interaction—"

"Dad, please." Matthew shifted, staring at his grimy boots. "I know you mean well, but I'm not ready. Not yet."

"The VA offered help if you needed it." Jonathan padded closer and placed a hand on Matthew's shoulder.

"I know, Dad. The famous transition." He spoke with derision, pressing harder against the handle "It's difficult to process what I don't remember. Look, I'll step back into the arena soon. If I don't, you can take me to task again." Matthew turned around slowly. "I'm almost ready, I can feel it." With his back to his father, he lifted the pitchfork and resumed his job.

Jonathan sighed, accepting temporary defeat. "All right, if you say so."

As soon as Matthew heard his father's footsteps fade, he slapped the handle. He hated lying, but he simply didn't want to reenter the social scene. What he wanted to do was scream in frustration. He'd lost almost a year, had turned twenty in that time. Hell, a life developed in nine months. Those elusive months ran like a subterranean river through his mind, hinting at their presence, yet completely inaccessible. A terrible sense of loss overwhelmed him, and he vented savagely against the pile of hay.

***

"Mother, where are you?" Jonathan called out, searching through the house.

"Over here. What is it, dear?" Ernestine answered from the family room. She sat on her favorite chair as her able hands crocheted in haste.

"It has to stop." He hated repeating himself. As he paced in circles, he set a fist on his waist. "He can't continue to hide. He says he's almost ready, but I don't see the effort."

"Jonathan, please sit down. Let's talk." Her emerald eyes, so like her son's, sparkled. "I want our son to be well. He needs time. I see his conflict and irritation." Ernestine stopped her work and placed the piece inside the knitting basket. "Dearest, try to imagine if you woke up in a hospital and learned from strangers you'd served in the Pacific, and didn't remember."

Jonathan sat silently, regarding the woman he loved and evaluating Matthew's loss. If by some twist of fate Ernestine's beautiful face or person was removed from his mind or his life… Jonathan shuddered.

"You're a wise woman. What do we do now?"

"We could jump-start the effort for him. Where's Johnnie Murdock these days? Is he still in town?" She stood, walked to her husband's side, and soothingly caressed his hair.

Jonathan smiled. "Why, yeah, he is. His injured knee kept him home."

"Let's throw a gathering tomorrow night. Nothing big, just a few friends."

"Dang, that's brilliant. We could ask Kathy."

"Absolutely not. If Kathy Miles returns to Matthew's life, it won't be through us. Are we clear?" She returned to her chair, sat with a thud, and primly recovered the abandoned afghan.

"Sure, Mother. I'd ask why, but I know better. A small party it is." Whatever angered his wife about Kathy, she had good reason. He let it go.

***

Friday night, Ernestine supervised the gathering of friends and their sons. By sheer coincidence, they were all Matthew's football buddies from high school. If Matthew saw through the ruse, he didn't let on. Perfect.

The barbecue was smooth sailing. The early March weather remained mild, and the evening was pleasant. There was only one hitch: Garth Miles, Kathy's brother, had come. Who invited him? It vexed Ernestine, and she followed his footsteps like a hawk. Garth, like his sister, was known for his drunken bouts. Ernestine wouldn't allow drunkenness in her house, least of all today.

Like clockwork, once Garth got a few beers in him, his discretion went south. He'd been watching a relaxed Matthew enjoying the party and discussing with Mr. Murdock a new brand of feed. Despite the warnings about the taboo subject of Matthew's lost memory, he plunged ahead.

"Hey, did you tire of the shweet youn' gal from Florida?"

Storm warning, batten down the hatches, Garth was slurring. Ernestine wanted to faint.

"What?"

Nonplussed, Matthew straightened, banging his bottle of beer with a loud chink against the chair. Mr. Murdock glowered and signaled to his son. Johnnie nodded, and in instant relay, he beckoned Stevie.

"Yesh. The li'l filly on Thanksgiving—"

Garth stopped. Johnnie and Stevie pulled him toward the door.

"Hey, careful wish the merch...andise." Garth chuckled.

"Which girl? What's he talking about?"

Ernestine grasped Jonathan's arm. Her husband looked ready to stomp on the fool.

"Shit, Matthew James. Why d'you listen to this drunk? He's goadin' you," Johnnie Murdock grumbled while he and Stevie subdued a squirming Garth.

"Yeah, yeah, ask Kathy, she'll tell ya," Garth slurred as they finally dragged him away.

The words struck a hidden chord in Matthew. He pivoted slowly around. As he turned, all eyes were trained on him, which was definitely odd. His father's brow had tightened. His mother's gaze was full of pity. Damn. Why?

Later that night, he asked his parents straight out. They answered lightly, some such about a casual date, no one important. Still, he sensed their underlying discomfort. True, Garth the idiot had always loved to beleaguer and antagonize him. But, the reaction from the guests had been evident. For the umpteenth time, Matthew cursed his damaged memory. Only one avenue remained, the one he'd been avoiding: Kathy Miles.

***

Saturdays were ladies' night at the Bronco Buster and the parking lot was packed. Matthew had to drive around a few times until he found an empty spot next to several trashcans. He parked the truck, and took a few minutes to fortify his resolve. He couldn't shake the untimely feelings; an ill wind blew tonight.

This mission feels bad. The man spoke clearly in his mind, familiar and unfamiliar. He shoved the steering wheel in frustration. What the heck was happening to him? Was it a lost memory, someone he'd fought with? He almost drove away. But Garth's words teased him. *"Did you tire of the shweet youn' gal from Florida?"* He wanted to know. He *had* to know. He stepped out, locked the truck, and went inside the club.

The first insult to his senses was the appalling smoke. Next was the sickly sweet stench of rotten beer. He winced, waiting for his vision to adapt. Matthew looked behind the bar. Yes, it was Kathy's night.

He wondered then, why was she still in Round Rock? With her ambitions, why not move to Austin? For that matter, why was she still in Texas? She should be in California or New York. He forgot the questions as he got closer. A year had definitely gone by. This Kathy was a different woman. She was terribly thin, with a sharp angularity and harshness to her features. Darkness and lack of fulfillment made a definitive statement in her features.

And wasn't he supposed to be in love with her? Why did he feel absolutely nothing? Matthew inhaled and approached the counter.

"Hey there, big boy."

How bizarre, she didn't seem hurt or angry. He recalled their last quarrel. Her pleasantness made him uncomfortable, for he had only come about the Florida girl. In the end, Kathy quelled his curiosity. Garth was a loon and the Florida girl a fantasy.

A celebratory round of beers appeared. Tequila shooters followed.

When her shift ended, Kathy walked around the counter and sashayed up to Matthew. Her lips came suggestively close to his face, and he pulled back. The scent was wrong, and the ruby lipstick looked offensive. Confused and slightly buzzed, Matthew wanted to go home. Despite the pull to escape, he remembered

Kathy. And his mind liked that. Besides, she was being unusually nice, so he didn't want to go yet. Still, he didn't want her to touch him.

A new round of beers arrived; more tequila shooters followed.

Fuck, I'm dizzy. Kathy smiled with four lips. Matthew blinked, and they fused into a pair. And now, the face of his dreams replaced Kathy's. *Oh hell.* Matthew had no real answers, no information, and not an active brain cell left. The bar was closing, and she proposed to take him home. Tomorrow he could claim his truck. He accepted. He wanted his bed and his room. He was wiped out drunk.

On the ride, he was plunged in a cauldron of discomforting stimulations. Unwanted hands pried and searched. The sensation was perverse, the feeling amiss, the odor repulsive. Moments later and nearly blind with alcohol, he staggered and pushed away, yet the hands insisted after him. He protested, but an expert, fetid mouth engulfed his unshielded member. He couldn't stop the shameful erection. God, did he desire? Yes, his angel.

In his fuzzy mind, his Gypsy beauty materialized, displacing the irritating seducer. Rich mahogany locks draped and soothed his anxious body and bewildered mind. The sweet-scented body hovered above him, and he took it in hunger and need. *Stay, please, love me.* He nestled in her warmth, desperate to ease his want and insanity. He cried out; her name teased at the edge of his lips, almost within reach. *Angel, don't leave me alone.*

***

Matthew stirred with the rosy morning light. He scrunched his face at the throbbing headache. His mouth was thick and dry, his stomach churned. He looked around, trying to recognize his surroundings as muddled thoughts crept into his brain. The dead weight of a golden head numbed his arm. He blinked, and snippets of the night surfaced. Finally, his short-term memory came to life.

Shit. What have I done?

Careful not to wake his sleeping partner, he extricated himself. Stealthily, as he'd been trained, he searched around for his clothing, dressed in the living room, left the house, and ran as if the devil chased him. In twenty minutes and with a fierce headache, he was in his truck He sped away like a madman.

Hours later, after repeated showers and multiple glasses of water, Matthew sat in his room, thinking. A thought passed, teased, but he was so nauseated, he let it go. How much had he drunk? There'd be a reckoning from last night. Kathy would come soon, asking for payment.

***

Richard's engagement with Vivian ended badly. It had left him with a bitter taste for relationships and a nasty scar from a knife wound on his back. From then on, he kept the door to his heart shut. As destiny would have it, the day he picked up the foursome at La Guardia and looked at Raquel's pretty face, alarm bells had gone off in his brain. Raquel was special. With her, his careful walls disappeared. She could crack his shields with a glance. Raquel was a heady combination for him: vulnerable, tempting, and innocent.

The young woman dismounted the bike, unaware of her grace. Without guile, she commanded his imagination at her unsuspecting will. It attracted him like a bee to honey. She waited for him, holding the helmet, her expression soft and questioning. *What was he doing?* Richard had cruised aimlessly, allowing his hands to take over the ride, and here they were, at his front door. He wanted her. It was all he knew.

He locked the bike, removed the helmet, and walked up to her. He reached down to her hand and brought it up to his lips. He kissed the small fingers one by one, peering into her enchanting eyes. Slowly, she lowered her lids, and he trembled like a schoolboy.

"Would you like to come in?" He spoke so low he wondered if she heard him. She had. A passing shadow clouded her expression. He knew her story and waited. When Raquel smiled and nodded, relief and happiness flooded Richard's soul. She had evidently reached acceptance, same as he had. He kissed her knuckles again and allowed her hand to fall. With a gentle pressure on Raquel's lower back, he guided her inside.

Raquel entered with a tremulous heart. The door closed softly, and the dull click of his boots stopped behind her. Richard's hands fell on the curve of her waist. Their warmth eased her trembling body. His hot breath caressed the nape of her neck.

She didn't wish to hurt him, yet she'd agreed to his invitation. *It's not Matthew.* Matthew was gone. Was it fair to Richard? He knew about her grief, didn't he?

"Richard," she began, turning to face him, and he placed a finger on her lips.

"Shhh, Lita. I know. If you're not ready, tell me. I'll take you home."

"No...I... Richard." She stumbled over her words, surprised by his admission. "I really like you. I don't want to hurt you."

"I understand," he said. "We'll go slowly, one step at a time. If it feels wrong, say the word, and everything stops."

Her lips moved to speak, but his descended on hers, warm and full, encompassing and possessive, in a wonderful caress. Not Matthew's kiss, though. His kiss would never return. Still, Richard offered what she had missed for months: life, emotion, and tenderness.

Wrong or not, she would allow the fantasy. Tonight, Matthew would live in her arms. She threaded her fingers through Richard's hair, he groaned and tightened the embrace. Sighing against Richard's lips, Raquel allowed her dream to take over.

***

On this beautiful late April morning, Jonathan sat in the kitchen, his attention half on the planting schedule, the other on his wife. Ernestine hummed, cooking bacon and scrambling eggs for breakfast. Her biscuits were already in the warming oven. She'd already called for Matthew to come before it got cold. The woman was fastidious about her meals.

Jonathan peered through the window; he could hear Matthew's loud clanking in the shed all the way from the kitchen. He emerged with a victorious smile. In one hand, he held a large chaff cutter, in the other, a rake. Thoroughly amused, Jonathan shook his head. He wouldn't try to guess what his son had in mind.

"Mom, I'm starving," Matthew exclaimed, moving around like a small tornado. "It smells delicious." He leaned toward his mother and planted a kiss on her cheek. "I love your biscuits. Mornin', Dad," he said and sat on the closest chair. "Can I have the recipe? I might wanna try my luck. I learned how to cook some."

Jonathan felt a tight grip constricting his throat. "Son, what did you just say?"

"Um...you mean the recipe for the biscuits?"

"No, the other thing, 'bout knowing how to cook."

"It started a while back. I seem to know things...though I can't remember how or when I learned them."

"It's a good sign, my boy," Jonathan said, but Matthew no longer looked at him.

"Maybe, but something wicked this way comes, Dad," Matthew said staring out the window. He pushed his chair back and slowly stood up.

"What is it?" As Jonathan turned, he caught a glimpse of an unfamiliar vehicle approaching. He frowned.

At the stove, Ernestine gasped. "Isn't that Kathy?"

Matthew had paled.

"I saw her over a month ago... Hmmm. Mom, Dad, go ahead and eat. Gotta take care of this." Matthew stiffened and walked out. He stood at the gate as the Dodge Charger approached.

"I don't have a good feelin' about this," Ernestine whispered.

Jonathan watched the scene. Kathy stepped out of the car and stormed toward Matthew, jabbering and gesticulating. Matthew stood impassive and silent. Kathy stopped abruptly, and he shook his head, his voice ringing out as he argued back. Jonathan became acutely aware of its timbre, deep, with a sharp, commanding edge to it. In that enlightening moment, he envisioned Matthew in jungle fatigues and giving orders. While he wasn't looking, his son had become a man.

Matthew grasped Kathy's forearm. Jonathan thought he'd have to intervene. Instead, she backed down, speaking softly. Kathy started to cry. What was going on?

Kathy lunged for Matthew, and he stepped back, waving his hands in front. She pursued him and finally desisted, heading for her car. Then she whirled and slapped Matthew across the face. Ernestine and Jonathan gasped. Matthew stiffened. Kathy entered her vehicle and drove away.

Matthew returned ghostly pale. His earlier happy expression had dimmed. "Mom, Dad, please sit. I have something to tell you."

Kathy was pregnant with his child. She'd asked for money to cross the border and have an abortion. Matthew refused, arguing he would raise the child. Ernestine and Jonathan Buchannan were about to become grandparents. And April Fools' Day had already come and gone.

***

Xavi arrived early at Emilio's home, and while he waited for the promised coffee, he glanced around in open admiration. The desk and bookcase in alder wood were a perfect set. Intriguing asymmetrical shelving housed books, objects d'art, curios and photographs in beautiful frames. Plush leather chairs pulled together the air of masculine comfort. Xavi pointed at a black-and-white shot.

"Is it Julie's?"

"Yes, I love her western works. Superstition Mountains, outside Phoenix."

"Do you have more of these?" This time he indicated a photograph of Matthew holding Raquel and Marité.

"Lots. Thanksgiving, last year."

"What'll you do with them when she returns?"

"We'll see. What matters is when she returns. Any news?"

They stopped with Julianna's arrival. She carried a ceramic coffee service and placed it on the desk. She filled two mugs with the aromatic liquid.

"Same as before?" she asked Xavi, passing a mug to Emilio.

"You are a goddess. I can't believe you remember."

Julianna tilted her head graciously, served him, and moved behind her husband.

"I overheard a little. Please go on."

Xavi stirred his coffee and took a sip. "His name is Whitlock. Highly recommended by several associates, and I read his file. He dug up people who'd vanished without a trace. I'm convinced the man has the dogged persistence we need. He's already on his way to New York."

"Expensive?" Julianna asked.

Xavi waved a hand. "This is a family effort, Julie. She's my goddaughter, and I've saved a ton of money living the single life, although the phase is ending soon. Jonas is also in, and he has ample funds. That's one reason why I came. To tell you money won't affect the search."

"Thanks, my friend. Now, back up a second. What does 'the phase is ending' signify?"

"I'm going to be a *papá*. Can you imagine? Isabel is past her first trimester. The Repulles line may continue after all." He slapped the armrest playfully.

"We're getting married as soon as I settle the business agreement between Ferguson and Jonas. We were going to wait for Raquelita, but Jonas and Coralina changed our minds. That's part of the news, the new partnership and our marriage."

"I'm so happy for you, Xavi." Julie grasped his shoulder as she headed for the door. "Meanwhile, if you'll excuse me, I'm going to finish breakfast."

"Wait, sweetheart." Emilio held on to her hand. "This is big. Bring your coffee, sit with us."

Julie smiled. "My tea is in the kitchen and it's getting cold. You can fill me in when we eat." She extricated her hand.

"Tea, Julie? You never drink tea, unless you're sick."

The smile didn't waver. "I'm fine, really I think I'll be drinking tea during the next few months." She gestured for Emilio to sit, then left.

Xavi didn't miss the glint in her eye. He looked back to Emilio and almost guffawed at the consternation on his face. *Oh, Emilio…*

***

"I am the liaison between the Reynolds and Ferguson joint venture," Xavi explained after breakfast. He rose, taking the empty dishes to the sink. Julie uttered a protest, but his raised eyebrow stopped her. He knew how to give orders with a simple expression. It brooked no argument.

"It's a perfect setup. I can move to Ocala and maintain the position in San Antonio." As he moved about comfortably, he washed, rinsed, and explained almost in the same breath. "I have one more surprise, Emilio. Isabel is granting joint custody of Marité." He settled the last dish on the drying rack, dried his hands, then flipped the dish towel on his shoulder before returning to the table.

"Isabel has been hit hard, between the fight against addiction and Lita's disappearance. Both have been bitter pills. Pity it had to be this way."

Chapter Thirty-Eight

Manhattan – April 24th 1968

> *With its ruinous task accomplished against Matthew, the Ancient*
> *soared, seeking adequate conveyance. True to its violent nature,*
> *it rode on the winds of a powerful eastbound storm. On the*
> *morning of April 24th the front dumped copious*
> *amounts of rain over the Eastern seaboard.*
> *The Ancient was now poised to release*
> *misfortune on its next two victims.*

Coffee. Dalia's first sleepy thought. *Coffee.* She stumbled out of bed, performed her morning ablutions, and dressed. She entered the living room and stopped. A statuelike Raquel stared at the sheeting rain.

"Lita, what're you doing?" Dalia touched her shoulder. It felt like ice. "Come, come with me." She pulled her friend to the warmth of her kitchen. "Sit," she ordered, and Raquel obeyed.

Dalia moved about the kitchen, setting up the percolator and pulling breakfast fixings out of the refrigerator. They needed food. She examined her friend. Damn, had she been smoking already? Dalia unleashed her anger.

"Are you high?" It had an effect, and her friend winced. Arms akimbo, Dalia said, "Don't lie." When Raquel stared back, Dalia almost winced. She'd seen this look before, in Ocala, after the news of Khe Sanh.

"You'll think I'm crazy."

Lita sounded more upset than high. Still, something was definitely wrong today. "Have you taken any pills?"

"No, I haven't. Okay? It's difficult to explain."

"Try me."

"It's Matthew, always Matthew. I can't stop thinking about him! I thought when Richard and I b-became intimate, t-that thoughts of Matthew would end. But they haven't. They grow stronger each day."

She jumped and walked to the sink. After opening the faucet to a full stream, Raquel cupped her palms, scooped up the ice-cold water, and splashed it on her face. She turned to her friend, wet fingers tightened over her chest, fisting the cloth of her night shift.

"He is here." She beat her chest. "Right here, like yesterday and the day before. It doesn't end. It's worse than a jealous lover. Matthew's dead, and yet he's in my waking thoughts and my dreams. When I'm with Richard, I see him… Christ, what am I going to do?" At length, Raquel murmured, "I need to join him."

Dalia had no words. They'd all prayed for a miracle. When Dickey showed interest, everyone's hopes grew. When they began to date, everyone believed she'd be okay. With this last outburst, Raquel squashed all possibilities. Maybe there would never be a miracle, or perhaps it lay elsewhere.

It was a humbling epiphany. She'd been so arrogant, fiddling with this soul, making decisions, convinced she had the answers and owned the key to Raquel's happiness. Her friend needed to go home, heal her grief in her father's home. The truth hit Dalia like a thunderbolt, she had to contact Emilio today, not wait until May. It would be her penance and an early birthday gift to Raquel.

Full of empathy, Dalia moved Raquel back to a seat by the kitchen table, placed a mug of coffee in her hand, and resumed making breakfast. Outside, the rain had turned to a drizzle. Dalia glanced at her still-silent friend; she seemed to have calmed as well. If the weather held, Dalia would take her for a walk. It might distract her out of this gloom.

"Let's go visit the guys at the shop. What do you say?" Dalia asked carefully, avoiding names and focusing on food. "Maybe they'll take us to lunch."

Raquel stared blankly. With a little more aplomb, Dalia continued. "By the time we get dressed and walk over, the guys will be ready to eat. Skippy left very early this morning. Looks like it's done raining." She was running out of inane chatter.

Without a word, Raquelita stood and left the kitchen. Seconds later, she answered, "I'll be ready in five minutes."

Dalia sighed with relief.

***

The morning storm was a distant memory. Clear skies heralded a glorious day. They walked so engaged in conversation they hadn't noticed they were a block away from the auto shop. The men were not in the repair and lift area, but someone in the garage had the radio on loud. The soft breeze carried the DJ's voice and then a tune.

"No." Raquel recognized the first hellish notes. "No." She stopped and swiveled. "No." She wanted to kick the radio.

A startled Dalia held on to Lita's hand. "What is it?" She tightened her grip.

"I need to go," Raquel shouted, hoping to drown out the plaintive promise of everlasting love through time and distance—Matthew's words. The song continued, unaware of the chaos it created. "Stop. I can't take it, not today!" she screamed, pulling against Dalia's hold.

Alerted by the commotion, Dickey and Skip came out of the office, saw the struggling women, and rushed to them. Raquel escaped Dalia, and, blinded by her internal conflict, she sped to the middle of the street, Dickey in close pursuit.

He shoved her to the sidewalk, away from oncoming traffic. "What's the matter, sweetheart?" He grasped her shoulders firmly. "Honey, please, stop fighting me."

On cue, the hag swooped down to whisper in his ear. For Richard was also an intended victim, a recipient of evil fortunes.

Richard stepped into the trap. "Angel, please tell me what's wrong?"

Chaos overwhelmed her soul. The cherished endearment tipped her over the edge to insanity. She wrestled away from Dickey's hold. "Don't ever call me that again. Never, do you hear me?" She whirled and fled down the street, away from Dickey, Dalia, Skippy, and anyone else who could hold her. She didn't look back.

Stunned, Richard watched her disappear out of his life.

All tasks completed, the Ancient soared again.

Raquel ran and ran, *Matthew, Matthew, Matthew* droning in her mind. What should she do? Where could she go? She remembered the plastic vial full of Tuinals. The plan was ready. She'd saved enough caps for an irreversible overdose, but if she went back to the apartment, Dalia would catch up with her. She stopped to think and realized she was at the Callahans' door. She struggled with the decision to knock. This place twisted her guts, but if she was committed to sending her soul to the void, she must return here. She prayed Linda would answer instead of her absurd mother.

Linda opened the door and stood to the side, allowing her in. Raquel rambled as she entered. "I need to escape Dalia, Skip, and Richard. I can't give Dickey what he needs or wants. When, when are you going back to the city? Would you take me with you?"

"Tell me everything," Linda said.

The Callahan's phone rang nonstop. All calls went unanswered.

Hours later, Raquel and Linda—armed with grass and assorted pills—rode the train for Manhattan. An invitation to a party in the East Village beckoned.

***

St. Marks Place, the heart of the East Village, historic and trendsetting, bustled with crowds, hippies, bohemians, artists, and shoppers. Raquel loved the unusual façades of little restaurants, performance centers, and famous shops, Limbo, East Side Bookstore, UUU, and more. Dalia hadn't exaggerated—if New York wasn't the heart of the world, it was certainly a vital organ.

There was a difference between East and West Village. When they turned south toward East 5th, the atmosphere became somber and darker. The streets were quieter; signs of life had abated. They walked along blocks of ill-maintained row houses and abandoned warehouses, until they reached a loft building showing signs of life. This must be the party.

The mood indoors echoed the outdoors, heavy and dense, a far cry from the cheery whoops and welcoming applause of Barrow Street. In a corner, two men argued, and one mediated. On a distant lounger, two women and a man giggled. A strange mishmash of guests ambled about the room, seemingly without purpose.

Linda walked away, and Raquel sat on an empty sofa. The question popped into her head as she observed the disjointed gathering. Why was she here? Soon followed by the familiar answer with all its skewed logic—to forget, to get high and get lost.

"Are you friends with Ari?"

The strange woman dressed in a long black sheath sat so close she was almost on top of her. Raquel wiggled to make space between them, but the woman persisted. She swayed, inched closer, and stared at her. A look Raquel wasn't certain she liked.

"Ari?"

"Yes, he owns this place," she explained, waving toward a man chatting with two others. "He's throwing the party." She leaned in, and her breath rolled out. "I'm Lilli."

This felt awkward. "Ari?" Raquel repeated. With the excuse to check out the man, she stood, abandoning insinuating Lilli.

Perhaps she spoke the man's name out loud, or maybe it was the move to get away from Lilli. The moment she stood, the man focused on her, and her soul shivered with an anguished premonition. He shifted, dismissed his guests with an indifferent wave, and focused his full attention on Raquel.

He wasn't tall, yet his stride across the room was long and fluid. Sleek as an eel, if eels could be compared to humans. His midnight hair was pulled back at the nape and gleamed with highlights of deep blue. His black silk turtleneck matched his black gabardine slacks perfectly. He was a peerless vision in black, made all the more severe by the thin, hard line of his lips.

Run, her thoughts screamed, but she couldn't, for the man named Ari walked between her and the door. His demeanor intent, he would obviously suffer no obstacles or interruptions.

"Mmm...gold... I like. I'm Ari. Welcome to my home. And you are?"

Raquel supposed some women would find this man attractive, but for her it was the polar opposite. For all his elegance, the man didn't emit one ounce of warmth or humanity. Rather, hints of curtailed violence danced behind the dark blue stare. He scared her to death.

Where the hell was Linda? She searched around quickly.

"I'm waiting for an answer, gold eyes. You're new to my stables."

Stables? "Raquel. My name is Raquel. I came with my friend Linda." On cue, she disentangled her eyes from the man's direct gaze and looked around the room again. "I don't see her now."

"You're not from New York, are you, goldie?" He came closer.

"N-no." She could smell the couture fragrance floating around him. Ari's scrutiny increased Raquel's discomfort and foreboding tenfold. She searched earnestly for Linda. Where was she?

"I'm over here, gold eyes." Ari smirked, turning her chin to face him. "Raquel. Nice name. Tell me, where are you from?"

"I'm visiting from Florida. I was born in Texas."

"Ah. It explains the soft accent." Without asking, the man's refined fingers reached for her hand and placed it around his forearm. "Come, let's search for this *missing* Linda. Meanwhile, you can tell me about yourself, gold eyes."

"My name is Raquel, not gold eyes," she protested, trying to tug away. His smoothness frayed her nerves.

He laughed, impervious to her outburst and ignoring her slight resistance. In fact, he seemed to enjoy it. "We have spirit. I like gold. If I choose to call you so, what could you do?" Sleet fell out of his lips and the midnight blue stare gleamed black in the shadows.

He wasn't tall or muscular like Matthew, Skippy, or Richard. In fact, he looked more like a reed, an aristocratic, smooth reed. The smile he affected was a blunt smirk, curving with imperiousness. This air of unquestioned authority terrified her.

She must have shown her edginess, for he patted her hand. "There, there, we don't want you to bolt just yet. Raquel, is it?"

She nodded as they continued to stroll through groups of people and several partitioned areas of a deceptively large loft.

"Do you have family in New York?"

She shook her head, and he smiled. Her answer seemed to please him.

A joint appeared in his hand. He tucked it lightly between his lips, and a lighter materialized out of nowhere. Raquel knew then, this man's wishes and demands were obeyed instantly. Ari inhaled deeply before he offered her the joint with a bland smile.

"Go ahead"—he winked—"take a hit."

She obeyed. It tasted funny. Scant seconds later, the room began to spin. People and furniture wobbled and changed form. Pins rushed through her body. Stars swirled in her vision. She blinked. Ari's distorted face examined hers curiously.

"What did you give me?" she asked. The spinning room picked up speed.

"Angel dust for a gold angel, and a little grass mixed in," he laughed.

Raquel stumbled, and he guided her to a large, cushioned chair. She closed her eyes and slid, down, down, down…

***

"Here, drink some water." A childlike voice spoke. The upheaval in Raquel's mind ceased as she stared at a hand holding a glass. She almost slapped the glass away.

"What, what? No, you… Get away from me," she groaned, crawling backwards on the bed.

"Don't be afraid. I'm not going to hurt you." A girl, with a pixie-like face, framed by a cap of carrot-orange hair smiled. "My name is Molly." She came closer. Raquel snarled.

"Easy, I'm going to help you. Drink a little, you poor girl." Molly placed the glass to her parched lips. "I brought you a robe. Ari's gone to his place uptown. His men are downstairs. Let me help you up."

Raquel reached for the robe Molly offered, wincing as she covered her naked torso. With agonizing care, she rolled her legs out and tried to sit upright. The room spun. "I can't. I'm dizzy."

"Angel dust is still in your system. Try again. You don't want to stay here." The deceivingly strong pixie helped Raquel to stand. Once Raquel was fairly steady, Molly fastened the sash around her waist, then led her through a maze of rooms and corridors. Molly stopped before a closed door.

"Here we are." She twisted the knob and gestured for Raquel to enter.

"It's not much, and a little messy," Molly said pushing aside some clothes strewn on the bed. "But it works for us. I stay here with my boyfriend. I also rent a studio on the West side. That's our refuge from this place."

Raquel slipped into denial. Last night's violence hadn't been real. The events hadn't happened to her. Not her, not her. She whirled to Molly and grabbed her by the arms. "Please, I need to get away. I don't even know where my clothes are." She released Molly to hug her body protectively. "I don't understand what happened. Where's my friend?"

She spoke louder as waves of realization buffeted her soul. She was freezing, her teeth chattered, and started to babble. "Please…help me. I don't have a lot of money but—"

"We don't want your money." A young man interrupted from the doorway. "Molly, get her under control. Her voice carries." He shut the door quickly. "Keep it down, or you'll get us all into a shitload of trouble."

Confused, Raquel shifted her focus to the man. "Why? He's taken what he wanted. I want to leave." She flopped onto the edge of the bed, shielding her face with her hands.

Molly sat next to her and placed a gentle hand on her arm. "Shhh… Easy, girl. This is Ralphie, my boyfriend. His bark is much worse than his bite." Molly turned to the young man. "Why are you scaring her?"

"It's frustrating to watch these starry-eyed women." Ralphie pointed at Raquel. "They fly like moths to a bright flame, lured by drugs and fame, but when it gets too hot, they beg for help, or worse, they burn to cinders. They never examine the consequences of hanging out with guys like Ari until it's too late."

"Yes, yes, yes. I was stupid, more than stupid. But I didn't know Ari, nor did I come here looking for fame. I did this to myself...because I was searching for a way out of this world. A foolish romantic notion. Oh God. I don't understand anymore," she whispered. "It's all so mixed up. Just yesterday afternoon, I wanted to die."

"I don't mean to be cruel, sweetheart. If suicide was your aim, there are easier ways. I could suggest a few." Ralphie sighed and walked to the edge of the bed. "Okay, I'll confess. Last night I saw the guests, and you seemed too innocent to be part of the new arrival. I wondered if you knew the sort of man you'd fallen in with, or how you got involved in this mess. Plus...I have something else to say."

He shifted his shoulders uncomfortably. "You were fortunate Ari called my brother Carlos. Any other member of his gang would've enjoyed hurting you."

"Carlos is the man who—"

"Yes, I'm sorry. Carlos is an idiot who follows Ari for money, but he doesn't like hurting or raping women. He told me he warned you. Did he?"

"Yes," she whispered.

"All right," he said. "I heard the bit about money. Do you have friends in New York?"

Raquel nodded, and he continued. "The deal's to get you out without a hassle."

"Ari's a problem. He seems to have a thing for you," Molly explained. "It's both good and bad. Good because he'll tire of you soon. Bad because until he does, or we find an opportunity to free you, you're stuck."

"What do you mean stuck? I only need some clothes, borrow a couple of dollars for the train. I promise, I'll return the money."

Molly shook her head, lips tight. "Ari's left word to keep you. His guys are downstairs. You're going nowhere."

"Hey, wait...the party on Sunday," Ralphie intervened. "That's our chance. Ari's rounding up a new stable of women for his political guests. While the place is catered and serviced, we could sneak you out. But until then, I'm afraid you'll endure hard times."

Molly took over. "Ralphie finished his time a year ago and was hired to do maintenance work as a favor to Carlos, who's in Ari's cadre. Ralphie's not a trusted member. He has to wait for the right opportunity."

"I can't bear another instant with that man," she moaned.

"It'll be difficult. Try to rest, because tonight you'll need all your wits and all the control you can muster."

Raquel shook her head, lifting a trembling hand to her messy locks. "Wits, control? I've been soiled to the marrow of my bones. I'm held against my will, and I have no clothes to wear. And why does that make me feel worse?"

Molly raised her palm. "I can get you clothes. They may not fit right, but who cares. Why don't you take a long, hot shower? I'll be right here when you come out. Maybe we can give you something to sleep. Ralphie?" He nodded, and Molly continued. "I insist, you need sleep, and trust Ralphie."

With the resignation of a condemned prisoner, Raquel shuffled to the bathroom. Molly had started to run the water and she entered the stall through a fog of steam. She stood under the spray for a long time, then scrubbed her skin almost raw. As if she could expunge each despicable act perpetrated against her. When her strength failed, she leaned her forehead against the tile. *Oh Matthew, could you ever forgive me?*

***

"He's asking for you. Hurry." Molly woke Raquel out of a dead sleep.

"I hate that guy, we don't know what's eating him. Before you go, I've brought something. It won't change anything, but it'll help you ignore what's ahead." She extended her palm, offering a pair of rainbow capsules.

Raquel remembered them. They were becoming old friends.

"Keep your eye on the brass ring and stay cool," Molly murmured close to her ear. "We won't fail you."

Dressed in an elegant black suit, Ari Bloomfield—she had learned—heir apparent to an alleged crime family, paced in circles. He stopped to examine Raquel, the now familiar sardonic smile lengthening across his face.

"Well, hello…goldie. It's about time you showed. I'm going on a business errand, and I'm taking you along." He paused and cocked his head. "To ease my tension. Do you want anything before we go?" he asked, sweet as molasses.

"M-may I have some water, p-please."

"Certainly." Ari walked to a serving cart holding crystal glasses and decanters. He filled a glass and handed it to her. She faked a cough twice, swallowing one of the Tuinals in each spasm. Soon she wouldn't care if the Apocalypse arrived.

***

The Dodge van raced up FDR Drive to the Harlem River, to the Cross Bronx and on to the Grand Concourse. In the midst of the drug haze, she recognized the streets and despaired. She was so close to safety, the people she'd fled from—Dalia, Skippy, and Richard—and yet she was miles away.

As the barbiturate rush continued, she rued how quickly her life had strayed. *Richard, please forgive me. I never meant to hurt you.* She sent the apology as if the wind could carry the message. *Dalia, my friend, will I ever see you again?* And the warm wave overtook her.

Behind half-closed lids, Raquel regarded the meticulous Ari as he descended from the van and entered a dilapidated building. She had no clue where they'd parked. From the looks of the sad buildings and barren streets, it wasn't an affluent neighborhood.

She'd started to doze, when several sharp reports woke her up, and the driver jumped up. A few minutes later, unperturbed and slick as always, Ari emerged. He tucked a glinting object into his jacket and waved a small packet in the air, smiling in triumph he slipped aboard. "Drive," he barked.

Ari turned to Raquel and sneered. Raquel's thoughts flew to Molly. Without her help, she'd never endure the night.

***

Three days after Raquel's disappearance, Dickey dialed Skip's number. "Any word?" he asked, already knowing the answer.

"Nothing. It's as if the city swallowed her. Linda claims she took her to a party. When it came time to leave, people told her she'd left with some guy. It's complicated. She's a minor, in New York without her parents' permission. If we report her missing, we get in all kinds of trouble. Dalia's beside herself, insisting we file."

"Maybe she found someone she liked." God, it hurt him to think so.

"That's not like Lita."

"People do strange things in this city. Listen, you once offered to buy my share of the business. Are you still interested in going solo?"

"That was a long time ago. Why ask now?"

"Because I'm getting out of Dodge. I can't stay another day in this town. I've reached my limit."

"Is this because of Lita? I know we'll find her. She'll show up."

"Nope, I'm done. Every time I enter this place, I see her. I can't take it."

"But, Dickey—"

"Nah, I'm packing and heading west or maybe south. When I stop, wherever I stop, I'll call. Hopefully, by then you'll have news of her. Skip, when she returns, please tell her I wish her the best."

Richard hung up and went around the house picking up the few items he'd need. He'd travel light and long. Above all, he'd leave behind the budding feelings he'd allowed to sprout.

In a few strides, he'd closed the door to his last home in New York, mounted his bike, and, with a deep rumble, sped away.

Ill or fair, he'd meet the wind head-on.

Chapter Thirty-Nine

Manhattan – April 28nd 1968

Raquel had always believed in guardian angels, the celestial defenders against evil and misfortune. She'd been right. Two had been stationed where she'd need them the most. Their rescue methods might have been less than orthodox. Thanks to a constant supply of downers, Raquel endured two more nights of Ari's sexual deviance and remained sedated throughout the daytime hours. It was a blessing she couldn't remember the numerous pairs of strange hands and other body parts, which probed, abused, and invaded her body. With the peculiar humor induced by a barbiturate high, she compared herself to a human pincushion.

Molly and Ralphie had promised deliverance, and she believed and waited. Freedom. A simple word full of meaning, it had forged revolutions and spawned eras. A word Raquel desired with every fiber of her soul and would never quite view the same way again. And now, the long-awaited morning of the party had arrived. She was on the brink.

The loft was abuzz with activity. She heard cleaning sounds, decorators discussing, and beverage suppliers hustling in and out. The moment was perfect to escape. Only, two men stood guard outside her door. As the afternoon progressed, the effects of the nightly Tuinals started to wear off, and anxiety ran its insidious course. Biting her fingernails, she paced, envisioning the worst. What if they couldn't get her out? She couldn't stand another night. Not another night.

Daylight waned, and evening darkened her little room. Raquel began to give up when a light rap made her jump. The door opened, and Molly walked in. She pressed a silencing finger to her lips, showed her a folded piece of paper and a plastic bag. She handed the items to Raquel and stepped out. Seconds later, Raquel listened to the conversation outside her door.

"Good night, guys. Try not to have too much fun." Molly, in a loud voice, was talking to her jailers.

Raquel's heart thumped.

"Is she all right in there?"

"Oh yes," she said. "Just making sure she's got everything before I go."

"Not staying for the party?"

"I work tomorrow. Ralphie's waiting. We're spending the night at my place."

Raquel panicked. They'd promised. They couldn't leave her.

"Too bad, Molly, it's going to be a big night."

"There'll be others." Molly giggled. "I'm sure this won't be the last of Ari's famous events. I'll see you over the weekend."

"Night, Molly."

Raquel was about to call out, when she remembered the clothes and the note clutched tight in her hand. She smoothed it out and read.

Put on the clothes and sneakers. Tie your hair in a bun. Be ready to go. You'll hear a diversion when the caterers arrive. He'll knock twice. Don't hesitate or speak. Follow him. I'll be waiting for you outside. Tuck this note in your pocket. Bring it with you. <u>DO NOT LEAVE IT!!!</u>

Molly had brought her a catering crew uniform, white sneakers, and rubber bands. She dressed quickly and tucked the note in her pants' pocket. Drumming her fingers on her lap, Raquel sat at the edge of the bed. She was uncertain of the time. The room had gone completely dark. Not a sound outside. *Any minute now, any minute now,* she intoned. Catering arrived an hour before the guests. The gourmet food and beverages had to be prepped. Ari was meticulous with his entertainment, and tonight was an important event. She'd overheard the conversation. Politicos and financiers had been invited, along with a fresh group of women for their entertainment. Details in a plan to maintain the status and power Mr. Bloomfield believed were rightfully his.

Outside her door, a busy shuffle began. Tables and chairs scraped the floor; glasses, cutlery, and dishes clinked. Familiar sounds from a recent past, she now remembered with fondness. Loud voices spoke, first frustrated, then angry. She tiptoed to the door and placed her ear against it, listening as the altercation intensified.

"This is unacceptable. Full payment on delivery," someone demanded.

"Ari's instructions, it's all you're getting."

"Okay, everybody, take it all down. We're leaving. You piece of—" Scuffling noises muffled the next epithet.

"Touch that fucking table, and you're dead." She knew Carlos's voice. He spoke above the tumult. "Hey. Guys. Need help here."

The hustle intensified: stomping feet, shoved furniture, thuds, yelling, and two knocks. She almost missed them. Scared witless, Raquel stepped away from the door. A hand reached in, seized hers, and yanked her out.

Ralphie pulled her out so fast her feet barely touched the floor. They ran in silence, thanks to rubber-soled shoes, through corridors, empty rooms, and down a set of stairs into a dim storage room. Ralphie shoved a large metal door, and a wave of cold night air hit her face. She stopped to inhale. Ralphie tugged at her again, his scowl clear. Raquel followed. He pulled her past several blocks. Just ahead, under a streetlight, a cap of carrot-colored hair sparkled bright as day.

Ralphie pushed her toward Molly "Get her away from here," he grumbled. "I'm going to check out if they've noticed her disappearance."

"Please be careful."

"They won't see me, and they won't be looking for me either. We left hours ago, remember?"

"Yes," she whispered.

"Go," Ralphie said. "Take her home; she's been through a lot. I'll meet you there later." He turned on his heel and jogged away.

"Hey, girl, you're free." Molly grasped her arms and laughed. Raquel sobbed. The two women disappeared through the streets of the East Village.

***

Molly and Ralphie had warned her. Withdrawal symptoms could be mild to medium. When the first waves of anxiety, muscle pain, and nausea rolled over her, Raquel questioned what exactly Ralphie and Molly had meant by mild to medium. For the next forty-eight hours, she fought with insomnia and severe anxiety.

On the third night, Molly gave her half a tab of Valium and news. As the tranquilizer coursed through her bloodstream and the punishing symptoms eased, the last traces of tension left her body. She listened to the news with some interest. Upon discovery of her escape, Ari, in a majestic display of anger, insulted his guests, caused the women to scramble, and ruined the party. She couldn't help the sense of gratification. Retribution tasted sweet on her lips. The remnants of her anger fled, and she finally slept for a few hours. The next morning, other than a lingering ache as if a two-by-four had pummeled her body, she felt better.

If she'd remained in Ari's clutches a few days longer, the severity of the withdrawals would've been staggering. Raquel shuddered at the thought of both scenarios, a prolonged, torturous captivity followed by a long, arduous recovery. Her angels had saved her. She could've been one more in the sad statistics of missing women.

Raquel sat on the trundle of Molly's Malibu daybed, considering much. Full of remorse, she remembered Matthew's last letter.

If I should leave first, do not fret. Live instead. I want you to live for both of us, promise me you will, and your heart will be my home until we meet again.

Did she not wish to carry his spirit within her? She'd rebelled like a child against his departure, instead of grieving like the woman she claimed to be. She'd disregarded his request and placed herself in danger, thereby dishonoring Matthew's wishes.

It was time to grow up. First, she would dislodge the shame, which rode hard on her back. Then she'd wash away the defilement, the result of her senseless behavior. Next, she'd find a way to earn money and go home. There, she'd start with a new slate and a new perspective. May 3rd would be her turning point. She walked to the windows overlooking the busy streets below. Pressing her forehead against the glass, she murmured,

*"I will rise now, and go about the city in the streets,
and in the broad ways I will seek him whom my soul loveth:
I sought him, but I found him not."*

She'd seek within, find whom her heart loved and rejoice, for he'd always lived in her soul, where she'd forgotten to look.

On May 3rd, Molly invited her for breakfast to a nearby coffee shop. There she received an unexpected birthday gift, a job offer—the way home.

***

Seventeen hundred miles away, dawn lightened the sky with a milky light as Matthew toiled and plowed his father's fields. He worked with the drive of a man pursued by demons. Not an unfair analogy, if his nightmares were considered.

It began a few nights ago. An amalgam of streets, faces, and scenes streamed in his sleep—fistfights, a couple fleeing an unseen peril, a fearsome man, and a brandished weapon. Through it all, the golden gaze remained. In the early hours, Matthew awoke with a start, covered in perspiration. A thought repeated. May 3rd—it was important—it was significant. May 3rd, May 3rd—but no answer. His unyielding mind guarded its secrets. Frustrated by the elusive date, unable to piece it together, and accosted by a headache, Matthew gave up and marched into his father's barn, ready to work into oblivion.

Hours later, an alarmed Ernestine sent her husband out in search of their missing son. Jonathan, as he expected, found Matthew in the fields. Matthew's shirt—drenched with perspiration—looked like a second skin. His light brown hair lay plastered to his forehead.

"What time did you start?" Jonathan was beside himself. Matthew's nonstop schedule worried him in the extreme.

"Early. I needed to work. There's something about the date." He groaned. "I'm trying to remember, but my mind only goes so far. Just when I'm about to reach it or touch it, it disappears. Why May 3rd? What's so important about the date?"

Jonathan shook his head. He had no answers. The date meant nothing to him.

It was the plan, the last preternatural interference.
The message went ignored, and the opportunity evanesced in the mists.

***

Skippy opened the door to an unfamiliar—albeit pleasant—face. As soon as the man presented card and identification, Skippy stiffened. The visitor must've noticed his wariness, because he raised a palm in a sign of peace.

"I'm sorry, Mr. Adams. You are Mario Adams, correct?"

Mario didn't answer.

"Please don't be concerned. I've no affiliation with New York's finest. My name is Robert Whitlock, PI. I'm searching for a young lady." Whitlock smiled pleasantly.

Intrigued, Dalia peered from behind Skippy. "What is it, Skip?"

"Miss Rodríguez, Dalia Rodríguez?" Whitlock asked. Startled, Dalia pulled back from Skip, and Whitlock held up his credentials again.

"I only need a minute of your time, if I may?"

"He's a PI, searching for a woman."

"May I come in, please?" Whitlock insisted. "I assure you, I'm not connected with the authorities at all. I'm following the trail of Raquel María Muro. Her family is searching for her. They're very concerned for her health and safety."

He said the magic words. Dalia slipped around Skippy. "Let him in, Skip." She glanced again at his credentials. "Mr. Whitlock, is it?"

"Yes, ma'am."

Robert Whitlock was in his mid to late thirties, by Dalia's estimation. With his casual haircut, sweater and jeans he'd fit in anywhere. His demeanor, however, was sharp and intelligent. In one sweep, he surveyed her house. She knew then he was ex-military and a professional. Better yet, he had the resources and had been entrusted to find Raquel.

That he would knock on her door, today of all days, she read as a good omen. Guilt had been a miserable companion since Raquel disappeared. In spite of Dalia's desire to report her missing, Skippy had convinced her against it. His arguments were valid. In New York, people disappeared daily. The investigation would be minimal at best. But once Raquel's age was noted, repercussions would fall upon them both. Skip might've valid points, but in Dalia's heart, they felt flawed. She couldn't shake off the shame; she'd aided a minor to flee, and then lost her. Mr. Whitlock could be the harbinger of salvation for all.

"Please, Mr. Whitlock, come in, sit down. May we offer a beverage?"

Whitlock followed her instructions; before he sat, he pulled a card out of his wallet and handed it to her.

"Please, call me Bob." He smiled. "I'd appreciate a glass of water, if it's not too much trouble."

"Not at all."

Within minutes, she'd returned with the water and taken a seat next to him. Without prompting, she explained, "You may be wasting your time. Raquel's no longer with us, and we've not heard a word." Dalia explained from the moment Raquel ran away and ended with her disappearance at the party.

"Thank you, I needed to know what happened. I also came to advise you of my involvement."

"Linda Callahan saw her last." Skip spoke from a chair in the corner. "Dalia's been angry with me ever since. I didn't want to file a missing person's report."

Whitlock smiled at Skip. "I understand your reasons, Mr. Adams. Information is what I need. If you remember anything later, hear from Miss Muro or from someone who's seen her, please call me right away. Ms. Callahan is my next stop."

"I told you everything I know. She took off like a wild creature." Her throat tightened. "I feel so guilty."

"Please, Dalia. May I call you Dalia? Don't berate yourself. Mix-ups happen when emotions are engaged and reliable information is unavailable." Whitlock stood.

"Reliable information?"

"Well, yes. The Muro family explained, and you have confirmed, that Raquel departed Florida believing Matthew Buchanan perished in Vietnam. She was likely depressed."

Dalia stood, fearing the investigator's next words.

"She left before news of Matthew Buchanan's survival arrived in the US. He's home, in Round Rock."

Dalia flopped down again on the sofa.

"He returned suffering partial amnesia. He doesn't remember anything or anyone from a certain date forward." He pointed at the card in her hand. "If you hear anything, however insignificant, from Miss Muro, please call me at the number on the card. It's my office. I check in every few hours or at the number on the back. It's the hotel where I'm staying." He walked over to Skippy and extended another card.

"I can't emphasize this enough. Should you encounter Miss Muro, do not disclose the information about Mr. Buchanan. The family would prefer to pass the information personally."

"Of course, Mr. Whitlock, if we speak to her, we'll not say a word about Matthew." As Whitlock walked out, Dalia pressed her forehead against her fingertips. "Matthew's alive. It all makes sense now."

***

In the attic of the four-story Walsh residence, Raquel unpacked the few pieces of clothing she owned out of her tiny bag. She'd been invited to spend the weekend with Molly, Ralphie and her relatives in Forest Hills, and was actually looking forward to a family gathering, a notion she had rejected months ago. As she admired the cozy room with its tilted roofline, single bed, plush pillows, and thick comforter, she couldn't help but think, how quickly life changed. She had arrived silly and naïve, seeking death in the big city. The horrid experience at Ari's hands had realigned her skewed perspective. Now she couldn't get far away enough from the siren song of the metropolis. This weekend would be a healing event. *Family.* She remembered her own and ached. Papá, Marité, Xavi, Julie, the Reynoldses, even crazy Isabel. Indeed, life had thrown her quite the curve ball.

Summer had arrived in the North East, and the Saturday morning sky was a clear azure, and warm enough for a dip in the home's elevated pool. Molly offered a bathing suit, but Raquel's tummy felt prickly and slightly bloated. Full of female self-awareness, she declined. More relatives arrived, and the ubiquitous barbecue began. Amid lively conversations, she forgot about her discomfort.

She was restless during the night, and her dreams returned. Poking, pinching hands, a dark stare, a fearsome glint, rushing footsteps… She woke up shaking like a leaf. She'd tossed the comforter on the floor, picked it up quickly, and fell back to sleep. In the morning, she awoke in a pool of perspiration.

Ignoring the internal furnace, Raquel went about the day, summoning enthusiasm and humor, but struggling through smiles and conversation. She refused a second invitation to the pool. This time Molly noticed her flushed cheeks. When she asked, Raquel blamed her upcoming menses.

The chills started late afternoon. Raquel excused herself to take a nap. At one a.m. the stabbing pain in her abdomen was so acute she couldn't straighten her body. Despite the fever, she managed to crawl down the steps but collapsed on the lower landing. Mr. Walsh found her and carried her upstairs while calling for his wife and daughter.

"Tell us what's wrong," Molly asked.

"I don't know. It hurts. I can't straighten. If I try, it hurts worse." She whimpered, curling into a ball.

"What do you think, Dad?"

"I'm no doctor. It looks like an appendicitis attack. Do you still have it, Raquel?"

She nodded.

"This could be dangerous. Call an ambulance. She needs attention, now."

***

When Raquel awoke, she didn't burn anymore, but the pain hadn't left. She glanced at the IV. The slow drip lulled her to sleep again. Sometime later, she was forcefully awakened. A nurse stuffed a thermometer in her mouth, wrapped a blood pressure cuff on her arm, and placed two fingers on her wrist. A young doctor grilled her with questions.

"Tell us the names of the men you've been with. We need to report your situation."

My situation? What men? No, some men she never wanted to remember, ever again. The questions didn't stop. Raquel shook her head.

"She's not ready." A different doctor spoke. He held her fingers lightly. "We need to stop the infection first. Raquel, is that your name?"

Raquel nodded.

"Can you hear me, Raquel?"

"Yes," she whispered.

"You have an infection. We need to suction your fallopian tubes. If we don't, it'll get worse. Before we proceed, we need your consent."

A nurse appeared with a clipboard and pen in hand. "Are you over eighteen, honey? Do you have ID?"

"I-in my bag."

"I'll check in a minute. Sign here, hon." The nurse held a pen and showed her a line where to sign. "Let's get you taken care of."

With a trembling hand, Raquel signed.

The nurse returned with a syringe and plunged the contents into her IV.

***

Raquel came to slowly, examining the curtained space as she tried to order her thoughts. She had no pain and felt cool. Whatever they did, worked. She had questions, but had to wait until someone showed up. She didn't wait long. Young, eager, and harassing, Dr. Levin initiated a round of questions. His explanations about her infection filled her with revulsion. She couldn't remember the names he wanted. Most were buried within a Tuinal-induced fog. And she'd die before she gave this jerk Ari's name or any details about that painful episode.

She did release Dalia's phone number, although she trembled at the thought of Richard hearing her ugly news. What would he think? He'd been so thoughtful with their intimacy. Her disease had come from Ari and his cronies. They could all take care of themselves.

***

"Whitlock has her," Emilio called out.

"Where?"

"Elmhurst Hospital, in Queens. She was admitted early Sunday morning. I don't have all the details. I'm on the phone buying a plane ticket."

"Emilio?" Julie pressed her forehead against his shoulder.

He threw an arm around her and squeezed tight. "Thank God," he whispered. "Thank God. Help me pack, darling, enough for a couple of days. As soon as she's released, I'm bringing my baby home."

Chapter Forty

Manhattan – May 27th 1968

Her room was full. With Molly, Ralphie, Dalia, Skippy, and even Linda. Raquel smiled, watching Dalia take up the baton and conduct the conversation through bland topics and ensuring no one asked indiscreet questions. Eventually, Raquel asked about Richard. His sudden departure from New York weighed heavy on her.

"There's no need to contact Dickey. He left loving you, not because he resented you. He wishes you well," Dalia explained.

"It's a relief," Raquel murmured, an odd sadness filling her chest. "I'll always think of Richard fondly. He's a good man. I wish I could have returned his feelings. He deserves to be happy."

"So do you," Dalia insisted. "No one dictates over the heart, Lita. It's the other way around. Life is full of surprises, sometimes there are reasons—"

Two men pulled the curtains aside, one a stranger, the other...

"Papá?" she asked, unbelieving. "P-Papá," she tried again.

Emilio rushed to Raquel, imbuing with his embrace all the healing a father can bestow. He murmured, "I'm here, sweetheart, and I'm taking you home, where you belong. We'll take care of you now and forever. No matter what, I'll be with you, through the worst and the best. I promise."

And Raquel embraced him back, knowing she would never run away, reject, or ignore his gift of support again.

Ralphie and Skip gave an excuse with choked voices and left the room. The women sniffed quietly. Standing in a corner like a hound keeping watch, Robert Whitlock surveyed the scene and gave Dalia a nod of thanks. She acknowledged it with a tentative smile.

The curtain moved, and Dr. Metzger, the attending physician, entered the cubicle waving visitors away. Bob Whitlock signaled he would wait outside. Dalia stood to go, but Raquel stopped her. "Please stay." She turned to the doctor. "She's my friend. She can hear this."

"It's about privacy, Raquel, Mr. Muro, and strictly your choice." Dr. Metzger moved to the foot of the bed. "The infection sped through the uterus and oviducts, prompting edema, pain, and fever. We've drained the tubes, and the massive doses of antibiotics will do the rest. I'd like to keep you for observation until tomorrow. Barring any complications, you can go home and continue with follow-up treatments." Dr. Metzger inhaled, tapping the chart, then continued.

"However, I want to tell you outright, gonorrhea damages tissues. You may have difficulty conceiving, I'm so sorry, my dear. Perhaps, after the inflammation disappears, the damage could be reevaluated. You're young, and anything is possible. And besides, medical breakthroughs happen daily. Anyway, I have to visit my next patient. If you have any questions, don't hesitate to ask." Dr. Metzger smiled kindly, nodded at Emilio, and left the room.

"I'm so sorry," Dalia whispered, her expression grim.

Raquel turned to her. "Why?"

"Because I could've taken better care of you. I should never've brought you here—"

"Please stop. Could and should only serve to make a person crazy. You can't take on my load. You had no control of what happened. I acted stupidly and plunged into danger head-on. Yes, I was depressed and disoriented with Matthew's loss. Still, I behaved like a child, and worse, I dishonored his request."

Dalia lowered her head and let her arms fall to the side. "You're too generous. Say what you will, you can't lighten my load either. I had a hand in this. I'm finished interfering in people's lives. I'll never forget nor forgive myself."

"When I leave this bed, Dalia Rodríguez, I intend to leave all darkness behind. I urge you do the same." Raquel extended a hand to Dalia, who squeezed it gently. "I don't want to see the past reflected in your eyes. It's the only way our friendship will survive."

"I understand."

"And you're leaving this bed tomorrow," Emilio interrupted. "No more recriminations or sadness. We're going home. Tomorrow. Where you'll heal. Your room is waiting. We're ending this pessimism now. I've lots of good news. It's a new beginning, Lita. For us all."

"Yes, Papá," she sighed. "I can't wait to go home. I have one request, though. Raquelita stays behind. I've earned my Raquel."

"That's easy enough. Raquel it is." He smiled and hugged her tightly. "My little girl," he murmured.

Raquel rolled her eyes. Some things would never change.

**

Tuesday morning, Molly and Dalia showed up bright and early to help her dress with a new outfit. Emilio said they could burn her old clothes for all he cared. It all went smoothly until Dr. Levin arrived, insisting on furthering his investigation, again demanding names and addresses. Instead of badgering Raquel, he met up with Robert Whitlock. Dr. Levin left, signaling the end of the Elmhurst episode.

The ride from Elmhurst Hospital to La Guardia Airport took minutes. Everything transpired in a frenzy of activity, and before she had a moment to think, they were at the boarding lounge. Dalia and Molly looked pale and weepy. Raquel carried nothing but her wallet, not even this morning's toothbrush, nothing tangible to account for or remind her of the past four months in the big city.

"Will you take care of them?" she asked Whitlock.

"Certainly, Miss Muro. I'll drive them both home."

"Thank you." Raquel smiled and opened her arms to Molly. The little pixie rushed into the embrace.

"I'll miss you," Molly said.

"I'll miss you, more," Raquel answered. "I don't have words to thank you. Without you and Ralphie, I—"

"You're safe. It's all that matters. I'm so happy you're going home."

"Molly," Emilio intervened. "I've a tremendous debt of gratitude with you and Ralphie. You both have a home and a job in San Antonio should you wish it. Keep it in mind."

"O-oh, Mr. Muro." Molly's face turned beet red. "I would like to visit one day."

"Whenever you like."

Raquel released Molly and turned to Dalia. Dalia reached inside her shoulder bag and pulled out a large envelope. She handed it to Raquel.

"I went through your things last night. I know you didn't want to leave Matthew's last letters behind. They belong with you…always."

Raquel pressed the envelope tightly against her heart. "Yes, they do. Thank you, my dearest friend. Thank you for remembering." She threw her arms around Dalia. "Forgive…forget. Visit me. I'll miss you. Who's going to eat Reuben sandwiches with me?" Raquel gave a little hiccup.

The loudspeaker called the San Antonio flight, and the women pulled away, smiling tearfully. Raquel turned to her father. He grasped her hand and led her toward the gate. She glanced over one last time and waved good-bye.

***

The aircraft banked over the city, and the wings tilted. Manhattan glimmered against a clear sky. She had admired it upon arrival with wonder and trepidation. Now, as the line of buildings faded in the distance, she couldn't help the odd thoughts.

Now it's behind me, the winter of my discontent.

I head for my Valinor, toward a hopeful, endless summer…

Outwardly she might not be as misshapen as the protagonist of the classic tragedy; inside, however, she was twisted and damaged. In keeping with that theme, she would never a lover be. With a deep sigh, Raquel nestled farther into her father's embrace. In minutes she was asleep.

Chapter Forty-One

Round Rock – June 1st 1968

As Johnnie Murdock predicted, the Bronco was packed, but it made no difference to Matthew. He'd find a niche for himself and his friends and proceed to get rip-roaring drunk. He hadn't glared murderously at the calendar for nothing. June 1st was a momentous day, and he was going to celebrate. Whatever happened during the night was up to the fates.

Matthew and his friends pushed through the doors, and the crowds made way. They were Bronco regulars; the status carried honor. Irregulars were shooed away from a corner booth and offered to Matthew and company. The owner was elated to see them. The first round of free drinks arrived in seconds.

The night promised to be fun, the music selection on the jukebox was hot, and so were the predatory ladies circling their booth. With charming smiles and revealing clothes, a daring threesome slithered in. One sat on Johnnie's lap, and the other took Stevie's. The third tried for Matthew's, although he genteelly denied her, she stubbornly stood next to him. Maybe she thought he'd change his mind, but flings weren't on the menu tonight. No sir, he was somewhere dark and angry, and girls were off-limits.

A peculiar wildness claimed Matthew's spirit. His war demons demanded freedom. In a twisted mass of shapes and colors, they gathered around the periphery of his vision. His pupils dilated in the dim light, and he loosened their reins. His devils would have their way, and when they did, he hoped to God his friends would forgive him.

A ruckus at the entrance caught Matthew's attention. Garth and his cronies had arrived. Matthew smirked, knowing Garth couldn't let a second pass without testing his mood or patience. Tonight, Matthew would play, the rules of engagement be damned.

Johnnie Cash and June Carter intoned "Jackson," and Matthew had to move. Cash's ripping, husky voice called to him. Politely, he pushed aside the young lady and stood to his full height. Johnnie Murdock and Stevie stared at each other. What was Matthew doing?

He smiled at Johnnie and winked, his voice rising above the general din. "Gonna shoot some pool. You in?"

"Keep yer pants on, boy," Johnnie said to Stevie. "I just saw Garth and friends at the tables. "I've a real bad feelin' 'bout this."

Stevie nodded. "I'm on it."

And Johnnie—bad knee and all—sprinted right behind Matthew.

Garth was full of liquor, piss, and vinegar, and couldn't resist Matthew's challenge. A few games later, Matthew and Johnnie were ahead. Garth seethed. Knowing how to irk his foe, Matthew waved his cue stick around while shuffling a victorious two-step to the tune of "Folsom Prison Blues."

Garth lost it. The edge of a knife gleamed, and men cursed. The glint hit Matthew's sight, and the bar disappeared in an explosion of lights. The flashback roared.

The injured man cut a bizarre indentation on the grass. Matthew's brain clamored. Protect. Protect. The NVA's obsidian eyes threatened. His smile taunted. A hand raised a grenade… A projectile flew. Matthew's knife chased it in the air. Blood splattered, the bulb rolled, deadly fragments dispersed. Matthew ran and ran and ran to his injured friend. NVA running…misfire…misfire… In a red haze, he engaged in a fight to the death. Fists flew again, again. Matthew gripped the man's throat. Kill. Kill. Kill.

"Matthew. Matthew, stop," Johnnie Murdock yelled. Multiple hands pulled at him, he fell back, and his butt slammed hard on the floor. He grimaced, bewildered. Between his knees lay a man. A battered, bloody face looked at him. Garth?

More hands reached for him. Matthew flailed his arms, shoving them away. Finally, four men overpowered him. With his demons now happy and spent, his mind started to recover. Slowly, as he unfolded his long frame, someone helped him up. The music had stopped. All eyes in the room were on him.

Garth's cronies were assessing the state of their buddy. Issuing threats, they carefully pulled him away.

Johnnie challenged, "Think y'all can make a case?"

Garth's friends looked around, but no one acknowledged them. This was an in-house brawl between men. It would remain as such.

***

Her first days in San Antonio were full of peace, without difficult discussions or questions. Today, however, Raquel couldn't evade them. Isabel's visit was imminent. The recent past had taught her much, and this meeting would tell her if their relationship had a future. Tragedy was life's great equalizer. All sentient beings bowed under its weight. A mighty hand had forced on them both similar ruinous events. Could this be the key to open a path between them?

Forgive...forget. Her words to Dalia... Could she follow her own advice? There'd been so much anger between them... The doorbell rang. Isabel had arrived.

Raquel stood but didn't get far before a speeding blur of outflung arms crashed into her.

"Lita, Lita."

She embraced Marité, burying her nose within the soft tresses and inhaling the honeyed scent. "My sweet Mari, I've missed you so," she whispered, then looked up.

Isabel stood at the door, smiling hesitantly, looking beautiful, and decidedly pregnant. Peace shimmered about her. Just behind, tall and protective, Xavier Repulles beamed, her godfather and stepfather, soon to be the father of her half sibling. Indeed, a man of many talents.

"Raquel María," Isabel whispered, but didn't move. Not until Raquel's smile gave wings to her feet. She then rushed to both daughters, crushing them within her arms and a thousand kisses.

***

Emilio watched the scene in delight. Perhaps there'd be resolution between mother and daughter. He'd already let go of any lingering resentment against Isabel. The past didn't matter. He had a promising life to look forward to, and he wished the same for his baby. Time passed in happy conversation, but soon tummies started to growl.

"I have an idea." Julie silenced the general chatter. "I could make lunch, but it's such a gorgeous day. Xavi, why don't you take them to the Hilton Palacio del

Rio? It recently opened to great reviews. You can grab a bite and stroll along the River Walk. If it's not too busy, you could visit the Coca-Cola pavilion."

Marité hopped and clapped her hands at the same time. "Yes, please, Mamá. I wanna see the Krofft puppets, please."

"We'll check it out after we eat, darling. It's the weekend, and it may be crowded. Emilio, Julie, will you join us?" Isabel asked quickly.

"Thank you, but not today. I have other plans. As you said, it's the weekend, and ever since the HemisFair opened, the bar's been busy. I have to prep before the waiters arrive. We've hired additional help. I want Julie to take it easy. She only comes to keep me company." He smiled and patted her belly.

"He makes it sound like I'm made of glass."

"To me, you are," Emilio countered, and Julie snickered.

"Well, I'm starving." Xavi clapped his hands and stood. He reached over to Isabel and helped her up. "Come on, lovely ladies. Let's go eat." He wrapped one arm around Isabel's ever-expanding waist and gestured for his stepdaughters to follow.

The little group had reached the door when Emilio stopped Xavi. "A word, if I may."

Xavi looked to Isabel and urged her gently forward. "Love, go on ahead to the car. I'll be right over."

"Does Isabel know?" Emilio asked after Isabel stepped away.

Xavi shook his head. "No. We agreed, she'll learn about Matthew when Raquelita does. They'll have to mend their differences with what they know."

"Fair enough," he agreed and closed the door.

**

For a weekend, the River Walk wasn't crowded. Raquel and Isabel weaved through lines of tourists along the bank, a few steps behind Xavi, who led Marité by the hand.

"Do you have any plans for school?" Isabel asked.

"Dad and I have looked into San Antonio College. I need to request my transcripts from Florida. I've been lazy, but I'll call soon."

The words floated between them like sheets drying in a gentle breeze. Still the spiny topics hovered, daring either one to address them. Isabel started.

"How can I earn your forgiveness? I'm not only talking about the letters, Lita... I mean, Raquel." Isabel placed a tentative hand on her daughter's shoulder. When Raquel didn't flinch away, they restarted their easy pace.

"I'm referring to my behavior with you and your sister. You, my dearest, took the brunt. I dumped my troubles on you. I should've protected and nurtured you. Instead, I abandoned and hurt you. I know it now." Isabel sighed and faced her daughter. "I'm so ashamed."

"Mom, you didn't abandon us."

"Yes, I did. I deserted you both emotionally. I knew you were in love. What I did to Matthew's letters is unforgivable. I destroyed a treasure, your cherished treasure. There's no way I can ever replace any of it. God, I'm so very sorry for my misdeeds, and your loss." Slowly, Isabel dropped her head. "I made you leave. How can I ever atone?"

"I want to know, understand why. I can handle your truths. Would you trust me with them?" Raquel reached out to Isabel and held her arms. "Look at me, Mom. It would help, and I could tell you mine. If what I've heard is true, you know the hole I'm in better than anyone. Would you help me climb out?"

"I would like that very much." Isabel grasped her daughter's hand and resumed their stroll.

Raquel listened to her mother's halting words. Her heart ached for the heinous abuse she'd suffered. She empathized and compared the differences, because through her own ordeal, two angels had mitigated the severity of her experience. But the eight-year-old Isabel endured it alone. Ingenuity was the sole refuge of a desperate, youthful mind. Instead of creating playful stories and games, it dug abysses in which to lose her pain.

Isabel listened to her daughter's words with obvious attention and deference. When Raquel finished, she grasped her hands tightly. "*Hija*, it's too late to mend our mother-daughter relationship. Maybe we can build a new bond, in friendship, respect, and trust. Is that possible?"

Raquel threw her arms around her.

***

Xavi flicked off the lights, slipped under the covers, slid an arm behind Isabel, and brought her to his chest. She didn't speak. She knew by now when he needed to order his thoughts. This trip to San Antonio had been fruitful. His project to reunite mother and daughter showed promise. The family was coming together and expanding. Even his old place at the Ferguson Ranch looked like a home, thanks to Isabel's decorating touches. Only one discordant item remained: his goddaughter's fortunes. He would abide Emilio's decision to do nothing...for now.

The tiny flame of the scented candle flickered, washing a tenuous light upon their embracing bodies, inciting and enhancing intimacy. His mood changed.

"I was so proud of you today," Xavier whispered. She rubbed her cheek against his bare chest, making small caresses. "Mmmm, I love when you do that little rub, *Tesoro*."

"Do you? Like this?" Isabel repeated the gesture.

Xavi arched a brow in mock disapproval. "Hmmm... Are you vying for my attentions, Mrs. Repulles? You know, we have to curtail our lovemaking until the birth of our child."

As he spoke, he slid Isabel's body to the bed and started to tug at her nightgown, rolling it upward, slowly baring her body. "But after the birth, all bets are off. It's back to our usual play."

He lifted the gown along with her arms; at the top, he placed her wrists together in his favorite position. "Yes, just like that, keep your arms up, *Tesoro*." With an indolent press, he turned her body on its side, her back toward him and he nestled behind.

"I've been thinking...after the baby's born, I'll build a special room for us." With languorous strokes, he caressed along her face and moved down. He pressed a palm on her shoulder, held it for a moment, and then slid his hand under a breast. He cupped the fullness, weighed it lightly, as a lazy thumb grazed the nipple until it spiked. Momentarily satisfied, he continued on past her waist and paused on her upper thigh. He tilted her body a little farther.

"Yes...that's beautiful."

"A special room?" she asked as a sensual lassitude invaded her body. He was a master. Xavi knew every inch of her body and what she liked. Every heated touch or singeing kiss had a purpose, to excite and entice her. He never rushed. This was his expertise, his art. He could converse and caress while mesmerizing her mind and seducing her body.

"What sort of room?" Her inner furnace blazed. He stoked her flames deftly.

Xavi reached under her knee and pushed it forward, deepening her tilt. With her arms raised, she had little balance and was entirely under his control. She felt wanton, exciting her further. He tucked a pillow under her belly, stabilizing her, and his hot palm returned to her upper back. Pressing lightly between her shoulder blades, he treated the spot with unhurried kisses.

"An adult playroom. You know I like it wild, rough at times. So do you, *Tesoro*. You love the sweet edge of pain, when I restrain you, when I give you pleasure at my pace. Like now."

He placed a pillow next to her face, settling her in a gentle position that protected her belly. Her beautiful buttocks were lifted, slightly parted and sensuously offered. He stood, discarded his pants and slipped behind her back, where he wouldn't place undue pressure on her or the baby. His hand roamed to her nipple, resuming its play.

"I can't wait to see you breastfeed our child." He rolled the tip gently between thumb and forefinger. "I want to taste it," he explained, and she moaned. "Will you let me taste the nectar from your nipples?" He released the excited pebble and moved to the swell of her belly as he rained kisses between her shoulder blades.

"You were wonderful with Raquelita today," he murmured.

Xavi grasped her knee and pushed it farther, widening her legs, splaying her buttocks. Trailing lightly along, he slid between her legs, his languid fingers explored her labia. Isabel gasped. The heat from his body was scorching, and her arousal was volcanic, yet he kept it controlled and at the edge. It was his plan, to plunge her into a never-ending burn.

"So honest and open."

Her fevered brain wasn't certain what he spoke of anymore.

"So very hot. And so very wet." His knee lifted, trapping hers securely. His body pressed against hers. His erection nudged. "Isabel, you want me in, don't you?" he groaned.

"Yes, Xavi. I'm ready, take me," she whimpered, half-insane with need.

"Hmm…what was that?"

The tip of his engorged penis teased her sheath, pressing with taunting little nudges.

She was at the border of insanity and begged, "Please, Sir, Xavier… Aaah." He'd reached within her sex, and his index and thumb pinched her sensitized nub.

"You're at the sweet edge of pain, Isabel." As he spoke, he filled her with a solid thrust, seating himself to the hilt. "Oh, Isabel. The emotions you make me feel. You humble me."

To her dismay, he withdrew, leaving her wanting and bereft. It didn't last long. Maintaining possession of her burning clit, he drove in. She moaned desperately.

His hips shifted and swiveled, extending the invasion until he could go no farther. He changed the angle of his cock, then searched and shifted. She released a throaty gasp and he renewed the sweet torment upon her clit. Isabel vibrated, racing toward the climax he incited. "Not yet, Isabel. You'll come soon, sweetheart," he murmured against her ear.

"Yes, Xavier Manel, Sir. I'll wait, oh God," she acquiesced and shivered. The penetrations were full, slow, and delicious. She was overcome and ready to explode with the unrelenting double stimulation but held on for her husband's word. He knew when her arousal had reached the edge better than herself. This man had shown her unimagined pleasures, had healed and remade her.

"That's my good girl." He bit down on the juncture of her neck and shoulder, holding her in place. He took her inch by insane inch, pulsed at the top and retreated at the same speed. He was in a laid-back mood tonight, and continued the deep-seated, leisurely thrusts, one after another, pushing and nudging, until she couldn't hold on.

She was ready. Her trembling body and contracting sheath told him. The tingle at the bottom of his spine warned him. "Give it to me, now," he groaned upon her skin. Unstoppable seismic waves raced between them, and their climax soared free, as they bucked against each other in a glorious release.

The moment overwhelmed him. She was making him a father, granting him undeserved gifts of love, family, and happiness. Xavi would worship Isabel until the end of his days.

***

Time passed like a whisper. As the end of the dog days approached, news of Isabel's impending delivery arrived along with an invitation for Raquel's presence. She hesitated to answer. How would it feel? Knowing she could never have her own?

Her father must have guessed her distress, for a few days later, he called her into his office.

"Have a seat, darling." Papá dragged a chair out and sat across from her. "This invitation to Ocala is troubling you, am I right?"

He'd gone straight to the point, and she could only nod, a sudden urge to weep strangling her.

"You received a terrible blow, and as destiny would have it, you have pregnant women all around you. This has to be traumatic. You don't want to ruin anyone's happiness, but if you go to Florida, you might, yes?"

He paused, and she nodded again. If she spoke, she would weep. Papá opened his arms, and when she stood, he patted his lap. She went to him, cuddling within his embrace. The bitter tears held back in a hospital bed inundated her. Sobs racked her body while he held on, letting the release take over.

"I'm feeling sorry for myself."

"You were very brave in New York. This reaction is long overdue. Whichever decision you make, I will support it." He rocked her back and forth. "I want to point out some facts. You're young, and your body is recovering with the speed of youth. Doctors can make mistakes. I can almost see it, sometime in the future, you with a baby."

"Not without Matthew."

"Ah, but life is full of surprises. Look at our ex-cantankerous Xavi, now the happiest man in the world. He never thought he'd have a family. Sweetheart, remember Dr. Metzger? He said anything is possible. Your miracle is out there, waiting for just the right moment to appear. If you don't go, you'll miss the birth of your brother or sister. Perhaps that little person will inspire you. Think about it."

"You're right, Papá. I'll leave with Marité." She nodded against his chest, her angst disappearing with each breath she took.

Emilio smiled, hiding the stream of troubled thoughts in his own mind. Not yet, he cautioned himself. *She's not ready yet.*

***

Raquel expected the worst upon her return to Ocala, but the family received her with the same exuberance, the same love and affection of a June night fourteen months ago. She'd always been right; their love would never be a quid pro quo affair.

In the morning of September 5th, an anxious family paced in the waiting room. The sliding doors opened, and a nurse walked through, announcing the birth of Jordi Xavier Repulles.

"Who's Raquel," she asked. Raquel jumped up. "Come, your mom wants to see you." She turned on her heels and sped away. Raquel hurried behind.

The scene in the maternity room left her speechless. A swaddled bundle upon Isabel's chest made soft, sniffly noises. Isabel nodded at Xavi, and with utmost care, he picked up the baby and approached Raquel.

"Hold out your arms, sweetie." Xavi placed the gurgling baby in the cradle of her arms. "Meet your brother, Jordi. Jordi, this is Raquel, your big sister."

"My brother," she whispered.

Xavi stared at her, the wisdom of the ages reflected on his serene countenance. "We all love you, Lita."

He understood. They all understood.

Gently, Raquel lifted the sweet-smelling baby close to her face, kissed his forehead, and whispered reverently, "Happy birthday, Jordi. Welcome. As long as I live, you can count on me."

"Do you mean it?" Xavi asked, surprising her. "Is it a serious vow?" he insisted.

"It is."

"Would you care for him if something happened to us? Would you be his godmother?"

Looking at the new life in her arms, the tiny curling fingers, the soft bud of his mouth, she didn't think further. Yes, she would dedicate herself to this little person; he would be her lifetime sweetheart. "I'd be honored."

***

After the debacle at the Bronco, Matthew resumed his recluse status, foreswearing all outside contact, frustrating his friends and parents. On November 28th Matthew awoke in the foulest mood, answering in monosyllables or moving about in silence. With uncanny intuition, his parents gave him a wide berth and pacified him as best they could. But peace would not be theirs to enjoy. At one in the afternoon, they received a call from the hospital. Kathy was having premature contractions, and dinner had to be postponed.

That night, after an exhausting day, Ernestine and Jonathan conversed quietly in the privacy of their bedroom.

"What a difference from last year, isn't it, dearest?" she asked, choked with restrained tears.

"Yes, Mother. I'm almost tempted to call Emilio. Maybe Lita has been found. Perhaps she might want to see Matthew? It could do the trick. God, I'll try anythin', he's so unhappy." Jonathan sighed, holding his wife tightly. "It kills me to see him so lost. How can this be? His mind doesn't remember, and yet his heart feels the strain of the separation. It senses her absence. He misses her every single day and doesn't know it."

"Let's wait after the birth and the holidays. It's only another month. In case she's not been found yet, don't you agree?"

"Sure, Mother. I'll wait till January."

**

The following evening, Jonathan listened in dismay to Matthew's report. "Dad, the hospital called. Kathy's contractions have stopped. Her doctor has ordered bed rest for the next four weeks. But he knows Kathy's willful and lives alone. So he suggested she should stay with us until the baby's born. I've agreed, pending your approval. Kathy has also agreed. What do you say?"

"Frankly, I'm shocked she accepted," said Ernestine.

"Of course, son, she can stay," Jonathan added.

"I can't believe she's gonna be here for four weeks. F-f—" Matthew stopped. "Sorry," he said and marched outside.

Plans to call San Antonio faded away.

**

Matthew received his beautiful baby girl in his eager hands. Her bright green eyes flashed, and Matthew was filled with a wondrous sense of belonging. She was entirely his, and he was hers. The feeling should have felt unique, yet it was oddly familiar. While her arrival should be enough to make the world complete for him, a lingering emptiness remained.

The following morning, Matthew arrived at Kathy's room. The discussion would be a mere formality. He knew Kathy didn't want the child. "Are you sure, Kathy?" Matthew asked three feet away from her bed, shuffling side to side and quivering in disgust. He wanted to put as much distance as he could between his child, himself, and the disturbed woman facing him.

"Yes. Take her."

"I thought you might've changed your mind, wished to bond with her," he offered while praying she wouldn't accept.

"I've no desire to bond with the brat. I can't wait for this milk to dry out. I would've aborted her months ago. Fuck, she's a burden and a bother to my plans. As soon as I'm able to travel, I'm leaving this cow town forever. Go away, Matthew. Take her, and let me get some sleep."

"I suppose you'll agree to sign this document."

That must've tempted her. Gaze gleaming, she turned back around. Matthew gestured to his father. "Dad, do you have it?" Matthew motioned to a person standing behind Ernestine.

"What is it? Who's this man?" she asked.

"It's a document by which you renounce and eschew all rights to the child over to me. I had it drawn up by an attorney, and here's a notary who'll verify your signature. My parents will serve as witnesses, or, if you prefer, we may call in two nurses."

Frowning, she extended a hand. He presented the document, and she nodded. "I'll sign. This isn't necessary. I told you I don't want her."

"So you said. I'm legally covering all our bases."

"I'm curious, Matthew," Kathy said, scribbling her signature. "What'll you name her?"

"Rebecca," Matthew said gently.

"Unusual choice. Do you have any women named Rebecca in your family?"

"I don't rightly know. It's the closest I came to a name I should remember but can't."

Tightening his hold on his daughter, he pivoted out of Kathy's room and her life. Forever, he hoped.

***

"These women are crazy, they talked about the delivery as if it had been a piece of cake. Well, maybe for them it was. All this nonsense about a first-time mother," Julie said in a mock huff while handling the feisty wriggler in her arms.

Another boy, Raquel mused. Two brothers in the span of four months. She crossed her arms on Julie's bed and watched, in rapt fascination, her father become a child while playing and cooing with Emilio Jr.

"Papá, when and where are you going to baptize him?" In her mind, she had a vision of the Spanish relatives crammed in the San Antonio home.

"I hadn't considered it, darling. Now that you mention it, maybe we could throw a big party in Florida. Coralina and Jonas must meet their newest nephew, and they have plenty of room." He hovered above Julie, one hand playing with his son's chubby feet, the other with his tiny fingers.

"I'll talk to Xavi. We'll coordinate a joint baptism and invite everyone."

"We'll take over the state," Raquel exclaimed. Her father smiled.

Chapter Forty-Two

Round Rock – April 6th 1969

Sundays in small towns are synonymous with peace and serenity. Mornings are dedicated to religious services, the afternoons to family and loved ones. This first Sunday in April presaged to be such a day, quiet and uneventful. Sunlight drenched the Buchanan's family room, and the plaintive notes of "Moonlight Serenade" filled the air. Ernestine sat in her usual chair. Her nimble fingers wielded a crochet needle as a delicate pink cape materialized out of her hands. Jonathan enjoyed the scene from his large recliner, listening to his favorite band and enjoying his weekend pipe.

Matthew worked in the toolshed, honing and repairing his tools while his pretty Rebecca cooed, aaahed, and gurgled at him from the cradle he'd crafted. They were always together, especially on beautiful days like these. Lately she'd begun to drool, a sure sign of teething, and she gnawed at her tiny fist in earnest.

"Those little gums are itching, right, honey?" he said sweetly, not expecting an answer.

Intent on him, Rebecca reacted to his voice and graced him with an enthusiastic flail of chubby arms and an appreciative *eeaah*.

Oh, he was smitten. Rebecca's arrival saved him, and not a moment too soon. The primordial instinct to care for his child rendered all other problems insignificant. In the beginning, Matthew was a bewildered tangle of thumbs and had to defer to Ernestine's experience in baby-care matters. Those early diaper changes, baths, and feedings were full of comical errors, yet Matthew would not be deterred.

For his dedication, he was blessed with an angelic child. She didn't fuss and was a pleasure to feed. Colics were rare. Little Rebecca had the sunniest disposition and the patience of the saints. Her bright gaze trailed her father's every move and, in the instances when he fumbled miserably, she would gift him with a dimpled smile and a soft burble of encouragement.

By the end of the first week, Matthew became so adept, he took over Rebecca's care, much to Grandma's disappointment. Rebecca was his daughter, his labor of true love, and much more. She reinstated his sense of worth, something he'd needed since the day he'd woken up without memory. They were an inseparable mighty duo.

Matthew moved to the slop sink, washed and dried his hands, tossed the hand towel aside and walked over to Rebecca's cradle. He bent over and wiped her drool while searching for her gnawing toy. He heard a distant engine roar and stretched to peek out the window.

A bright red Pontiac GTO flew toward the ranch, a dust cloud sprouting in its wake. What fool sped on a private road? Frowning, he picked up Rebecca and stepped out to investigate further.

***

Brian MacKay drove in a state of anticipation. He'd waited nearly fifteen months to accomplish this errand. As the Buchanan ranch came into view, his mind whirled with memories: the terrible premonition and the deadly skirmish, unending surgeries, the sentence against his right limb, and his miracle. A talented and daring orthopedic surgeon offered to reconstruct his shattered bones. He warned Brian's recovery would take time and grueling therapy sessions. Brian would always have a limp, but he would keep his leg.

Brian tightened his grip on the steering wheel as he thought of Matthew's amnesia. The friend who'd risked his life to save him didn't remember him. Didn't matter, Brian had vowed to thank him personally, as soon as he was up and running, so to speak.

He recalled the afternoon when the Army package arrived. He had casually tossed the war relic in a corner of his bedroom. Soon he realized his mistake. The box—as if endowed with an unnatural voice—kept calling out to him. Finally Brian opened it, only to be stunned by the content. This was more than a fortuitous mistake. The thing vibrated in his hands just like the ring in the famous novel: the item sought its master desperately. Brian couldn't get well fast enough.

He abandoned his thoughts as he drove through the gate of the Buchanan ranch. On the other side of the fence stood his friend and brother-in-arms, Matthew Buchanan, tall as he remembered, perhaps thinner, with surprisingly long hair and a few extra facial lines. Brian prayed he carried Matthew's miracle in his pocket.

Shading his eyes from the sun, Matthew repositioned his daughter in his arms and stared as the shiny sports coupe came to a full stop. The driver's side opened, and a man about his own age stepped out, he reached inside the car, unfolded a walking stick, and with a mild limp, headed in Matthew's direction.

"Hey, there." The stranger grinned.

Matthew nodded. Out of nowhere, his father rushed toward the visitor. The men spoke a few words, and, in a vigorous exchange of back slaps and hugs, they greeted each other like old friends. Jonathan pulled away and walked quickly to Matthew.

"Son, give'r to me." Jonathan extended his arms to Rebecca. "I'll take her to Mother."

Silent and bewildered, Matthew handed his daughter over.

"Son, this is Brian, Brian MacKay. Yer Vietnam buddy's come to see you." And tucking his granddaughter in his arms, Jonathan sped inside the house.

Matthew and Brian stared at one another. "Brian McKay." Matthew enunciated the name slowly. Rolled it around, testing it for accuracy as if a hidden truth lay within it.

"That's my name," Brian responded.

The kitchen door slammed, and Matthew winced as his mother flew past him. "Brian, Brian." It was Ernestine's turn to rain a deluge of kisses upon the man. "It's so good to see you. You look wonderful."

His mother sounded choked up. Was she crying?

"Were we really good friends?"

"The best kind. You saved my life, Matt James," Brian drawled. "And I hope to return the favor."

"Where are your manners, son? I taught you better," Ernestine said. "Come in, darlin', let's get you something to drink and eat. You must be exhausted." She fussed, pushing Brian toward the house.

With mild resignation, Matthew smiled. So much for a peaceful Sunday.

***

Ernestine sped around the house. The family room was rearranged to accommodate Brian and his injured leg. Coffee, finger sandwiches, and sweets popped out as if a genie cast spells in the kitchen. Matthew settled Rebecca in her carriage, while Jonathan and Ernestine took up their places, ready for conversation. Matthew was the last to sit. His head spun with all the activity. But once everyone settled, he plunged ahead.

"I'm sorry. I wish I remembered."

"Don't worry yer purdy li'l head. I didn't think the sight of my gorgeous face would snap yer memory back." Brian snickered with good humor.

The banter felt easy and familiar. Yes, Matthew could see how they had been friends.

"I came prepared, brought the big gun."

Jonathan's expression tightened. Ernestine's lips rounded in a questioning moue.

Brian reached inside his shirt pocket and pulled out a small case. This was the big gun? Matthew almost laughed. But then...something strange happened. Like the night at the Bronco, shadows gathered around him. The white box on Brian's palm gleamed. Matthew's fingers trembled. Slowly he picked it up.

"Go ahead, open it."

Matthew started to lift the cover. Hesitating midway, he glanced at Brian, and his skin prickled. Brian leaned back, a quirky smile on his face. The shadows roiled... Matthew opened the box.

And stared at a woman's oblong charm—about the size of a quarter—strung on a thin chain. He felt weak. Perspiration dotted his forehead, and his stomach plummeted. The shadows picked up speed, spinning fast, faster... He lifted the chain, and the charm twirled. He peered at the religious design of a crowned Madonna and child.

"It's actually yours." Brian's voice drifted from some distant place.

Yes, it was familiar. Damn it. He'd seen it before. He flipped it around; a name and a date were inscribed. "Raquelita. May third," he whispered.

A painful stab attacked his temples. As if wielded by a mighty hand, a prodigious sledgehammer pummeled the battlements of his mind's wall. Sparks flew under the punishing blow. Shards of concrete and mortar exploded, and the structure cracked.

"May third," he repeated. The hammer descended anew with merciless purpose and the crack lengthened. The pain in his temples was excruciating. Wincing, he pressed a hand to his forehead.

Ernestine moved to stand. Brian stopped her. "Please, let it be. The wall is falling. It's the only way."

"*La Virgen del Pilar, Matthew.*" A woman's voice swept through his mind and soul. Matthew wanted to yell at the severity of the pain, the crippling wave of nausea. He collapsed against the sofa.

"*I commend him to your care. Please keep my Matthew, my heart, safe.*" The voice continued... Her voice...

The wall gave way. Through the wide breach, a river of memories rushed out.

"Raquelita." Matthew's cry reverberated in the room.

Everyone jumped except Brian, who'd obviously expected it. Jonathan gasped, little Rebecca whimpered, and Ernestine shushed her softly as she witnessed the return of Matthew's mind.

"Raquelita," he murmured, clutching the medal to his chest, an anchor in a storm of memories—caramel eyes, an irate woman, a wondrous kiss, Fort Benning, Special Forces, Brian...Vietnam.

He stared at his friend. "Bri, you're alive."

"Thanks to you."

The images roiled and surged in his mind: Brian wounded, the explosion, falling to the ground...and they kept on coming. "Dad, I remember, I remember." Yes, the memories were returning, one triggering the next, and as they did, the pain lessened. He lifted the little medal and stared at it for a few minutes.

"Raquelita," he whispered. "Oh Lord." He examined the faces around him. "Where is Raquelita?"

"Son, we need to talk. You've been lost for a long time, and there's much you need to learn."

***

With Ernestine's and Brian's contributions, Jonathan filled in Matthew's blank spots as best he could. The most difficult were the volatile events between late January and March of 1968, starting with the hostilities between Raquel and Isabel, and ending with Matthew's amnesia.

"She believed I was dead? Why?"

"It was a nasty set of circumstances," Jonathan explained. "You two had a special connection, right from the start."

"Ain't it the truth?" Brian said with a grin. "I remember trainin' and Nam. You sensed her trouble even before her letters arrived, and you thought *I* was weird."

"The link got you both in trouble. Yer group missed its return date at Lang Vei, the siege of Khe Sanh began and everyone worried. Everyone but Lita." Jonathan shifted in his chair. "She insisted she could sense you. Just before the tragedy at Lang Vei, yer link was severed. She couldn't *hear* you anymore. Tet exploded, Lang Vei was overrun, and my inside guy silenced. The media in the States went nuts. After some ugly developments at home…well, one mornin' she left without a word."

"What? Where did she go?"

"Emilio believed she fled to New York."

"Of course. Dalia," Matthew murmured. "When did she leave?" The question ached in his throat.

"Emilio said mid-February, when I saw him last."

"And you haven't spoken since? Why the hell not?"

"Several reasons." Jonathan frowned. "You didn't remember anyone or anythin'. Suppose she was found, should Emilio tell his daughter you were alive, but didn't remember her? I think not. Not after what she'd been through. None of us knew how you'd react to her."

Ernestine slipped to his side, held his hand, and Jonathan eased.

"In fact, a few weeks before Rebecca was born, Mother and I had resolved to call Emilio. We were desperate, son. You were a walking misery. With Kathy, and Rebecca's birth, it slipped my mind. Brian, thank God, stepped in."

"I'm sorry, Dad. I shouldn't lash out at you. I just woke up to this ugly tale, a nightmare that should have happened to someone else, not me, not us. Raquelita, my angel, alone in New York. Damn it, I feared this." Matthew jumped to his feet and began to pace the room.

"So," Brian said after a while, Matthew whirled around to stare at his friend. "What'll you do now, Romeo?" He laughed. "San Antonio's a little over an hour's ride from here." Brian batted his eyelashes repeatedly.

Matthew smiled and stopped pacing. "You know me so well. Even though I didn't know it, I've missed you, man. It's too late to drive now. By the time I get there—"

"You can always call," Ernestine said.

"No phone calls. People hide behind them. I have to see Emilio and Julie, personally gauge their reactions. Then I'll know the truth."

"We'll go first thin' in the mornin' o' dark thirty," Brian said. "You'll love my car on the road."

"Are you coming with me?"

"Of course I am. Who else will hold yer ugly hand if Raquelita's not back? 'Sides, I've missed yer nasty mug."

"No," Matthew said thoughtfully, returning to his seat. "She's been rescued. The link still works. I feel her. Lord, do I feel her, and she's not far. The feeling's growing by the second."

"Great, early it is. Ye'r drivin', my leg cramps at times. I'll be there for emotional support, and 'cause I love teary-eyed reunions."

***

"She's beautiful," Brian said as the sleeping baby made soft, raspy noises in the cradle of Matthew's arms.

"She is, and special too. I'm not talking like a besotted father, though I am. My child has an old soul. On days when I've despaired, she watches me like she knows." He shook his head in bewilderment. "Then she smiles and everything changes. Burdens lift and the world brightens. It's amazing."

"I'm changin' my mind. Think I'll git me one of those."

"When you're ready, it'll happen." Matthew pushed the rocker back, resting Rebecca on his chest. She shifted and snuggled, her rosebud lips puckering slightly. "How did you know?"

"Soon after the package arrived, it called to me. I saw the medal, and I remembered it meant so much to both of you. I knew once you saw it, yer mind would be released."

"It was. Thank you."

"I was entrusted with the key and given the opportunity to pay you back for my life. My brother, I'm here to thank you."

***

Soon after Brian retired to the guest room, Matthew deposited Rebecca in her crib and proceeded—besieged by anger and guilt—to toss and turn through the remaining hours of the night. Sleep was not a friend.

Merciless thoughts presented all possible hazards his girl might have endured while he recovered, and later, when he wandered lost and idle through long months of utter blankness. How could he forget her? No, that wasn't entirely accurate; his heart never forgot. It always missed her. It persisted and summoned her every night. She was the Gypsy of his dreams, the beauty with the golden gaze.

A soft whimper returned his attention to the crib. Rebecca... It made sense now. The name he'd tried to remember. Raquel, Rebecca. Then a new set of worries beset him. The weight of the past year and all its complications fell heavily upon him. Would Lita accept his child? What did he know of her after such a long separation? What if she'd built a new life? She believed him dead. There might be another. No, his heart asserted. There was no other. Not for her and not for him. And yet, there'd been a woman. Rebecca was undeniable proof. How could he explain his insanity, the loss of faculties, or the glorious vision that night? No, losing Raquelita wasn't acceptable. His mind was no longer fractured. He'd drive to San Antonio and present his case. Raquel was his other half. She would understand. His heart was certain.

***

Flexibility was the keyword in the adventures of bathing Emilio Jr.; the child's moods dictated the event. If he was serene, one came out fairly dry. Conversely, should he be frisky and playful, the bather needed a rain slicker. This morning he wanted to play, and when the doorbell rang, Julianna cursed the inopportune arrival. She almost ignored it, but it rang insistently. She decided to answer.

Wrapping the baby securely in his oversize towel, she marched quickly to the door, calling to the visitor to cool his heels. She sped toward the door, patting and fixing her wet locks as best she could, reshifted the culprit of her pitiful appearance—the wriggling rascal—to the other arm, and spied through the peephole. Julianna almost dropped the baby.

"Matthew." She yanked the door open. Emilio Jr. squeaked a protest. "Oh Emi, shush, sweetie," she murmured, easing the baby and her shock. "Lord in heaven. Come in, come in." She tugged at Matthew's arm with her free hand.

Matthew gave a thumbs-up toward a car parked at the curb, and shrugged. "Brian's waiting outside. We weren't sure if you still lived here."

"Brian? He's here as well? This is wonderful. I must call Emilio this instant. I can't believe it, you're here." Julianna's hand flew to her mouth. "But, you know me?"

"Yes, I remember, Julie," he said. "Please, don't call Emilio yet. Let's talk for a moment. Okay?"

"Of course, of course... Here's Brian. Are you fully recovered?" Julianna kissed his cheek. "We heard your injuries were extensive."

"I'm well, 'n happy to see you, Julie."

She waved toward the living room. "Sit, please, both of you. Let me get you something to drink. "I'll put Emi in his playpen, and I'll get us some coffee."

Matthew held Julie gently by the arm. "Julie, please sit. We know you're surprised. We're fine; we've had plenty of coffee." She did as he bid, while Brian headed for an armchair, plopped down, and straightened his injured leg with a sigh of relief.

"Who is this handsome man?" Matthew extended his hands toward the baby. "May I?"

"Are you sure you wish to hold my troublemaker? He may be a little damp from his bath."

Julianna deposited Emilio Jr. in Matthew's arms. The child studied him like his father would. Matthew smiled and cooed, but instead of rejecting the stranger, the child grinned. She watched Matthew's ease with a mixture of curiosity and awe.

"He's gorgeous. You both must be so pleased. How old is he?"

"Three and a half months. He was born December twenty-sixth."

"He's a few days younger than mine."

Matthew spoke in a casual way. But when he noticed Julianna's horrified expression and her obvious search for a telltale ring, he explained quickly. "It's not what you're thinking. I'm not married, nor do I have any commitments. Still, there's a lot to discuss. For now, I'd prefer if you didn't call Emilio. I want to speak to him in person. What about Raquelita? Any news? Is she all right?"

Perhaps sensing his anxiety, Emi began to squirm. Julianna took the child back in her familiar arms. "Of course you don't know. Raquel's here assisting her father with the business, a short ten-minute walk from here."

***

He covered the distance in five. The front door was unlocked, as Julie had promised. He pushed it open and peered into the gloom of the empty bar. His sight adjusted in a few seconds. He stepped inside.

On the far side, through a partially opened door a beam of light spilled out. The distance to the office and his goal appeared impossibly far, almost unreachable. As he walked across the floor, the click of his boots on the wood echoed throughout the silence, and his heart pounded so hard he felt the pulse in his ears. He reached the door and pushed it in. Father and daughter discussed something about wines. Emilio faced him. Raquel faced away.

Emilio saw him and blanched.

"Dad, you didn't answer me. What about this wine account?" she asked. "Don't you think the quality has suffered?"

Raquelita's melodious voice... A hand squeezed his heart, and a new rush of memories filled his mind: a yellow dress, a soft question, a poem exchanged, and tears blurred his vision. He remained still, listening and filling his sight with the silky hair, softly curved back, and the toned arms, the small, delicate hands shuffling papers.

"Papá?" she insisted.

"Raquel," Emilio whispered.

"What is it? Are you feeling all right?"

Matthew spoke at last. "Your father is fine, angel. I, on the other hand, am not."

Raquel stood, a marionette pulled by unseen strings. Refusing to succumb to another devilish delusion of Matthew, she didn't turn. But the look on her father's pale face... Had he seen the ghost as well? She replayed the last words and almost relished the familiar tone. She shook her head, refusing to accept.

"Papá." Hot tears burst out. "I think I'm losing my mind."

"No, you're not, angel. But I will, if you don't look at me soon." The phantom sound came closer. Her crazy ears insisted...*it's real.*

No. Don't do this. Stop dreaming. It's not possible.

Raquel pivoted, ready to dispel the fantasy. Instead, she looked into Matthew's beloved emerald gaze. She took one slow step, then another, delicately touched the whiskered cheek.

Swirls of stars closed her vision.

Chapter Forty-Three

San Antonio – April 7th 1969

The delusion pounced on Raquel like a panther. Not because she'd been careless, but because it felt real. Her fingers had touched warmth, human skin. Did she have the guts? Was she brave enough to see? Her eyelids fluttered. *Not yet, not yet,* her lonely heart argued. *Wait a little. Give us another moment; enjoy the dream.* Would it be so bad if she indulged the fantasy another second or two? The gentle caress on her forehead, the fingers threading through her hair and the murmuring voice…

That's enough. Raquel's eyelids flew open.

The eyes of her dreams and memories stared back with deep concern. Raquel frowned. "You're still here," she accused.

And now little crinkles appeared at the edges of his eyes. "Of course. Where else should I be?" he asked amused, and a dimple appeared on the whiskered cheek.

"I don't know," she huffed, her hand waving a dismissal. "With the others, wherever it is fantasies live. Go, shoo."

A warm fingertip lifted her chin, and her heart jolted. The unforgettable, delicious breath caressed her face. "Angel, I'm real. This is where I belong. Don't send me away."

His lips brushed hers with the lightest touch, and Raquel's breath hitched at the contact. He pulled back, linking his heart to hers through his gaze. *I'm here. I'm back.* His lips descended again, this time ravenous and decisive.

Releasing a strangled moan, Raquel swan-dived cleanly into the mirage, ghost or insanity. She would take it all. She wanted it all. Her hands flew to his chest. Fisting his shirt, she pulled him tight, seeking warmth to survive, fingers clutching with the desperation of one who's lived in the tundra of oblivion.

"Matthew," she whispered. "If this is a dream, I couldn't bear it."

"It isn't a dream, Raquel," Papá's steady voice explained. "Matthew didn't perish in Vietnam."

And reality slammed in. Matthew stared with concern. A few feet away stood Papá, his countenance echoing Matthew's expression.

"How?"

Matthew grasped her hands and brought them to his lips, kissing them lightly. "I was injured, and my memory was erased for many months. That's the short explanation." Matthew spoke to Emilio. "Can we take her home now? Make her comfortable. Wouldn't you like that, angel?"

"Yes, yes." She was still dazed. May God forgive her, she still doubted. What would it take for her to believe, sunlight, fresh air, perhaps faith in miracles?

"My car is parked out back," Papá said.

"Lead the way." Matthew lifted her in his arms and followed Emilio out. In minutes, she was settled in the cradle of his arms.

She had resigned herself to his loss. Which unexplained portent had returned him to her? So she examined him as if he would disappear: the chiseled jaw, the graceful muscles of his neck, and his hair. Raquel had never seen Matthew's hair long. Locks of light brown with a profusion of gold strands fell on his forehead, the back brushed the nape of his neck. His cheekbones had sharpened. Tiny creases had appeared.

She lifted her hand, and her fingertips alit gently upon his cheek. A tenuous smile eased his features, and his gaze brightened, yet a haunting shadow lingered. The flames of old had dimmed. What had he seen? What had he experienced? Life hadn't been kind.

***

With Raquel in his arms, Matthew rushed through the house until he reached the sanctuary of her bedroom. He shoved the door shut, closed the distance to her bed, and set her down gently.

"You gave me such a scare," he whispered, propping pillows behind her neck. With a feathery touch, he caressed her temple, her cheek, back to her temple. He could do this for hours. "What an exquisite sight you are. To think I could have lost you forever."

"B-but...w-what happened?"

"Amnesia, induced by a head injury."

"Are you well now?" she asked anxiously, pushing herself upright. "Tell me, please. I need to know everything."

"Everything?"

"Yes...only..."

"What, sweetheart?"

"Please, hold me. Let me feel you, and don't let go."

God, more than holding her, he wanted to inhale her. "Never, angel," he murmured. But shock was still strong upon her. She needed time to adapt to his sudden return. He restrained his need, allowing a lone fingertip to resume the slow and easy touch on her face.

"I'm going to hold you forever." He could barely speak; words and tears had tangled in his throat. "I can't exist without you. It's not an empty declaration. For the past fourteen months, I've been less than an aimless shadow. My brain may not have remembered, but my heart broke without you." He slid next to her onto the bed. He couldn't bear the distance. Gently, he circled her shoulders. "Is this comfortable? Do you want to hear?" he asked, tucking her head on his chest.

"Yes," she sighed.

Like an ancient narrator, Matthew lulled her into his story. Raquel released her imagination and soared over the mountains, mysterious and majestic despite their treacherous dangers. She visited the camp and learned about the men who struggled daily. She experienced the loneliness and homesickness. She relived the months of anguish and frustration when his brain locked away vital knowledge.

"Through the appalling emptiness, you were always there. You came to me every night. It also drove me mad, because your face was hidden."

"But...I saw yours as well. I questioned myself. I thought *I* was going crazy. I should've known you were alive."

"Don't do this, angel. You didn't know, because I couldn't answer your call." He shook his head. "If anyone's to blame...it's me."

"Blame? You? You were wounded. I ignored your wishes. I made terrible decisions and so many mistakes. I am so ashamed." She turned her face into his chest.

"I don't want us to end. If you left now, I couldn't go on. But you have to know. And when you do, you won't look at me the same way again. I'm soiled goods," she whispered, starting to move away from him.

His arms tightened like iron bands. "No." He swung her around. Her back fell on the bed as he hovered above her. "Don't ever say that in front of me again. Our bodies may have endured detestable moments, but only the quality of the soul matters. I see yours, and it's perfect."

Control disappeared. Matthew crushed her body to his, and his mouth devoured hers. This was what he'd needed from the first, to be entwined with his angel, fusing into one. She received him in kind. Breaths, lips, and tongues merged in frenzied kisses, arms and legs twined frantically around each other, hips thrust against hips, chest against chest, all in a twist of need. Raquel arched against Matthew, seeking instinctively the penetration that would clean the filthy remnants inside her. Could they, could they love this way?

A glimmer of sanity returned to Matthew, and he gradually eased their motion. He smiled, pulling slightly away. "Sweet Jesus, baby, I'm sorry. I lost myself."

"I did too," Raquel said, out of breath, fisting his shirt again. "I've missed you so."

Matthew flipped sideways, and, leaning upon a forearm, he stared at her. He wanted to speak, tell her everything, but opted to wait until he brought her home, showed her the beautiful child waiting for him, his other perfect girl "Angel, I have a load of sins to confess. Such has been our journey, separated by life and events beyond our control. We're blessed. Our paths have rejoined. We'll share our stories of woe and start fresh. Can we do this? What do you say?"

Raquel didn't care about his professed sins. She had her own mess to confess. Whatever happened was in the past. She only cared about a future with him. With the promise of renewal and redemption in the air, she answered without hesitation. "I say yes."

***

Pulling Matthew by the hand, a joyous Raquel returned to the family room. Her bright smile was for everyone, but her eyes searched for Papá. Emilio had waited for her return, standing like a sentinel or a man awaiting sentencing. Soon he would have to confess, and when he did, he hoped the long-held secret wouldn't rupture their relationship.

"Papá, it's like a dream." She rushed into his arms.

"Raquel, honey, look at me."

The tone of his voice alarmed her. "What is it, Papá?"

"Baby, please take a seat. We have to talk."

Matthew frowned when Emilio pushed his daughter back to him. Recalling his conversation with his father, Matthew had an idea what Emilio was about to disclose. He guided Raquel to a large recliner and dragged a chair over for himself, then threaded his fingers with hers and waited for a very pale Emilio to speak.

"Raquel, I…" He paused. " When you look at me like that it's difficult to speak."

"Papá, please, it can't be that bad."

"It's worse." His voice dropped an octave. "I knew Matthew was alive, Raquel. I've known since February of 1968, soon after you disappeared."

He sat next to Julianna, and with obvious discomfort, Emilio continued. "Jonathan came to see me. He told me Matthew and Brian were badly wounded. Matthew's prognosis was inconclusive. The amnesia could last hours or a lifetime, and you, my daughter, were in the forgotten period, same as Brian and Vietnam."

Matthew exhaled forcefully, and Raquel's head snapped to him. He'd pressed her hand against his lips. She'd not felt it, so intent was she on her father's words.

"Whitlock found you in New York—"

"And you came to get me," she said. "You knew I was very sick."

"Yes, Raquel, I—"

"No, Papá, wait." She stood, pulled her hand from Matthew's hold, and stepped toward her father, who stared at the floor, fists clenched tight. Raquel placed a gentle hand on his hair.

"I was fragile. You heard Dr. Metzger and decided not to tell me about Matthew. You knew I would've fled to him. You feared if he didn't remember me, I'd be devastated." She dropped to her knees before her father and asked softly, "Am I close, Papá?"

Emilio's tear-streaked face looked at her, the light of comprehension illuminating his features. He opened his arms, and she rushed into them. "You were protecting me, Papá. The only way you could."

"Yes, I meant to tell you, Raquel. When you were stronger, but then I'd look at you and…didn't have the heart. I reckoned if Matthew recovered, Jonathan would call."

"Yes," Matthew intervened. "Just yesterday, Brian arrived with the medal."

Raquel swung around. "The medal?"

"The medal you gave Matthew," Brian explained. "He wore it day and night, except on clandestine ops. He wasn't wearing it the day of the NVA clash. In some missions, we didn't wear tags. It's what we did."

"The medal remained at Lang Vei," Matthew continued. "Later, when patrols reentered the camp, personal belongings were collected. What was salvaged was sent home, and in the confusion, my medal was sent to Brian."

Raquel returned to the recliner and dropped into it. "This is unreal," she whispered.

"Ordained, not unreal," Brian emphasized. "The medal could've been sent to any of the other families and never returned to Matthew, its purpose foiled."

"As soon as I saw the Madonna and read your name, the mental walls crashed. No earthly entity can summon such power." Matthew tapped on his chest; the medal was back in its rightful place.

The memory of an enigmatic dream returned to her, the Lady's promise. "Yes. Thank you, *Virgencita*. Thank you."

***

The Pontiac hummed along H290, and Raquelita's heart vaulted with the familiar surroundings. They were getting close to the ranch, and to their confessions. She almost feared the moment, but no, she was done living in fear. Their turn for happiness had come. It would work out. It had to work out.

"I heard every word." Matthew squeezed her hand. "New York was hard on you, wasn't it?"

She pressed her lips and jerked a nod.

"We won't talk about it yet. My turn comes first. Don't worry, I've my share." He pressed her hand to his lips. "We're almost there."

Matthew drove through the gate and parked the car near the kitchen door. He turned to Brian's oblivious form in the backseat, reached for his leg, and tugged it lightly. "Mornin', sunshine. We're here." He pulled the leg harder.

Brian yelped. "What? What is it?" His arms flailed, and his eyelids flitted.

"He sleeps like a rock"—Matthew snickered—"even in Nam."

"Right, hold yer horses. I'm awake now." Brian huffed; after opening the door, he unfolded his cane and stepped out.

All three descended from the vehicle. Lagging behind, Matthew allowed Brian to enter the house first. He grasped Raquel's arm, detaining her. He lowered his face to hers and whispered, "People make mistakes and commit sins they regret, deeply. The fallout, however, is inescapable. Debts must be paid. After you learn everything, I pray you'll forgive me."

He paused, looking bemused. "How can I explain? I hate my transgression, but not the outcome. It's strange how it all works out. I'm about to show you my second most precious gift on earth. What you must never doubt is my love for you. I love you, in all the possible ways a man can love a woman. You'll always be my luminous Vega, the sweetheart of my soul," he said, staring into her eyes. "Do you believe me?"

When Raquel listened to his explication, it sounded like her disaster, except for the second part. She had a bizarre intuition about this gift, but she wouldn't jump ahead; she'd wait. What mattered was her response. With her whole heart, she answered, "I believe you."

Matthew smiled, and his gaze twinkled. Was it her imagination, or did the nasty shadow finally dissipate? "Let's go inside. My parents are likely going nuts." He gently ushered her through the door.

***

She'd barely stepped into the Buchanan kitchen when she was rushed by the affectionate whirlwind of hugs and kisses called Ernestine. From around her arms, Raquel spied Jonathan; his dark blue eyes gleamed with evident pleasure.

Raquel allowed Ernestine's effusive tenderness to rain upon her until she was drenched. She now understood the second component to her former grief—the absence in her life of Matthew's wonderful parents. The concept settled in her soul, and Raquel tightened the embrace

"Oh, child," Ernestine whispered, dabbing at her face and pulling away. "Let me look at you. Beautiful as always. We've missed you so much." And she tightened her embrace again.

"Come, Mother, don't keep her all to yourself. It's my turn for a kiss," Jonathan said, resting his hands on Ernestine's shoulders.

"Of course, of course."

She led Raquel into Jonathan's arms. They felt solid and warm, much like her father's, always steady in their affection.

"Thank you for bringing Matthew back to us," he said.

"Oh, I didn't do anything. It was Brian."

"You both did. You gave Matthew the medal, and Brian brought it to him. I owe you both for my boy's return."

"He's back for all of us. Back for good." She placed a kiss on his weathered cheek.

"Okay, sweetie," Ernestine fussed. "You must be thirsty. Did y'all eat before leaving San Antonio?"

"I'm fine, really," Raquel answered, but her attention was somewhere else. She'd caught a unique sound in between Ernestine's chattering, and her woman's ears locked on to it. Her gaze swept the kitchen and stopped on the incongruous stroller next to Matthew. Raquel extricated herself from Ernestine's hold and padded toward the pale green baby carriage. She reached for the cover and lifted it. A pair of chubby arms with cute little fists moved playfully. Bright green eyes examined her. A wondrous one-dimple smile appeared.

The bond was instant.

She could never explain how the sense of ownership and protectiveness kindled and took over. Her soul welled with an unspeakable emotion. She reached in, and the baby's arms extended toward her at the same time. Without asking, she lifted the child into her arms.

"She's beautiful."

Matthew touched his child's forehead and gently caressed the silky strands of golden-brown hair. "Her name is Rebecca. I'd like to add María, when she's baptized, if it would please you," he whispered.

"If it would please me? How could it not?" She lowered her face, inhaling the baby's sweet aroma. "Wait a second," she exclaimed with a sudden snap. "What about the mother's opinion?"

"There is no mother. She renounced all her rights."

***

The silvery light of a waning quarter moon filtered through Matthew's bedroom window. Shrouded in shadow, Raquel and Matthew stood over the crib, watching the sleeping baby inside.

"Will you tell me now?" she whispered.

"Yes." Pulling her by the hand, he sat on the leather recliner next to the crib, where he'd spent many a night lulling Rebecca to sleep. He lifted Raquel to his lap, slipped his arms around her, and pressed her gently to his chest. He explained about the fateful barbecue and Garth, the search for the mysterious Florida girl, the night at the Bronco, and the resulting fiasco.

When he reached the part about Kathy's wish to abort Rebecca, anger filled him anew. "I couldn't let her destroy my child. We made the mistake. Why should Rebecca pay for it? Kathy wanted money for the abortion, but I bargained with her. 'Carry the baby to term, and I'll take her off your hands forever,' and she agreed." He paused, drawing a deep breath. "Something niggled at me through those months. A boy's name came easy. Then I thought, what if it's a girl?" He laughed softly.

"The search for a special name began. My mind gravitated to the letter R. I was so confused, and so were my folks. I pored over books. Rosalind, Regina, Raphaela, but none clicked. I don't know how I missed Raquel, but I found Rebecca. I think the Hebrew meaning caught me—bound, tied, faithful one. So appropriate for us both. From my fractured point of view, she'd be tied solely to me."

"Matthew, I'm so proud you had the fortitude to take on the responsibility."

"Perhaps. But how do you feel about it? Can you forgive my loss of judgment? Do you resent my error with Kathy? You must know I didn't want her. I was almost insane, so lost in those days. Would you believe I was overcome by a fantasy that night? I was making love to you, my mysterious beauty with the golden eyes."

"Shush." She pulled away from his chest and placed two fingers on his lips. "I understand all about delusions. I believe you, and I'll forever be in debt to Kathy for Rebecca."

Matthew gasped at the unexpected answer and started to speak, but she increased the pressure on his lips.

"Now it's my turn." Her expression silenced him. He nodded, and she took over the mantle of storyteller. Although intricate, her tale wasn't at all wonderful or mysterious or romantic as any offered by Scheherazade. She started strong, but when the tale took its downward course, her voice lowered. She finished in a bare whisper.

"So you see, I'm grateful for the miracle of Rebecca. I can't offer you a child. I told you earlier, I'm damaged goods. No family option for Raquel María Muro. It's my lifetime payment for my mistakes. I ask you now, am I still your Vega, the sweetheart of your soul?" she asked, averting her eyes, deathly afraid to see the rejection in his face.

Matthew had listened in silence. Holding her tighter, he stood and stepped to his bed, where he placed her with utmost gentleness. Her lips opened to speak, but he placed a quelling finger on them, shaking his head. She wouldn't be allowed to protest, not tonight.

"Buchanan," he whispered.

He saw her bewilderment and smiled. His lips returned to her ear and kissed the lobe. "Raquel María Buchanan. You have a family option. Or are you rejecting us?" He tilted his head in the direction of the cradle.

"But...you still want me?"

"I told you earlier. I can't exist without you. Will you let me show you?" he asked.

Slowly he pulled back from her, gazing down the length of her body. He twirled a long tress around a finger, ran his knuckles along her face, gliding gently to her jaw, to the curve of her neck, to her blouse, where he paused briefly. He began to release one button after another as he placed soft kisses on her lips, her chin, and between her breasts. His fingers trembled, same as his murmuring voice. "I need to love you, angel. I can barely contain myself. Will you give yourself to me?"

"Yes."

He closed his eyes, envisioning the approaching delight and his purpose tonight. With the gentlest touch, he removed her blouse and wispy bra. Her rosy nipples peaked, and he kissed each one in reverence, undoing and erasing the contemptible abuse inflicted upon them. With the gentlest nip, he reminded them of his ownership. In turn, they recognized him; eagerly, they reached for his caresses.

He slipped his palms down her body. When he reached her aggrieved pelvis, he pressed gently, hoping to infuse his warmth, and Raquel moaned in pleasure. Matthew deposited more slow kisses along her belly, continuing with the healing and cleansing process. His quest didn't end there. He removed the rest of her clothing, and returned to caress the soft skin of her thighs. Onward he glided, slowly up and around. He stopped under her knees.

"I want to touch and taste all of you, Raquel. Will you let me?"

"Please, make me yours."

"Angel, you've always been mine." The whisper rolled out. He stared into her eyes as he lifted her knees, slowly widening her legs. She flushed shyly. With trembling hands, she reached for him, and he smiled, shaking his head. Releasing one silky thigh, he captured a hand in midair, brought it to his lips for a delicate kiss, and placed it above her head. He repeated the action with the other. "Easy, my love. I wish to pleasure you tonight."

He returned to her legs, widening them a little farther, while he traced the silky inner skin from her knees to the juncture of her thighs. With the softest touch, he ventured through the tender inner lips eliciting her soft gasp. Matthew lowered his body between her legs and settled his shoulders beneath her knees. He pulled at her hips, brought her labia to his lips, and kissed the heart of her sex. Tenderly, he nuzzled her open, and with the hunger of almost two lonely years, he lapped and sucked thoroughly. "I've missed you," he murmured. "So beautiful."

Every gesture and caress had a purpose, to blot out and expunge all insult and injury inflicted upon her. He had to reinstate what was lost, what had so brutally been wrenched away. Everything he'd bestowed upon her the first day they'd loved: tenderness, passion, respect. His mouth continued its mission. His lips covered her clit, and he suckled, extending the healing, and obliterating the shame imposed on her.

"Will you allow me in?"

"Please."

He smiled. His need of her raged within him, but he couldn't forget his mission: to claim her from the darkest pits of hell. Controlling his impatience, he stood, and as his eyes absorbed her beautiful body, he discarded his clothing. He returned to the bed and to a kneeling position between her legs. With deliberate tenderness, Matthew slipped his palms around her hips and brought her closer. His erection nudged her sheath, and her liquid response received him. She was eager, pliant, and desirous.

Raquel gasped and tightened her legs around him. "Take me," she pleaded.

At her honest reaction, he knew he'd won her back, had wrested her from the dark, and Matthew thrust forward, reclaiming all of Raquel. With the full force of his rightful penetration, he dislodged any remaining poisonous debris. He pressed her hips against him, burying himself deep in her warmth where he belonged. He bent forward and kissed her chest.

"Yes, Raquel María," he murmured. "You'll always be my luminous Vega. You're the reigning sweetheart of my soul. I love you, and you're entirely mine," he declared, thrusting rhythmically. The release he'd lovingly initiated burst into a million stars, illuminating the whole universe.

Epilogue

Ocala — December 16th 1969

"Your father is insane. All Andalucía is in attendance."

"Just about," Raquel answered, struggling to fit Rebecca's playful chubby feet into her first pair of sandals. "He's not the only one insane. Xavi plotted with him to coordinate the baptisms, since the birthdays are so close. Jordi had to wait the longest. Next year he can celebrate his birthday with yours." She wiggled her eyebrows.

"Xavi didn't mind waiting. It gave Bob a chance to return from his latest mission, after my rescue he's become a member of the family. Besides, December in central Florida has wonderful weather. Folks in these parts will hate us for years to come. We've overrun them with relatives." She sighed.

"Please, sweetheart, uncurl your little toes," she coaxed Rebecca gently. "Come on, baby. Mommy wants you to look real pretty."

Matthew watched, entranced, as his wife fought to fit the sandals on Rebecca. Once he'd thought Raquel was beautiful; now she was breathtaking, and she owned his soul. Raquel had accepted her physical condition; resignation added a special brilliance to her aura. The chestnut of her hair had become richer; the gold in her eyes burned deeper. He understood her pain and grieved privately for it. But Matthew was a man of faith and, as Emilio often insisted, miracles happened. Men's decrees were not necessarily written in stone. And Matthew hoped and believed.

"Ah-ha," Raquel exclaimed, changing the course of his thoughts. "Gotcha." The cute, tiny sandals were effectively buttoned.

"We talked about it once, but it's been a while. Are you happy with one child? We could adopt. The baby would be ours."

She didn't even look at him. She carefully spread the lacy skirts of Rebecca's baptismal gown. "Matthew James Buchanan, you're steering for trouble. Are you suggesting Rebecca's not ours? Where have you been the past eight months?"

"W-well, no, it came out wrong."

"Rebecca is your biological daughter. But she's also the daughter of your heart, which makes her unquestionably mine, because you are my heart. And she loved me right away. If anyone contradicts me, I will rip their little hearts out." She finished by batting her eyelashes.

"I only pray to be a good nurturing mother for her. I learned by force what nurturing means. I remember what I missed most from my mine, and Rebecca will not be lacking. However, I'm not opposed to adopting a child. It's a great idea, a brother for Rebecca."

"Hmmm... Maybe I'm being premature. Yes, we should continue with the normal methods, quite often, I might add. Testing your dad's theories a while longer. We have time." He winked.

It dawned on him then, he was the most fortunate man in the world. He remembered the long days of war and lost memories and how they transformed to this happiness, to this peace and fulfillment.

"Are my beautiful women ready?" He bent over his wife and daughter, kissed the baby's head, and deposited a lingering kiss on Raquel's lips.

"Ahh," she whispered.

"Let him kiss me with the kisses of his mouth: for thy love is better than wine."

"Behold, thou art fair, my love; behold, thou art fair; thou hast doves' eyes," he answered.

"Matthew... You memorized it, the Song of Songs," she exclaimed.

Full of satisfaction, Matthew Buchanan ushered his little family toward the festivities.

***

Later that night, Raquel and Matthew reposed in each other's arms, waiting for sleep to overtake them both. "It was a beautiful ceremony," she whispered.

"Yes, I loved watching y'all, you with Emilio holding Jordi, Coralina and Alejandro with Emi, and Marité with Brian cradling our daughter. The lighting of the candles and the congregation's response was so moving it gave me the chills."

"The babies were so good. They didn't cry with the chilly water."

"Marité is so poised, isn't she?" he said.

"Yes, she's on her way to womanhood."

"Your momma and Xavi look so happy together. Man, she was something." He chuckled. "And Xavi, you called him a crank-ass."

"Yes. Love changes everything and everyone. Even aloof Lorrie is now enthusiastically engaged."

"Look at us."

"We had our trials and were lost to each other. I count my blessings each night," she murmured, nestling closer to him.

As sleep descended, snippets of the past two and a half years flashed in quick succession. The faces of friends; some present tonight, others absent. The road had been long, arduous at times. Tonight, despite the challenges, she was with her little family, in the arms of her beloved. Nothing else mattered.

***

The following morning, Raquel awoke to a silent guesthouse. Matthew must've taken Rebecca out, always the mighty duo, although Matthew insisted they were the mighty Buchanan trio. She stretched lazily, donned her robe, and stepped out to the kitchen. Thoughts of coffee beckoned. Waiting for the bubbling percolator, she gazed out the windows. It would be another spectacular day. Later, she would walk over to the old oak. She owed it a visit. It had once shaded her in hope, another time in sadness. She must return in happiness.

She glanced at the breakfast nook and noticed the package, a thin case, and a folded note on top addressed to her. She brought her coffee mug and sat down to read the note.

Angel,

It's been a long time since you wrote. It's time you started again. It was always your desire. Please don't give up on your dreams.

With all my love,
Matthew

She removed the paper covering the beautiful, leather-bound journal, and her heart jolted. Matthew was right; it had been a long time since she'd picked up a pen. To her further surprise, the long box held a Montblanc. Her husband was serious about her writing and most generous.

She sat for a long while, sipping her coffee. Finally, she lifted the pen, and, opening the journal to the first page, she began to write.

> *On a moonless summer night, a Greyhound bus rushes along a lonely stretch of road, its headlights penetrating the blackness. In the thoughts of Men, a bus is an innocuous conveyance, transporting all sorts of strangers. But in that single moment, all are joined in an unspoken united purpose: to reach their destination. The simple act of moving from point to point is taken for granted. It is on these rare, unintended occasions when paths cross, lives intersect, and the Fates intervene. Directions, once solidly set, change. Destiny is fickle, humbling human arrogance. It spins, It weaves, and It cuts lives at a whim.*

Thanks for reading!

If you enjoyed *Destiny's Plan*, please help other readers find it, too. Consider leaving a review wherever you bought the book.

You can connect with me at:
www.VictoriaSaccentiWrites.com

OR

Sign up for my Newsletter
Like my Facebook Page
Follow me on Twitter

Acknowledgements

A million and one thanks go to Laura Caine, my friend, mentor, outstanding cheerleader, and staunch supporter. Your faith in the project gave me the strength to finish. Linda Ingmanson, copy editor extraordinaire, her humor and sharp eye taught me much; my wonderful beta readers—Lynn Latimer, April Cleaver, Teresita Reynolds, Lauralee Owen, Jaime Jacobs, and Nadine Winningham—for their outstanding input and advice; María Elena Alonso-Sierra my sister, author of The Coin and The Book of Hours, for holding my hand through the harrowing process of searching for a literary agent; Angie Waters for this beautiful book cover and to Mari Christie for her guidance and formatting the manuscript. In the technical-historical department additional thanks go to José Meléndez-Pérez, who served two tours of active duty in Vietnam (1965-1966 and 1969-1970). Through his words the struggle and vicissitudes of the war came alive and Dr. Kenneth Finlayson, historian with the US Department of Defense for providing details about Special Forces training. Lastly, to my husband John, who tolerated many lonely hours while I wrote locked away in my office. He takes the final thank you, because without his patience this book would've never been written.

About the Author

A native of Cuba, Victoria acquired a love for books from her parents, and the thirst to see the world from her father. As a result she has been around the globe by her count, at least twice. From her journeys she has gathered a varied collection of stories and anecdotes, which now serve to inspire her muse. Central Florida is home, but if she could convince her husband, she would pack her computer and move to Scotland, a land she adores.

www.VictoriaSaccentiWrites.com

Coming Soon from Victoria Saccenti:

Destiny's Choice, the sequel to *Destiny's Plan,*

Continue on to the first chapter.

Chapter One

December 1969

You're late...you're so late. Where the heck are you? Out of the corner of her eye, Marité Muro scanned the right hallway of the chapel, but a small group of attendees and a column blocked her view. Human anatomy can only go so far, and soon, a dull pain at her temples and a million sparks clouded her vision. So she gave up and looked toward the altar and the marble baptismal font; otherwise, she'd end up half-dizzy with a headache. The temptation to simply turn around and search the faces behind her was strong, yet she managed to control the impulse. She had an important role and should appear composed and focused on the ceremony—same as Brian, her cosponsor—or at least pretend. Still, she couldn't stop thinking of Michael. *Why aren't you here?*

Shifting to the left, she tried again, seeking a body, a shadow, some movement, anything that might indicate her cousin's arrival. Nothing. Zip. He couldn't miss the triple baptism. It meant a lot to everyone. The entire family had flown in from the Old Country, not to mention friends from all over. *You're going to ruin it if you don't show up.*

Her instinct was to stomp and protest out loud, but she kept her growing discontent silent. She'd dreamed about this occasion for weeks, had bought a special dress. She wanted to show off. She wanted him to see her among adults, doing adult things, like a young lady. Be proud of her. And to think, not so long ago, he would've insisted on driving her and would've been full of advice on the ride over. He used to be so protective and supportive, so affectionate, but lately—

Father O'Leary's prayers snapped her attention back to the ceremony. Moving from infant to infant, he uttered the blessings, dabbed a little salt in their mouths, sprinkled the tiny foreheads with holy water, and finally anointed them with chrism. And now, Rebecca María, the adorable child cradled in her arms, came next. Marité glanced at the beaming parents standing off to her side: Raquel and Matthew Buchanan, her sister and brother-in-law. Dismissing her earlier preoccupation, Marité sent a silent prayer on their behalf for a life full of well-deserved happiness. They'd struggled enough.

The questions to the godparents began, and she answered in unison with Brian. His voice, deep, full of emotion, and self-assured, rang in her ears. Something strange happened then. Either the solemnity of the moment or the misty spirals of the church incense wafting past the stained glass windows must've affected her, because with each *I do* response, she was overcome by a dreamy feeling. A sense of déjà vu transported her to a different moment and a distant place, nowhere she knew or had seen before. She shivered and peeked Brian's way, wondering if he felt it as well. He grinned down at her, and the vision-like sensation dissipated.

With his sunny smile, Brian MacKay, Matthew's best friend and ex-war buddy, was the happiest person she'd ever known, from her almost-fifteen-year-old perspective. In these days of the Vietnam War, men who survived the jungle came home either physically damaged or with broken spirits, sometimes both. Not Brian. His cheerful disposition had carried him through exhausting physical therapy sessions—she'd heard Raquel and Matthew talk—and conquered his wounds. She watched in awed respect as he moved or walked about, displaying his faltering step like a badge of honor and the ever-present cane like a scepter.

Brian didn't condescend, despite the eight-year gap between them, and she liked that quality best. He treated her as an equal. So, she'd been thrilled to learn he would be her cosponsor in Rebecca's baptism. The sacrament would not only bind them to the child but to each other as *compadres* in a very special life-long relationship, almost like parents. She remembered her absent cousin...and yep, she was back to where she started.

"What is it?" Bending closer, Brian nudged her arm. "That frown's ruinin' your purdy face."

Marité knew he'd tried to keep his voice down but was also certain folks at the last row heard him. "Shhh," she whispered and, suppressing a rising giggle, bumped him with her shoulder.

Brian jerked up to his full height and snapped two fingers in mock salute. "Yes, ma'am."

In that moment, Rebecca decided to join the fun. Her rosebud lips puckered, releasing a loud half raspberry, half spit-bubble.

"Not very ladylike," Marité murmured. Brian snickered, and the priest shot them both a warning glare.

Her sister, Raquel, heard the sound and flicked a signal to Matthew, just in time for the lighted candles. As a taper was presented to Marité and Brian, Matthew retrieved Rebecca in exchange, rescuing everyone from the priest's displeasure. With little Rebecca's explorations in sound effects successfully silenced, Father O'Leary nodded, and the baptism proceeded in its ordered sequence.

Boom! The sound of a fallen kneeler reverberated throughout the chapel like a discharged cannon. This time she tossed composure out the window and turned, searching above and beyond the curious guests to the source of the commotion. *You know how to make an entrance, don't you?* There he stood, hands pressed against the last kneeler, leaning forward. His jaw-length hair, tilting in the direction of his body, concealed his features. On her next breath, Marité evaluated the situation in the room: A pale Aunt Coralina directed a wife-to-husband plea for serenity to Uncle Jonas, whose gaze emitted ice-blue fury toward his disrespectful, noisy son.

An unexpected censuring scoff out of Brian startled her, and Marité pivoted, beginning to feel like a spinning top. The disapproving frown was a rare departure from Brian's affable countenance. Confounded by it all, Marité swiveled back around just as Michael looked up, tossed his leonine mane in obvious defiance, and smirked. Ignoring everyone present, he stared at her. A chill ran down Marité's spine.

***

As the black sedan sped along the festooned perimeter fence, Marité ignored the incomprehensible chatter of accompanying Spanish relatives and focused instead on the folks who lived in and around the Ocala area. Most were familiar with her aunt and uncle's lavish celebrations. But this time, the festivities would surpass everyone's expectations and likely be remembered as *the* party of the century. And with good reason—all four families had much to be happy and grateful for. The last two and half years had tested each one in different ways. The Reynoldses, Muros, Repulleses, and Buchanans had experienced the anguish of loss and the joy of recovery, the heartbreak of discord and the peace of reconciliation. For their trials, life had rewarded them with three beautiful children.

Today marked that occasion.

The chauffeur made a turn into the private road heading toward the shimmering glow ahead. Before she knew it, the vehicle had stopped. As she accepted the solicitous driver's hand to step out, her relatives emerged out of the car and melted into the gathering.

For weeks, she'd listened to the extensive plans between Aunt Coralina and Mamá about the yay-long list of invitations with a menu that included Texan, Spanish, and Caribbean entrees. Despite all the description, her imagination had come up short.

The ranch blazed with lights. Guests populated the grounds, some under the tents, others congregating around the buffet tables and open bars. A few traversed back and forth between groups. Elegant servers dressed in black and white maneuvered through everyone, offering hors d'oeuvres and bubbly champagne out of silver trays. The happy cacophony of laughter, conversations, and clinking glasses mixing with soft music filled her ears.

She didn't know most of the people standing around her. At the end of the ceremony and with all the Michael-related hubbub, she'd been separated from her inner circle. She would have to negotiate the crowd to find her family. Marité stepped forward, and someone exclaimed, "The young godmother," and from then on, she felt like she'd been thrown into a wash-and-rinse cycle. She was passed from effusive well-wishers to more relatives she'd never met, on to kissing friends. Finally, she was released at the end of the line, where she took a moment to straighten her mistreated dress, pat her hair, regain some decorum, and search again.

She considered heading toward the house, but that also meant threading through yet another group, and she was still dizzy from the last one. No, first she had to gather her wits, but…there'd be no gathering of wits, no peace, no calm, not when her thoughts were still consumed with Michael. She'd seen him stumble out of the chapel as soon as Father O'Leary said the last blessing, then lost him in the ensuing tumult.

Oh Michael…how can I help you?

The question had troubled her for months. Ever since she noticed the slow separation between Michael and his family, between Michael and her. She missed him, her cousin and buddy, the friend who'd accepted and taken her under his wing right from the start. He'd been a big brother then. With a twinge of nostalgia, she remembered the night, over two and half years ago, when a tired and bedraggled little group—Raquel, Mamá, and she—had arrived at the Ocala bus station. Lord, a lifetime had happened since…

As the ache aroused by the memories started to constrict her throat, she shook her head. No, none of that. Not on this happy night. She'd not dwell in the past. With the resolution firmly in mind, she stiffened her shoulders and moved forward.

"Mari!"

Raquel's voice. Marité pivoted in that direction. "Hey, sis. I could trek the Amazonian jungle or climb the Himalayas, but I'll never get lost, because you'll always find me. It's comforting, you know," she exclaimed.

Her older sister laughed and waved while repositioning Rebecca from one hip to another. The smile on her face didn't need explanations, and neither did Matthew's look of pride as he stood behind his wife and daughter. Marité approached them with a slow step, and again, that gnawing feeling tightened around her throat. The stubborn mix of sadness and joy almost won, and she felt the twinge of tears, although these felt like happy tears for her sister and Matthew. This day evoked so many conflicting emotions. In fact, her heart filled with jubilation for everyone who'd overcome life's tests…then she paused, the moment of exuberance dwindling as she realized the group ahead was incomplete.

The Buchanan trio—surrounded by acquaintances and relatives fussing over Rebecca—smiled and waved at her. Where was Brian? The constant presence, the always-together buddy, was missing. She frowned as irritation pushed happiness aside. Brian was probably roaming around, checking out and flirting with a pretty girl. He was famous for loving the ladies. Funny how the notion churned in her stomach. What, had she expected, for Brian to be glued to her through the night? Such nonsense. He'd never, and yet—

"Come over, Mari. Abuela Alicia wants to see you."

"Oh crap," she grumbled under her breath, "another relative who I can't understand."

The first meeting between the Spanish relatives and the American-born generation had been *interesting*, since they couldn't communicate with each other, except for Raquel. A lot of hand language had been used with the unavoidable, hilarious misunderstandings. Compared to Abuela Nieves—Papá's stately mother— Abuela Alicia was a little thing, although she had a light of inner power that made up for her short stature. Here was a woman who really didn't need a translator. Her intelligent brown eyes watched everything. She grasped and took in every last detail. Marité squirmed under her knowing regard. Could Abuela read her bewildering thoughts?

"*Niña, María Teresa, acércate*," Abuela murmured. "Come close," she repeated in her heavy, slightly lisping accent. Abuela epitomized contradiction. For someone her age—she had to be close to sixty—her speech was soft and velvety. Her fingers rounded Marité's forearm with a deceptively strong grip and pulled. In response, Marité gasped and resisted the tug. Abuela's smile deepened as if Marité's reaction had been exactly what she'd expected. Bemused, Marité relented. It was obvious who'd given Mamá her stubbornness.

"You have his look," Alicia said, glancing up and down the length of her body. "*Hermosa*, beautiful. You take after him. Seve, your grandfather. Did you know?"

Marité did know. Her mother had explained a year ago when she'd hit her first growth spurt. She'd inherited his good looks, except for his green eyes, and height. She wasn't too keen on that idea, though. Everyone knew girls shouldn't be too tall. It was easier to find dance partners; one could wear high heels without threatening the male ego. Although Michael's ego wouldn't suffer, because, like Uncle Jonas, he towered over everyone. Her brow tightened with the thought of her missing cousin.

"*Niña*, why the concern on such a pretty face?" Abuela patted her cheek.

Marité winced and turned to Raquel. "Please, help me out, sis. I can't talk to her like you can."

"Of course, Mari. What would you like me to say?"

"Tell her...tell her I'm not concerned. I was curious, wondering where our cousin had gone."

Raquel arched an eyebrow but didn't pry further. She handed Rebecca over to Matthew, turned toward the tiny woman, and a flurry of words, accompanied by hand gestures, escaped her lips.

"Damn, I need to brush up on my Spanish." Matthew burst out laughing.

Abuela nodded as Raquel spoke, though her regard remained intent upon Marité.

"That's right, Abuela," Marité said, uncomfortable with the visual examination. At her grandmother's unchanged expression, she added, "*Sí, Abuela*."

Now that is pathetic. The extent of her vocabulary was meager at best. Feeling wholly inadequate and a little miffed, Marité shook off her grandmother's grip.

"I'm going to look for Mamá. Have you seen her? I lost track of everyone after church."

"I saw her and Xavi under the pergola," Raquel said. "They were discussing something that looked pretty serious with Aunt Coralina and Uncle Jonas. I can help you find them, if you like. By the way, have you seen Uncle Jonas? He's in a terrible snit. You wouldn't happen to know why?"

"Me? Why would I know?"

"Oh, silly. Don't get all twisted up. I was just asking," Raquel said, slipping an affectionate arm around Marité's waist.

"Wait a minute, sis. You can't leave. Abuela, Matthew, and Cousin Almudena need a translator."

"Gosh, I guess you're right. You'll have to find Mom and Xavi on your own," Raquel said, releasing Marité.

Whew… Close call. The last thing Marité wanted was her sister's company. It wouldn't take long before Raquel wondered about Marité's behavior or asked a million pointed questions. Now Marité could continue her recon around the house and grounds in search of her elusive cousin. Smiling to the group, she mumbled a few words and left. However, as she walked away, she caught one last glimpse of Abuela Alicia's penetrating gaze. Language barrier notwithstanding, she hadn't fooled the old lady.

Read the rest of the story coming soon in print and for e-reader at all major online retailers.

To make sure you are the first to know, sign up for my Newsletter: www.VictoriaSaccentiWrites.com

Made in the USA
Columbia, SC
30 March 2018